i

Also by Gary Paul Corcoran

The Trip Into Milky Way
The Last Love of Eleanor Sands
It's Always Christmastime In Cratchitville
Postmark: Paris ~ Destination: Unknown
The Twelfth Commandment
Afghan's Lipstick Warriors: First Chronicle
Afghan's Lipstick Warriors: Darkness Falls
Afghan's Lipstick Warriors: The Deadly Sins

From The Michael Devlin Series

South On Pacific Coast Highway
Love In A Dying World

With Gary Paul Corcoran

The Slow Train to Rishikesh
Purgatory: Origins

THE TRIBE

A Novel

by

Gary Paul Corcoran

Stargazer Press
Charlestown, Rhode Island

Published by Stargazer Press
Charlestown, Rhode Island
http://garypaulcorcoran.com/

Printed in the United States of America
ISBN 978-0997126501

Visit us and blog with the author at
http://garypaulcorcoran.com/

Acknowledgements

Michael, for the exquisite cover, Patricia for her wry and heart wrenching tales of life in corporate America, Elise for her work on the farm, Tyler for his laughter, you are sorely missed, Dancing Rabbit, Three Rivers, Earthship, Breitenbush, Earthhaven, and to all those unnamed here, for their boots on the ground work in alternative living and to everyone in this world who sees the ecological writing on the wall and is working to turn our species around before it hurtles off a cliff.

For all those good and enlightened souls,
Who know that humanity must change its ways
and have done their part To protect our dear planet,
Mother Earth...

THE TRIBE

The Tribe

1

It had turned out to be one of those days along the northern California coast; cold, damp and dreary with a steady drizzle falling and low gray clouds woven in among the forested hills. If you have ever been up to that neck of the woods, you know what I mean. There are days when it rains hard but once the storm has broken, the sky is scrubbed clean and the whole world seems to be brand new. Then there are days like that one, when it's simply cold and wet and dreary and you want to crawl in a hole.

I had driven down to Eureka about ten that morning, my mood more or less in keeping with the dreary day, and had not gained much ground on that front by the time I stepped into Stella's Café around two that afternoon.

Inside, I found the place deserted, save for a lone waitress wiping down the lunch counter, a cook scrubbing his grill in back and an attractive brunette with short cropped hair seated alone at a window table. The brunette had her hands cupped around a coffee mug, the remnants of various sweetener packages scattered about the mug, a Corgi curled at her feet, two large gym bags on the floor next to the Corgi and no signs of a meal. She was staring out the window with a funereal air. The scene had shopping cart written all over it.

1

I said hello to the waitress and ordered an espresso. While she went to work, the cook nodded curtly from in back. Neither of them looked all that happy to see me. The place did not serve dinner and no doubt they were both just wanting to go home.

Waiting for my espresso, I stole another glance at the brunette. She was a delicate little thing and appeared to be in her early thirties, as best I could tell. The light dusting of freckles on her face brought to mind young girls in plaid skirts and white blouses, carrying their books home from school.

I was off on that reverie when the waitress returned with my espresso. I paid for it and headed for the door.

Halfway out onto the sidewalk, I stopped. Hell. The scene cried for intervention. You could feel the despair from forty feet away.

Back inside, the woman looked up at my approach and quickly back out the window. When I pulled to a stop across from her, she looked up again. Something resembling a smile crossed her face but failed to stick. Meanwhile, her hands had started to rearrange things on the table, as if building turrets and ramparts against all would be intruders, me included.

I gestured at the opposite chair.

"Mind if I join you?"

"Oh, thanks, but I'd really rather be alone."

I sat down anyway. The Corgi shifted away from my invading feet. The woman's turret building assumed a new fury. When she looked up again, it was with the fierceness of a hawk, both enraged and helpless over being cornered with its broken wings.

"I'm Steven," I said.

The woman continued with her turret building. I shrugged when she looked back up. Yeah, I'm still here.

"Oh, Colette," she said and looked out the window again.

"Colette. That's a beautiful name."

She nodded. I waited until she looked back.

"So, it's probably none of my business, Colette, but it sure looks to me like you're having a roll in the barrel here."

I glanced down at her two bags on the floor. Her eyes followed mine and came back.

"It's that obvious, huh?"

I shrugged.

"Something doesn't feel right."

"And that's your job? Checking on the needy and downtrodden."

I shrugged again.

"You look like you're taking it hard. What's a man supposed to do under the circumstances? Ignore you?"

"That's usually how it works, isn't it?"

With another one of her failed smiles, Colette looked back out the window. A moment later, she was wiping at tears.

"Hey," I said with a touch of her arm. "It's all right." I handed her one of the unused napkins from the table. "If I have this pictured right, we can fix it."

She looked back, her eyes clutching at hope from a sea of despair. The Corgi, having sensed all the emotion, sat up and looked from her face to mine.

"What's his name?" I said.

"Hugo."

The big ears pricked up. I called and he waddled gloomily over to my side of the table.

They were a pair, those two.

"So, you were saying?...About fixing this?"

"Oh, if you need a place to stay, I have a spare cottage you can use."

"And?"

"You mean, the catch?"

She nodded.

"There isn't one. Just don't burn the place down."

She shook her head slowly from side to side.

"This is starting to feel like a reality TV show or something. You're not secretly filming this, are you?"

3

I smirked.

"Of course not."

Colette looked back out the window.

"The truth is, Hugo and I were down to sleeping in my car tonight."

"And now you don't have to."

Colette looked back and reached for my hands.

"Please tell me you're not making this up."

I squeezed her hands in return.

"No. Why would I yank your chain about something like that? You need a place to stay and I happen to have one."

Colette bowed her head and mouthed the words 'thank you'.

"Truly, Steven," she said with another squeeze of my hands. "I don't know who you are or why you're trying to help me, but even for one night off the streets, I'd be eternally grateful."

"Hey, it's all right. Everything's going to be all right now."

Colette let go of my hands and looked back out the window. I stared at her, realizing that if you were broke and down to the streets, platitudes about everything 'being all right now' might tend to rub you the wrong way.

"Are you hungry?" I asked in place of more platitudes.

"Oh, no…Really, I'm fine."

"No, no, it's all right," I said and went over to grab the waitress' attention again.

A moment later, I returned with the last three muffins of the day.

"Thank you, Steven…Again. And forgive me for being so cynical. I just don't seem to have any hopes or dreams left in this world."

"It's okay. I feel the same way half the time."

"Yeah? And why you?"

I held up my hands.

"I mean, does it feel like the world's coming to an end or what?"

4

"Please. Don't get me started."

Colette broke off a piece of a muffin and pushed one of the uneaten ones my way. I held up a hand.

"Thanks. I'm fine."

She nibbled.

"So? You were saying?"

"What? About the madness?"

Colette nodded.

"Well, I'm loathe to speak this out loud but it just feels like the bullet of modern civilization has been spent. You know, we're like Rome at the end? I was reading a biography about Caesar the other day and found myself thinking, Jesus, this is us. The parallels are frightening. The institutions of government had become so completely effete and useless in the years before the republic collapsed, you couldn't get a goddamned thing done."

I gave Colette a look of feigned alarm.

"Sound familiar?"

"Please. Don't get me started," she said again.

"Yeah. Makes you want to find a cave and take up the wood flute."

The hint of a real smile crossed Colette's face.

"But it's true, isn't it? I don't know what's worse, the state of this world or trying to keep all of our anxieties about it stuffed inside."

Colette nodded and looked out the window.

"Steven. Everything that could possibly have gone wrong in my life over the past few years *has*. Then I walked out of a job three weeks ago." She looked back. "I know…foolish of me but I just couldn't take one more day of working for the Mastuh."

"What?" she said at seeing me smile. "You mean about *the Mastuh*?"

I nodded.

"It's true. That's how it is in the corporate world."

5

"I know. Or, I should say, I understand. I've never actually been there."

"Well, I definitely never wanted to be there *either* but I was and finally could not take one more minute of it. I had this asshole of a manager who was forever looking for a chance to grind me down. Then he'd ask me out for a drink. Like I was going to work my way up the corporate ladder by letting him screw me."

"So how did you find yourself in that situation in the first place? You don't look like the corporate type."

"Oh, I can assure you. I'm not."

I stared.

"I'm a Julliard trained dancer, if that's what you're wondering."

"Wow. Okay. So what happened?"

"The Russians."

"The Russians. Really. What did they do?"

"They came."

I laughed.

"Yeah. Real funny."

I shrugged penitently.

"Okay. Explain."

"Oh, I had run my own private dance studio for a number of years. Successfully, mind you, but once the Soviet Union collapsed, thousands of refugees from the Russian dance troupes started emigrating this way. And they're so cutthroat, they've made it impossible to make a decent living at it."

"The bastards."

"Tell me about it. So, I became a lackey in the business world."

Over the next half hour, Colette filled in the details. How, after five years of being kicked around on the lower rungs of corporate America, she had been chewed up, spit out and left with an aging car and fifty grand in credit card debt. Forced to give up her apartment three days earlier, she had started up the coast, with no idea where she was going.

Driving off a cliff had become an option. And there we were.

"I have a great book idea for you," I said when she stopped.

Colette looked up from her muffin.

"The Confessions of a Julliard Trained Bag Lady."

Seeing my words were a knife in her heart, I quickly reached out a hand.

"Sorry. I suppose that wasn't very funny under the circumstances."

She sighed deeply.

"Please. I'm so fucked up right now, I..."

My jaw almost hit the floor.

"Oh, yes," she said. "*Fuck* is one of my favorite words."

"I would have expected a nun to swear first."

"Yes...well...we all have our dark sides, don't we?"

I acknowledged her point with a nod and a shrug.

"So you were saying."

"Oh. I was going to say, please explain about this cottage of yours. I'm so afraid this bubble is going to burst."

"It's not going to burst. I have some land up the coast and the cottage is tucked away in the woods. And, as I said, you're welcome to use it."

"With running water and everything?"

I chuckled.

"Ooohhhhhhhh, so you wanted the one with running water and electricity. Well now, that's a different story."

Colette was staring at me again from her sea of despair.

"Yes, running water and every little amenity. I can assure you, it's quite cozy."

"And?"

"And what?"

"And when would I have to leave?"

"When would you want to leave?"

"Probably never," she said with another nibble at her muffin.

7

"Well, I suppose we'll both be dead before that eventuality comes along."

She reached for my hands again.

"And you really mean this."

"Of course."

"So, is it too much to ask? Can we go look at it right now?"

"Sure. I was heading back up to the ranch anyway."

I stood up. Colette took the last bite of the muffin she had been eating, gathered the remaining two into a napkin, stuffed them into her purse and grabbed her espresso. I downed the last of mine and grabbed her two bags. They felt like they had rocks in them.

"I did a splash bath and change of clothes in the bathroom," she said.

I nodded. Colette had one last look around the table and joined me in heading out the door.

It was a quiet street, and particularly so at that hour.

"Are you parked nearby?" I asked.

"It's the convertible Celica over there."

I nodded. It was a '90s model with the red paint rusted down to metal in places and the top held together by duct tape.

"Come on, let's get you loaded up," I said and walked her across the street.

With Colette and Hugo safely inside the car, she hit the power window. It required an extra hand to get it down

"So, I guess I'm following you?" she said.

"You can lead if you want."

She took a playful swipe at me.

"I'm in that truck up there," I said with a laugh.

She glanced at my brand new rig with another pained look.

"So which way are we going?" she said.

"North up the coast a few miles. Just follow me."

Seeing Colette's hesitancy, I touched her forearm.

"It's okay. Come have a look and if you're not comfortable, turn around and leave. I can assure you there are no strings attached. And I'm not a serial killer."

"Okay."

I smiled, touched her arm again and headed up to my truck.

All the way out of town and up the coast, I kept an eye on Colette in my rearview mirror. She was looking nervously this way and that as if she might lose heart and turn back. For all she knew, I *was* a serial killer.

When I turned onto a gravel road that disappeared off into the redwoods, Colette paused for a long moment before following me in among the trees. No doubt she had been expecting a driveway, not a mile long journey into the forest.

I kept to a slow pace, so as not to spook her any further, and kept a constant eye on the rearview mirror.

2

In time we came to a gravel parking area, graded into one side of a rolling meadow. I pulled to a stop and climbed out. Forest ringed the meadow and the scent of pine filled the air.

Colette parked next to me and climbed out with Hugo. The sounds of sawing and hammering echoed from deeper in the forest. Several gravel roads and foot trails led from the parking area off among the trees.

"What is this place?" Colette said, nodding at two cottages visible along one of the meandering trails. "It looks like you're starting a retreat or something."

"Not exactly."

"What then?"

"To be honest with you, I'm not entirely so sure anymore."

By way of a face, Colette made her puzzlement clear.

"You must have some idea. My god, the money you're spending."

"Yeah. Half the town thinks I'm crazy. The other half thinks I'm nuts."

Hugo suddenly caught a scent and bolted off.

"Hugo!" I called out and he stopped. "Better keep him near," I told Colette. "We're not alone out here."

She grabbed his leash from the car and put him on it.

"Let's have a look," I said and we started off towards the first cottage.

The trail wound off into the woods and every hundred yards or so, another cottage came into view, tucked away among the trees, each one built around a Craftsman theme and each one whimsical in its own unique way.

"Oh, I love that one!" Colette said of the fifth cottage we passed.

It was a bit more whimsical looking than the others, and tucked a bit further back into the woods.

"Let's go have a look then," I said.

Unlocking the door, I allowed Colette to go in ahead of me. The interior was commensurately whimsical, in keeping with the outside, but the kitchen and built-ins and bathroom were still built along a basic Craftsman's theme. All the rooms were furnished with a matching Craftsman style of oak furniture.

Colette went around opening cupboards and drawers in the kitchen, as a lady is wont to do.

"My god. Look at the dishes and silverware. What wonderful, old fashioned stuff."

"I thought the forties would be a fitting touch."

I went back to the living room and flopped down in an oak and brown leather chair. Colette had a quick look at the two bedrooms and bathrooms and took a seat opposite me on a matching oak and leather sofa. The forest was alive with bird song around us. The sound of construction echoed now and then from farther off.

"Peaceful, huh?" I said.

She shook her head.

"I feel so restored in just these few minutes."

"And you like the cottage?"

Colette nodded.

"Then it's yours to use for as long as you wish."

"Thanks...I'm still waiting for the catch."

"I told you. Just don't burn the place down."

Colette glanced out the door.

"And I'm it? I mean, nobody else is living here?"

"Not yet. It's just you and me, kid."

11

She shook her head again.

"So, help me here. I'm still struggling to understand where this thing is headed."

"Oh, I guess I had envisioned a tribe of people gathering together."

"And what would said tribe be doing, once it gets together?"

I stared, drumming my fingers.

"You would have to bug me about the fine details." Colette smiled. "Look, go back to our earlier conversation. You know, about the world being so fucked up?"

She nodded.

"And the path we're heading down being unsustainable?"

She nodded again.

"Everybody knows it, right? Somewhere deep down inside, all of us know we're hurtling towards the abyss but we just put our heads down one more day and forge ahead, with some vague notion that the big Kahuna up there in the sky is going to turn this thing around somehow. But of course that never happens."

Colette sat there biting her lip in thought.

"You know what I mean, right?"

She nodded.

"See? Deep down in our guts, we all have the same feelings. How is this madness ever going to turn out okay? The population keeps exploding and we keep pumping more fumes into the air and despite all the good folks out there fighting the good fight, those fuckers in the petroleum industry keep winning the battles."

Colette sat there staring.

"Did I lose you at *fuckers*?"

She smiled and shook her head.

"Well, forgive the rant but this stuff drives me crazy. I lie awake at night, thinking about it. Anyone with half a sense knows we need to change course but even the best of our leaders seem to be bought off and we just keep hurtling towards the abyss like everything's dandy."

I paused and took a deep breath.

"See? Don't get me started."

"No, it's all right, Steven. I'm totally with you. But what are you going to do?"

"Well, there I was at a crossroads a few years back, wondering just that. You know. Do I sit here Buddha like and accept that there's no fixing the mess? It's all in a dream anyway, right? So why am I worrying? Or do I roll up my sleeves and try to do something about it? And this." I waved my arms at the forest around me. "Whatever you want to call it, is my meager attempt at an alternative path."

"By being sustainable?" she said.

"What? Like that's not a big deal?"

Colette feigned repentance.

"Sorry."

"Yeah, well, being sustainable is a big part of it but beyond that, it's not easy for me to explain. I just figured we'd get some people together and see what comes of it."

"Like a commune?"

"Well, yeah and no. I pictured everyone retaining their individuality while gathering around a common core."

"And doing what?"

"I don't know."

Colette looked askance with her dubious smile.

"You still have to go out there and compete with everyone else. Right? You still have to try and make a buck."

"You and your details."

She laughed.

"Sorry. Just trying to be realistic."

"Yeah, well, call me naïve, but as Roosevelt once said, try something, and if it fails, try something else, but keep trying."

We stared.

"So I take it you have a lot of money," she said.

"Yeah. There's that."

13

She kept staring.

"You're wondering how much."

"Well, yeah, but…no. It's really none of my business."

"No, it's all right. My old man passed away and left me his fortune."

"Oh," Colette said as if I had just thrust another sword through her heart. "I could only wish for such luck. My parents died in poverty."

"Well, you're on the team now so you don't have to worry."

"Oh yes I do," she said with glass in her voice. "You want a rant? I'll give you a rant. I worry about money every single day. There is no greater yolk of oppression than being poor in this world. You may as well be a slave. The well-off can smile at this or that calamity, but when you're poor, you shrink at every dismal event, expecting it's just one more ball and chain around your neck. You struggle through every ordeal, with no idea how things will work out. It's a slow, sad, dismal, hopeless form of torture, so don't tell me not to worry."

We sat staring at each other.

"Did you want to go back to the café?"

Colette turned her head askance.

"Bastard."

"Well? I did say you're part of the team, didn't I?"

She nodded and looked out the open door.

"I do feel safe here."

"And that was the basic idea."

She looked back.

"Then, thank you."

I nodded. We sat there for a spell in the quiet of the forest.

"But Steven, I still don't get where this is headed. You know. Those pesky little details?"

I shrugged and stared back out the open door, playing with my lower lip in thought.

"I'm winging it, but I think for good reason. It just seems to go against the grain of what I'm trying to create, cluttering up

14

things with a bunch of rules beforehand. First we have a tribe of people. Then we start deciding things."

Colette tilted her head with a forlorn smile.

"It is very sweet of you, you know. Using your money to help others in this way?"

I nodded. Helping others had not been my first impulse. A destiny undone had led me to this place, but I had no interest in talking about that.

"Like to see the rest of the spread?"

"Sure. What else is there to see?"

"Lots." I stood up. "Come on. I'll show you."

I helped Colette to her feet and we went out and started down a path towards the sea. Hugo trotted along ahead of us, his stubby little legs working overtime.

"By the way," I said, pointing back. "The roof shingles on the cottages? They're all solar. It's part of an overall system that helps us to stay off the grid."

"I do like that part a lot," Colette said.

"Thanks. I'm greatly relieved."

She took another playful swat at me.

Eventually, we passed through a dense thicket of trees and stood above an array of solar panels, four small windmills and some heavy machinery.

"Wow, impressive," Colette said. "And what's that tank and machinery for?"

"It's a waste recycling plant. There's electric power for backup but it's designed to run off of the methane in those tanks. Which comes from us."

I smiled wanly at Colette.

"Not much raw material at the moment but we're gunning for more."

She smiled back.

"The methane also supplies fuel for heating and cooking in the cottages. My truck runs off of it too."

"Wow, it's just marvelous what you're doing, Steven, but I can't help but wonder. Why didn't you do this in a place like New Mexico, where it's really sunny?"

"Oh, well, let's tear the whole thing down and start over."

"Oh god, Steven. I'm sorry. I just keep talking off the top of my head."

"Well maybe you shouldn't talk off the top of your head so much."

"Well maybe you shouldn't be so sarcastic."

"Well? 'Why didn't you just do this in someplace like New Mexico, where it's sunny?' "

She looked away.

"Oh Christ," I said. "This is ridiculous."

"Well, you started it."

"No I didn't."

"Yes you did."

I walked away, beginning to regret that I had invited the woman out here, and maybe regretting even more this goddamned pipedream I had embarked on.

I steamed for a spell and finally walked back.

"Look, Colette, I'm sorry, and you're right. I'm totally impractical at times but I didn't want to live in New Mexico. I can't stand the hot, dry weather. Or being that far away from the sea. And I wouldn't have met you if I was in New Mexico, now would I?"

Colette shrugged.

"I guess you're right about that. And I'm sorry too."

I reached out and touched her shoulder.

"Look, it's hard enough battling the world and my own demons. I was hoping for a little support around here."

"Okay, I'll try to be more supportive." She made a sad face and rubbed my arm. "I guess we're both being a bit sensitive today."

"Yeah. I guess we are."

She studied my face.

"You having a rough time too, Steven."

16

"Oh, Colette. I look back at my life sometimes and think the whole thing has been a total waste. If not for the money, I'd have nothing but regrets."

Suddenly, Colette was in tears again.

"Hey, what's the matter, kid?"

"Well, think about it. All I have are regrets. *And* no money."

She broke down then and I held her. I held her for a long time until her emotions were spent, then pulled back to look at her.

"Are you okay now."

She wiped at her cheeks and nodded.

"Truce, then?"

She nodded again.

"We're in this together now, okay?"

She nodded again.

I gave her another big hug and a kiss on the forehead and we started back up towards the cottages. Hugo went out ahead of us with his stubby little legs still working overtime.

"Maybe we should just concentrate on getting more people out here," Colette said.

"Now there's an idea."

"Do you have any thoughts?"

"Keep hitting that café?" Colette smiled sarcastically. "Seriously, I don't know. I was thinking to run an ad or something."

"Couldn't you just spread the word around town? It seems to me that you'd have this place filled up in no time."

"Yeah but we have to be selective. Get a cross section of skills and talents out here, you know? Otherwise things will never work."

"Yeah, I guess you're right."

"Yeah. I've given it *that* much thought."

She smiled.

A minute later, we had arrived back to the cottage area.

"Okay, then. I imagine you'll be wanting to grab some supplies in town but if you'd rather not drive back today, I can serve you dinner. And breakfast in the morning and supply you with whatever necessities you might need to get through the night. Coffee. Tea. Dessert. Whatever you like."

"Thanks. I think I'll take you up on that. I need to look for a job but I'd rather stay here and enjoy the peace of the woods for the rest of the day. If that's okay with you."

"Of course. Let's walk back down to your car and I'll show you where you can park."

Once there in the meadow, I pointed to a winding gravel road that ran along behind the cottages.

"If you follow that, it will lead you up to the back of your place. You'll find two parking spaces there. Oh, one other thing. I have some lingering zoning issues with the county building department, so if you take a walk, come this direction, away from the construction noise up there, okay?"

She nodded. I glanced down at Hugo.

"And keep him on a leash. The coyotes are wary, but you let him wander off the beaten path and all bets are off."

Colette nodded.

"So which of the cottages is yours?"

"None of them...I have a tree house."

Colette smiled.

"Seriously?"

"Seriously. It's the other way. Down that path over there. It's a good distance back but if you keep walking, you'll come to it. Stop by for dinner. Around five? Or if you need anything in between."

"Thanks but I'm fine for now. I have some bottled water and the rest of those muffins."

"Okay. We'll see you for dinner then. It's gowns and black tie."

Colette smiled.

"Hugo too?"

"Neah, he can skip the black tie for tonight."

"I mean is he welcome?"

"Of course. We'll bring him up in the basket."

18

"Oh god no."

"Just kidding. There's a proper set of stairs and all."

"Okay. See you later then. And thanks again. From the bottom of my heart."

"Sure. Just relax and enjoy yourself and we'll discuss the bigger picture later on."

I reached for the door of my truck and waited to make sure Colette was headed in the right direction before climbing in.

3

I started my truck and paused there with the window rolled down, listening to a woodcock call off in the forest somewhere. A bee buzzed by overhead and continued on its way across the meadow. I heard the strike of a hammer again and was just dropping my truck into reverse when I saw the building inspector Dan coming up from the direction of the highway. He turned down an access road towards the current cottage in construction. I backed up in a rush and sped off after him.

By the time I had pulled to a stop in front of the cottage, Dan was already marching up to the door, his wiry frame stooped over, a dour look on his face. You struggled to picture Dan having fun with the kids. The man had been a thorn in my side since day one.

"Hey Dan," I called out after him.

He glanced over his shoulder without responding. I hurried to catch up. As much as I didn't like the man, my contractor Dale liked him even less, so running interference was one of my primary duties.

Dan checked his clipboard and went into the kitchen first. The cottage was roofed and sided but otherwise still in raw framing. Dan had a quick look at the plumbing and moved on to the electrical.

"What the hell is this?" he said, squatting down to inspect a row of wall plugs. "You're supposed to be running 2/12 in the kitchen, not 2/14. These should be GFI plugs. All this will have to be torn out and redone."

Dale came in, as taciturn as Dan, but with shaggy hair and a heart. I looked at him for answers.

"It's the dining room," Dale said matter-of-factly.

He whipped out his tape measure, marked off where the kitchen counter would end and measured over to the last wall plug. It was just a tad over four feet. Dale looked up at Dan.

"That's code."

Dan harrumphed and went about inspecting all the wiring above the kitchen counter area, taking each section in hand and turning it around to read the label, clearly hoping it wasn't 2/12, when anyone who knew his stuff could see at a glance that it was. Dale and I watched him.

Dan jotted down something on his clipboard and headed for the bathroom, where he again checked the wiring, as if still hoping to nail us on that issue. All through the cottage, he performed his duties without cordiality or mirth.

Finally, Dan went outside to sign the inspection card.

"Asshole," Dale muttered under his breath as soon as Dan was out of earshot.

"Careful," I said and went out to check on Dan.

"You're lucky those floor plugs were over four feet away," he told me, looking up from the inspection card. "Next time, don't cut it so close."

I nodded, holding my tongue. There was no point in arguing with the man.

As Dan was climbing back into his truck, something caught his eye down towards the finished cottages and he climbed back out. I stepped out from under the covered porch and saw Colette coming up the path, chasing after Hugo, his leash dragging along behind him. Down at Colette's cottage, some of her belongings were scattered around on the front porch. It looked as if she had been outside sunning herself.

Dan was already on his way down there. Again, I hurried after him.

21

He barged inside before I had chance to catch up and was already storming back out as I arrived. Colette had Hugo gathered up in her arms and looked horrified as Dan brushed by her on his way back to his truck. I reassured Colette with a wave of my hand and rushed after Dan.

"Look, it's not what you think."

"Yeah, right," he said with a quick look my way. "You know you're not supposed to have anyone occupying these places yet. This whole circus of yours is still under zoning review."

"Look Dan. She was down to living in her car so I told her she could freshen up in there until I figured out something more permanent."

"So you're running a homeless shelter now."

"That's not what I said."

"Well, that's what it sounds like and if that's what you're doing out here, you'd better get the right zoning permits."

With that, Dan sped up even faster. I reached out to grab him by the shoulder.

"Goddamn it, Dan. Haven't you ever been down on your luck?"

He shook himself free.

"Keep your hands off of me."

Off he went, full of steam.

"What the hell is wrong with you?" I said, catching up again. "You got a rock for a heart?"

"Don't give me your bleeding heart crap. There are codes and ordinances and it's my job to make sure that everyone lives by them."

"So I'll have her stay at my place until things are settled with zoning. Let's not make a big deal out of it."

"It's already a big deal. She's living there and I'm red flagging the entire development. I don't want another nail pounded around here until you get things straightened out with zoning and the council."

"What's the deal, Dan? You've had it out for me since day one of this project."

"I don't have it out for you. Or anybody. I'm just doing my job."

"Your job? You know what? Fuck your job for a moment."

That spun his head around.

"Yeah. What do you think? St. Peter's going to be up there with a clipboard at the Pearly Gates. 'Oh yeah, Dan did his job all right. Come right on in'. The only thing you're going to be known for is being a petty little man who couldn't see the real life around him."

"You're treading on thin ice there, buddy."

"Yeah? Well fuck thin ice, Dan, and fuck you."

Dan reached his truck and quickly had a red tag card in hand.

"Why don't you answer me? What the hell happened to you? Had a rough childhood and you're taking it out on everyone else?"

Dan was writing away furiously. I nearly tore the red card out of his hands.

"Forget the goddamned paperwork for a second and look around you, Dan. There's life. People, destinies, real flesh and blood hardship. That woman was down to sleeping in her car. That's what some people have to go through these days to survive, but I guess that doesn't matter to you, huh?"

Dan took his notice back, tacked on the wall next to the front door and went inside to announce that all construction was to stop. Dale and his helper looked at me. I motioned for them to hang loose and followed Dan back outside.

"Why don't you answer me, Dan? Never been down on your luck? Never had a tough break? No guilt whatsoever about sticking it to people who have?"

Dan threw his clipboard into the truck and jumped in with it.

"I've given you every break I could over the past two years and now I'm done."

"Yeah right, Dan. The truth is, you haven't been cordial to me for one goddamned second. You showed up with a hard on the first time you came out here and you've had one ever since. What do you think? I'm building a getaway for bin Laden?"

"He's dead."

"Funny. You know what I mean."

"You know, you rich people are all the same. You come in here throwing your big time money around like you own the place. No respect for the rules or local traditions."

"Oh, so that's it. Us rich people, throwing all our money around."

"I don't want to see another nail being pounded around here until you get this straightened out."

Dan slammed his door shut, started his engine, and backed out in a cloud of dust. I watched to make sure he had turned back down towards the highway before going in to talk with Dale. He was already wrapping up.

"Fuck him. Just keep working."

"Hey, I'd just as soon shoot the fucker but I've got a license to protect."

"I'll protect you. I'm calling my attorney right now. I've had it up to here with that son of a bitch. I'll sue the county if I have to. I don't know exactly what for, but I'll come up with something."

Dale stood there staring at me with his power cord in hand. I whipped out my money clip and counted out ten, one hundred dollar bills.

"Here. That's a show of good faith. Take your wife down to Frisco for the weekend. Give Jason here a bonus. Whatever. Just don't quit. I don't care if I lose. I'm going to put the fear of god in these fuckers. When Mayor Twilling gets a whiff of the city's legal expenses, he'll come suing for peace."

"You hope."

"Yeah, well, like I said. I don't care what it costs at this point. I figure I've got more money than they do, so screw 'em."

"If I end up with attorney fees, you're paying."

"I'm paying. Absolutely. Have I ever left you hanging?"

Dale nodded warily and started rolling out his power cord again. I headed for the door.

"Excuse me. I have a lady in distress to comfort."

Sure enough, Colette had packed her bags and was carrying them down from the porch as I pulled up. I rushed to intercept her.

"Colette, wait," I said.

She set her bags down.

"I'm sorry."

"Don't be."

"No, I shouldn't have let Hugo run off."

"Colette, that bastard would have found some other reason to fuck with me, with or without you."

She looked unconvinced.

"Seriously. It'll all be fine. Let's just sit down here for a minute and I'll explain."

I grabbed the bags and encouraged Colette to take one of the Adirondack chairs on the front porch. I sat opposite her and rubbed my temples in thought. When I looked up, Colette was staring at me.

"Look, I don't even know where to start with that man. The fucker's been nothing but trouble...See, everything's currently hung up over a zoning hassle because I don't know what to call the place. Smoke would come out of their ears downtown if I suggested I was starting a *tribe*. We left off with me getting a hotel license, which I don't want to do, so we're still slugging it out."

"Is that a big hassle? Getting a hotel license?"

I rubbed my thumb and fingers together.

"Which is not the real issue. I certainly don't want to spend any more than I have to but it's more about the paperwork

25

and all the hoops I'd have to go through if we called it a hotel. Anyway, that's not what this is so we battle on. My lawyer suggested that I start a foundation. Purportedly that would give me the wiggle room I need but I've got a neighbor out here who's going to make a stink, no matter what I do."

"Which neighbor?"

"Exactly. You could live up here a hundred years and never see the bastard but if you're in this neck of the woods, it probably means you've got money, which probably means you're a prick."

Colette smiled.

"Yeah, trust me. They do tend to go together. Attend one of these local board meetings and you'll see what I mean. That son of a bitch spends half his life making sure no riff raff moves into the neighborhood. And to him, I'm riff raff."

"Fucking world," she said.

I smiled, a smile that quickly faded.

"What?" Colette said, seeing my face grow dark.

"Oh, just realizing. I'll probably have to apologize to that fucking Dan now for going off on him."

"Why? Would someone at the city make you do that?"

"Well, maybe, but it's more about my own conscience. I'm trying to live in a world where we don't start wars over our petty differences."

"There's a dream for you."

"Yeah, well, it's the one I have. Anyway, once you realize something is wrong, you can never go back to doing things the way you once did. And this *is* how wars get started, if you hadn't noticed."

Colette nodded and sighed.

"Well, I'd best get going. If Hugo and I have to sleep in my car tonight, I need to scout around for someplace before it gets dark."

"Colette, please. You don't have to leave."

"But I heard him say he wanted me out of here."

"Yeah, this place, but you and Hugo can come and stay with me."

"Oh, Steven. Really, I couldn't."

"Nonsense."

She went to stand up again and I stopped her.

"Colette, look, let's establish some ground rules right here and now, and rule number one is, if I have a problem with something, I'll let you know. In the meantime, please stop trying to run off at every turn. This is your new home."

Colette bit her lower lip and stared.

"All right?"

"Oh, Steven. You know how fucked up I am."

"I know. You're so beautifully fucked up."

She smiled.

"But this is your new home and we'll make it work. It may take a bit of shuffling but we'll make it work. Okay?"

Colette shook her head doubtfully.

"No, we'll make it work."

I stood up and offered her my hand. She took it and stood up with me. I went inside to check the kitchen. It was clean. I went back out to the front porch.

"I gather you have the muffins."

She patted her handbag. I locked the door.

"Okay, off we go then."

Colette had Hugo on his leash. I grabbed her bags and we went around back to her car. Once everything was situated inside, I jumped into the ragged front seat.

"Let's go grab my truck and I'll lead you around to my abode."

We drove up to the cottage in construction and Colette followed me from there back down to the meadow and up another narrow, winding lane that led to my treehouse.

"Oh my God," Colette said, getting out.

"Nice Valley Girl imitation."

She laughed at herself.

"But how whimsical and wonderful. And big."

27

"You were expecting a kid's fort, no doubt."

"Something a bit closer to that, yeah."

With her bags in hand, I led the way upstairs and opened the door. Colette stopped on the landing to wait for Hugo. He was struggling with his stubby legs to make the climb. With every other step, he stopped and looked up at us mournfully. Finally Colette went down to retrieve him.

I took the bags inside, set them down in the living room and stood staring out the windows at the forest. The sea would have been visible off through the trees, had it not been for the gray, dreary day.

"God, this is so enchanting," Colette said, coming in with Hugo. "Oh, the drawings."

She immediately went to the Japanese ink drawings on one wall.

"Sumi-e, isn't it?" she said.

"Yes. Actually, Suibokuga, but they're more or less of the same school. I suppose to be entirely accurate, you'd call them of the one-corner school. A figure over here, set against the vast emptiness over there."

"Yes. It's very Zenny, whatever you want to call it. Stops you in your tracks."

"That's the idea. Please, god, awaken me from the prison of my own mind."

She smiled.

"Oh, and originals too."

"It's not very Zenny to talk about that. The rest of the tour?"

"Sure," Colette said with a final look back.

I took her upstairs to my personal quarters and work area first. At my request, the architect had designed it at the far end of the structure. The lower landing of my stairs was bordered by a quiet room and library to ensure my further privacy and quietude.

Back downstairs, I grabbed Colette's bags and led her through the kitchen and great room to the three bedrooms and three baths on the other end. I dropped the bags in a bedroom decorated especially with a lady in mind, showed Colette the rest of that wing and we returned to the kitchen.

"Anything you want, it's here," I said with a wave at the refrigerator. "I presume you have dog food."

She nodded.

"Well, please, make yourself at home and feel free to cook up anything you'd like. Mi casa es su casa."

Colette blushed.

"I said make yourself at home, okay?"

She nodded.

"Okay, I need to go take care of some business upstairs. As in, call my attorney."

"Oh god, I'm feeling awful again."

"Remember our pact?"

"I do. It's just so hard to accept."

"Accept it. This was going to come to a head, sooner or later, and maybe it's just as well that you've sped up the process. Everything happens for a reason."

"I guess."

"Are you okay then?"

She nodded. I swept a hand over the house, offering it to her again and headed up to my office. Richard was on the phone a few minutes later. Richard the Lion Hearted, I liked to call him. He was a short, stout Irishman with a florid face that could be merry one minute, then utterly dark in the next. For the most part, he was very cerebral, but if something got in his way, cannons roared and steeds galloped.

I explained the situation.

"And you want from me?"

"Sue the bastards."

"For doing their jobs?"

"There has to be something we can nail them on. That bastard has a hard on for me and I'm tired of taking his crap."

"I think you'd have a better chance incorporating than you would beating the building department in court."

"Okay, then we'll incorporate."

"I meant, as in your own separate city, and I'm being facetious."

"All right, you son of a bitch. How about that foundation?"

"I'm looking into it."

"Well quit looking and do something."

I heard Richard sigh.

"Look, I don't care how you go about it, but put the fear of the lord into these bastards and get me some way to move people in. I have this lady here who needs a place to lay her head. And there will be others soon. I need this vacancy issue resolved or I'll go mad."

"I think you already are."

"Fine. Then it's all the more pressing that you do something."

"I'll work on it tonight and give you a call."

"The sooner the better."

"I'm busy today but I'll work overtime tonight on your behalf. That's the best I can do."

"You get this done and I'll send you down to Cabo fishing, all expenses paid."

"And I'll take you up on it."

"You've got a deal. I'll talk with you tomorrow."

I hung up the phone, kicked my feet up and stared out at the forest. The sky had cleared with the afternoon wind, revealing the sea, very blue and white-capped off in the distance. It appeared to be both stationary and drifting continuously south down the coast.

My thoughts fixated back on Cabo. Why hadn't I gone down there as originally planned? I could have built a lordly place overlooking the Pacific, bought a big boat, gone fishing every day and sat back watching the sea from my favorite bar in the afternoons. Let go to the Zen of the moment. Accept that this world is what it is and you're never going to change it.

It was nothing anyway, so there was nothing to change.

Fitzgerald's Folly. That's what I had. Chasing your wild dream and look what it's brought you. Nothing but trouble.

But some deep rooted instinct that I did not understand or particularly trust told me to hold steady and go forward. Hell, I had to now. I was in so deep, there was no turning back.

I sat there reaching for Eden while slouching on my way towards Bethlehem.

The Tribe

4

While working away in my upstairs office that afternoon, I occasionally heard Colette moving around on the main level but when I went down to start dinner at four-thirty, she and Hugo were gone. A short while later, I heard footsteps coming up the stairs and looked over my shoulder. Colette stood outside the half opened Dutch door.

"Hi," she said.

"Come in, come in," I said, waving to her from the kitchen.

She did so tentatively. Hugo stood at her feet looking up, mirroring her energy.

"Please," I said and waved again. "And you can go ahead and close both doors."

She did and came towards the kitchen. Hugo followed along, his nails tapping against the hardwood floors, his ears pricked up at the scent of my cooking.

"Smells wonderful," Colette said with a peek around my shoulder.

Her cheeks were flush from the walk.

"Just a Thai vegetable stir with shrimp."

I let her taste it.

"Mmm, very good. With mint?"

"And lime and coconut. Put the lime in the coconut and fill you right up."

Colette chuckled and went to wash her hands.

"You're being careful with Hugo out there, right?"

"I am, thanks. Oh, I came across this wonderful cottage up the lane the other way," she said while drying her hands. "Who lives there? Or lived there? It looks like it was inhabited at some point in the past."

"Oh, that's a long story…Did you want to give me a hand?"

Colette stared.

"How about slicing the bread?" I added with a smile.

As I went back to work, I heard the sound of the hard crust bread cracking against the cutting board, like ice breaking up.

"Mmm," I heard Colette say behind me. "So good. Where did you get this?"

"There's a French gentleman in town. A regular boulanger."

Colette brought over a bite for me.

"Butter?" I said.

"Oh, so we're really going to get sinful."

"Well, we're in this deep already."

Colette came back from the fridge with the butter and we had a minor orgy while I finished the salad.

"I don't usually eat at this hour, but with the time change."

"God, I know. It suddenly gets dark so early."

Colette wandered over in the direction of the French doors and the adjacent balcony.

"So lovely, though. This hour of dusk in the forest."

"Yes. Spirits are afoot. You're welcome to go out and have a look."

"Thanks but I'm enjoying the warmth inside. By the way, I hope you don't mind. I threw Hugo's waste in the trash enclosure around back."

"Not at all. I trust you used a plastic bag," I added over my shoulder.

"Of course. I have my own supply." She came back into the kitchen. "That's quite a fortress you have back there. I mean for the trash cans."

"We have bears around here, too. Maybe even wolves. They tracked a male crossing over into the Siskiyou's this past

33

spring. Apparently he marched all the way down from a pack they introduced in northern Oregon."

"And they didn't shoot him?"

"No. This isn't Wyoming. They're actually hoping he finds a mate. It's the first wolf sighting in California since 1924."

I continued tossing the salad.

"Should I get the plates out?" Colette said.

"Sure, thanks. They're in that cupboard."

With the table set, Colette filled Hugo's bowl with dried dog food. I placed the salad on the table. There were two covered bowls with the stir fry and brown rice already waiting.

With everything on our plates, Colette was suddenly overwhelmed with emotion and touched my hand.

"I don't usually do this, but a little prayer of thanks seems fitting."

"Sure."

She bowed her head. I closed my eyes.

"Thank you for your many blessings, God," Colette said.

While I waited for more, I heard Colette buttering up more bread.

"That's it?" I said, opening my eyes.

"Short and sweet."

"Okay. Works for me."

I too buttered up a piece of bread and dug in.

"So please tell me more about how you came from Julliard to the current state of affairs."

"I'd rather forget."

"Okay."

"No, it's all right."

I listened to a somewhat typical story of a marriage in Manhattan that went south, then a westerly trek, with stops in upstate New York and New Mexico along the way. Other men had come and gone, but mostly she had concentrated on building up her own dance studio down south, only to see the Russians sink her.

34

I found myself chuckling frequently as Colette described the details of her foray into the corporate world.

If only I had been willing to fuck this guy. If only I hadn't slammed the lid of the scanner down on this guy's hand.

"Actually, if I had been willing to utter the word Mastuh out loud, I probably would have gone far."

I chuckled again.

"So, tell me about you, Steven. You haven't said a word about you."

I waved a hand at the forest around me.

"I was a bad person in my last life and this is my punishment."

"Some punishment."

I smiled and bit into my bread. Colette stared.

"What?" I said.

"You still haven't answered my question."

"Oh, I was hoping you hadn't noticed."

"I did."

"Yes, well, here's how it is for me. I wake up every morning with a gasp. Then I somehow get myself pointed in a positive direction. Then I wake up the next morning with another gasp. It's like Groundhog Day. Every morning, I wake up to this fucked up world and can hardly believe it. Like, is this really it? Of course I realize that I'm not alone and feel driven to try and do my part to make this a better world. Maybe as a form of penance? I don't know but then I wake up the next morning with another gasp."

I shrugged and dug back into my meal. She studied me for a long moment.

"I guess I feel the same way."

"Yeah. It's going around."

She laughed and we ate.

"Actually," I said. "I've been planning to build an arts center out here as part of the project and it's occurred to me that…given your presence…maybe we might want to add in a little dance studio?"

35

Colette was quickly wiping at tears again.

"Is there anything I can say that won't reduce you to tears?"

"Oh god, no. I can't tell you how happy that idea makes me feel. Are you really serious?"

"Sure. We've got to have some *cultuah* around here."

Colette chuckled while wiping at her cheeks.

"Where would you put it?"

"Oh, somewhere down near that meadow and parking area. That's the basic idea. Folks scattered about in the woods and a central community area."

"You really mean to do this?"

"You mean build the arts center?"

She nodded.

"Of course. The arts are essential. Probably the most essential part of humanity, don't you think? Consider. What was the first thing man put up in a cave? Not an accounting ledger. It was a painting. Maybe art *is* our humanity."

Colette smiled, bit into her dinner and then dabbed delicately at her mouth with a cloth napkin.

"What about rules?" she said. "You'll have to have rules, right?"

"Oh, yeah. We'll have lots of those." She laughed. "But that's the age old question, isn't it? Like Madison said, first you need some means of governing the people. Then you need some means of controlling those who govern."

"So, any ideas?" Colette said with another bite of her meal.

"My motto is, when all else fails, attack the neighbors."

Colette gave me a look. I shrugged.

"It helps to keep your mind off your own problems."

"Seriously, Steven."

"Oh. Well, I suppose if chaos evolves, we'll hold a town hall meeting."

"It will, you know."

"What, chaos?"

She nodded.

"So? We'll deal with things as they come along…No? You're not buying it?"

"I don't know. It just seems to me that you're being awfully Rousseaunian. Is that a word?"

"It is now."

"But you know what I mean."

"Sure. I admit it. I'm a seat of the pants kind of guy but I did poke around a bit into the history of communes and it appeared to me that there was always a tendency to overdo things. The rules, I mean. 'You're required to do this. There's no doing that.' Even those sixties' communes had their ten commandments but that seems totally counterproductive to me. You know, from one state of bondage to another?"

She nodded.

"Probably those early Israeli kibbutzims are the closest thing to my own vision. At least in terms of structure. Or lack thereof. Everybody just chipped in as necessary and made it work."

"Were you ever in one?" Colette asked.

"A kibbutzim?"

"No, a commune."

"God no. How old do you think I am? I've just heard the stories and seen some of the documentaries and everything seems to support my impressions. It was a short trip from hippiedom to fascism."

"Banished for drinking a Coke."

"Ah, so you *have* been in one."

"Well…yes, briefly. While living in New Mexico."

"Yeah? Make your skin crawl, did it?"

"A bit."

"Yeah. I prefer a simple premise. Everyone has to do his or her fair share. Beyond that, there are no rules. We'll just deal with stuff as it comes along."

"I foresee a lot of town hall meetings."

I laughed.

"The fact is, I'm not even sure about the 'contributing' part. At least there has to be some latitude at the start. What if we drag in a helpless soul who's not capable of doing anything?"

"Like me?"

"Well, Colette, I expect there are people in a lot worse shape than you are."

"A few," she said. "Maybe."

"Yeah, yeah."

She smiled facetiously.

"But you get the idea. Create a sense of community and trust that everyone will get into the spirit of it. It's that or you get booted off the island. You included, Hugo."

That got Hugo up from his prone position. Colette gave him a snow pea, which he chewed with a curious expression.

"So, back to acquiring more volunteers," she said.

"Yeah, there's that and getting approval from the powers that be."

Colette looked down and played with her food.

"Hey, don't worry. You can stay here until we get things straightened out. In the meantime, we'll set up an appointment with the architect and see what we can do about moving this arts center forward."

"Do you have any ideas for it?"

"What do I know? You're the artist. I'm sure I'd like to add my two cents at some point but it's up to you. Envision whatever you think we could possibly need for the arts and we'll go from there."

"Do you have any idea how big this structure would have to be?"

"Some. We'll want a good sized theater and spacious rooms for the dance and art studios. Why don't you draw up a list of the separate spaces you think we'll need and some approximate idea of the square footage for each and we'll go see Connor."

"That's the architect?"

"Yeah. Scottish fellow. It's a kick just listening to him talk."

"And you don't care at all about the cost."

"I believe in being frugal wherever possible but if you're asking me whether or not this project is going to break the bank? No. Not hardly."

She stared.

"You're dying to know, aren't you?"

"Oh god," she said. "I shouldn't be prying."

"It's okay. I'd be curious too. Let's just say, far more than a man could ever spend in a lifetime."

Colette looked as if she had just watched someone else win the lottery.

"Look, I can't change what happened but I can surely do something more constructive than hording it. Consider. If you had a billion dollars, you could live on a million dollars a year for a thousand years. I mean, how much fucking money does one person need?"

"I've often asked myself that same question." Colette shook her head and looked out at the now dark forest. "It's just so incomprehensible. Especially when you're worrying over your next tank of gas."

She suddenly seemed very sad again. I reached for her hand.

"Hey. I'm really, really glad you came along. It's just the perfect fit for the first member of the tribe. Someone in the arts. That's really the kind of focus I wanted to see. Concerts at night, dance and stage performances, an art school. Whatever."

"It does sound wonderful."

"It will be wonderful and you're going to help me make it happen."

Colette looked out at the forest again.

"What?"

"Oh, I don't know. I still feel like this bubble is going to burst any minute."

"Look, Colette. I'll go you one further. Let's establish a fair salary and I'll put you on the payroll. That way this situation

39

won't seem so nebulous to you. You'll have a job and responsibilities and we'll forge ahead, okay?"

"Oh, Steven, honestly. I couldn't."

"Why not? Let's just decide on a figure. How about thirty grand a year?"

Another tsunami of emotion washed over Colette and she turned away with her napkin.

"Jesus, Colette. I'm going to stop giving you good news if this is how it's going to affect you."

She smiled through the emotions and touched my hand.

"I'm sorry. It's just like some dream, everything that's happened today."

"Yeah, I can see that."

She waved the napkin at me.

"All right, all right. I understand. You've had a thousand pound weight on your shoulders."

"Oh god. You don't know. Right, Hugo?"

He looked up, baffled but caring, as all dogs are when confronted by human grief.

"So, we'll call it thirty grand a year. It's a bargain for me and with the housing thrown in, it's a good deal for you, right?"

She nodded and shook her head all at once, still not knowing how to take her good fortune. I reached out to shake her hand and she threw herself at my shoulder instead.

When her emotions were somewhat spent, she pulled back and looked in my eyes.

"Thank you. Again."

"It's all right. I'll go see my accountant tomorrow and make sure your checks start flowing right away. Okay?"

She reached out impulsively to kiss my cheek and looked out at the now darkened forest.

"Oh god, my mind is already spinning with ideas for the building design."

"Hey, feel free to brainstorm to your heart's content and we'll arrange to meet with Connor this week, as soon as he's available."

I took another bite. Colette was playing with her meal.

"Did you want a title?" I said.

She made a face.

"How about, Grand Director of the Trinidad School of Arts & Dance. I'll have some cards made up."

"Please don't."

"All right. Just trying to bring a bit of levity to the situation."

"I know, but trust me, I'm truly excited."

"Good. That's what I wanted to hear."

I buttered up another piece of bread.

After the meal, I led Colette and Hugo up a trail to the creek and fern grotto.

"Oh, how lovely. Did you ever think of building the cottages up here?"

"Yes, but that would have triggered some serious watershed issues. Anything that has plumbing within a couple hundred yards of that creek and you're now dealing with the federal government."

"Too bad."

"No, no. I'm all for protecting the environment and I've already had enough roadblocks with the county as it is. Building the cottages up here would have penciled in two more years of review. Lovely, though, isn't it?"

"Very."

"So, we'll consider it a place of sanctuary for all to use. I think once the dust settles, I'll see about building a simple Zen pagoda out here. With one of those Zen sand gardens. We'll have gongs and incense and that sort of thing."

She smiled and we continued our walk.

Later, back at the treehouse, I poured two brandies and we sat up late in the living room, talking about life and the arts center. Colette had curled up on the sofa and was seemingly at home as a cat now, contentedly twitching its tail.

At a bit past one, I glanced at the clock, yawned and stood up.

"Better hit the hay. Much to do tomorrow. Richard doesn't know it yet but he'll be seeing me first thing in the morning."

"Is that the attorney?"

"Yes."

"I feel awful again."

"Don't."

I leaned over and gave her a kiss on the forehead.

"Sweet dreams. I'll see you in the morning."

I gave the spellbound Hugo a rub on his head and went upstairs.

In the middle of the night, I awakened to a gentle rain and with my head going round and round. It was the same old stuff. What have I done to myself? Like I could change the world, when nobody else has much succeeded. I had done little else but upend my cherished privacy. A tribe, indeed. Well, not that I needed a multi-million dollar pick up line, but Colette was certainly a fine first member

I found sleep again a short time before dawn and awakened a few hours later to find the storm had broken. White clouds marched across a cheery blue sky and the sea danced with white-caps far off through the trees.

I headed downstairs and found Colette seated at the kitchen table with the remnants of an omelet in front of her, along with a cup of coffee. With a quick glance at the clock stove, I saw it was 9:30.

"Well, now you know all my dirty secrets."

"It's all right," she said. "I used to sleep in too but from all those years as a corporate hack, I'm now an early riser."

I smiled and went for a cup of coffee.

"There's more omelet."

I uncovered the pan.

"Thank you."

I quickly nuked the eggs and sat down with my breakfast and coffee.

"I see broccoli and cheese. What else is in here?"

"A bit of tomato, garlic and onion."

I dug in.

"Hmm, delicious. Thank you again."

"Thank you."

"We can sit here and thank each other to death."

She smiled. I continued eating and chatting with Colette and had quickly finished up.

"So, did you want to join me in town today?" I said while depositing my dish in the sink.

"And do what?"

Go see the accountant."

"I'm so totally embarrassed somehow."

"Okay. Let's see if we can find you another job in the corporate world."

"So when did you want to go?" she said.

I laughed.

"Let me shower and I'll be ready."

With a last gulp of coffee, I dashed upstairs and dashed back down fifteen minutes later.

"Ready?"

"Sure."

"And did you want to take separate vehicles? You'll probably want to do some running around on your own after we hit the bank, yeah?"

"Probably, yeah."

"Yeah. Anyway, I've got a million things of my own to do, so…ready?"

"Sure. Let's go."

Colette started to gather up one of her bags and I grabbed it for her. Hugo followed us out the front door and I locked it.

Downstairs, I started my truck and waited for Colette to get her car going. I saw the brake lights go on but nothing else happened. Finally, I climbed back out and found Colette with her head against the steering wheel. I opened the door. She looked up at me in tears.

"What's the matter?"

"It won't start."

She beat her hands against the wheel. I got down in a crouch.

"Hey, hey, come on. Let's not get worked up about it. I'll call AAA and have it towed into my mechanic."

"And then what?"

"We'll have it fixed."

"With what?"

"Your new salary."

Without further warning, she completely broke down. I pulled her into my arms and held her tightly until her grief was spent.

"Hey," I said.

She looked at me, wiping at tears.

"Look. I know there's a great burden upon you right now but it's just a goddamned car repair."

"Easy for you to say...She wiped at more tears. "I'm sorry. I've just had so much grief of late. I don't know if I can take any more."

"It's all right. I understand, but look. I've got so much running around to do in town today, it doesn't make much sense, me dragging you along. Let's just wait until I've arranged an appointment with Connor. That way we can get your first check from the accountant and this arts center moving forward all at once. Okay?"

Colette nodded and dabbed at her nose with a tissue.

"Then let's go back upstairs."

I grabbed her bag, she grabbed Hugo and we went back up to the house.

"Make yourself at home."

Colette nodded.

"You're sure you'll be okay?" I said.

She tried to smile.

"I'll be fine."

"Okay. I'll set up that appointment with Connor and your checks will be flowing in a couple of days."

"Please stop talking about it. I feel so embarrassed."

"All right. Why don't you work on some preliminary sketches for the art center? There's a desk and computer in the library. Paper in the drawer. You can go online and poke around if you want. Whatever. Just make yourself at home and I'll have things rolling here in a couple of days."

Colette reached out to touch my hand.

"Steven, I can't thank you enough."

"Hey, you're helping me too."

"I don't see how at this point but I so appreciate everything you're doing for me."

"No, don't you see? It's all meant to be. Our meeting and everything?"

"Well, we did meet. I can't argue with that."

Determined to make my point clear, I leaned forward in my chair.

"Did you ever read Vonnegut's *Cat's Cradle*?"

"Oh god, somewhere long, long ago. Yes."

"So, you remember Bokonism, right? And the karass?"

"Vaguely."

"So, I've often felt that way when certain people come into my life. This is a really profound connection. Sadly, so many of them drifted away and disappeared which makes me all the more determined to make these new connections stick. So, karass or whatever you want to call it, that's the whole idea of the tribe. We work together so we're no longer alone in this world."

"It sounds lovely," she said with a sad smile.

"No, we're going to do great things out here together. Trust me. And I'm telling you all this because I want you to feel like you're on solid ground. Not like the rug is going to be pulled out from under you every time you turn around. Okay?"

"Okay."

45

"Okay. So, I'll probably be in town until late afternoon. Make dinner if you want or wait until I get back. Either way, I'll call AAA on my way into town, so look for a tow truck."

"Thanks again."

"No problem. Just make yourself at home in the meantime."

I gave her a final hug of assurance, patted Hugo on the head and went out the door.

The Tribe

5

On my way out to the highway, I called AAA and arranged for the tow, then called my mechanic.

"Louie, Steven here."

"Hey buddy. What's up?"

I explained about Colette's car.

"Do I smell love here?"

"Come on. She's a doll, sure, but that's not really the point. It's just somebody who's been kicked around by life for too long and needs a break."

"The man on a white horse."

"Yeah, that's me. So, look. What I want you to do is run the car next door to the body shop as soon as you're done, have it painted and then have somebody take care of redoing the top and upholstery. And feel free to tack on whatever you need to make it worth your while."

"Consider it done, my friend. Three or four days and it'll be ready."

"Thanks. Oh, and fix the power windows. You need a monkey to help you move them up and done."

Louie laughed and said he would take care of it.

In town, I stopped at a bakery and left with a dozen espressos and a lavish assortment of muffins for Richard's office staff. Richard was in his back office when I arrived. At the sound of all the commotion, his door promptly opened.

"I just laid odds in Vegas that it was you," he said with a hand on the doorknob. "Come on. Get in here."

"Espresso? Muffins?"

"I'll take one of those espressos, thanks."

Richard frowned at the orgy in progress behind me and waved again.

"Gloria, let's get that brief done. I'm due in court in two hours."

Richard closed the door and took his princely seat. I sat in the wood and leather chair opposite him.

"I suppose you'll want this before the Supreme Court by next week."

"The 9th Circuit will do." He nodded sarcastically. "Look, I just need to settle on a course of action and get it done, that's all. Whatever you think will get me residency permits the fastest."

"Adopt everyone."

"Funny."

"I jest not. If you want the most expedient way of moving folks in, adopt them. No one can stop a family member from living with you."

"Fine. I don't care how at this point. Just get it done. I have that woman staying at my place and I want to get her situated in one of the cottages."

"All right, all right. Just hold your horses. I had a talk with Toni and she thinks she can get at least four of her fellow board members to sign off on the foundation idea. Then all you have to do is make everyone living up there with you an employee of the foundation and you're good to go."

"Good. Then do it."

"You understand that you'll have to abide by *all* the requirements of a foundation. It's like a corporation, only on steroids, as far as the paperwork goes."

"Fine, fine. You set it up and I'll adopt some son of a bitch who knows how to run a foundation."

Richard's eyes twinkled ever so slightly, the corners of his mouth moving up a bit in unison. With him, that was the equivalent of a serious guffaw.

"Go talk with Toni," he said.

"Fine. I'll go see her right now. I trust you can have everything ready for the board meeting tomorrow night."

"Christ, Steven. I can't get this done by tomorrow night."

"Richard, how much do you want to draw up a charter?"

He shrugged and drummed his fingers in thought.

"Rough estimate? Twenty, thirty grand. Probably on the higher end of things if the board throws this back at me for some tweaks."

"Fine. Now you double that and put everyone on overtime. I want an answer this week."

"You don't ask for much."

"I only ask for what my money can buy me."

"Fine." Richard hit his phone intercom. "Listen up everyone. We're on overtime as of this minute."

There was a chorus of groans.

"Be prepared to sleep on the floor tonight."

Richard clicked off, had a second thought and clicked back on again.

"And you can thank Mr. Fitzgerald here for the privilege."

I heard sounds of mutiny. Richard smiled. I flipped him off.

"Anything else, your highness?"

"Yes. About that prick Dan red flagging the project. Please get him off my back."

Richard shook his head. I stood up.

"Just have your secretary send me your dates for that fishing expedition."

"It'll be a party of four the way things are going."

"Fine."

Richard called out to me as I opened his door.

"Just curious," he said. "This dame. Is she…uh…?"

He motioned with his hands.

"Yeah, she's a doll but that's not the point. She's part of my karass."

"Karass?"

"Yeah. Look it up. It's in a Kurt Vonnegut novel. Anyway, she's Julliard trained so I'm making her the director of my art center."

Richard shook his head.

"I'd say you have more money than sense, but I know you're really serious about what you're doing out there."

"Yeah. Just look at all the good it's doing you." His eyes twinkled again. "I'll let you know how things go with Toni, but I trust you'll have everything ready for tomorrow night's board meeting."

"Semper Fi."

"Indeed you are. Well, off on my steed here."

On my way out of the office, I dodged a gauntlet of insults. And I could have my espressos and muffins back.

I drove straight downtown to Toni's office. She ran a small consulting firm out of a two story historical building, upstairs in back with a view of the harbor. It was definitely low key. Much of the time she was leveraging her days on the Coastal Commission to help folks work through the review process.

Toni had her liberal allies on the county board, but none were as liberal as she.

Toni peered over her glasses as I barged in, her wide-set eyes sparkling above a glorious smile. She had a pencil in her auburn hair and a set of blueprints on her desk.

"Well, sunshine," she said. "How goes it up there at your Valhalla?"

I sat down and explained my run in with Dan.

"Oh, that's not good."

"Yeah. I'd like to put him on the rack but I'll probably end up apologizing instead."

She smiled.

"So, I had a chat with Richard yesterday about a foundation. Is that what you've settled on?"

"That's what he recommends. My next best option is adopting everyone."

"I'm available."

"Everything's on the table if it solves my problems."

She smiled.

"So, the question is, can we run this by the board tomorrow night?"

She raised her eyebrows.

"You don't ask much."

"That's what Richard just said. I'm paying him and his staff overtime to get the paperwork done."

I looked around as if checking for cameras and leaned forward.

"Any way I can bribe you and the board."

"You'll have to be more subtle than that."

"I'm giving away free fishing trips to Cabo."

"More subtle yet."

"I was thinking to make a large donation to the Natural History Museum."

"Really? Do tell."

"Yes. In fact, I think I have the check right here."

I produced my checkbook and wrote one out for fifty grand.

"Well! How generous of you, Mr. Fitzgerald."

She reached for the check but I held it back.

"I'll be there at the meeting tomorrow night with my proposal."

"Well, I'm sure the board will be very deferential under the circumstances."

"I trust they will."

I handed her the check and got up to leave.

"I'll see you tomorrow night."

"Oh," Toni said before I could close the door. "I've always wanted to take a fishing trip to Cabo."

"You'll have to be more subtle than that."

I winked and dashed back down to the street. The day was brisk and cold and sunny after the rain, the kind of day that lent itself to optimism.

On my way over to Connor's office, I stopped for two more espressos and found him alone in back when I walked in, his tall, wiry frame hunched over his drafting table. With a look up, he waved for me to join him. He had cut his black hair short a few months back and it remained that way. His chiseled, Rock Hudson good looks came with an impish smile.

"Ah, a cuppa. Thank you, sir," he said, taking the espresso. "How is it? Still Baltic like outside?"

"A bit shy of that, but chilly, yeah."

I sat down and explained everything that had taken place over the past twenty-four hours.

"The man sounds mental," Connor said of the inspector.

"Ya 'ave a fine way a puttin' things, McTavish," I said in my best Scottish accent.

"And I was being kind at that."

"Well, that's business for the attorney. I'm here to set up a meeting about that arts center."

"Oh aye, any time you like. Is she a fine lass, then?"

"Lassie enough, and let's say tomorrow afternoon? I want to introduce you two and pass it along. She'll be on point. Entirely. I'd like to be kept in the loop and I might offer up a few suggestions, but this is her baby."

"Terrific. We'll put together a proper Opera House."

"Something this side of the Met will do."

"Aye, already footering in the works, he is."

"I'll footer ya." I stood up. "What time tomorrow?"

"Say threeish like. That'd be fine on my end."

"Threeish it is then."

Back down on the street, I made for Tillie's office on foot. Her place was two blocks up and one over, hardly worth getting back into my truck.

On that fine, crisp day, all the shops were done up in holiday spirit. Seeing a lady's red cashmere sweater, I thought of Colette and went in to buy it. Red seemed to be her color.

Back out on the street, my phone rang. It was Richard again.

"Done already," I said, stepping out onto the sidewalk.

"You have a fine imagination. We haven't even started."

"So, what's up?"

"Your neighbor, Chaplin. I received a call from his attorney. He wants to meet with you."

"What for?"

"To talk, I am told."

"And you would recommend this?"

"I don't see why not. Just comb the place for bugs first."

"I'll leave that to you...So where and when did he want to arrange this?"

"Lunch today at the Baywood Golf and Country Club.

"Christ."

Richard chuckled.

"At least it's hard to bug. Can you make it?"

I weighed things for a moment.

"All right. Tell the bastard I'll be there. What time?"

"He said at 12:00 noon."

"Fine. I'll see him there."

I stepped into Tillie's office a minute later. She looked up from her desk with a smile. Tillie was the white queen, all chin and jowls, but as smart as a whip and equally honest. I had never caught her filching a penny, and she had millions of mine to filch.

"What's up?" she said with her nervous laugh and a look at the box in my hands. I set the box down.

"I put somebody on payroll and need you to set up regular salary checks."

"Oh?"

"Don't give me that."

I explained about the arts center. Tillie laughed nervously.

53

"What?" I said.

"Well, just worried about you and your money."

"Think I've lost my head?"

She laughed nervously again.

"Yeah, well. Just so you know, it's not what you think. She is a doll but that's not what's going on here. Every community needs the arts and she fell into my lap. Believe me, if anyone ever deserved a break, she does."

"Well, it's your money."

"Exactly. Just put her on as an employee of my company for now and once the foundation is set up, we'll make her the full time art center director."

"And when did you want all this to start?"

"Oh, she's broke so we'll pretend she started last week."

Another nervous laugh.

"Look, I know this goes against the grain of your fine-tuned sense of ethics."

"My fine-tuned understanding of the tax law," she said with yet another nervous laugh.

"Okay, whatever you need to do to cover your butt, but do it. Put it in writing and I'll sign it. Just get it done, please."

"Ooookaaaay."

"Thanks. I'll be by with her tomorrow to pick up the first check. Say, about two?"

Tillie nodded.

"Okay, we'll see you then." I stopped at the door. "You can make them biweekly after that."

She grimaced as if seeing prison orange. I winked back, grabbed my box and went out the door.

The drive out to the country club took about ten minutes. The golf course itself was dotted with shallow lakes from the rain. Several members of the grounds crew were out there with power equipment, furiously trying to dry things out for the landed gentry. The early lunch crowd was just heading out to the first tee. A gaggle of ducks made its way across the course as I pulled into parking lot.

Inside the clubhouse, I announced my name and a hostess promptly led me to Chaplin's table. He stood up and shook my hand.

"John."

"I know. Steven."

"Something to drink?" he said.

"Scotch," I told the hostess.

Chaplin made sure she was bringing the most expensive brand.

"Please, have a seat."

I did.

"It's a hundred grand just to get in on the ground level here these days so I try to make good use of my money. I had to earn every penny of it."

With that jab at my ego, he tipped his glass my way and sipped his Scotch. I was considering which water hazard to toss him in.

"Have you ever enjoyed my line of products?" Chaplin asked.

I shook my head.

"Of course I've sold out and retired now but we revolutionized the boutique wine market. Particularly to the 18-30 crowd. We also had our pinot noirs and chardonnays and zinfandels for the more sophisticated connoisseur. When we came out with a line of flavored olive oils, even I was amazed at how well they sold but it's all in the brand, as you know, and the Chaplin name still has enormous cachet, all these years later."

I nodded.

"So, you wanted to see me?"

Chaplin looked taken aback by my lack of interest in his royalty BS.

"Well," he said, blinking. "Let's not get off on the wrong foot again. It just occurred to me that, as neighbors, we ought to get along. That's why I'm holding out the olive branch here."

"You've been harassing me for the past two years. At every step of my project. Is that your idea of getting along?"

"Well, let's face it, Steven. That circus of yours...or whatever you wish to call what you're doing out there...it is highly unusual. You can hardly blame me for being concerned."

"Circus or not, Chaplin, you filed a complaint against me and that leaves us at war, as far as I can see."

"I'd rather not think of it in that way."

"Okay. You tell me how I should think about it. You're the one who arranged this meeting."

"Well, to be completely frank, I was wondering if I could somehow prevail upon you to drop the whole thing. For the right price, of course."

"Drop the whole thing. Really?"

"Yes. As I said, I'm willing to offer you some sort of generous dispensation. Something to help take the sting out of it."

The Scotch came and I leaned out of the way for the obligatory cocktail napkin.

"Are you gentlemen having lunch?"

"I don't know," I said. "I'm not so sure we can put up with each other for that long."

The waitress blushed. Chaplin tossed back his Scotch.

"Bring me another. I'll let you know about the meal upon your return."

She thanked us and scurried off. I smiled back at Chaplin.

"So, you were saying."

"Good god, man. Have you no civility?"

"Perhaps not, but I do know how to be honest, so why don't we start with that and see how things go?"

"Then why don't you give me your take on our situation."

"I don't like you. You don't like me. You want the world your way and I'm goddamned well determined to have it mine. That doesn't seem to leave us much wiggle room, does it?"

"Honestly, I don't understand you, Steven. I assumed we all came up here to get away from the clutter down south. Why on earth would you want to drag it up here with you?"

"Maybe that's why *you* came up here. I wouldn't speak for me or anyone else."

"You know I'll simply file another complaint against you. And I'll keep filing them until I get this nonsense of yours stopped."

I nodded and leaned over the table.

"I presume you know how much money I have, Chaplin."

"I have a vague idea." He flung a hand at space. "So?"

"So, I have a vague idea how much you have and it's simple math. I can outspend you roughly a hundred to one. I can spend you right into the ground and still have enough money left over to live like a king for ten thousand years. And I'm quite prepared to do that, if that's what it takes."

With one fist clenched on the table, he looked like a tea kettle ready to boil over. I smiled and tossed back the rest of my Scotch.

"So, now that we've laid our cards on the table, I guess we can call it a day."

The other Scotch came and Chaplin quickly tossed it back. Then he leaned over the table.

"Listen, you bastard."

"Oooohhhh. So the polo club veneer finally comes off. Now we're getting somewhere."

"Yes, be forewarned. I know your deepest, darkest secrets. Like that little incident over in the Mediterranean? How would you like to see that getting leaked to the press?"

I stared.

"Yes. You see? You think you want to play rough with me but you don't. You think I've been a thorn in your side so far? I haven't even taken off the gloves yet."

"Chaplin, you pompous ass. You fancy yourself Hemingway, the great white hunter in khaki pants and leather

57

riding boots but you're actually Macomber, the guy whose knees went weak when he saw a lion."

"Listen. I'll drive you right into the…"

"No, you listen to me, you phony piece of trash. You think you can buy me out? I could have built a palace big enough to fit your whole place in my foyer, but I didn't. I set about trying to help a few lost souls. And maybe build a better world in the process. But you had to come along and fuck it all up. And why? Because it doesn't comport with your hunt club image of the great northern coast. Frankly, I can't stand the sight of you, you arrogant prig, but I forgive you. Because you don't know any better. I'd even make peace with you, if there was some way to do that. But let's face it. You don't want peace. You just want to order me around, the same way you've been ordering people around your entire life. Well, screw you and your façade of respectability. I know underneath it all, you're just a two bit crook."

The waitress reappeared about the time I was standing up. I smiled at her. She had instinctively found a safe spot several feet away. There were two glasses of water on her tray and Chaplin noticed me eyeing them. It did occur to me to toss one in his face but I wasn't into that kind of theatrics. I was more inclined to punch him. Instead, I threw some bills on the table.

"It appears Mr. Chaplin and I were unable to stand each other's company after all."

The waitress stood there mortified as I headed for the exit.

6

Out in the parking lot, I jumped into my truck and grabbed the steering wheel. My heart was pounding. My entire being felt nauseous from that adrenalin fueled episode. The implications of Chaplin's threat raced through my brain. I didn't give a damn about the notoriety, but if that bastard dragged my dirty laundry out into the open, my struggles with the county could become that much knottier.

The dirty rotten bastard.

I started for home but quickly redirected my course towards Trixie's Diner. I needed something in my gut.

The tables were all taken when I walked in so I grabbed a seat at the counter. The café was buzzing with conversation around me.

A tall young man to my right offered up a cheery smile as I sat down. He was a bit overweight, in the manner of athletes who have let themselves go to seed in recent years. His big cheerful face was the most noticeable thing about him. It could have seconded for a sun calendar.

"Hey, how are you doing?" he said.

"Oh, fine. And you?"

"Oh, wow. I just pulled into town and I'm totally digging this place."

The waitress arrived with a menu and glass of water. I held up my hand to both.

"Make it a club sandwich and a Becks."

She left. I sat there staring straight forward in thought.

"So, rough day, huh?" the man said.

I nodded with a quick glance his way. He appeared to be in his late twenties but still a big puppy in nature, all paws and eagerness. I stared forward again, trying to ignore him. When my beer came, I drank from it earnestly, and drank again.

Finally, the silence was too much so I spoke up.

"You were saying? You just pulled into town?"

"Yeah. From LA. Long Beach, actually."

"Big change, then."

"Oh wow, yeah. I can't even believe the difference. I mean, just three days ago I was stuck in traffic with all this smog and a frigging heat wave. Now it's like just blue skies and clean air and like some little town out of the Midwest or something."

I nodded and looked forward again. The high school vocabulary aside, he seemed like a hell of a nice guy.

Just then, an old couple abandoned their window table so I stood up.

"Hey, I'm grabbing that table over there. You're welcome to join me."

"Hey, sure, far out."

We settled in with the remnants of their lunch still littering the table. We backed out of the way when a busboy appeared. As soon as he was gone, I held out my hand.

"Steven."

"Kyler. Yeah, this is way cooler," he said, taking in the view of the street. "So, like what do you do up here?"

"Oh, this and that. I own some acreage up the coast a few miles."

"Yeah? Far out. I'm totally ready to move up here. I'm so sick of LA." He leaned farther over the table. "See, I was just..."

The lunch counter waitress appeared with Kyler's burger and he backed away again.

"Sorry," I told Suzette. "You know me. See an opportunity and seize it."

"Yeah," she said quietly. "Tell that to Rhonda. It's her table."

Rhonda came whizzing by just then and gave us all a curt look. Suzette made big eyes in her wake.

"Tell her I'll to tip enough for both of you."

"Thank you," Suzette whispered and left.

"Far out," Kyler said. "So you like know everybody up here?"

"Pretty much. It's a small town."

"That's so totally cool."

"Most of the time, yeah. So you were saying."

"Oh, yeah." Kyler finished the bite of burger in his mouth and leaned forward again. "I got fired from my job a few weeks ago. I had been working as an aide at this hospital for the past three years and they caught me stealing pills."

"Bummer."

"Yeah. The bummer part is, I got clean and sober and quit doing that shit a year ago."

"So why were you stealing pills now?"

Kyler finished another bite of his burger and wiped his mouth.

"I wasn't. I guess they had me on videotape for a couple of years and were just waiting to see if I would like lead them to some big drug dealers or something."

"That sounds fucked up."

"Yeah. Tell me about it."

"So, that's it? They're not going to charge you?"

Kyler leaned back over the table.

"See, that's what I don't know. The DA said that since I was clean and sober, he didn't see the point in pursuing it but he didn't say *no* for sure, so the question's still hanging over my head now."

My sandwich came.

"Thanks, Suzette."

She winked and left. I bit in and looked over at Kyler. He was taking another bite of his burger.

61

"So you're worried they might still come after you?"

"Yeah," he said, wiping his mouth. "There's no way I could go to prison. I think I'd fucking off myself first."

"Jesus, why throw away the rest of your life over a couple of years. It wouldn't be that much, would it?"

"Fuck, they told me they had about six counts. They could lock me up for twenty years, I think."

Kyler shook his head dismally and bit back into his burger.

"So, what's you're status otherwise? Are you broke?"

"Oh, no," Kyler said, wiping at his mouth again. "I've been saving up my money. Plus I have this inheritance. I get a check every three months and then there's a big payout in a couple of years."

"That's nice. So you weather this storm and you have a pleasant future ahead of you."

"Yeah, I don't know. Even if I forget these problems for a minute, sometimes I just feel so totally lost. Like what's the point of living? All we do is screw each other over. You know what I mean?"

"Sure."

"So, what keeps you going? I mean, don't you ever get up in the morning and think, fuck it, I may as well jump off a bridge? Like none of this shit makes any sense to me?"

I finished the bite in my mouth and measured my words.

"There was a time, a few years back when I felt that way, yeah. Like a withered branch. I was just wandering around completely lost and I've been trying to figure out how to fix that feeling ever since."

"Far out. So what have you come up with?"

I studied Kyler.

"I'll tell you what. Why don't you drive out to my place with me and have a look around?"

"Cool. Sure. So how far up the coast is it?"

"About fifteen miles. A little less."

I finished up my sandwich and pulled out some bills for the check.

"Here, I can get my part," Kyler said when I left three twenties."

"It's all right. I've got it. It'll cover your gas for the drive."

"Wow. You totally don't have to do that."

"No. It's fine." I glanced at the clock. "I just need to get back, if you're ready."

"Yeah, sure."

Kyler gobbled up the last of his burger and wiped his hands.

"I just need to take a leak."

He smiled his big sunny smile.

"I'll be waiting for you outside."

I went out to the sidewalk.

"Where are you parked?" I asked Kyler when he reappeared.

"Right over there. The Forester."

"Okay. I'm in this truck so I'll wait while you turn around. Do you need gas or anything?" I called after him.

"No, I'm cool."

As with Colette the previous day, I kept an eye on Kyler in my rearview mirror. When we came alongside Trinidad, I could see him rubbernecking over the rocks that girded the coastline, like Easter Island moai, standing guard over the sea.

When I turned up the road to my place, Kyler held back a bit to stay out of my dust. When I pulled to a stop at the meadow, he was right there.

"Far out," he said, getting out. "Do you like own this whole parcel? I mean from the coast all the way out to here?"

I nodded.

"Actually, it goes another mile or so in all directions."

"Wow. So how many acres is that?"

"A little over twelve hundred."

"Wow. I guess you do have some serious dough then, huh?"

I nodded.

"Come on, I'll show you around."

As we headed up the path, I heard the sounds of Dale and Jason at work.

"Wow, cool," Kyler said at seeing the first cottage. "Oh, wow! There's another one. What are you building? Like a retreat out here or something?"

"More like a military boot camp."

Kyler laughed.

"Wow, cool boot camp. So in exchange for one of these places, we'd goosestep around saluting and shit?"

I laughed.

"Actually, it's about creating a place where people can live together in a new kind of way."

"Wow, far out. So it would be like a little community."

"Yeah. I like to call it a tribe, but that's the idea."

"Wow, far out. So are you asking if I'd like to come live out here?"

"Would you?"

"Oh yeah. Totally. So how much would I have to pay?"

"There's no charge for living here. I just haven't worked out all the details yet. Like what the hell we're going to do, once we actually have enough people around. You know, the minor stuff."

Kyler laughed.

"You know what I think would be really cool? If we raised our own crops and made our own stuff and kind of lived just like the pioneers did."

"That's partly the idea, but utilizing modern technology. Come check this out."

I walked Kyler down to the treatment plant and power center, explaining how things worked along the way.

"Oh wow," he said, seeing the plant and solar panels and windmills.

"Yeah, it's pretty much self-sufficient, energy wise. Now all we need are some people and to have a pow wow and figure out where to go from there. I'm not a big fan of laying down a bunch of rules and regulations in advance."

"Far out. Me either."

I spent a few minutes showing Kyler around the area and then we headed back up towards the cottages. When we came to the one in construction, I waved Kyler in with me and introduced him to Dale and Jason.

"Any word yet?" Dale asked me.

"No. I sicced Richard after him."

Dale looked skeptical.

"Don't worry about it. I've got something permanent in the works with the city council. Everything okay here with you? Got everything you need?"

"We're good."

"Okay. Well, Kyler and I are back to our tour of the property."

"Here, this way," I said to Kyler outside, pointing the way up a path towards the creek and fern grotto.

"So, what? You're like having trouble with the city or something?" he said.

I explained about Dan and having lunch with Chaplin and the zoning issues.

"That sucks. So now you have to spend a ton of money on attorney's fees and shit."

"Yeah. There are people in this world who would love to have my problems, Kyler, but it's definitely getting to be a pain in the ass."

We had come to the creek and Kyler went down to the edge.

"Wow, far out! I just saw a big fish swim off!"

"Rainbows. I had it stocked when I moved in."

"So we can totally go fishing."

"We could. I've been trying to give them a little time to mature."

"Oh wow! There goes another one!"

He was like a big kid on his first day at camp.

We sat down beside the creek and talked with the water gurgling past us. Eventually we got back to our feet and started down the trail towards my treehouse.

"So, if you're wondering whether or not I want to move in, I'm totally on board."

"Okay. You're tribal member number two and you're about to meet tribal member number one."

"But aren't you like tribal member number one?"

"I suppose, officially speaking. Anyway, I ran into this gal yesterday in town, basically the same way I met you."

"Cool. Is she good looking?"

"Yeah, but she's also pretty screwed up in the head right now so..."

"Hey, I'm sorry, man. I'm just being stupid..."

"No, it's understandable but it's probably best to tread lightly on that front for a while."

Back at the meadow, we jumped into our vehicles and I led Kyler up the winding lane to my house. I noticed Colette's car missing first thing so the tow truck had come.

"Oh wow! Far out!" Kyler said upon getting out of his car. "Are you kidding me?" He laughed. "This is just so far out! Now I want one."

He laughed again.

"Yeah," I said. "It's actually been on my mind the past few days. How is everyone going to take me having a treehouse? The idea was for everyone to be equal around here."

"It's cool, man. It's like you're his lordship and we're the peasants."

"Ha ha. The fact is, the treehouse came along well before this tribal business, so..."

"It's cool, man," Kyler said. "You're like paying for everything, so screw 'em."

"Yes, in the true spirit of the tribe, screw 'em."

We had come to the stairs and started up side by side. Hugo commenced to bark inside at the sound of our approach.

66

"You have a dog?"

"No. He comes courtesy of member number one."

Hugo really went off as we walked in through the Dutch door.

"Hugo! Stop it!" Colette said.

She was stretched out on the living room sofa reading and remained that way upon our entrance. She glanced at the box in my hands. I set it down on the credenza.

"I just came up to introduce you to tribal member number two. Or three, as he rightfully points out."

Colette took the news a bit painfully. Meanwhile, Hugo had accepted me back in the room, but not Kyler entirely.

"Hey, little poochie," he said and crouched down to pet him.

Hugo growled low and deeply. I went over and helped the two of them get acquainted.

"Sorry," Colette said. "He thinks it's his place already."

"Understandable. Oh, Kyler, Colette, Colette, Kyler."

"Hi," Colette said, still acting a bit territorial.

"Hey, hi," Kyler said with his usual sunny smile. "Isn't this place far out? It's like an enchanted cottage in the clouds or something."

Colette smiled with a glance at me.

"Kyler's from the LA area too."

"Long Beach," he said.

"Oh. What a small world. I lived in Belmont Shores."

"Oh wow! I totally wanted to live in that place. It's so cool."

"Where were you living?"

"Oh, my condo is over by Cal State."

"Well, you weren't that far away."

"No. I could totally ride my bike down there in the summertime. It's just…you know…my condo's a cheesy little place with all this traffic rushing by."

"At least you have a condo."

Kyler laughed.

"That's true, huh?"

"Hey, well, I need to use the restroom and make a couple of calls so I'll leave you two to get acquainted. Kyler, whatever you want, help yourself. There's plenty to eat and drink in the refrigerator."

"Cool, thanks. Maybe a Coke or something?"

"Help yourself. I'll be down in a few minutes."

Kyler was heading for the refrigerator as I headed upstairs. I heard the sounds of Colette and Kyler talking as Richard came on the phone.

"How did it go?" he asked me.

"You mean with Chaplin?"

"Yes."

"We basically threw Scotch in each other's faces."

"Great. Who started it?"

"Depends on who's telling the story."

"Christ. So there's no hope for détente."

"Chaplin's idea of détente is telling me what to do. And offer me a handout for the privilege."

"All right, so it's back to the trenches."

"More than that."

I explained about Chaplin's threat.

"I want you to hire a private investigator and dig up some dirt on him."

"Oh Christ, Steven. Haven't you had…"

"No, I haven't. And I want the dirt in my hands before that board meeting tomorrow night."

"I don't know. By tomorrow night?"

"Just do it, Richard. Please. I'll pay some son of a bitch five grand to get it done. Just find somebody down there in Sonoma, dangle the money in front of him and get the son of a bitch to drop everything else."

"I'll see what I can do. And you talked with Toni?"

"Yeah."

"So? I trust you two didn't toss Scotch in each other's faces."

"Hell no. Toni's civilized."

68

"And? What did she have to say? I don't need to be going through this overtime exercise for nothing."

"I made a donation to the Natural History Museum and Toni assured me that we'd be on the docket tomorrow night. Not that she'd ever admit the two things are connected."

"Fine. We'll be on it then. Call me tomorrow afternoon. Everything will be done by then."

"Thanks. Any snags, be sure to let me know. Otherwise, I'll be in touch around two. And get me that dirt. Oh, and I believe I'll be needing fifteen copies of that foundation proposal. Nine for the board, four for the building department and I'd like to have two for myself."

"I'll run off twenty copies. That way you'll have plenty of extras if something comes up."

"Thanks, Richard."

"Sure. Oh, I'd bring more peace offerings before you show up here again. The natives are restless. They're using your photo for a dart board."

"What? They haven't hung me in effigy yet?"

"They'll probably hang you in the flesh if you show up empty handed."

"Okay. I'm on it."

I called to check on having my teeth cleaned and headed back downstairs. Kyler and Colette were chatting away as I appeared. It was a good sign.

"Hey," he said. "We've already got everything figured out for your place. Zip lines. Eco tours. A camping area to generate income. Community garden. A factory to make guitars and shit like that."

"Most of these are Kyler's ideas, not mine. Particularly the zip line…and the shit like that."

"What? That'd be so cool. We could start them way up there on that hill and land their asses right into the Pacific."

He let out a good laugh. Colette smiled sardonically at him. I was just glad to see the two of them getting along.

"Well, all joking aside, Kyler, I'm still waiting on approval for people to move in around here, so I'm hoping you have someplace to stay tonight."

"What? You mean I can't move in with you guys? — No, just kidding. I rented a room in town for a week. I figured to be here for that long anyway and got a better deal."

"Okay, so here's what's happening. Tomorrow night I'm taking my foundation proposal before the county board. We should have an answer right there on the spot. If it's a yes, we'll get you two settled into your own cottages. If it's a no, we'll have to make some contingency arrangements."

"Hey, I'm cool with whatever," Kyler said. "I've got money. I can hang loose somewhere until things work out."

I looked at Colette. As expected, she looked duly forlorn when it came to the subject of money.

"Look, one way or the other, we'll sort this out. Maybe I'll rent a house in town until things get settled. In the meantime, Colette, you and I are going to see the accountant and architect tomorrow afternoon. Get things rolling. How about you, Kyler? Do you have any plans?"

"No, man. I think I'll just check out the area. Go to the beach. Maybe come up here and go hiking in the woods tomorrow afternoon."

"Sure, you're welcome but just so you know, I'll be tied up all day and into tomorrow night, getting this board business resolved."

"Yeah, cool. Then I'll just hang around town or something."

"How about this? Give me your phone number and I'll call you as soon as we have a decision. If it's a go, we'll meet someplace in town and have a big celebration."

"Yeah! Cool!"

I checked my watch.

"So, I'm frazzled. I think I'll go for a run. You two, feel free to hang out or whatever."

Kyler looked at Colette.

"I could use a walk," she said. "I'm sure Hugo could too."

"Cool, let's do that," Kyler said.

"All right. Enjoy. I'll be back here in half an hour or so."

I dashed upstairs to change and dashed back down. Kyler and Colette were already down on the forest floor and wandering up the trail in the direction of the forbidden cottage. I had been thinking to head that way but decided not to meddle. The last thing I wanted was to make the damned situation more obvious. With a last look their way, I headed for the meadow, followed the path past the cottages and took a trail from there up into the hills. Forty minutes later, I was bent over in front of my stairs, drenched in sweat and catching my breath.

Upstairs, I found Kyler and Colette busy making dinner.

"Hey, I hope you don't mind," Kyler said with his big smile.

"No, not at all. Saves me the trouble."

I went over to have a look.

"I found some pork in the freezer," Colette said, "so we're having carnitas tacos."

"Cool, huh?" Kyler said.

I tasted the pork.

"Hmm. Good. Guaranteed to skyrocket your cholesterol levels. Guess I'll take a shower and see you two down here for dinner. How about you, Kyler. Did you want to clean up?"

"No, I'm cool. I'll take a shower when I get back to my motel room later on."

Everything was ready when I arrived back downstairs. I grabbed a beer from the frig.

"Hope you don't mind, Kyler."

"Not much...you bastard."

He laughed but it was not exactly the same laugh as before.

"I'll have a Perrier with you," Colette said.

They were bantering away as I sat down to the meal. When they sat down with me, I held up my beer as a toast. They held up their two Perrier bottles.

71

"Great. I'll just sit here and feel sorry for myself," Kyler said.

He laughed again but clearly the presence of a beer was bothering him.

"Are there many meetings here in this area?" I asked over my first bite.

"Yeah and I'll need one after watching you drink that beer."

"Is it really that difficult for you?"

"No. Not really. Well, sometimes. Like right now." He made bug eyes. "You know, beer and Mexican food."

Kyler laughed again.

"Let's talk about something else then," I said.

"What else is there?"

"I saw Henry IV is playing at one of the local playhouses," I said to Colette. "Like to go see it with me?"

"Oh, that would be grand. Part One, I'll wager."

"Always is."

"So what?" Kyler said. "You have to like go back to see what happens in part two?"

"Yes," I said. "It was all a big marketing scam by Shakespeare."

Colette chuckled.

"All right. Now I feel totally ignorant."

"It's all right, Kyler. Don't take it to heart. I've read all of Shakespeare's histories and I'm not so sure I agree with the popular consensus but all the fuddy-duddy experts in academe will tell you that Henry IV, Part One is the quintessential Shakespearean history. For its unique mixture of sweeping events and pastoral charm. Right, Colette?"

"Yes, lots of swordplay, sack and bawdy women."

I smiled.

"I know what bawdy women are but what's sack?" Kyler said.

"Sherry, basically, in modern terms."

"Oh man. Can you picture it? Some old inn in the forest with singing and wenches?"

"Better get to a meeting," I said.

"No kidding."

Kyler quickly had his phone out.

"Far out. There's one at 8:00 o'clock tonight."

"And what about the play? Did you want to join us?"

"I don't know. I've never been to a Shakespeare play before. Maybe that would be kind of cool."

"Just let me know and I'll buy three tickets."

"Yeah. Cool. I'll go and yell out some program shit when they start drinking."

I chuckled.

"Oh, to be sixteen again."

Colette and I went back to talking about the arts center and soon after, Kyler was getting up to leave.

"So, were we going to exchange phone numbers?" he said to me.

"Yeah."

I reached for my phone.

"I'll just call you if you want, boss man."

"Sure."

I gave Kyler my number and a moment later the phone rang.

"Cool. Now we're connected." He stood there entering my contact information into his phone. "Okay, so I guess I'll see you guys tomorrow night. Hopefully it'll be good news."

"If not, we attack the neighbors."

"All right!"

Kyler shook my hand, said goodbye to Colette and started to leave.

"Oh, hey, Colette," he said from the door. "Get my number from Steven and call tomorrow if you get bored and want to do something."

She smiled and waved as he left. I waited until Kyler's footsteps had disappeared down the stairs and his car was pulling away before speaking up.

"Nice guy."

"Yes. Like a big, lovable puppy dog."

"Yeah. After that encounter with Chaplin, Kyler's sunny countenance restored my faith in the human race a bit. I figured there had to be a place for him around here somewhere."

"But doing what?" Colette said. "From what I could gather, he doesn't possess any particular skills."

"I kind of picture him with a clipboard, organizing things."

"Kyler?"

"Sure. He'll like be our totally cool summer camp organizer."

Colette gave me a look.

"Well, let's not be too uppity here. We definitely need our share of doctors, lawyers and Indian chiefs but there has to be a place for misfits too."

Colette nodded petulantly.

"Present company excluded, of course."

"Yes, of course."

"Hey, you don't know about being a misfit. I dropped out of school. Never any direction. Pretty much a failure at everything I touched. If not for my old man's money, I'd probably be out on the street."

She stared glumly.

"What?"

"It's just, every time you talk about money, it's like a knife in my heart."

"Oh shut up."

I leaned forward and whispered, as though in secret.

"Just so you know, I had the accountant fudge the books a bit so your first paycheck will be waiting for us tomorrow at her office."

"Oh god, Steven. Now I feel even worse. I haven't done a damned thing to deserve it."

"Consider it a signing bonus for your design work on the arts center."

"Hmm. Maybe I should have negotiated a better deal."

I guffawed, had the last bite of a taco, chased it with a gulp of beer and pushed away from the table.

"So, they came and grabbed your car."

"Yes. I have no idea where it is, or if I'll ever see it again."

"The mechanic did say it might take a few days. Otherwise, I wouldn't worry yourself."

"I worry. All this takes money, which I don't have."

I pretended to frown at her.

"Okay, okay…Oh," she said brightly. "I forgot to show you my sketches."

She went off to her bedroom and came back.

"They're a bit rough but you get the idea."

"Very nice," I said and flipped through to page two and three. "I like it. You're sure you didn't go to the Julliard School of Architecture?"

"I had a minor in design. Did my paper on Frank Lloyd Wright."

"I can see that. Very earthy but functional. Why this big cantilever, if I may ask?"

"Well, here. Look again at the floor layouts. I have the dance studio on the lower floor. Otherwise it would always sound like a herd of buffalo stampeding overhead. Then I cantilevered the arts studio so there would be even less transference of noise between the two. That leaves all the first and second story classrooms and offices centered over each other, acting as a further buffer."

I stared at the layout in thought.

"You don't like it?"

"Yeah, but I was thinking to have a museum area, so maybe we should have three floors? That way the classrooms and offices could be arranged so that all of them have a view.

Either outside or into a central atrium. Otherwise, one whole row of these classrooms would be stuck between a wall and a hallway on both floors."

"I was trying to be modest about the budget."

"That's very kind of you, but if we're going this far, we may as well go all the way."

"Fine. I'll redraw them."

"No, no. Don't worry about it. I think this is a fine start. Let's take what you have here to Connor and let him have a go."

I went back to her elevation drawing of the exterior.

"Definitely a good start, though. I like this. I can see it blending in beautifully with the surrounding forest."

I looked at Colette. She was still staring at the elevation and seemed more content than I had yet to see her. When our eyes met, I reached out my hand.

"You see? You're already earning your keep."

That brought on the predictable misty eyes.

"I'm going to guess those are tears of happiness."

"Oh yes." She squeezed my hand. "I do thank God for all of this. That I found you or you found me or whatever it was. I was absolutely filled with despair but two days ago."

I patted her hand, went to grab a bottle of Courvoisier from the liquor cabinet, poured two aperitif glasses half full and held up mine to her.

"Here's to laying the first cornerstone." She touched her glass to mine and we drank. "This is going to be fun. And edifying."

"Oh, it will be absolute magic for me. I have to pinch myself. We'll have to talk. I mean about the direction. There are so many things we can do."

"I know. We'll deal with that once this zoning business is resolved."

I filled the glasses half full again and we toasted.

"Hmm. Good stuff."

"Delicious," she said.

Remembering something, I jumped up and grabbed the sweater box.

"Nearly forgot this."

"What?" Colette said. "For me?"

"No, for Hugo. Of course for you."

She gave me an embarrassed look and opened the box.

"Oh Steven," she said as the red cashmere came out of the tissue paper.

"Nice, huh? Let's see the color on you."

She held it up to her chest.

"Oh, it's really your color."

"You shouldn't have."

"But I did."

She took it down and felt the softness.

"This must have cost a small fortune."

"Very small."

"Thanks," she said with another squeeze of my hands.

I winked and squeezed back.

"So, back to tomorrow. It's going to be a long day so I'm figuring to leave about noon. We'll have lunch, go see Tillie and Connor and then we'll be in limbo for however long in the afternoon until the attorney has my paperwork done. Then it's on to the board meeting."

I made big eyes. She shook her head.

"So you're saying I can cash this check tomorrow?"

"Sure. Somewhere in all that, we'll set up your bank account and go shopping to grab whatever food and sundry items you need."

"And should I plan to join you at the board meeting?"

"Yeah. As painful as it may be, you could be dealing with these folks directly at some point down the road."

I winked and went to place the Courvoisier back in the cupboard.

"So, up for a movie? I have a couple of good ones here from Netflix."

"Sure. Let me use the bathroom and take Hugo down for a pit stop first."

I used the bathroom too and was queuing up the movie when Colette and Hugo reappeared from down below.

"Popcorn?" I said.

"No, I'm fine," she said and curled up on the other end of the sofa. "What are we watching?"

I told her the title.

"It's about Reagan and the CIA funding the Nicaraguan Contras."

"And selling arms to Iran to get the money, let us not forget. That bastard."

Colette went into a minor rant about Reagan and his minions. I listened to her droll, acerbic take on things with admiration. As much as Colette had disclaimed any affection for politics, she was marvelously informed.

"Well," I said. "If the movie's going to upset you that much, we can watch something else."

"No. I really love hating the man. And to think they wanted to put him on Mr. Rushmore."

"The movie's beginning."

"Okay, I'll shut up."

I smiled to myself. The hawk I had discerned in Colette at the coffee shop the other morning had risen from the ashes, and appeared to be anything but wounded. In fact, I feared for any board member who got in her way.

Late that night, I lay in bed, aware that a beautiful woman was curled up in flannel sheets downstairs, an awareness that hurtled my thoughts back to a fine spring day long ago, when an ancient and long dormant urge had stirred in my heart and I had called a contractor and had furiously set about bringing the first little gingerbread cottage to life.

Then, like a bowerbird, having fashioned its talisman of sticks and stones and colorful flowers, I sat back to wait, not at all certain I could live with a woman under the same roof, or that I wanted to, but knowing the warmth of her lights down the lane from my treehouse would warm my heart as evening settled over the woods. And soon, a woman had appeared, her windows burnished with lights at dusk, our evening meals shared over fine conversation, our dear, sweet passions indulged by a roaring fire.

But, now, five winters later, all that was gone. The cottage was boarded up and the subject was as taboo to me as voodoo was to a Kansas preacher.

The Tribe

7

A brief storm raced through overnight, leaving behind another blustery day along the northern coast. I sat in my upstairs office, handling a flurry of morning phone calls with the white-capped sea off in the distance.

Around ten, I took my empty cup of coffee downstairs and found Colette and Hugo off for a walk. Scrambled eggs and bacon greeted me on the stove. I gobbled them down, showered and dressed. It was going on noon when Colette and I finally headed out the door. She was wearing her new red sweater.

"It looks stunning, dear," I said.

"Oh, thanks." She touched my arm. "It was sweet of you."

Down on the forest floor, I helped Colette into the truck and jumped behind the wheel. She was holding Hugo up so he could see. Motoring south down the coast, I put on an old Beatles' album and we sang along with the songs. By the time we arrived in town, we had replayed *Love Me Do* a half dozen times.

"It must have been magical to be alive back then," Colette said.

"A much different world. Simpler, I imagine. It's what I love about the music. Clean and straightforward."

"My father was a draft dodger," she said. "I was actually born in Canada."

"Faaarrrrr out," I said. She smiled. "So you truly were a child of the sixties."

"Well, I was born in the eighties but I've always felt like belonged in that earlier generation."

My phone rang before we had a chance to go on. I saw it was Richard and held up my hand.

"Hi Richard. I hope there aren't any snags."

"Nope. We're right on schedule. I'm calling you about that business with your friend, the inspector."

"I'm still boiling over about the bastard. So what's up?"

"I've arranged a meeting for you with Frank, the head of the building department. The inspector will be there too. Frank promised to do whatever he could to straighten things out."

"Would that include a firing squad?"

"If that's your goal but I've worked Frank into a cooperative mood and would recommend you not screwing that up."

"I'll do my best. So when's all this planned?"

"4:30. Basically when Dan gets back in from the field this afternoon."

"Okay. Thanks. That actually fits in very well with my other plans. As soon as I'm done in town, I'll head over your way."

"We should be ready by then."

"We should? I don't like the sound of that."

"We'll get it done. You may be racing back across town at the last minute but we'll get it done."

"Okay. Thanks. And that Chaplin business?"

"I've got a man working on it."

"Great."

"Just don't forget the baubles and glass beads for the natives."

"Oh, I'll have baubles and glass beads galore. Don't you worry about that."

I got off and explained the call to Colette.

81

"So, are we hungry yet?" I said.

"Not really but I think I'd better put something into my stomach. All that coffee has given me the jitters."

"A bowl of soup maybe?"

"Yes, that sounds perfect."

I drove over to a little soup and sandwich place down by the coast and parked in front. Colette let Hugo relieve himself before we went in. I ordered clam chowder. Colette ordered the broccoli soup. The waitress brought a big bowl of chowder crackers to go with mine. Colette began slipping a few of the crackers to Hugo. We had a good laugh at the look on his face while he ate them.

"Hmm, delicious," I said once my chowder arrived.

"Yes, this broccoli is delicious too. Thick and hearty."

I smiled and looked out the window. The sun glowed yellow in the ashen blue sky. The boat riggings clanged in the harbor.

"We've got half an hour to kill," I said when we were done and back on the sidewalk. "Care for a walk?"

"Sure."

We followed the boardwalk down along the harbor. The wind was cold. The gray and white water lapped against the shoreline. We walked all the way up to the Bay Bridge and turned around.

At two, we were walking into Tillie's office. Both women took awkwardly to the introduction, Colette because she wasn't entirely comfortable with her ersatz role and Tillie because she just seemed to be eternally uncomfortable around people. She was the Nowhere Man in a dress. Facts and figures. Logic and economy. To the point. To the point. I pictured her home alone on Friday nights, pouring bottles of wine over her unspoken loneliness.

Then what did I know? Perhaps she was the wiser one when it came to these human affairs.

With all three of us shifting our feet, Tillie handed Colette her first check. A nervous laugh came with it.

"So, every other Friday from now on?" she said to me.

"Yes, but we'll consider this last week's pay, so the Friday after next will be her second pay day."

Tillie smiled to gloss over her grimaced look.

"Just make it work, dear. As far as the IRS is concerned, she's been on my payroll since Monday, a week ago."

Tillie shrugged.

"Okay."

All three of us stood there smiling awkwardly again.

"So now you ladies know each other. You know where to pick up your checks, Colette, and you know how to reach me if there are any problems, as always, Tillie."

I gave her a cautious, one armed hug and headed out the door with Colette.

"I don't think she likes me," Colette said downstairs.

"I wouldn't worry yourself. She's just type A. By the book. You'll find her picture with that phrase in the dictionary."

"I'm already dreading my next check."

"I told you not to worry. When it gets right down to it, I'm the one writing the checks, not her."

We had jumped into my truck and were heading across town. Hugo sat in the middle. Poor guy couldn't see anything but the sky and the tops of buildings going by. Colette finally put him in her lap again.

"You know, I had this vision of Tillie as the Nowhere Man while we were standing there."

"Woman," Colette said.

"Yes. Nowhere Woman."

"Facts and figures. Facts and figures."

"Exactly my thought. I begin to wonder if she's ever been laid. But...I won't' even go there."

"You already did."

"So I did. Let's just say she's a good soul and leave it at that. Anyway, our next stop should be far more entertaining."

"This is the architect?"

"Aye, lassie. The laddie from the highlands of Scotland."

Colette smiled.

"He'll be wearing his kilts, no doubt."

"Is he really that avid?"

"No, but there's no mistaking the accent."

I had come to his office building and parked in front.

"Can Hugo come with us?"

"Sure. Connor's informal, if nothing else."

Colette carried Hugo up the stairs and I followed. Connor must have heard us coming up because the door opened before I had a chance to knock.

"Grand!" he said. "I've always wanted me own Short Legged Scottish Sheep Dog."

Hugo gave him a low growl.

"Well, I see the feeling's mutual. You must be Colette. Connor. Come in, come in. Steven had let on you were beautiful but I'm afraid he didn't do the matter justice."

While Colette blushed, Connor shook my hand.

"Good to see you again, mate. Come in and let's have a look."

I followed Colette in and Connor closed the door.

"May I suggest we have a sit down here at my desk for starters and knock things around?"

Colette looked at me and I waved for her to proffer her sketches.

"Connor, I had asked Colette to work on some ideas for the layout and she did these drawings."

"Terrific," Connor said, taking them. "I see the mark of some training here. A regular Frank Lloyd Wright, she is."

"Yes, I like the feeling of it but she was being way too modest with my wallet. My first thought is, let's go three stories instead of two and have a museum of sorts as a centerpiece."

"Absolutely. Smashing idea. Come, since we've already got a start here, let me show you my take on things."

He led us back to his drafting table and quickly sketched out an elevation with three stories.

"See, if we take your basic idea and stretch it out a bit, we'll have your central museum space here on the ground floor, Steven, along with a viewing balcony completely surrounding it from the second floor, which would allow some further gallery space on these second story walls. What do you say to that?"

I looked at Colette. She nodded.

"Also, this vaulted space will continue all the way up to the third floor. It will be quite dramatic."

He drew a bit more, adding in Colette's cantilevered second story dance floor.

"A viewing deck and offices above it here. We could even add a little kitchen to serve the bloody patrons tea and crumpets. Do you like it?"

"I like it," Colette said with a look at me. "But it's your money, Steven."

"It's your art center, Madam Director. Connor, I'll leave you two to settle on the matter of offices and classrooms and this little refreshment area. I hadn't thought of it but that's a great idea. Add in whatever you want and let's all sit down again to have a look together before we finalize things."

"But do you like it?" Colette said.

"I love it. I wasn't looking for the Met but I absolutely wanted a grand feeling. It's supposed to be the art center of a community, so above all I want it to feel spacious and inspiring. If that means adding ten feet here or twenty feet there, by all means go for it."

"You've got it, mate."

Connor jotted down the words, offices, classrooms and kitchen on his sketch.

"Maybe even a kitschy little gift shop for the tourists," he said with a wink at me.

I frowned.

"Well, you had said something about a self-sustaining community." Connor pretended to scratch off the idea and looked back at me with a smile. "I'll work up a preliminary drawing over the next few days with Colette's input and then we'll have another sit down together. Right?"

"Right," I said. "You'll be fine with your current retainer then?"

"Absolutely. Let's say I work up an overall cost and bill you for the initial drawings when we meet again?"

"That's fine."

I looked at the clock and started to get up all in one motion.

"Listen…we need to hit the bank and I need to go knock heads with the building department at 4:30 so…"

Colette stood up with me.

"Make sure he has your number?" I said to her.

"Oh, right, mate," Connor said and handed Colette one of his cards. "Check in with me tomorrow, luv and we'll go from there. Thanks as always to you, sir."

"Thank you. So it's onward with building the Met here."

"Right you are. Cheers, mate. Luv. A pleasure meeting you."

"A pleasure meeting you."

With more handshakes we backed ourselves out of the office and headed downstairs.

"He's quite charming," Colette said once we were out on the street.

"Yes, quite dashing, and available, I would imagine."

Colette frowned at the suggestion.

"So, what's your preference in banks? I do most of mine with a local credit union. A pox on 'too big to fail' and all that."

"I'm all for screwing them too," she said.

"Great. Let me get you started there and then I'll have to dash off to this meeting at the city." We jumped into my truck. "You'll be downtown and surrounded by shops so you can do all your shopping."

"What? No mall?"

"Oh yes. The Great Northwest Discount Outlet is just up the street here. Gaudy as hell and everything guaranteed to be made in China."

Colette pretended to swat at the bees about her head.

Four blocks over, we were parking at the credit union. I accompanied Colette inside and introduced her all around.

"She's on the payroll so take good care of her. Got to run, luv." She smiled at my Scottish accent. "I'll call as soon as I'm done and we'll connect back downtown here. Thanks, all!"

I started for the door and stopped.

"Almost forgot," I said, rushing back to over to Colette. "Kyler's number. Why don't you give him a call?"

She copied it from my phone to hers. I dashed out to my truck with five minutes to make the meeting on time. I was five minutes late walking in and made sure to look fashionably out of breath.

"Sorry, gentlemen. A thousand appointments this afternoon and things got a bit out of hand."

Frank Wheeler, the department head offered up a disgruntled smile and leaned forward in his seat to shake my hand.

"Dan," I said, sitting down.

Dan nodded for an answer.

"So," Frank said. "I've heard Dan's side of the story. Let's hear yours."

"Well, I'd say what happened yesterday was my case in point. He sees a woman with a few of her belongings spread out in one of the cottages and assumes she's moved in."

"Well, she had. There was food in the kitchen and clothes spread out all over the place. And a dog."

I stared at Dan until he looked at me.

"May I?"

"Let him finish his side of things, Dan. You'll have plenty of time for a rebuttal if necessary. Go ahead, Steven."

"Look, I'll admit. It was a lousy idea on my part, letting her stretch out and clean up a bit in that cottage, but move in? She had a couple of bags and what was left of some muffins we had purchased in a café downtown."

"And a dog," Frank said.

"And a dog."

"And where are said dog and lady now?"

"Staying at my place."

"Hmm."

"Look, Frank. My point is, chew me out. Tell me to run the gal off, but shut down the entire project? Dan's actions the other day are symptomatic of his attitude towards me from the very start. As far as I'm concerned, he came out there with a hard on that first day and he's had one ever since."

"I'm there to perform a function on behalf of the city, not to win a popularity contest."

I stared at Frank. He motioned for Dan to back off and for me to go on.

"Dan's right. He's there to perform a function on behalf of the city, but in the normal course of human affairs, is it unreasonable to expect civility? This sort of crap goes on in a marriage and you get a divorce. What am I supposed to do here?"

"So what would you propose?"

"Assign another inspector to my project."

"Damn it, Frank! Are you going to let him run roughshod over us like this? Every time a person doesn't like what they hear, we assign a new inspector?"

"He has a point, Steven."

"I'm not arguing the code or the law here. I'm just saying, this whole thing has become poisoned and there seems to be only one solution to that. Reassign Dan. What am I going to do? Move? I own twelve hundred acres out there."

"Well, if you hadn't started building that circus of yours out there in the first place, we wouldn't be in this situation, would we?"

I shrugged at Frank.

"I rest my case."

Frank sighed heavily while shaking his head.

"Dan, look. No one's telling you not to enforce the code but it does seem like you've gotten yourself a bit too emotionally invested in this situation. Maybe a change of personnel would be in everyone's best interest."

"Fine. Fuck it." Dan bolted out of his chair. "I'm filing a formal complaint with the employee's union. You can't do this..."

"Dan!!!" Frank said.

Frank stopped in his tracks.

"Sit your ass down!"

Slowly, Dan settled back into his seat.

"Now you go right ahead and file a complaint if you want, but if you do, I'm going to file a report on you. Look at yourself. It's like you're on a goddamned vendetta. You're right. It's your job to enforce the building code. It is *not* your job to meddle in zoning and the likes. We have a department for that and capable people, who can handle these situations."

"Oh, so if I see a zoning issue, I'm not supposed to report it?"

"No, you report it to the proper personnel and get back to the job you were hired to do."

Dan sat there steaming.

"Look, I'd say let's shake hands and part in peace but I can see that's not going to happen so you're dismissed. Do whatever you think you have to do but you're off the Fitzgerald project. And I say the rest of this with real concern. We're here to serve the public good, not to run a witch hunt so I suggest you go home and take a long hard look tonight at just how you've gotten yourself to this point."

Dan continued steaming.

"Go on. You're dismissed. I have a few things I'd like to discuss with Steven in private."

Angered and wounded in equal proportions, Dan stormed out of the office without closing the door. I got up to close it.

"Sorry," I said, sitting back down.

"Christ," Frank said under his breath. "I've always known the man to be wound a bit tight but this is on another level altogether. You're sure you didn't say something to egg him on?"

"Not a goddamned thing, Frank."

"Well, I guess it doesn't take a rocket scientist to figure out what got him started."

"I don't even have to guess, Frank. He said it for me. And I quote here. 'You rich people are all the same. You come in here throwing your big time money around like you own the place. No respect for the rules or local traditions'."

"He really said that?"

"I won't swear it's verbatim but it's pretty damned close. If anything, it's slightly abbreviated."

"Jesus. He really said that?"

I nodded.

"It sounds like the man's in need of some counseling."

"By his own admission, he's targeted an entire class of people...Not that I blame him in this case."

Frank shot a satirical look my way and looked back out the window.

"What I put up with around here."

"Sorry. So am I free to go?"

"Oh, sure." Frank got up to see me out. "You know, you're going to have to deal with these zoning issues, sooner or later."

"I'm being dragged before the Inquisition this evening, as a matter of fact."

"The Inquisition?"

"In a manner of speaking. I'll be trying to ram a foundation through the board. It's that or adopt everyone who comes to live out there."

Frank shook his head with a perplexed smile on his face.

"Well, I'll be goddamned if I can see where you're going with this, but I guess it's your money and your business."

"Actually, the lady who instigated this great kerfuffle?"

"Hmm hmm?"

"She's a Julliard trained bag lady."

Frank chuckled.

"Laugh, but I've made her my arts director and once we get that place up and running, we'll have an open house so you can come out and see for yourself."

"Well we'll just have to do that."

"I'll look forward to it. In the meantime, please assign someone with an open mind to my project. That's all I ask."

"Anyone you prefer?"

"Oh, hell. I wouldn't pretend to make that choice. I don't even know them. Just anyone but Dan at this point is good enough for me."

"Well, don't worry about it. Just make sure your boys build to code and we'll be fine."

"Dale's as fastidious as they come."

"Yeah, no. He's a hell of a builder." Frank patted me on the shoulder. "You'll be fine. I'll try to pick someone who fits the project and you let me know how it goes."

"Thanks again, Frank."

"No problem."

It was one of those goodbyes that didn't seem to have a proper ending so I smiled and headed down the building department corridor with Frank staring at my back. Halfway down the hallway, I heard his door close.

The Tribe

8

On the way out to my truck, I called Colette's number. She answered after several rings.

"So how did it go?"

"They reassigned Dan to cleaning latrines at the state park."

I heard her laugh, the phone being muffled briefly, a voice in the background and then she was back.

"What's going on?" I said.

"Oh, Kyler's here. I called him as you had asked and he came right down to meet me."

I heard Kyler say something about hanging the guy in the background.

"He's all excited, as you can imagine. So were you coming back to meet us?"

"Yes but I may have to stop by my attorney's office first. Let me call him and I'll call you right back."

Richard came on the phone as I was jumping into my truck.

"So, how did things go at the city?"

I explained.

"Splendid. Let's hope your streak of good luck continues tonight."

"And? How's it going on your end?"

"We're almost there. Give me another hour and things will be ready for you to pick up."

I checked my phone.

"So around six?"

"Thereabouts. You may have to wait a few minutes."

"And the dirt on Chaplin?"

"It's here but I don't want to lay a hand on it personally. Let's just say I've learned that the man had a less than sterling reputation down there."

"Gee, I'm shocked."

"Yeah, well. I heard enough to know you'd be kicking up your heels and beyond that I asked no questions. I had someone in the office package up the report for you and read no further."

"Fine. The last thing I want is you losing sleep over this."

"Thank you."

"Okay. I'll see you in a bit."

"Don't forget the peace offerings."

"I'm not drooling on my chin yet, Richard."

"Just wanted to remind you."

"I got it. So, how many folks am I accommodating?"

There was a pause.

"The usual. Eleven. Clarke left to pick up his kids about an hour ago but he was here all night too."

"Eleven it is. I'll see you soon."

I called Colette back.

"Where are you?"

"Oh, it's an area of boutique shops by the waterfront. I can see the marina from here. Kyler, what are the streets?"

"Waterfront and F Street," I heard him say in the background.

"Got it," I said. "Just go on with what you're doing and I'll call the minute I'm in your neck of the woods."

I hung up and headed for a nearby gourmet market. Inside, I grabbed someone in the wine shop and had him box up a case of Perrier-Jouet Belle Epoque, Brut, 2006 vintage. While he did, I went over to peruse the gift card rack. One of the finer local restaurants seemed to be the best option. I started to reach for the $100 cards, thought better of it and went for $200 instead. $100 would hardly get you past the drinks and *hors d'oeuvres* at that place.

With everything paid for and loaded into my cab, I headed towards the waterfront and called Colette back. She guided me into a coffee and chocolate shop over on Opera Alley. Kyler gave me a high five when I walked in.

"All right, dude. Yeah! You beat his ass!"

"Yeah, well. I wouldn't get too excited. Dan was a gnat buzzing around my head. I'll be dealing with crocodiles tonight at the board meeting."

"Wow. Cool. Want me to bring a baseball bat or something?"

"That's exactly what I *don't* want you to do."

"Oh. I get it. Like I should lay low and pretend I don't exist, right?"

"That's the general idea." I glanced up at the clock. "Excuse me. Think I'll give my jangled nerves with another jolt of java."

I glanced again at the clock as I returned and sat down.

"What? Are you late or something?" Kyler said.

"Yes and no. I need to be at my attorney's office around six. So, are you really planning to join us at the board meeting?"

"Yeah! I want to see you get pissed and start a brawl or something."

"You might see a brawl all right, but it won't be me starting it." I sipped at my coffee. "You know, I'm thinking, Colette. There's no need for you two to come with me to the attorney's office. Why not just hang out with Kyler and we'll all hook up later on at the board meeting?"

"Fine but you'll have to give us directions."

I quickly pulled up the location on my phone and Kyler punched the address into his. I had another sip of my espresso and kicked back to watch twilight rush over the world.

"So tell me more about this Chaplin dick," Kyler said.

"Oh Christ. The Duke of Trinidad."

Kyler laughed and punched his fist.

94

"Yeah!"

"Actually, my attorney had a private dick dig up some dirt on him down in Sonoma."

I noticed Colette studying me.

"Yes, all my mortal sins laid bare for the world to see."

She smiled and sipped from her espresso.

"Anyway, if Chaplin decides to play hardball with me, I'll be ready to play hardball with him."

"All right!" Kyler said. "I love it!"

"We'll see who's loving it in a couple of hours."

I took another gulp from my espresso and stood up.

"So, if you two are okay, I'll see you over at the meeting later on. Just lay low in the back and no outbursts from you, Kyler. Especially if we win. I don't want it to look like I'm gloating."

"Damn," he said laughing.

"All right, you knucklehead. The meeting starts at seven."

I headed for the door. The evening had turned bitter with a wind blowing down from the north. I grabbed the sheepskin coat from the seat of my cab and pulled it on. Ten minutes later, I was walking into Richard's office. Between the coat and box of champagne in my arms, a split second went by before his frenzied staff recognized me and a general razzing set in. I waved as though the conquering hero and started passing out champagne. Between that and the gift cards, the tide had soon turned back in my favor.

Richard met me at his door with cheers at my back.

"All right, everyone. Come on. Let's get this done." Richard checked his watch. "Steven has less than an hour to make that board meeting."

He waved me into his office. I handed him two bottles of champagne and two gift cards.

"One set is for Clarke. The other for you. Wouldn't want you to feel left out."

"You pay me enough already," Richard said.

"I know."

He eyed me, and then one of the bottles.

"Nice stuff."

"Nice stuff."

"Thanks. Sit down."

I did.

"So what do you think?" I said.

"I think it'll all come down to those two swing board members, as usual."

"It's like the Supreme Court. Everyone's fate hanging on the bastard in the middle."

"Yes. In any case, you'll know in a few hours."

An attorney named Byron knocked lightly and popped his head in the door.

"We're binding the copies right now. Five minutes and you're out the door."

Richard thanked Byron and he disappeared.

"So, the damage?" I said.

"Don't know yet. A bit less than what we had discussed."

"That's fine. Any time you want a check."

"I'll have my secretary bill you next week."

"And send me your dates for that fishing trip."

Richard smiled.

"I will, thanks. After Christmas sometime...Oh," he added and reached into his desk. "Here's that dirt. I decided it was my duty to read it after all. Most of it's public record. I'd tread lightly on that last page. Unless you like defamation suits."

I thumbed through the public record part quickly.

"No, this will do. I assume you have a copy?"

He nodded.

"Good. For now, I just plan to drop this in his lap. 'Just so you know that I know'. I figure it'll back the bastard up a few paces."

Richard held up his hands.

"Hey, he threatened mud, not me."

We chatted about life and politics and the winter weather in Cabo for a few minutes. Then Byron knocked and popped his head back in the door.

"All done."

I slapped my knees and stood up.

"Thanks again, Richard. You're a scholar and a gentleman."

He nodded and accompanied me out front. I took the box of copies, thanked everyone one more time and headed for the door.

Ten minutes later, I was walking into the board meeting. A woman clerk took the foundation proposal copies and set one in front of each of the name tags around the long, crescent table.

I saw the portly Chaplin already seated in the front row, girded up by an entourage, wearing his khaki jump suit and high leather boots and channeling silent picture stars. He had just quelled a disturbance among the natives in the African bush and was back for a gin fizz before dinner.

Colonial toad. Arrogant pretender. He liked to drop the last name, as if it implied royalty, even though the lineage had come down through the famous actor's cousin. I figured Fatty Arbuckle was a better fit.

Everyone in Chaplin's entourage looked up as I approached their row of seats. I asked him for a private word and waited until we were alone against a far wall before handing over the report. Chaplin quickly turned red as he thumbed through the pages.

"Just so you know, Chaplin. We all have a past. You want to fight over the merits of this case, fine. You want to dig up dirt..."

I gestured.

"Then all's fair in love and war."

I gave him a final nod and took a seat opposite him in front. When Chaplin's wife inquired about the folder with a whisper, he snapped at her. I smiled and looked forward.

97

There was a growing buzz from people pouring into the meeting behind us. At one point, I glanced back and found Colette and Kyler seated in the last row. When I waved, Chaplin looked back with a frown. You could see him visibly harrumph. Riff raff. A tiger pit was too kind for the bastard.

A short time later, the board members entered the chamber and the head of the board, Chairwoman Parch, rapped her gavel. The usual crap ensued. The reading of minutes. Honors given. Announcements made. A few minor points of business were discussed and then it was my turn.

As I stepped up to the podium, Toni smiled at me. The other board members were busy thumbing through their copies of the foundation proposal. There were several asides whispered among them.

Chairwoman Parch pulled her microphone around.

"From what I can glean of this proposal, Mr. Fitzgerald, it's all quite properly drawn up. I just question whether this is the kind of thing we want to have in our community."

"With all due respect, Chairwoman Parch, I believe this question of usage was already ruled on in an earlier zoning matter. As long as I maintain a 2000 foot distance between construction and my property lines, I am free to build as I choose, subject to all applicable building codes and local ordinances, of course."

"But this foundation of yours, it allows for all sorts of…how shall I put it…unusual forms of activity."

"Unusual? As I hope my foundation charter points out, I intend to do a number of things through One Earth, which are designed to assist the most vulnerable in our society. Is that unusual? Maybe far too unusual these days but I don't see where that makes it illegal."

"Well, I just…well…as I said, it just seems a bit out of place to me."

"If I may interject here," Toni said. "We currently have an animal rescue foundation up on the Deming Ranch and I don't remember anyone complaining about that when it came before the board. Now, here, we're talking about trying to help some disadvantaged people and I for one would be ashamed to think that we'd vote unanimously to help animals in need and reject the notion of helping our fellow human beings."

"Well, yes. I guess when you put it that way," Chairwoman Parch said. "It would seem a bit mean spirited. Does anyone else wish to comment?"

A florid faced geezer named Watson reached for his microphone with less than steady hands.

"I do think this board has a right and duty to voice its concerns about density issues and I don't see a thing in your charter here about that."

"It's on page seven. Any development would be subject to all local zoning and ordinances. I can assure you I have no intention of building a megalopolis out there. My vision is of something quite bucolic."

"Hmm," Watson said as he continued thumbing through the charter.

"Ladies and gentlemen, I'm not asking for a blank check here. I'm only asking that you approve the use of my own land for the purposes of this foundation so that I'm free to inhabit the existing cottages I've built. All future construction will be subject to the usual review process."

"Very well," Chairwoman Parch said. "We'll go ahead and allow public comment and then vote. Does anyone wish to voice their opinion?"

Chaplin was quick to raise a hand.

"Yes, Mr. Chaplin. You may take the podium."

I passed him as I was sitting down. He gave me a condescending look and took the microphone.

"Mrs. Chairwoman. Members of the board. As you well know, I owned and operated a highly successful winery in Sonoma County, along with a highly successful line of olive oils. I sold those businesses and retired here, to what I had hoped would be a quiet sanctuary for the remaining years of my life. I bought my parcel of land in large measure because of its zoning. I expected that my fellow landowners and I would agree to maintain the rustic nature of the land, if nothing else. Then along comes Mr. Fitzgerald, intent on starting god knows what kind of circus out there and I'm not going to lie down and watch him destroy the peace I worked so hard to achieve. Not without a fight. Now, I have a petition here, signed by several of my fellow landowners, stating our opposition to the use of his land for anything other than residential purposes and I must warn you that we are prepared to go to court, if that becomes necessary. I would just conclude by stating that while operating my businesses down south, I went out of my way to work harmoniously with my neighbors and that is all I am asking of Mr. Fitzgerald. If he wants to start a foundation or whatever he wishes to call it, let him start it in some appropriately zoned commercial area. Thank you."

Chaplin shot another condescending look my way and took his seat.

"Anyone else?" Chairwoman Parch said.

No one spoke up.

"Well, Mr. Fitzgerald, I suppose it's only fair to give you an opportunity to respond to Mr. Chaplin's remarks."

I returned to the podium.

"Let me be the first to congratulate Mr. Chaplin on his successful career. There is no question he worked hard to make his fortune. That does not, however, give him license to dictate land uses in this county. I would suggest that, if he doesn't like the local zoning ordinances, then sell out and move elsewhere. All I'm asking is to be treated fairly under the existing laws. Now, as to Mr. Chaplin's threat of a suit, if he persists in his efforts to deny me the free and fair use of my own land, I will have no choice but to file suit against him."

I turned to look at Mr. Chaplin and then back at the board.

"Did you have a response?" Chairwoman Parch asked Chaplin.

He shook his head.

"Then are there any other comments?"

There was a great deal of murmuring among the citizenry but no one stood up. Parch banged her gavel.

"Then I recommend we proceed with a vote."

The board members went down the line, announcing yay or nay. Watson came out against it, as did his fellow Republican, Avorres, but the final vote was 7-2.

With that, Chaplin sprung out of his chair and fairly well bellowed out.

"You've not heard the last of me, rest assured of that!"

A hush fell over the crowd as he stormed out of the meeting, his wife and entourage in tow. Chairwoman Parch looked a bit shocked. The entire board looked stunned, save for Toni. She winked at me over a suppressed smile. With a buzz of conversation continuing amongst the masses, Parch banged her gavel again.

"Mr. Fitzgerald. You are free to occupy your property, per the terms of your foundation proposal. I wish you well with your...enterprise. I'm confident that if we stick to all the pertaining codes and ordinances, we'll be just fine."

"Thank you, Chairwoman Parch. I assure you I will. And thanks to all the board members for your time and votes."

Parch had to bang her gavel yet another time as I headed down the aisle. Some of the old guard hippies held out their hands in support as I went by. Otherwise, the response was fairly muted. Some of the old timers would never understand what I was trying to do out there, but I had conducted myself as a responsible neighbor and few around town wished me ill.

Approaching Kyler, he was unable to restrain himself from punching a fist in the air. I herded him out the doors before he could make any more impulsive displays.

"Yes!" he said once we were out in the hallway. "Does that mean we can move in?"

"Yes, let's go get drunk and celebrate."

"Oh wow. I totally hate you now."

"I understand. So, are you all right with joining us for a couple of drinks?"

"Yeah. Sure. Sort of. I'll have my Ivanhoe and hate you two."

"Very well. Let's go hit The Quill. It's a civilized place to grab a drink."

Out in the autumn coolness, Kyler resumed his displays of victory.

"Yeah! All right! You creamed that sleazy bastard!"

I put a hand on his shoulder.

"You might want to save a bit of that energy, Kyler. We've won a battle, not the war. I have no doubt that fucker has more mischief up his sleeve."

"Yeah, you're right," he said, pretending to be chastened.

Then he was pumping his fists in the air again.

"How do you turn him off?" I said to Colette.

She joined me in my truck and Kyler followed us across town. Colette and I talked but my mind was on other things. This vision of mine had acquired substance now. It was becoming something real, with new people in my life and new responsibilities to face and far flung repercussions I did not pretend to understand. I had succeeded in mounting the wild wind with no idea where that wind was about to take me.

The Tribe

9

At a little past midnight, the three of us made our way back out onto the sidewalk in front of The Quill. A steady drizzle was falling. Pleasantly high, Collette propped her head sleepily against my shoulder.

"I know," Kyler said, still all ginned up over our earlier victory. "Let's go grab some new recruits so I can whip them into shape."

He pumped his fist in the air.

"How *do* you turn him off?" I asked Colette.

"There's a button in back."

"Yeah!" Kyler said with a big laugh. "Can't wait to put the fear of the lord into our new recruits!"

I smiled and patted him on the shoulder.

"All right, young man. You come by tomorrow around noon and we'll get you set up in one of the cottages. Everything you need is there, save for food and sundries."

"Don't ever forget your sundries," Colette said with the humor of a drunk.

"Yeah, sundries, baby. I'll stock up and see you there."

He gave me a hug and then Colette.

"This is so far out, man. I can't even believe this is happening. Our own tribe. Wow. I am so totally going to make this work."

"*We're* going to make it work."

"Hey, that's right. Like we say in fellowship. It's a 'we' program."

"It's a wee program, laddie," I said with a Scottish brogue.

Kyler laughed. Colette had chuckled against my shoulder.

"All right. I'll see you tomorrow, Kyler."

He started down the street to his car. As I was helping Colette into my truck, Kyler broke out into an Indian rain dance.

"Tribal, baby!"

He looked back with a laugh. I waved one last time and climbed into the cab. Colette and I looked at each other.

"He's so wonderfully innocent," she said.

"And mostly harmless," I said.

I started the truck and looked over at Colette.

"I think."

We had a good laugh as I drove off.

Back at my place, Colette took Hugo up the path to relieve himself. I went upstairs and unlocked the front door. I was putting away the morning dishes when Colette came in.

"I was ready to nod out in the bar," she said. "Now I'm all wound up again."

I went to the cupboard and returned with the brandy and two aperitif glasses.

"Just what I needed," she said.

"I have sleeping pills if you'd prefer."

"No. This is fine."

I filled both glasses and offered up mine as a toast.

"To the tribe."

"To the tribe."

We drank.

"So, still no idea where this thing is headed?" she said.

"Not really. You know what they day about fools and their money."

Colette smiled lazily and sipped again. I looked back out at the forest.

"You know of Paul Bowles, I presume."

104

She nodded.

"Well, I am reminded of this vignette he once shared, regarding his novel *The Sheltering Sky*. He was living in one Arab city or another while working for the British foreign service and described how, having had this vision for the book, he hurried back to his room and by that afternoon had outlined the entire story. My god, I thought. How boring. Wouldn't it be like coloring by the numbers after that?"

Colette smiled.

"Some artists need more structure than others," she said.

"Apparently so, but that's not me. I mean, you just left a corporate job where everything was already mapped out for you."

I waved my hands around.

"What's the point of this, if it's only to find the same sort of rigid structure?"

Colette pumped a less than enthusiastic fist in the air, a la Kyler.

"Yay. The tribe."

"Thanks…You know, for me, I think it just comes down to left brain, right brain, and whatever that logical hemisphere is, I'm the other side."

She chuckled.

"You, no?" I said.

"I find my life is a constant battle between the two. I suppose that's mostly fear driven. The potential for catastrophe seems enormous if I ever give in entirely to my creative side."

"Fair enough."

We sat there for a spell with our thoughts.

"See, my sense from the start was, every new member will bring something to the table and their talents and energy will help to influence our direction."

I polished off my brandy.

"Of course, Kyler was right about one thing. Food is essential to survival so we ought to start with a garden. Everyone chips in or they don't eat."

"This is beginning to sound like one of those communes."

"So? It's back to being a hack in the corporate world."

"When do I start?"

"That's the spirit."

"Ha!" she said.

I smiled and played with my empty brandy glass.

"But seriously, Steven. I'd love to get my hands into the earth. Man cannot live on ballet alone."

"Touché," I said and stood up. "So, are we all right until the morning?"

"I'm wonderfully fine and sedated now. Thank you."

I went to a mission desk by the door and dug out a collection of keys.

"Here, this is for your cottage. If you're up before me, feel free to go down and set yourself up."

"Thanks. What with Kyler showing up today and our other adventures, I never did get around to my shopping. And of course, I'm without a car."

"I'll check on it for you tomorrow."

"It is a rather helpless feeling."

"Don't worry. You can steal whatever you need from my kitchen and we'll drive in as soon as it's ready. Connor knows the drill in the meantime. Complete the elevations for design review, and while they're signing off on that, we have a week or two to finish the rest of the plans. Then it's a final dash through the building department before we break ground."

"How exciting."

"Yeah. So, dare I install Kyler next door to you?"

Colette got big eyes.

"Maybe a few doors down?"

"You never know, Colette. The next tribal member might be even less to your liking."

"Oh, don't get me wrong. Kyler's a doll. It's just that, I kind of fancy some space right now."

"Sure. Understood. Anyway, I think I have just the spot for him. A cottage befitting the camp director."

We smiled. I started for the stairs.

"See you tomorrow then."

"Thanks again, Steven. This is a most wonderful adventure you've created."

I shrugged.

"I'm only slightly terrified by I've wrought."

She waved a hand at me as I headed upstairs.

Once lying there in the darkness of my room, the image of Colette's nakedness entered my mind, but that only made me think of Catherine and those nights when I had delicately stripped off her clothes in the moonlight, down to her pale flesh, and the way she had giggled as I slipped a pair of high heel sandals onto her fair feet.

What the hell was I going to do? I was unable to escape the old feelings, the old bonds, the old devotion. I wanted intimacy but my mind would not be where my body was. I would be looking into Colette's eyes and thinking of old love.

Fuck.

I rolled over and tried to put the thing out of my mind. Outside, the pines moaned and serenaded my thoughts.

In the morning, I found Colette gone and a stack of buckwheat pancakes next to the stove. I buttered up four, laced them with maple syrup and nuked them in the microwave. While they heated, I started a pot of coffee. While that was brewing, I got my vitamins out. I took enough supplements every day to choke a horse. I had to hope it was doing me good. I could assume to have my answer in thirty or forty years.

While eating, I stared out towards the sea through the forest, my mind racing here and there about what to do next. I had been so consumed with the zoning battle, there had been scant time to focus on more practical matters.

Talented people, I thought. If this tribe is going to be self-sufficient and thrive, it will need people with skills to fill in the gaps.

Pushing my plate aside, I opened my laptop and looked for places to post job opportunities. After a bit of poking around, I settled on one professional site and the local Craigslist. Local people would be ideal for the situation, but you never knew. There might be a guy or gal in Detroit, just dying to get out of the city.

The ad basically said that there was a unique situation for professionals and craftsmen. A great living environment on the northern California coast. Doctors, programmers, biologists, whatever. Inquire for more info.

With that done, I called my landscape contractor. The phone rang while I rinsed off the dishes at the kitchen sink. When Kevin answered, I turned off the faucet.

"Kevin, it's Steven. How's it going?"

"Well, not so good, actually." Kevin laughed his yuk yuk laugh. "I went down to Baja on a surfing expedition for a month and it's been pretty much raining ever since I got back. I can't get any work going."

"Well, I have something for you."

"Yeah? Wow, that would be great. So what is it?"

"I need a couple of new roads put in and some fencing done. Maybe a few other things."

"Great. So when did you want to meet?"

"Today? Say one o'clock?"

"Wow, sure."

"Good. There's somebody out here I want you to meet. We'll go over what I want done and he'll give you a hand from there."

"So when were you thinking to get this project started?"

"You can start right away if you want."

"Yeah, sure. I'd love that."

"Great. In fact, get your gravel trucks lined up and bring your grading equipment out here today, if you'd like."

He chuckled.

"Didn't you want me to give you a bid first?"

"It's not necessary. We'll settle on a figure as soon as you've seen things."

"Wow, great. So, get right on it."

"Get right on it. I want this done by the end of the week."

"Wow, thanks." Kevin laughed. "So I'll see you at one then."

"I'll see you at one."

I called a local golf cart operation next and arranged for them to deliver four golf carts, two strictly for passengers and two for maintenance work. With a bit of arm twisting, the sales manager agreed to deliver them at two.

With that done, I settled back at the kitchen table and stared out at the coast. What next? I was a runaway train, looking for the next station to blow through.

Having another idea, I ran upstairs to brush my teeth and dashed down to my truck. A minute later, I was pulling to a stop in front of the last cottage. I found Dale and Jason inside banging away on the pick up framing.

"How's it going?" Dale said with a look up from his work.

"Good. Hi Jason." He smiled while cutting a block for Dale. "Look, you guys. This is going to be the last cottage for a spell."

Dale paused with a glance at me. Jason looked dejected.

"Take a break for a second. I need to discuss something with you."

Dale reluctantly set his nail gun down and came over.

"What's up?"

I explained about the arts center. Dale raised his eyebrows while listening. Jason now looked delighted at the prospect of even more work.

"My point is, I'll need you to ramp up. Get some more bodies out here. I'll pay you overtime if necessary but I want the building done by spring."

"You're talking miracles," Dale said.

"Maybe, but all I'm asking is, give it your best shot, okay?"
Dale shrugged.

"I have no problem with that."

"Good. I'll make sure you have every resource you need. You tell me what it is and I'll make sure it's here on the ground immediately."

"Let's have a look at the plans and go from there."

"I'll run them by you as soon as I have something in hand." I started out but stopped. "Oh, and we'll start right back in on the next cottage as soon as we're done with the arts center."

That got a nod from Dale and another big smile from Jason.

I jumped back into my truck and checked my watch. It was almost noon. I headed home and found Kyler leaning against his car, smoking. He gave me a big smile as I parked and got out.

"All right. I'm ready to start cracking the whip around here, boss man," he said. "No, just kidding."

"Well, you may indeed be cracking a whip around here tomorrow."

"All right! What's up?"

"Jump in the truck and let's go settle on a cottage for you first."

"Cool. I want the one right next to Colette."

I pulled away with a look at Kyler.

"Like I said, you're probably barking up the wrong tree with that business."

"Like what? She probably said, 'Don't put Kyler next to me.' Fucking bitches. They're all the same."

He laughed.

"Kyler, Kyler, Kyler."

"What?"

"They're not all bitches and they're not all the same. You just need to get it through your head that Colette's a wounded bird. Not that I pretend to know what she wants in a relationship, but I'm pretty sure she doesn't want to get involved with anyone right now."

"Yeah. Fucking bitches. Okay. I'm just kidding."

"All right, knucklehead. Let's just find you a cottage and get on with the business at hand, which is starting the community garden."

"Wow, far out. I don't think I've grown anything since I was a kid."

"Well, this is your big chance. I'll put every resource at your disposal and hopefully we'll have some fresh bodies around here soon to help you. I even ordered a couple of those maintenance golf carts."

"Wow, cool. You mean like they have at golf courses and shit?"

"Yes. Like they have at golf courses and shit."

"All right. I'll get one of those straw hats and start talking in Spanish."

I laughed at him.

"Just for today…"

"Yeah, that's what we say in AA."

"I know, so just for today, I have a landscape contractor stopping by and I want you to work with this guy putting in a new road out to the garden."

"Cool. We'll make a little Le Mans that I can whip around on."

I shook my head and pulled to a stop in front of a cottage.

"I think this one would be the perfect for you, Kyler. It's close to the meadow but still really secluded. What do you think?"

"I love it. It's the perfect place for me to keep an eye on the peasants." He pretended to crack a whip. "Yeah, get a move on, suckers."

"You knucklehead. Come on, let's go take a look."

Kyler was his usual ebullient self, checking out everything inside. There could have been wooden bowls and orange crates, for all he cared. The cottage was merely a prop for his shenanigans.

"Wow, man. Thanks," he said and gave me a hug. "This is so cool. I am so jazzed about being a part the tribe. Yeah."

He pumped his fist in the air. I checked my watch.

"Okay. Let's get back. We don't want to miss Kevin."

Back at the homestead, I had just enough time for another cup of coffee before Kevin pulled up. I quickly introduced him to Kyler.

"So, you didn't bring your equipment."

"Oh, I'll hit the ground running in the morning."

He laughed his yuk yuk laugh.

"Fine."

We climbed in my truck and headed further up into the hills. I pointed out the general area where I wanted the roads as we passed through the forest.

When we came to a high meadow, I parked and we all jumped out. The flanks of the hills rose up behind us, bare in places where they had been logged in past years but dotted now with younger pines and green with grass, their crests capped with old growth and the higher hills behind them towering into the pale blue winter sky.

I kicked around the rolling meadow with Kevin.

"So what I want you to do is build a fence around this area. Follow the contours. Make it fanciful. I don't want it square. I don't even want the garden level. Then dig out the soil inside the fence and mulch it thoroughly. We're going to plant a community garden.

"Far out," Kevin said with his characteristic chuckle.

"You know you're going to have a lot of critters out here trying to get inside."

"I know. So what I want you to do is build some kind of barrier that goes underground and cap the fence in a way the big critters can't get over it."

Kevin chuckled.

"Yeah, it's not as easy as it sounds."

"I know, but here's an idea. I saw this on a nature channel one night. You cap the fence with a sheet of plywood three feet wide. That way raccoons or whatever can't reach over the top."

"Okay, cool. I guess it'll work."

"It will. I saw it. Now as far as the fence goes, use redwood with a 2X12 cap. That should provide enough support for the plywood. And make it nice plywood. Put a router edge on it. Some kind of embellishment on top. Whatever. I want it to have a nice feeling."

"Sure, but we'll also have to place the pickets really close together or use some kind of wire mesh to keep all the critters out."

"I think wire mesh is the trick. Use something heavy duty and galvanized and run it down into the ground a good 18" or two feet. I don't want anything shy of a goddamned mining engineer to get under it."

Kevin laughed a real laugh.

"So, that's it," I said.

"So what about a price?"

"What about it?"

"Well, there's enough going on here that I don't know if I can finish up a bid by the morning."

"So, we'll do it cost plus. The only thing I'd ask is, get the fence started simultaneously and put Kyler to use in any way that you can."

"Sure. You got it."

Kevin chuckled and bumped fists with Kyler.

"So, tomorrow?" Kevin said.

"You can start today, as far as I'm concerned."

"Well, it's a bit late now but I can definitely get started first thing in the morning."

"That's fine."

We jumped into my truck and headed back down the hill. The driver with the golf carts was parked alongside the main meadow and waiting when we arrived.

"All right," Kyler said. "My low riders."

Tyler and I hummed a few bars of the song.

I climbed out and greeted the driver. His helper set up a ramp and started backing off one of the maintenance models while I signed for the carts. As soon as it hit the ground, Kyler jumped in and did some figure eights. Kevin stood there chuckling.

Finally the truck was gone and the show was over.

"Shit," I said, staring at the golf carts. "I just realized. We'll need to build a storage shed to house the equipment, which means having more plans drawn up and more approval from the building department. Fuucccckkkkk!!!"

Kyler laughed.

"Wow, brother. That's like the first time I've seen you lose it."

"Yeah, well. I'm guessing you haven't seen anything yet."

In the pause that followed, Colette and Hugo appeared off through the woods. The three of us watched them come down the path until they were standing before us. I introduced Kevin to Colette.

"And who's this little guy?" Kevin said.

"Hugo."

Hugo's ears went up. Kevin petted him.

"I just saw Steven lose it for the first time," Kyler said to Colette.

"Do tell."

Kyler explained. Colette smiled at me.

"A presage of things to come?" she said.

"All right. Enough with this crap. We need to get two of these golf carts over to Kyler's place and two of them over to mine."

"Hey, don't mess with my ride, baby!"

I held out the invoice to him.

"Shakin' the bush, boss man, shakin' the bush."

"Yeah, I thought so. Colette, why don't you give Tyler a hand and Kevin, you can help me."

"What about dinner?" she said. "That's why I walked over here. It seemed rather pointless to cook all by myself."

"Sure. What about you, Kyler. Are you hungry?"

Kyler checked his phone.

"I've got an hour and a half to make this meeting in town."

"I'm sure we can whip up something by then. Come. Let's go eat. Then you and Colette can drive two of the golf carts back to your place on the way home."

We were soon caravanning together through the woods.

Back at my place, Kevin said goodbye and drove off. Colette and Kyler and I paused there in the fading light. A hush had come over the forest. I felt a fine breeze tickling my face.

"Did you talk with Connor today?" I asked Colette on our way upstairs.

"Yes."

"And how did it go?"

"Fine. We hit a wall when it came to adding a banquet facility."

"Indeed. Whose idea was that?"

"Mine, but incorporating it into the arts center turned out to be completely untenable."

"Why do I smell another building in the works?"

"I know. You see? You've gotten me into the habit of spending your money and now I can't stop."

"Hey! While we're at it, let's do that zip line!"

"Get out of here."

"Oh, man. Come on."

Colette looked back down the stairs. All of us looked that way and found the forlorn Hugo stopped near the bottom. With a sigh, Colette went down to retrieve him.

The Tribe

10

As soon as Colette had departed that evening, I jumped into my jogging togs and ran off into the woods. My head had begun to go around and around about her. Her scent, her wooly patch, that first moment of penetration, everything about that cloistered world was becoming visceral to me. And yet my heart was still with Catherine, the same as it had been for the past five years. Solitude was my only true mistress, that and the rain. Perhaps I loved the rain so much because it wept in place of my own grief.

Consumed with these thoughts, I was jogging back down the hill, wondering how it would all end, when I saw Kyler from a distance, slipping into his cottage with a woman. What the fuck? You just moved in and you're already dragging a strange woman home with you? My impulse was to go beat on his door. That was followed by reluctant restraint. So what did you expect, Steven? To dictate the personal life choices of every tribal member?

That high valley in the Alps was calling to me again. Why hadn't I gone for simplicity? I'd head into a little village every few days, have some laughs with the townsfolk and return to my peace and solitude. Instead I had thoroughly complicated my life.

I fell asleep struggling with my destiny.

A bit after eight the next morning, someone knocked on the door as I was sitting down to a bowl of cereal. I answered and found Kyler with a frail, blonde waif of a woman standing next to him. She had rosy cheeks and large blue eyes that seemed to suggest clairvoyance. That, or madness. It was hard to tell which one. She was bundled up in several garments, including a nylon parka, beneath which she could not have weighed more than 90 pounds. Her oversized jogging shoes grabbed my attention, that and her silent stare.

"Hey!" Kyler said with his typical ebullience. "This is Camellia. Steven."

I shook Camellia's frail, delicate hand. Her penetrating stare did not waver.

"We met at the meeting last night and thought maybe she could become part of the tribe. She says she knows all about growing gardens."

I nodded with another forced smile for Camellia.

"Well, listen, Tyler. I was just sitting down to breakfast so maybe we could we discuss this later?" I looked at my watch. "I'm expecting Kevin here any minute and need to gobble down my cereal."

"Oh sure," Kyler said, his ebullience faltering. "I guess I'll just have Camellia hang out in my cottage today until we're done."

"Sure, sure." I held out my hand again. "Nice meeting you, Camellia."

She stared for another moment before Kyler encouraged her back down the stairs.

"All right! Time to crack the whip!" Kyler said with a big laugh on their way down.

I offered him an obligatory smile and wave of my hand when he looked back up.

Fuck, I thought, closing the door. That was one thing I had failed to foresee. Members of the tribe taking it upon themselves to invite new members. How was I going to tell Kyler to get rid of her? I returned to my breakfast and ate while brooding.

Hearing Kevin's trucks rumble up from the highway, I placed my bowl in the sink, rushed upstairs to brush my teeth and dashed down to my golf cart. Kevin was already unloading equipment as I pulled to a stop in the meadow, with Kyler lending a hand and pretending to crack a whip with a laugh. Kevin chuckled with a look up from his work.

"So I'm guessing we'll have to build these roads a bit beefier than the previous ones," he said.

"Yeah. They'll have to carry some weight."

"So, say six inches of compacted base and six inches of gravel?"

"You're the expert but that sounds good to me."

"Yeah. With the compacted base, that should be fine. As long as you're not planning to run dump trucks up and down it all day long."

Kevin chuckled.

"No, just golf carts and regular traffic and the occasional delivery."

"Okay, so my plan is to clear some brush and make a path up to the top with my grader and we'll start from that end. That way the dump trucks won't be tearing everything apart on their way down."

"Sounds brilliant to me. What's Kyler going to do?"

"I'm cracking the whip, man."

Kevin chuckled.

"Okay. Seriously."

"So, I'm going to have him help back the trucks in, for starters," Kevin said. "Then as we're digging out a trench, he can set aside any small boulders we find and we'll use those to line the road or do something artistic."

"Sounds good. Just do as we've done before. Wind here and there. You don't have to go crazy but I don't want any straight lines."

"You got it. So, I'll start up with the grader. My guys are already up there with a generator and our compaction equipment. Kyler, you can help clear any brush out of the way as I go, if you want."

"Sure." He laughed. "I guess there goes my whip."

I grabbed Kyler by the arm before he took off.

"Go ahead, Kevin. Kyler will be with you in a minute."

"Sure."

As soon as he was out of earshot, I spoke up.

"Kyler, I know you had good intentions but we can't go dragging everyone we meet on the street up here."

"Yeah, I guess I should have talked to you first, huh?"

"Yeah. I hate to be a dick but think about it. What happens when we have twenty or thirty members and they all start dragging people up here on a whim? It becomes exponential. If nothing else, there has to be some kind of agreed upon process."

"Yeah, I know. I was thinking about it after we left your place this morning. Sorry, Steven. I'm just a fuck up."

"No you're not. Shit, I'm sorry. The last thing I want is to dampen your spirits, Kyler. Or crush her hopes. What the fuck is with her, anyway? She acts like she's had shock treatments or something."

"No. She shared a bit about her life in the meeting last night. Her only son killed himself a few months back. She was already struggling, trying to put him through college on what she made at a health food store. Then they fired her because she was just walking around staring at people in the store. Fucking sad, huh?"

"Yeah."

"So, that's why I invited her out here. I talked to her after the meeting and could tell she was totally lost and thought, shit, isn't that what we were trying to do out here?"

"You're killing me, Kyler."

"It's cool, man. I can take her back into town at the end of the day. I guess she's got a bed in a shelter."

I kicked at the ground and looked back up at Kyler.

"You say she knows how to tend a garden?"

"Yeah. She was telling me all this shit about how to grow organically and stuff. It sure sounds to me like she knows what she's doing."

"So she actually talks."

Kyler laughed.

"Yeah. There's like a string in back."

I laughed.

"All right, Kyler. This one time."

"All right!" he said and gave me a big bear hug. "I know she'll be cool and really help out."

"Yeah. I don't know if could sleep with myself, sending the poor thing away. But from now on we have to have a pow wow and discuss things before we decide to bring on any new members onboard, okay?"

"Yeah, cool. You're totally right, brother. And thanks."

"Sure. Just to keep her out of harm's way for now. I don't want to see her run over by a grader."

"Yeah, I told her she could hang around my cottage for the day."

"All right. You'd better go catch up with Kevin."

"All right! Crackin' the whip, boss man, crackin' the whip."

I started back to my place, shaking my head. So now we were a collection of four misfits. Meanwhile, I had not received a single inquiry from my ads. Without my money, this entire thing was a joke.

After making some phone calls, I headed up to check on progress. Kevin already had two guys setting posts for the garden fence. Meanwhile, he was personally grading out the path. Every fifty feet or so, he would let a truck back in and dump a load of base. There were four guys spreading the gravel with wheelbarrows and two more compacting. By noon they already had a hundred yards done.

When everyone broke for lunch, I headed home to make a turkey sandwich. Colette popped in as I was sitting down to the table. I gave her half the sandwich and we talked. Connor had completed a preliminary set of plans and wanted to meet with us the following day.

I told her about Camellia.

"You've now officially relinquished your title as resident bag lady."

Colette gave me a sardonic smile.

"Is she really that bad?"

"I won't know until she actually speaks." I looked at my watch. "I'd better get back up there and see how things are going. So, are you good for now?"

"Just fine, thanks to you. Perhaps I'll go introduce myself to Camellia. The two of us can chip in with the community garden."

"Kyler swears she has a regular green thumb."

"Maybe she does."

"Maybe she does."

I had started upstairs to brush my teeth but was stopped short by the sound of Kyler's frantic shouting in the distance. I hurried back down to the front door, fearing someone had actually run Camellia over. Kyler came to a stop at the bottom of the stairs outside and bent down, out of breath.

"What's going on?"

"Fuck man. There's some radical dudes up there by the garden and they've got a gun."

"What? What are you talking about?" I started down the stairs. "What dudes and what kind of gun?"

"It's actually a chick and two dudes and the one guy has a shotgun. He was telling us to get off of his land."

"Off his land? What the fuck? Are we talking biker dudes or something?"

"No, man. They're just some hippie freaks."

"Hippie freaks with a shotgun?"

"Yeah."

"And they just sauntered up?"

"No, look. When everyone sat down for lunch, I went for a walk out in the woods and stumbled across this camp. I just figured I had wandered over onto someone else's property and turned back. Next thing I know, these freaks showed up with a gun so I'm guessing they had seen me and followed me back."

"So how did *you* get away?"

"I had started down to wait for the next truck and ran off while they were cornering everyone else."

"Shit. So they're holding Kevin and his crew hostage?"

"Yeah."

"And what about all the dump trucks?"

"It was lunch and all the drivers were taking a break too. I don't think any of them saw what was going down."

"All right, let's go deal with this."

"Man, I wouldn't go up there without the cops or something."

"Kyler, after all I've been through with the county board, getting my project approved? I do not need the cops up here. In fact, I don't want a word said about this to anyone outside the three of us."

I looked from Kyler to Colette and back.

"All right?"

"Hey, you know I'm cool. I would never say a word."

Colette nodded.

"All right. Let's go find out what this is all about. Colette, I'll drop you off in the meadow and you make sure to keep Camellia out of harm's way. In fact, stop any of the dump trucks from coming in. Tell the drivers we've had a bit of a snag and that everyone needs to hang loose for a few minutes."

She nodded and came down the stairs with Hugo. We piled into my truck, I dropped Colette off at the meadow and Tyler and I raced up through the woods.

The guy with the shotgun had Kevin and his crew sitting on the ground by Kevin's equipment when we pulled up. He pointed the shotgun our way the minute he saw my truck approaching. The young woman standing beside him looked equally hostile. Some hippies. The other guy was standing about thirty feet away, as if he wanted no part of the scene.

I jumped out and headed towards the guy with the shotgun.

"Just stop right fucking there, dude or I'll blow you away."

I kept walking.

"I'm warning you, dude."

"Fuck you," I said and stopped about three feet shy of the barrel. "Who do you think you are, pulling this shit on my land?"

"This is our land, man. We're homesteading it."

"Like hell you are. I own this place for a mile in every direction."

"I told you, dude. Either back off or I'll blow you away."

"Yeah? Well go ahead." I pressed my chest up against the barrel. "Go on. Put yourself behind bars for the rest of your fucking life."

"Come on, Brad," the other guy said. "I told you we should just get out of here."

"Yeah. Maybe you can talk some sense into your friend here."

"We don't want any trouble," the woman said. "We're just trying to protect our claim."

"What are you talking about?"

"We've got a…"

"Shut up," Brad said.

"You've got a what?" I said.

When they didn't answer, I looked at Kyler.

"Do you know what the hell's going on here?"

"Fuck, I think it get it. These guys are up here growing a crop of weed."

"Ohhhhhh," I said, looking back at them. "So that's it. Hippie growers with a crop of bush. And this is your idea of the new age? Pointing guns at people? Shit. You're an embarrassment to higher consciousness. Now get the hell off my land before I do call the cops on you."

"Let's just go, Brad," the other guy said.

"Fuck you. I've got three grand invested in that crop and I'm not walking away from it. I know the law, man," he said to me. "Once we homestead the land for five years, it belongs to us."

I shook my head with a smile.

"First of all, buddy, you've haven't been here five years and secondly, they repealed that law in 1976."

"Oh wow," the woman said.

I looked at her and back at Brad.

"I'm cutting you some slack. Just pack up your shit and be out of here by tomorrow morning and there'll be no cops and no trouble."

"Let's go," the other guy said and started to leave.

"Fuck it. What about my investment?"

"All right. What's your name?" I said to the guy leaving.

"Donny."

"Okay, look Donny. You come by my place tomorrow at noon. I'll have Kyler check on your camp in the morning. If everything's cleaned up and gone, I'll hand you three grand cash."

"Yeah, right," Brad said.

"It's that or you deal with the cops. Or you can blow us all away and see how that works out for you."

"Let's just take the deal," the woman said.

"Fuck, how do I know this guy's good for his word?"

"Look, let's just trust him," Donny said. "He could have called the cops and he didn't, so I believe him."

Brad backed away a few paces with the gun still pointed at me.

"All right, fuck it. I'll trust you that far, but if you don't fucking produce, I'll come back. You can bet on that."

"Come in off Coast Highway," I said to Donny. "It's the first turn past McKenna Road. When you come to the big meadow, take a hard right. You'll see a treehouse about a quarter mile back."

"Okay. I'll be there at noon tomorrow."

Brad backed himself off about fifty feet and turned away into the woods with the woman. Donny looked back once before disappearing.

By then, Kevin and all his crew had all stood up and were gathering around me.

"Fuck, duuuuudddddde," Kyler said with a nervous laugh. "I thought sure that guy was going to blow you away."

"Man, I thought he was going to blow all of us away before you showed up," Kevin said with his own nervous chuckle.

"Yeah, fuck. Sorry."

I held out my less than steady hand.

"Just glad that son of a bitch didn't have an itchy trigger finger."

Everyone exhaled and wandered around a bit, looking lost.

"So what now?" Kyler said.

"What? I'll pay him and let's hope that's the end of it. In the meantime, not a word of this, to anyone. I just went through hell getting my plans through zoning and that's the last thing I need, news of this spreading around town. I mean it, Kevin, and all you guys. Please keep your mouths shut and I'll make sure there's a nice bonus in it for you when you're done."

"Not to worry," Kevin said.

"Okay. Are we all good then?"

"Yeah, we're good."

Kevin and his crew slowly drifted back to work.

"Come on," I told Kyler. "We'd better head back down there and get the trucks rolling again."

Colette was at the head of the truck line when we pulled to a stop in the meadow. A couple of truckers had gathered around her. Camellia was standing off to one side, staring.

Kyler and I jumped out.

"Go ahead and take over. And remember, not a word of this to anyone."

I greeted the truckers and led Colette off to the side, away from Camellia.

125

"I thought you were going to keep her out of harm's way."

"She followed me," Colette whispered. "Did you know she has a degree in fine arts?"

"How could I?" I whispered back. "I have yet to hear her speak."

"So, what do you want me to do?"

"Get her back to your cottage. Maybe help her pick one out. I don't care. I just don't want her standing around here with all these trucks coming and going. Okay?"

Colette nodded.

"Okay. Figure out what she needs in the way of supplies and we'll grab them when we're in town tomorrow. Just get her out of harm's way."

Between the rush of trucks and general commotion, I found myself face to face with Camellia. She stared. I managed a smile and reached out a hand.

"Welcome. Colette here will help you pick out a cottage."

She stared back without speaking. Jesus. I managed another smiled and turned to Colette.

"I have some work to do in my office. You know where to find me. Once you pick out a place, just come and get the key."

When a truck passed, Colette guided Camellia across the meadow. I had one last look at them before climbing into my pickup.

What madness. I found myself secretly envying that bastard Chaplin. He was probably next door, enjoying snifters of Sherry and ordering around the servants in his landed gentry outfit.

11

Around eight the next morning, Kyler appeared outside my opened Dutch door again.

"Hey, duuuuuddde!" he said, making light of the previous day.

"Yeah, right. Did you check on their camp?"

"Yeah. They're gone but they totally left a bunch of trash up there."

"Yeah, let's not worry about it. I'll have Kevin send a crew up there to clean things out. Is everything else okay?"

"Well, that's why I came down. Camellia's up there, trying to run things."

"Run things?! Run what?"

"The garden."

"It isn't even started yet."

"I know but Kevin was getting ready to haul away all the brush and limbs and shit he had shredded and she told him not to. He had to leave it for the garden."

"For compost, I gather."

"Yeah."

I shrugged.

"Makes sense."

"Yeah, but she's like going around talking to herself. 'We need to test the soil for PH.' Blah, blah, blah. All kinds of shit. It's like she's totally obsessed now."

I smiled.

"And who do we have to thank for that state of affairs?"
Kyler laughed.

"Yeah, I guess I kind of blew that one, huh?"

"Who knows? Maybe it was meant to be…Look, my main concern is keeping her out of harm's way. You guys are well out of that area now, right?"

"Yeah. We're halfway down through the woods. I just know you were kind of freaked out about her so I thought I'd better let you know."

"Yeah, it's fine. Just keep an eye out. And maybe jot down whatever the hell she's babbling about. We might actually need it for the garden."

"Yeah, cool, boss man. Shakin' the bush, shakin' the bush."

"Hey, whatever you need, just let me know and I'll arrange the finances."

"Will do…So, do you ever think to yourself, 'why didn't I just buy a big yacht and a place down in Cabo'?"

"That thought crosses my mind about every other minute."

"Yeah! All right! Let's just go fishing down in Cabo."

"All right, back to work, sucker."

"Yeah, crackin' the whip, boss man…Hey," he said on his way down the stairs. "I think it's totally cool what you're doing with your money. I always thought, if I win the lottery, I'm like totally going to try and help people and do good shit."

"Yeah. I don't know how a person can be in this position and not try to help."

"You'd have to be a really greedy prick."

"And sometimes I wish I was."

We laughed.

"The important thing is, are you having a good time, Kyler?"

"Yeah, man. I'm totally digging it. I just think we need some more bodies."

"I know. I'm working on it. Some skilled people, though. They can't all be idiots like us."

Kyler laughed.

"Well, at least the garden will help us to become self-sustaining."

"Oh yeah, that'll help big time."

He laughed.

"Yeah. We'll all be living off of radishes and shit."

"You knucklehead. Get back to work."

Just then, we heard the rumble of more trucks coming up from the highway.

"Oh shit, I'd better get back down there."

"I'll be up as soon as I'm done with Donny."

"Oh yeah. He's coming by at noon. Did you need some extra security? Someone to bust some knuckles?"

"No. Donny won't be any trouble."

"Okay, boss man." Kyler hurried down the stairs off through the woods. "I'm shakin' the bush, shakin' the bush."

I shook my head with a smile and went back inside.

Promptly at twelve noon, I heard tentative footsteps coming up the stairs. Assuming it was Donny, I hustled down from my office. He was just coming up to the Dutch door as I arrived.

"Hi," he said through the opening. "I'm not early, am I?"

"No, right on time, Donny. Come on in."

"Wow, this place is really far out. And cool drawings."

"Yeah. Here, come in and have a seat. Can I get you something to drink?"

"No, I'm good. Thanks."

Donny took a spot on the sofa and sat forward. If not for his shock of long dark hair and the peach fuzz growing on his chin, he was the kind of young man who would have gone far in a corporate boardroom; a pale, finely chiseled face with a neat nose and nice ears. He appeared to be both intelligent and quietly perceptive.

I sat opposite him in a chair.

"So, you guys are all moved out up there."

"Well, we left a lot of trash behind but Brad and his girlfriend wouldn't help me clean it up. I can totally do it myself but I don't have a truck or any way to haul it off."

"Don't worry about it. I'll have my landscaper guy send some of his crew up there. Brad seems like a jerk but I could tell your heart was in the right place."

"Well, I was definitely against using guns but, you know, this was Brad's gig. I was just up there to help him out and get a share of the profits."

"Don't worry about it. It's done."

"Thanks."

"So, tell me about yourself. You seem like an educated guy. How did you get mixed up in this situation?"

"Yeah, how did I? I have a major in eco-biology so that's why Brad brought me in."

"And you couldn't find any better use for your skills?"

"I tried working down in Silicon Valley for a year after college but just kind of freaked out one day. You know, it's all about the 1%."

"Yeah, I know."

"It is and it totally sucks so I ended up here, working in a co-op and struggling to pay my bills. Then I ran into Brad and thought, far out, at least I can put my education to use. That guy quickly freaked me out, though. I could see how unhinged he was but decided to hang in there, hoping to get my share of the profits before I moved on."

"So what now for you?"

"I don't know. I've always wanted to do something good for mankind. That's what I was thinking when I took my major in eco-biology. I also have a minor in software engineering but that was just to keep up with the times. You're screwed if you can't do computer modeling these days."

"Well, the fact is, Donny, I need people out here. Good people. Intelligent people with skills who can help to bring this project to life. What do you think of that?"

"Like doing what?"

I explained as best I could, particularly about the green energy.

"Far out. So, I would get a cottage out here and work in exchange for food and stuff?"

"For starters, yeah. That's all I can guarantee is a roof over your head and something to eat. Once we get this tribe generating income, then we can talk about salaries or whatever. In the meantime, I'm willing to fund anything that gets us headed in the right direction."

"You mean like making pottery or something?"

"That's a possibility but I've got other ideas. Look, if you're interested, the best thing is, let's sit down and have a brainstorming session with everyone. See what we can come up with. Take the best ideas and run with them. So?"

"So you're wondering if I'd like to get involved?"

"Yeah."

"Totally, yeah. I mean, this is exactly the kind of thing I had wanted to do. Help mankind."

"Yeah, well, I'm trying not have any illusions. I've learned that there's always the potential for disaster when you're dealing with your fellow human beings but I think we can do some good out here and maybe have some fun in the process."

"Cool, man. And, hey, I'm sorry about the other thing."

"It's all right. Don't worry about it. I knew right away that you were different from Brad. Let's just see what we can do to make this thing happen."

"Yeah, I'm totally onboard."

"Good." I stood up and Donny stood up with me. "Let's go see if we can find you a cottage."

I grabbed the keys out of the mission desk and we headed out the door.

"This your car?" I said down below.

"Yeah."

I glanced at the interior. It was an aging, black Honda Fit but clean inside. That was a good sign.

"Go ahead and follow me. I need to get back here soon for another meeting."

As we were parking in the meadow and getting out, Kyler spotted us from afar and made a gesture across his throat. Donny didn't see him but I made the same gesture back at Kyler. Like mind your own business. I was unable to hear him over the trucks but saw he was laughing.

Donny and I started down the path towards the cottages. The lower end of cottage row was already populated by Kyler, Camellia and Colette so I thought to install Donny somewhere on the far side of them.

Coming alongside Colette's cottage, we found her reading a book on the front porch. I introduced Donny.

"Eco-biology. That's a great major," Colette said.

"It's a struggle. I had better luck with my software engineering but then you're basically stuck in the corporate world."

"Another refugee, are you?"

"Yeah. You too?"

"Yeah. Put 'er there, partner."

They shook.

"But I should think your major would be a great fit out here, Donny."

"Actually, I'm taking him down to see the recycling plant right now. He'll be our...er...eco-maintenance engineer."

"That sounds dignified," Colette said.

"So, we're off," I said.

"Nice meeting you," Donny said.

"You too. Oh, are we still on for that appointment with Connor at two?"

"Sure. As soon as we pick out a cottage for Donny, I'll swing by and grab you."

"Okay, see you then."

Three cottages up, Donny said "wow" so I showed him inside.

"Wow, the whole thing's like out of a movie from the forties."

"Yeah. So you like it?"

"Yeah, totally."

"Okay." I handed him the key. "Let's go take a look at the treatment plant."

We walked down a path through the woods and towards the sea.

"Far out!" Donny said upon seeing things.

"So you understand this?"

"Oh yeah. It was one of my dreams, setting up this kind of recycling plant in developing countries. You can run everything off of the methane. Cars, stoves, furnaces. Create electricity with the compressed gas."

"You got it. It's all there and you're in control."

"Cool. I can totally handle this equipment for you."

"Great. Oh," I said and dug out the three grand. "Almost forgot about this."

Donny took it reluctantly.

"You're sure you're okay with this?"

"Of course. I gave my word. The trash aside."

"Hey, I'll totally go help clean things up."

"Maybe. Look, let's just plan on having a pow wow tonight over dinner. Either at my place or at some restaurant in town. Let me get you into my phone here."

We exchanged numbers and started back down the path.

"So, go take care of Brad and I'll call you as soon as I know what's going on for tonight. I'll be in town anyway for this meeting with my architect so we'll probably hook up there. Feel free to stock up on supplies for your cottage or whatever you like. It's a long way out here. You do have money, right?"

"Not much. It depends on whether or not Brad gives me some of this three grand."

"Well, don't worry about it. I'll make sure you've got whatever you need."

We came alongside Colette's cottage.

"Ready?" she said.

"Yeah."

She set her book inside and locked the front door. Hugo came down the path with a curious look at Donny.

"Meet Shorty," I said. "AKA, Hugo."

"He's cool," Donny said and petted him.

"He's still trying to figure out how come he's so short, right Hugo?"

Colette laughed.

"Don't. You'll give him an inferiority complex."

"Oh yeah. Like he doesn't have one already."

We went down the path with me cracking jokes at Hugo and Colette defending him.

We came to where the passing trucks were kicking up a cloud of dust in the meadow. Kevin had made good headway down through the woods and Kyler was out there, having a grand time directing things. He waved and we waved back.

"So, I'll call you later," I said to Donny. "And good luck with Brad."

"Yeah. It was nice meeting you," he said to Colette before climbing into his car.

"Oh, hey!" I said before Donny drove off.

He stopped and rolled down his window.

"Don't say a word to Brad about this situation. I don't want him knowing what's going on up here, period."

"Yeah, I kind of figured that."

"Yeah, I figured you did but I didn't want to leave anything to chance."

"Don't worry. I'll keep my mouth shut."

"Thanks."

I patted his window opening as he drove off.

"Seems like a nice guy," Colette said.

"Yeah. It was kismet. He knows all about that equipment down there, so, perfect match…"

"So, are we off right now?" she said.

I looked at my watch.

"Yeah. Let's get going."

I called Kyler on our way down to the highway.

"Shakin' the bush, boss man, shakin' the bush," he said, answering the phone.

"Yeah, yeah. I installed cameras out there and can see you're screwing around."

Colette smiled at me.

"Shakin' the bush, boss man, shakin' the bush," Kyler said again and laughed. "So, what's up?"

"You know that list you were making for Camellia? I'd like you to text it to me. I'll stop by this garden supply place while I'm in town and set up a delivery."

"You got it."

"And stop with the boss man routine. It's going to my head."

"Shakin' the bush, shakin' the bush."

Kyler laughed again. I shook my head at Colette.

"Just send me the list."

"I will. Oh, here comes another truck. Gotta run."

"Oh, hey, Kyler," I said before he could hang up.

"Yeah," he said.

"We're having a tribal pow wow tonight. Probably at a restaurant in town. Either there or at my place. I'll call you as soon as I know which but be prepared to bring Camellia with you, either way. We need to start talking about direction."

"Zip lines, baby!"

"All right. Get back to work and I'll call you later."

"What did he say?" Colette asked when I got off.

"Zip lines."

"You know, it's not such a bad idea."

"Ha! I'm not turning the place into a tourist attraction."

"Maybe just one little corner of it?"

"No."

"Just for our own entertainment?"

I glanced over at her.

"Maybe. But there has to be a better way to generate income. I'm thinking something techy. Something to do with the internet. The minute we start talking a heavy footprint, I'm back to fighting with the county board. And probably the Coastal Commission."

As we neared Coast Highway, a heavy fog enveloped the road. All was gray and grizzly along the coast. I turned south and flipped on some Latin jazz.

"Oh, that's lovely," Colette said. "Who is it?"

"Cachao." I looked over. "A Cuban bassist and orchestrator."

"Very nice. Lovely rhythms. Do you mambo?"

"A bit. This music does make your feet restless, doesn't it?"

"Yes. I used to teach it."

"The mambo?"

"Yes. The mambo, the rumba."

"The tango?"

"Oh, that's very different. Far more difficult and stylized. It's beautiful when done right but I much prefer the mambo. The mambo is just as elegant when two people know it well and are in tune with each other."

"We'll have to try it someday."

"At the new dance studio."

"Oh, I imagine we can get something off the ground before then."

The two of us went down the road with the Latin jazz bursting through the gray, foggy day like sunshine.

The rhythms and melodies were still going around in my head as we walked into Connor's office.

"Drawing's on the table, luv," he said to Colette, welcoming us in.

She went back to look.

"There'd be a secret in there somewhere," Connor whispered to me.

"In what? The smile?"

Connor winked. I scoffed, getting his drift.

"We were listening to some Latin jazz on the way down the coast."

"Looks to have the same effect then."

"You lascivious old man."

"Lascivious young man."

"Yeah, yeah. Let's go have a look."

I guided him back towards the drafting table. Colette stood in front of it, flipping through the elevations. I joined her and nodded in agreement with each new page.

"What do you think, Madam Director?"

Colette nodded.

"I like it. A lot. I like the way you've created these secluded patio areas, Connor. Nice places for people to retreat and talk about the arts."

Connor reached in and flipped to the floor plans.

"Here you are, luv. Office spaces, an ample sized cafeteria. Everything else we discussed."

Connor noticed me lost in thought

"What's on your mind, mate? You don't look all cheery like."

"No, I like it. It's rustic but elegant. It's just, I'm thinking all of a sudden about our need for a tech center."

"Don't you dare try to incorporate your tech business into my arts center," Colette said.

I glanced at her.

"I could have figured you to say that."

"Well."

"Well, I'm just thinking of the review process that awaits me if I have to build a separate structure for every need."

"Look, if I catch your drift," Connor said. "We can rearrange some of these offices on a temporary basis. Ya see, I've designed this center core so that none of the walls are bearing. These 18 spaces are divided equally just for show. We can easily move the walls around. Bigger, smaller, whatever you like."

Colette groused. I reached over to comfort her.

"Let's plan on at least having the tech center in here on a temporary basis. We'll shove them over in a corner somewhere and give them a derogatory name. Like Skunk Works or the Wrecking Crew."

"Nerd Works," Connor said.

"Perfect. Your arts people can treat them like outcasts, Colette but I can't house them in a cottage or tent until the next structure is approved."

"You won't."

"All right. We're mincing phraseologies here."

"Cheer up, luv," Connor said. "We'll get you a queen sized corner office. You'll have a title. Servants. The lot."

Colette looked over with a beleaguered smile. I chuckled.

"So we're good then, aye?"

"Probably not but why don't we do this? Assign the tech department to this one little corner over here by the cafeteria. Then work out the rest of the office space to suit Colette's vision of things. Like he said, Colette, it's all flexible. Someday we'll have a separate tech and science building, but for now, just get something down that we can submit to the city and let's roll."

"You've got it, sir."

"So, about the money?"

"Right."

While Connor and I settled on a price and a down payment, Colette went to stare out Connor's windows. A few minutes later, Colette and I were seated down in my truck.

"Are you all right there, luv?" I said, imitating Connor.

"Wounded. But still standing."

"Would it help to say I'm delighted over your commitment to the project?"

"A bit."

"Eh, don't worry. It'll be all right."

"And my car?"

"Oh, yeah. I talked with the mechanic this afternoon. One more day, he said."

"I can't imagine what's taking so long."

"I don't know. He's been swamped, I guess."

I felt my phone vibrating and pulled it out.

"Ah, here's Kyler now with the gardening list. Jesus Christ! We'll need a semi-truck! Wow. Okay. Care to join me on a shopping expedition?"

"Sure. I was thinking to plant some flowers around my cottage anyway."

"Oh, that sounds nice. A window box or two?"

"If you don't mind."

"Why should I? It's your cottage."

I drove over to the garden center and went about filling Camellia's list of supplies. Meanwhile, Colette loaded up a cart of her own.

"So, what do you think?" I said when we were done and back in my truck.

"About what?"

"About the meeting. Here or back at the ranch?"

"I vote for here. A bit of laughter and tinkling glasses?"

"Sure. I'll tell you what. I know a great seafood place. Old school. Darkened atmosphere. Piano bar. Towels over the arms and all that."

"Sounds wonderful."

A few minutes later, we were seated in a booth in back, with a view of the coast through the tinted glass. I ordered a Scotch. Colette ordered a glass of chardonnay. While waiting for our drinks to arrive, I called Kyler and told him where to meet us, then called to update Donny too.

"To our growing tribe," I said, holding up my glass of Scotch to Colette.

The two glasses touched and we drank.

"You know, Tyler told me about that 'shotgun in your chest' incident. My god, Steven. What were you thinking?"

"I hope this son of a bitch doesn't fire accidently?"

"Steven, don't. You scare me at times."

"Yeah? Worried about me?"

139

"When you do stuff like that, yeah. It's like you have a death wish."

"I did once, but not anymore...I'm just an ornery old SOB."

"You won't be for long at that rate."

I smiled and was about to offer Colette a retort when my phone rang. With a glance, I saw it was Richard.

"I'd better take this," I said. "Yes, Richard. What can I do for you?"

Colette watched me listen with increasing concern.

"Goddamn it," I said out loud. "You'd better get ready because I'm suing that bastard. Hell, I'll sue the city and whole state if I have to. One way or the other, I'm going to put that haughty little prick in his place."

Richard had a few more words for me before signing off. The people in the next booth were stealing glances when I hung up. I almost told them to shove it.

"What is it?" Colette said cautiously.

"It's that bastard, Chaplin. He filed a complaint against me with the Coastal Commission."

With murder on my mind, I tossed back the rest of my Scotch and called for another one.

The Tribe

12

Colette listened patiently to my harangue of Chaplin. A few minutes into it, she cleared her throat and offered an apologetic smile over my shoulder. I looked back to find Donny standing there.

"Hey, how are you doing? I said and stood up to shake his hand. "Please, have a seat."

He did.

"I'm not too early, am I?"

"No, no. And you already know Colette."

Donny said hi and returned his stare to me.

"What? Don't worry. I'm just having a little snag with one of my neighbors."

Donny kept staring.

"He filed a complaint with the Coastal Commission about my project."

"Bummer. So does that mean everything's off?"

"Not at all. I'll deal with that prick. Did you want a drink?"

"Sure, I'll have a beer."

I got the attention of the waitress and Donny ordered something from a local micro-brewery.

"Did you want to see the menus now?" the waitress asked.

The three of us shared looks and shook our heads.

"Not right this second," I said. "We're waiting for some more people to arrive."

"Okay. Just holler whenever you're ready."

"Will do."

I looked back and found Donny still staring at me.

"So how did the money drop go off with Brad? Did he cut you in?"

"Yeah, a little. Enough to survive for a week."

"Don't worry. You'll be all right."

Donny's beer arrived and the three of us held up our glasses.

"To our brave new world," I said.

We toasted and drank. Colette spoke up.

"Steven said that you went to Humboldt. How did you like it?"

"It was cool. Kind of strange. There's a fine line between eco-consciousness and just being flaky."

Colette laughed.

"And you? Where did you go to college?"

"NYU, and then Julliard."

"Wow, that's different. What was it like?"

While they discussed college education, I considered the hellhounds on my trail. Unable to ignore them, I stood up.

"Look, I need to make a couple of phone calls. I'll be right back."

Out in front of the restaurant, I got Toni on the line and explained the situation.

"So what are you proposing to do?" she asked.

"What can I do?"

"File a counter claim."

"Sure. And then everything will be tied up for the next two or three years."

"Possibly. Probably. It depends on how legitimate his claim is, and of course how much money he's willing to spend."

"And no doubt you know my answer to that one."

Toni chuckled.

"And now, in my present capacity, I am finally free to discuss that trip to Cabo."

"You get this SOB off my back and I'll buy you a villa down there."

"It may take that."

"And I'm prepared to spend it."

"All right. I'll poke around a bit. Sound some my allies on the commission and see how they feel."

"Thanks, Toni. Get back to me as soon as you can."

I called my real estate agent Jolie next. She was just coming on the line when Kyler and Camellia appeared down the sidewalk.

"Hey, Jolie, just a second." I cupped the phone and shook Kyler's hand. "Go on in. Colette's in there with Donny. I'll be with you in a minute."

Camellia stared at me before following Tyler. As soon as they had disappeared, I returned to the conversation.

"Sorry, Jolie. I'm here in town meeting some friends for dinner."

"No problem. So what can I do for you?"

"You had mentioned that piece of property just up the coast from me the last time we spoke."

"I did. It's still for sale, if you're interested."

"I am."

"Wonderful. You know, there's another piece of property for sale up there too. On the inland side of the Chaplin property."

"Perfect. That's just what I was going to ask you. I'll buy that too."

"Do I smell mischief here?"

"I don't know. How far does your fiduciary obligation to me reach?"

"If it's nothing illegal or unethical, I keep my mouth shut. If it is, I pretend I never heard you and you can try another agent."

"Okay, let me explain. Chaplin filed a complaint with the Coastal Commission about my project here, so my plan is to

143

box the SOB in and make his life so miserable, he'll pay me to retract his complaint."

"So far, I don't hear anything illegal. And not necessarily unethical."

"Don't worry, Jolie. Whatever I do, it will be by the book. I'm not about to give that SOB another out."

"Okay."

"So, can you draw up something right now?"

"Tonight?"

"Yes. I'm not leaving anything to chance on these properties."

Jolie sighed heavily.

"Or I can find another agent."

"Okay, okay."

I arranged to meet Jolie at her office in two hours and returned to the restaurant.

"Fuck, dude," Kyler said under his breath as I sat down. "I can't believe the great white hunter is back to making your life miserable."

"I can't believe you thought he'd do anything else."

"Yeah, he is a total dick, isn't he?"

"So, what are we going to do?" Colette said.

"Look, it doesn't affect anything we have in place right now. Whatever the board has approved remains in place unless revoked by the commission. Which they won't. It just ties me up on future projects for now."

"Like the new arts center," Colette said.

"We'll go ahead as planned with the design and the building department review, but actually building it? Yeah, that's out the window until this complaint gets resolved."

"So, there goes my job."

"There's always the garden."

"Great."

"Look, let's not get down in the dumps about this. I'm setting some things in motion right now that'll have that toady begging to me to relent."

"Cool!" Kyler said. "So tell us about it."

I did.

"See, the thing is, I've agreed to all kinds of setback conditions with the tribal property but none of that will apply to these other two parcels."

"All right! We'll get out there banging pans and shit."

I smiled.

"I'm thinking more like bulldozers and jack hammers."

"Zip lines, baby!"

"Whatever. I want him to feel like there's a swarm of bees around his head."

"Oh, the wild tempests of the heart," Colette said.

"Yeah." I ordered another Scotch as the waitress flew by. "Hope you don't mind, Kyler."

"I hate you."

"I know. I can feel it. Now look, everyone. The purpose of this meeting is to discuss forward progress. The art center plans will go ahead. Donny, just so you know, we're planning to dedicate some office space upstairs to a tech department."

Colette wrinkled up her nose.

"Okay, Colette wants you to know that as soon as we build a proper science and tech center, she's kicking you out. Hell, for that matter, we may be running both operations out of a cottage at first."

Colette made a face.

"Okay, two cottages. Whatever. The point is, let's move the ball forward. Now as far as the tech thing goes, I'm looking for ideas. I'm looking for people. We need to find a way to start generating income and I'm thinking an online platform. So anything you've got, any people you know, let's hear it."

"Well, I don't have any ideas off the top of my head. I just know it's all about traffic statistics and the money you can make from advertising. Unless you want to start some kind retail store."

"No, no. That's too much of a footprint. Too much traffic. I want something that's basically cyber based."

"So, like I was saying…"

"I know. The more traffic, the higher the advertising rates. So what about people? Do you know some folks who might be willing to throw their lot in with us?"

"Yeah, actually, I do. I was thinking of this couple I know today. They're really cool. Good people. We went to college together and they live in town here. She runs a local food co-op and he's the tech guy for a local business. He's super techy. Way more than me."

"Great. So, you think they'd really want to join us?"

"Join us, like in salaries?"

"Hey, I want a salary," Kyler said with a laugh.

"All right, everybody. Let's get this straight right now. I'll fund any enterprise that is for the betterment of the tribe, and anything that has a real prospect for generating income but this thing has to become self-sustaining at some point or it's a joke. In the meantime, I'll guarantee you a roof over your head and food on the table. I'll even guarantee you shoes on your feet and clothes to wear but incomes are all going to be based on profitability. We make money, it goes to the members of the tribe and to building up our operations. So basically, as long as you're part of the tribe, you have nothing to worry about, and you're part of the tribe, as long as…well…"

I knocked back the rest of my Scotch and looked around the table.

"The fact is, I don't know when the hell you'd cease being part of the tribe. I guess that would be for the tribe to decide."

"Yeah! Someone screws up and we kick 'em off the island."

"The plantation," Colette said.

"Yeah!" Kyler said. "Kick 'em off the plantation!"

"You know, Kyler, it might just be you who gets kicked off."

"I'm shakin' the bush, boss man, shakin' the bush."

"You knucklehead. All right. Why don't we set up another meeting so we can meet your friends, Donny? Say tomorrow night? Same time, same station? Do you think they'd be available?"

"Probably. I can call them right now if you'd like."

"Please do. In the meantime, is everyone ordering?"

Donny nodded.

"I'd like something," Colette said.

"I'm starving," Kyler said. "I've been shakin' the bush all day, boss man."

"How's that going, by the way?"

"Oh, cool. Kevin's almost done with the path and said something about being done with the fence in a couple of days."

"Good. And you, Camellia." She stared. "Something to eat?"

"I don't know. I'm vegan."

A miracle. She had spoken. I wasn't too thrilled about what had come out of her mouth. I heard 'vegan' and thought of the food police.

"Let's see what they have," I said and got the attention of a nearby busboy. He said she would bring us menus and disappeared.

When I looked back, Camellia was still staring at me. It was an intense but faraway stare. I made a mental note to find out what kind of medication she was on.

Meanwhile, Colette and Kyler were discussing ideas for the website. Donny got off the phone.

"Yeah, my friends are cool with meeting us here tomorrow night."

"Cool. What are their names?"

"David and Anne."

The menus arrived. Everyone ordered and the conversation resumed. My mind was as far away as Camellia's gaze. I was preparing to spend another hundred million or so, just to put the fear of god into Chaplin. I felt half mad about having the wherewithal. But wait until that bastard finds out I have him

147

surrounded. There'll be bellowing over in the Chaplin mansion all right.

Later, Colette joined me at the meeting with Jolie in her downtown office. Jolie was an attractive, plus sized blonde with hair that was forever plastered tightly to her skull. I thought by this hour that she would have let it down, but no. Perhaps she slept with it that way.

"I've drawn up everything but the price," Jolie said after the introductions. "Did you want to make a counter offer?"

"No. I don't want to give them any reason to shop around. In fact, I want it stipulated that my offers are to be kept confidential until escrow closes or they will be retracted."

"Okay."

Jolie smiled while filling in the amounts. When she was done, I signed the papers and wrote out two checks, one for five hundred thousand and one for five million.

"Are we good?"

Jolie glanced at both checks.

"We're good."

"Great." I stood up and both women stood up with me. "Whatever you can do to expedite things, including the escrow, please do it. I want to start banging pots and pans along his property line as soon as possible."

Jolie shook her head with a smile.

"You're sure you don't want to just disappear down into the South Pacific somewhere?"

"Don't remind me…Anyway, I'm already in too deep. Read Shakespeare's histories. You'll know how I feel."

"I haven't read them. Is it anything like the Hatfield's and McCoy's?"

"Oh yeah, but on a grand scale."

I shook Jolie's hand.

"Thanks for coming down and getting this done tonight."

"You're welcome. And nice meeting you, Colette."

"Nice meeting you."

"That bottled spider," I said to Colette outside. "That elf-faced monstrous toad."

She laughed.

"I'm practicing up," I said.

Back at the property, I stopped in the meadow.

"Did you want to come up for a night cap?"

"Sure. I need to walk Hugo."

"No problem. I'll join you."

I made the turn up to my place and parked. Colette and I climbed out and started up the path on foot. Hugo went out ahead of us on his leash. It was a cold, clear night with a full moon peeking through the pines.

Once Hugo had relieved himself, we headed back to my place.

"About my salary," Colette said as I poured two snifters of brandy.

"What about it?"

"I feel guilty with everything on hold."

"I understand, but don't." I held out my glass to her. "I want you here and no one else needs to know the particulars of our arrangement."

"Okay, but we can always amend it if you want. Set it up for less money? I just feel all wrong about thirty thousand a year when I'm not doing anything."

"You're doing something. You're helping me to get this arts center designed and built."

"And then?"

"Don't worry about it. When his lordship next door gets wind of my flanking maneuver, I'm pretty sure he'll fold and we can get back to business."

"Are you really going to harass him with heavy equipment and the likes?"

"It will be the threat of heavy equipment." I smiled and drank. "I'll probably file for a subdivision. Make him think his little Valhalla is at risk of being invaded by a two hundred home development."

Colette shook her head.

"I know. I'm mad by five hundred pounds."

She smiled, understanding the reference.

"I wonder how it feels to have that kind of money and the power that goes with it."

I shrugged.

"It helps…and it doesn't. I still lie awake at night with my head going around and around. The Duke of Gloucester has nothing on me."

She smiled again. I drank.

"Anyway, please stop worrying, all right? Forge ahead with Connor on the arts center design and we'll submit the plans. In the meantime, I'll deal with his lordship."

"You really think he'll buckle?"

"I believe *cave* is the right word. *Capitulate*. But, yes. I think when confronted with the lesser of two evils, he'll come around. I certainly hope so."

I splashed some more brandy into my snifter and offered the same to Colette but she declined. I drank and leaned back on the sofa with a sigh.

"It is overwhelming at times. I keep throwing money at this thing, thinking I can persuade people that there's another way of going about this life when all they want is their SUV, Sunday afternoon football and a backyard barbecue Who gives a crap about my little project? Meanwhile I'm turning into a Kaczynski character. Wild hair and all."

I closed my eyes and threw my head back.

"Fuuucccckkk."

Colette laughed. I opened my eyes and looked at her. She stared back.

"Come here," I said.

She turned her head askance.

"Please, come here," I said again.

"Steven. Do we really want to be doing this?"

"I don't know. Just come here and hold me. Please."

She came over, curled up on the sofa and tucked herself under my arm.

"I've been haunted lately. About the many terrible choices I've made. It seems pretty clear that I don't know what's best for me, but I like you. My feelings for you seem healthy and good. So why don't I just respond to them?"

"Because it will probably fuck up everything?"

"There's that word again."

She shook me.

"You know what I mean."

"Worried about your job security, are you?"

"It's more than that."

"I know."

I leaned over and kissed her forehead.

"I'll tell what I envision. That you and I would be like brothers and sisters of the universe." I pulled Colette's chin up. "We're trying to save humanity here. The problem is so much bigger than we are. Why in hell would we fuck it up over the need for a little affection?"

Colette put a finger to my lips.

"There's that word again."

"Yes."

She stared into my eyes.

"Do you really think we can keep things simple? Do you really think there's some way for us to keep from complicating the crap out of it?"

"I don't know. I think so." I looked at her. "I mean, why do relationships always become so complicated? Jealousy? Possessiveness? The need for control?"

"All of the above?"

"Yeah, and so far I'm not feeling any of those things. And you?"

"Not really. I just know that, once I start, I don't want anybody else playing with my coconuts."

I chuckled.

"Yeah, well, I can promise you that much. Not forever. I can't even think in those terms anymore but no one else will be playing with your coconuts."

"And yet I worry."

"I know, but maybe that's good. With both of us knowing how easily things can get fucked up, we'll go in with our eyes wide open."

"I think we've just bled the romance right out of it."

I kissed her lips.

"How's that for romance?"

"Hmm."

I kissed her again, and again, and then her ears and neck. When I pulled back, I noticed Hugo staring at us.

"Does he watch?"

Colette slapped at me playfully.

"Oh, I feel like I'm selling myself somehow."

"Don't. It wasn't my intent when I first saw you."

She threw her hands up to the heavens.

"Come on. You're a beautiful woman. I'm just saying, my intentions were purely altruistic at first, but you've grown on me. And that feels completely natural. I think it would be unnatural not to respond at this point."

"Hmm."

I shrugged and gave Colette another tentative kiss, but she was soon pulling away.

"What are we going to do in the morning?"

"Fry up some eggs."

She slapped at me playfully again.

"You know what I mean."

"Yes, and I will be glad to see you. Or you can go home tonight, if that makes you feel safer."

"I think it would. Would you mind?"

"No. I think it would be kind of fun. The lady who lives down the lane."

"Like the one who lived in the enchanted cottage?"

I pulled back.

"Please don't ever bring that up."

We sat there in silence, neither one of us knowing what to say next. Finally, I took hold of Colette's hands again.

"Look, it's taken me a long time to get to this point. Where my mind is here in this moment and not somewhere else."

"Is it?"

"What can I tell you? I loved someone very dearly once. It didn't work out and it's taken me all these years to accept that fact. That that's just the way things go sometimes but..." I shrugged. "Life only moves forward and I'm doing my best to move forward with it."

I was about to add something more but Colette put a finger to my lips.

"Come. Let's stop talking now."

She took my hand and rose to her feet and I followed.

"What about Hugo?"

"He'll be all right. Let's put some water out and I'll give him a bone."

I found a suitable bowl and filled it with water. Colette took a bone out of her purse.

"Stay here," she said as we headed upstairs. Hugo sat staring at us with the bone in his mouth

Behind the closed the bedroom door, Colette stood staring at me. I kissed her.

"Let's just take off our clothes and curl up in bed together, all right?"

She nodded. We took opposite sides of the bed and started to undress. Then we were beneath the flannel sheets and flesh to flesh.

"Oh, Colette. It feels so heavenly."

I lay still with her for several minutes, just gently caressing. Then I was drawn to kiss her face and ears and neck. Then I started down her belly. Colette was soon making wonderfully melodic sounds.

Some minutes later, she came and I crawled back up. We both gasped and stared when I penetrated her. Colette was so small and delicate, I was able to lift her up in my arms and rock her gently against my loins. When she came again, I set her back down and went at her with unrestrained hunger.

"Oh god, so good, so good, so good," I said in coming.

We lay there for a long time afterwards, gently kissing and caressing in the moonlight. Finally I rolled over onto my side and found the other woman there in the darkness. As much as I tried, as much as I wanted her to be gone, she was not.

"Did we ruin everything?" Colette said in the silence.

"No."

She curled up close to me.

"Shall we keep this a secret?"

"If you want. I suspect it will become all too apparent, whether we like it or not."

"I need to pee," Colette said a short time later.

While she was gone, I lay there staring out the window at the moonlight in the pines.

"I'd better drain Hugo too," Colette said when she returned.

"You're leaving then."

"I think so."

When she was dressed, I got up and threw on a bathrobe. Hugo was sitting at the foot of the stairs when we opened the door, in the same exact position we had left him, but without the bone.

"You don't think we've ruined everything?" Colette said at the front door.

"Please. Don't think that way. Let's just concentrate on the tribe and our mission and be thankful for the companionship."

Colette eyed me for a long moment, reached up to kiss me and headed down the stairs with Hugo on her leash. There was one last look back before they disappeared down the path. I waved and closed the door, still haunted by the memories of the other woman.

13

I awakened the next morning with both women still on my mind. In an effort to cleanse my soul, I sent Colette a text.

I want to kiss you. Above, below, before, behind.

Being words from a Donne poem that I had already used with the other woman, I felt anything but cleansed. I was in the bathroom when a note came back from Colette.

Thank you. Sweet memories too, but still I worry.

I wrote back.

Don't. I'll be on the phone but please come see me soon.

I went downstairs to make coffee, my thoughts as restless as a pit of snakes.

With the coffee brewing, I bit into a banana and dialed Kyler's number. He answered a moment later.

"Shakin' the bush, boss man."

I smiled.

"Good movie, wasn't it? 'What we have here…is a failure to communicate'."

"Yeah!" Kyler said.

"Well, look. I'm just checking to make sure you're ready for that load of garden supplies."

"You bet, boss man."

"Is Camellia up there with you?"

"Yeah."

"Okay. Keep an eye out and as soon as those supplies arrive, have Kevin assign some of his men to help stock everything next to the garden. Whatever our little soothsayer wants you to do. In fact, if you need my truck to move things around, feel free to use it."

"You got it. Oh, here comes another dump truck right now."

"Oh, hey. Make sure that delivery truck goes nice and easy up that new road. It wasn't built for racing."

"You got it."

I hung up and poured the first cup of coffee. My attorney was next in line. Richard's secretary soon had him on the phone with me.

"Pray tell. What mischief are we up to now?" he asked without saying hello.

"Hi Richard. Did you get your tickets to Cabo?"

"I did. Thank you, and I already heard about the Coastal Commission complaint."

"Small town, isn't it?"

"It is."

I explained about the land purchases.

"You're mad."

"Probably. As I told Colette, I'm channeling my inner Gloucester."

"Explain."

I did.

"Next time you see me, I'll have a hunchback."

"Duly noted. So what is it you want from me?"

I explained about the subdivision.

"You are mad."

"I don't intend to follow through with it. I just want him to think I will."

"If you love throwing your money away, I'm sure we can find better ways of doing it."

"I can't think of anything that would bring me greater joy in this world than to see Chaplin begging for mercy."

"I suspect he'll fight back. Harder than you think."

"Good. Since I can significantly outspend him, I'll be glad to engage that prick in an arms race."

"You are mad."

"I know. So please draw up the paperwork. Whatever's necessary to make my bluff look official."

Richard went silent.

"Look, I suppose you'll be wanting some kind of cover so I'll send you a note with my intentions. Then it'll be in the official record book."

"I'd appreciate that."

"Consider it done. I'll dash off something as soon as we get off the phone."

"In the meantime, please don't say you want this done yesterday."

"I do but I'm not going to drop that one on you. Just as soon as you can will be fine. Simplify the filing maybe? Any way you can expedite things will be appreciated."

"That's fine."

"Thanks. I'll send you that note straight off."

As soon as we hung up, I dashed off something to cover Richard's butt and leaned back in my chair, hands behind my head. The sea along the coast looked all simple and cheery off through the trees. My heart was anything but.

After a moment, I called Jolie.

"What's the good word?"

"I was going to call you in a few minutes."

"So? Is it all a go?"

"Yes. There was a moment of hesitation on the part of the owner with the smaller parcel but it's all a go now."

"Hesitation? What the hell for?"

"Oh, I'm just reading between the lines here but I suspect he saw someone offering full price and thought to himself, maybe I'm asking too little."

"Jesus. Well, did he sign?"

"Yes. I'm sending over some paperwork right now. As soon as you sign it, we'll be in escrow."

"And does everyone involved know to keep their mouths shut?"

"The two owners agreed as part of the offer and I'll make that abundantly clear to Gloria, the owner of the escrow company, as well."

"Okay. Then make this abundantly clear to her too. There'll be a 20% bonus if she can get it done this week."

"You don't ask too much."

"So I've been told. Get this done and I'll make sure there's a bonus in it for you too."

"I'll do my best, Steven."

"Thank you."

"I've got to run," she said.

We got off. I leaned back and stared out at the cheery looking coast again, considering what to do next. There being nothing more to accomplish on the phone, I sprung to my feet, gobbled down some vitamins with a muffin, chased that with a bit more coffee and ran upstairs to get dressed.

I texted Colette before going out the door.

I'm going up to play in the dirt. Would you like to join me?

Her reply came back a moment later.

Sure.

I wrote back.

I'm on my way over. Wearing boots and old jeans.

Five minutes later, I was pulling to a stop behind Colette's cottage. She was curled up on the sofa when I walked in, reading Dorothy Parker. I noticed Colette's pale, delicate feet with the red toe nail polish and sat next to them.

"You know, a woman who will tell you her age will tell you anything."

Colette smiled and set the book down.

"Do you like her?"

"I do. Her essays more than the stories. It seems to me that her stories were written for the privileged class and her essays to skewer them."

"Probably had to pay the bills."

158

"Probably."

I leaned over and kissed Colette. And kissed her again. And felt her body and held her head in my hands.

"I want you again."

"I thought we were going to go play in the garden."

"Maybe I want to play in your garden first."

Colette pretended to sag playfully.

"Okay, fine. Go change."

She gave me a peck and went off to her bedroom. I followed and stood in the open doorway. When she was down to her bra and panties, I couldn't resist and went to hold her. The passions quickly spun out of control from there.

"God, I do want you."

"Oh, you fucking men," she said.

"Yes, us fucking men."

"Come here," she said and sat on the bed.

When she went to pull down my zipper, I told her to wait and rushed to her opened closet. There was pair of Marilyn Monroe shoes on the floor amongst the others. I placed them on Colette's pale, delicate feet.

"You crazy man."

I nodded. She proceeded.

"Oh god, yes."

Ready to come, I went to mount Colette but she held me back.

"No, just this."

"I'll feel guilty all day if I don't please you."

"It's okay. I'm still vibrating from last night."

"Okay."

She proceeded and soon I felt weightless and swept up into the clouds.

"Oh, I do feel guilty," I said afterwards.

"Good. Now let me get dressed."

When she was done, I kissed her face and neck.

"There's something I want to do for you."

"What?"

"Pay off your credit cards."

"No. I'm already feeling guilty about everything else."

"Colette. It's going to take you years to pay them off."

"I'm figuring four or five."

"Yeah, and in the meantime, you're paying what, 24.99%?

"29.99."

"Jesus. Look, just call it a loan and you can pay me back at zero interest if the guilt is too much."

She eyed me askance.

"Steven, why are you doing all of this for me?"

"Because I..."

She rushed a hand to my mouth. I waited until she took it away.

"Because I like you."

I rubbed her nose with mine.

"Okay?"

"All right. God, how will I ever repay you?"

"You already have. Trust me, you already have."

She touched my face.

"You dear sweet man."

"Thanks. I've missed hearing that. I've forgotten how good it feels."

She kissed me.

"Let's go play in the dirt."

When we spotted Kyler in the lower meadow, I stopped the golf cart. Three men from Kevin's crew were tying the last leg of the new path into the parking area.

"So, how goes it?"

"We've been shakin' the bush, boss man."

"I can see that."

"Hi Colette," Kyler said.

"Hi Kyler."

"So what's next?" I said.

"I was going to ask you, boss man."

"We're heading up to play in the garden. Care to join us?"

"Sure, but I need to stop by my cottage first. I'm starving!"

"I take it Camellia's still up there?"

"Yeah, she's mulching away."

I smiled.

"That must be something to see."

"It's definitely a trip, boss man. That wheelbarrow looks like a dump trunk in her hands but she's shoveling away."

"Well help is on the way. We'll see you up there."

Kyler gave Colette what looked like a knowing wink as I pulled away.

"I think he knows," Colette said.

"Oh god no," I said with a look of terror.

She made a face back at me.

"Sorry, but I still cherish my privacy."

"So do I, but then, we're all just one big communal family out here now, right?"

"I suppose I hadn't properly considered all the ramifications of that fact."

"Neither had I...until yesterday afternoon sometime."

I made a face and she chuckled, and was still smiling as we pulled to a stop next to the garden. Camellia was out there shoveling away at the pile of manure and failed to look up. Kevin was nearby finishing up the fence with his crew and waved for me to join him. I climbed out and went that way. Colette went over to help Camellia.

"What's going on?" I said, shaking his hand.

He chuckled.

"Well, I thought I should tell you. Camellia's been telling me this and that about how to build the fence."

"As in?"

"Well, the main thing is, she says we need to bury a board all along the base of it and top the board with a copper strip."

"Sounds like old almanac stuff."

"Yeah. Well, just so you know. If we do that, the board's going to rot unless we make it redwood. And that means it's going to cost quite a bit more money."

"How much more?"

Kevin spelled out the cost, which came to about six grand.

"Maybe a little more," he added. "If you want it painted."

"So do it. Paint it. Whatever the hell she wants. Just forge ahead and I'll cut you a check as soon as you're done."

I slapped Kevin on the shoulder, which elicited another one of his chuckles.

"Well, we're out here to help Camellia with the mulching so I guess I'll jump in."

"Yeah, that's another thing," Kevin said in a lowered voice.

"What?"

"I offered to help her mulch everything with my machine but she said no, it has to be done by hand."

I glanced over at the garden.

"It'll be one hell of a work out, won't it?"

"Yeah. You'll be here all week."

"Oh well. I guess that's how folks use to do things. Like raking leaves instead of using a blower. You get a workout and don't ruin the planet in the process."

"I guess."

"Well, at some point, we'll have as many as a hundred people living out here so it won't be that much of a chore then."

"Yeah. I guess."

I slapped Kevin on the shoulder again and headed over to help the ladies. Camellia and Colette were busy loading up the wheelbarrow. I grabbed a shovel and pitched in. When it was full, I grabbed the handles.

"Tell you what, ladies. Why don't you let me fill the wheelbarrow and you go ahead and spread things around. Sound like a deal?"

Camellia stared. Colette wiped the sweat from her brow and said, "Be my guest."

I dumped the wheelbarrow and returned to fill it again. Camellia went about spreading the mounds of mulch like Hercules. Colette appeared to be spreading lead. I smiled and got back to my work in the sun.

Kyler showed up a few minutes later and chipped in.

"You're shakin' the bush now, boss man."

"Shakin' the bush."

"All right!" he said while shoveling. "Who needs a gym?"

By lunchtime, all four of us were drenched in sweat and smelling of cow manure. A quarter of the garden had been covered. That meant two days, just spreading the manure. Then you had to mulch it into the soil. I eyed Kevin's tilling machine with envy, even as the saga of mankind's evolution raced through my head. We had been seeking the easier, softer way for five thousand years, only to find that easier, softer path leading us to ruin.

I dumped my last load out in the garden and dropped the wheelbarrow.

"Done shakin' the bush, boss man?"

"I've got some other bushes to shake. What about you, Colette?"

"Am I excused?"

"Of course. The same for both of you. No need to kill ourselves. We'll keep chipping away at this and get it done over the course of the week."

Camellia continued shoveling away. I shrugged at Kyler.

"It's cool. I had a quick sandwich before coming up here. I'll keep shakin' the bush."

"Okay. Well don't forget. We're having another tribal council in town this evening. Same place, same station. We'll be meeting the potential new members of the tribe."

"All right. I'll be like Donald Trump. You're fired!"

"You're insane, Kyler."

"Yeah!"

"All right. We'll see you tonight. And be sure to bring Camelia."

I looked back at her, working away. As frail as she appeared to be at first glance, you had to marvel at her strength and endurance.

That evening at the restaurant, the four of us were looking at menus when Donny walked in with David and Anne. David was a few inches under six feet, lithe in body, with light brown, collar length hair and an intelligent, elfish looking face that seemed cheerful even when he was serious.

Anne was not beautiful, but with her long brown hair and lean physique, she was elegant and sexy in some way that transcended everything else. She had an aura of grace and regal presence that drew you in.

I stood up and shook both their hands.

"Welcome. I'm Steven and this is Colette, Camellia and Kyler."

Anne said "hi" with a slight New England twang and smiled warmly at everyone. In a flurry, they sat down, more drinks were ordered and the laughter continued as we got acquainted. I noticed Anne stealing looks at Camellia.

"God, she has such beautiful blue eyes," Anne said of her. "Doesn't she? They're like lagoons in the Caribbean somewhere."

Anne looked around the table with a laugh, completely sincere. Meanwhile, Camellia stared back with her impenetrable gaze.

"So, David," I said, breaking the awkward hush that had fallen over the gathering. "The word is you're super techy."

"I guess," he said with a self-effacing smile. "It's what I do for a living."

"A degree?"

"Yeah, yeah. Computer science, software engineer."

"Great. So we left off last night with somehow making our first million on the internet."

"That's what everybody's trying to do."

"We're very tribal," Colette said.

"Yeah! Our tribe against yours!"

"I'm being somewhat facetious but how *do* you make a buck online?"

164

"Donny was telling me you don't want to do retail," David said.

"I don't think so. I can't see how it would work. Something wholesale maybe. One truck coming and going each week? But we can't have all kinds of traffic. The county won't have it and I don't want it either."

"Yeah, it's tough," David said. "The internet's already so saturated with ideas. It's hard to come up with something that creates a truly unique niche."

The waitress came with more menus, interrupting us.

"Do you need more time?"

"Give us five more minutes," I said and nodded at David over my menu. "You were saying."

"That's it. If it's not something completely unique and different, it's more of a vanity project at this point, in terms of the value."

"And you? You have any ideas? Nothing that's been percolating around in your brain?"

"I was thinking we could do a website on living green," Anne said.

David smiled.

"There are lots of those."

"Yeah, but I mean about the whole tribe and how we're living an alternative lifestyle and all that. I think that would really resonate with people."

"Yeah, I could see that," I said. "It might go viral."

David seemed skeptical but Anne went on smiling as if indifferent to reproach. I looked around the table in the silence.

"National roll call," Camellia said out of the blue.

"What?" I said.

"National roll call. Have a site where everyone in the country can vote on an issue at the same time."

"There are all kinds of blogs already doing that," David said.

There were shrugs and the conversation careened off in another direction. I kept thinking about Camellia's suggestion.

"No, wait a minute," I said, interrupting everyone. "Maybe Camellia's onto something here. There's been talk about this sort of instant democracy for years. Push a button and your vote counts right away. We could take the most debated issues of the day and let everyone have their say. Wars, the environment, tax breaks for the wealthy. Boom and you've taken the nation's pulse. Everyone could feel like their voice was being heard."

"There's just so many ways that people could game it," David said.

"Like what? Voting twice?"

"Yeah, or a hundred times."

"But that's your job, isn't it? Building safeguards into the software?"

"Yeah, but it would take a monster program."

"So, I'll pay you. I think it's a great idea. All right, Camellia."

I cautiously went to high five her and was thoroughly surprised when she high fived me back. Then she stared around the table again with her clairvoyant gaze. You had to wonder what was going on in there.

I looked back at David.

"You don't look too enthused."

"Well, it's just, you know. The younger generations, they have the attention spans of a gerbil. I just wonder if this is the kind of thing that would really take off. Everyone's into Tic Toc and stuff like that. Instant gratification. I don't know if anyone would take the time."

"Well, I like the idea and I'm willing to take a chance."

"Okay. It's your money."

"Look, let's just knock it around. We could take whatever issue is most prominent in the nation's mind week by week and have a vote. Invite two guest journalists, one right, one left, and let them offer up their opposing opinions. Then we'd open up the vote for X number of days and post the results. Shit, if it took off, the whole goddamned nation might be talking about it."

"Yeah," David said. "I can see a lot of ways for it to fail, but I guess there are a lot of ways that it could take off."

"Sure," I had started to say when the waitress came to take everyone's order.

As soon as she was gone, I continued with my thought.

"So, I was saying, I see it as a great way to get people focused on what's important. It doesn't have to be perfect. You find a glitch, you fix it. Isn't that what companies do all the time?"

"Sure."

"So?"

"So, I guess the real trick is to get it all designed and ready to launch, and then come out with a big splash. That way you're the go to site whenever anybody thinks of the idea. You come out half assed and somebody with big bucks will roll you over."

I looked around the table and back at David.

"At the risk of sounding arrogant, I can do that."

"We're talking about major money."

"Like what?"

"Like ten, twenty million, minimum."

"Okay. Consider it done."

David looked around the table with a smile and back at me.

"Really?"

I nodded to let him know I wasn't kidding.

"Hey," Anne said with her phone in hand. "I just checked and the domains are all available. NationalRollCall.com, dot net, dot org."

"Cool, grab them." I pulled out a credit card. "Better do it now before the hoarders beats us to it."

There were laughs.

Within minutes, we had secured those domain names and a dozen or so like them. Our food came and we all dug in with the discussion continuing.

"David," I said between bites. "Would it be possible for you to come by my place tomorrow night so we can discuss this thing in more detail?"

He looked at Anne. She smiled and said, "Sure."

"Cool. In the meantime, if you can, make up a list of whatever you'd need to get this off the ground. And whatever the rest of us here can do to help. I'm thinking we could even set up a rolling blog so readers can voice their opinions."

"*That's* where I'd draw a line. I don't care how much money you have. You're talking hundreds of people just for quality control. You've seen what's happened to what used to be Twitter. You'll have Nazis doxing everyone on the other side."

"Yeah, fair enough. I'll grant you that one...Anyway, I'd like to see this thing up and running as soon as possible so let's get to work."

Amidst the ongoing chatter, I found my mind racing with the countless possibilities. This was what I had been looking for, something of substance, something with big potential.

I looked over at Camellia and found her staring back at me.

Well, god bless you, I thought with a smile. You lost and homeless little waif.

14

Braking to a stop in the meadow that night, I looked at Colette. I had been dreaming of her coconuts all evening, but with the old memories still stalking me, like wolves circling just outside the glow of our campfire. I was beginning to accept that it would always be that way. There seemed to be no escaping where my heart had once been.

"So, what'll it be, my dear?" I said.

Colette leaned her head against my shoulder.

"I'm sorry. I keep worrying."

"Yeah? And that's because?"

"Because...It's easy to see how things could become all messy and entangled."

Given my own thoughts, I was inclined to agree but reached out with my arm and gently pulled her head closer.

"All we can do is take it day by day."

"I'm trying, but it occurred to me this evening that, sooner or later, sex will become rather drab without the romance."

I nodded, again, knowing she was right. Colette reached up to touch my face tenderly without looking at me.

"That *word*. It begins to stir in my heart."

I knew she was right about that too but shrunk from speaking my own thoughts. I had loved once, in a way that I felt sure I would never love again. What the hell was I going to do?

I leaned over and kissed Colette's lips, then her freckled face and ears and neck. She looked at me now and ran her hand through my hair.

"Oh Steven."

"Yes, dear. Sorry to have placed you in this quandary. Leaping back into the fire or not."

She studied me.

"Oh fine. Let's leap back into the fire."

She touched my face again and we kissed.

"Your place or mine?" I said.

"Your place. I'd feel like Kyler was watching us."

I put the truck back in gear and started for my place.

"I'm sure Tyler has his hands full enough with Camellia."

"You don't really think they're...Do you?"

"Why not? They're both human...I think."

Colette slapped at me playfully.

We were soon in bed naked with me crawling down beneath the covers.

"Oh god, oh god," Colette said "How sweet you are. Oh god, yes..."

I went about my work as one needing redemption and felt much better when I heard Colette orgasming. When she was done, I crawled back up.

"I want you this way," I said and gently rolled her over onto her hands and knees.

Childless, Colette still had the anatomy of a sixteen year old so I struggled to penetrate her, but what a fine place it was when I finally did. Wanting the ecstasy to last a good long time, I worked slowly and gently until the two of us were coming together.

With a final collapse onto the bed, I spooned Colette and ran my hand along the contours of her body. There were so many lovely hills and valleys. That word did creep into my heart but I shoved it away and out of sight.

"I like the idea," Colette said in the darkness.

"You mean for the website?"

"Yes."

"Did you want to chip in?"

"I don't know how. I'm not very techy."

"You could help on my end. I need to line up a list of guest bloggers and advertisers. A bunch of stuff. Maybe you could even work with David on the design end. You have a touch for that."

"I'm game on all but the advertising."

She looked over her shoulder at me.

"That's fine. I don't blame you. I can take care of it myself."

She rolled over to face me.

"About the design. I was thinking of two heads in silhouette. Like Jefferson and Hamilton. Left and right."

"Yeah, I like the idea but I don't know how many people would recognize the images. Jefferson, maybe, but I'm not even sure about that. Hamilton? I don't know if I could make him out in silhouette."

I got up on one elbow.

"How about two cartoon images of Roosevelt and Reagan? Fists at the ready, Irish style, about to duke it out. That seems to be more where the battle line is drawn these days. The New Deal and those who have been trying to undo it for the past forty years."

"Okay. I'll work on the advertising."

"Oh, what? It was a grand idea." She was silent. "Come on. It just needed a little finessing." She was still silent. "This is how wars get started, you know."

"Okay. I'm over it."

I laughed.

"Aw, and that is how peace is maintained."

When she still failed to respond, I tickled her and made her laugh.

"Honestly, I love the idea. It will never be about the soap opera of the day. It will always be about what's really important in this world. Is there global warming? Should we wean ourselves from fossil fuels? Should we be meddling in

171

the Middle East. Maybe I'm being grandiose here but I can picture the whole nation tuning in. This won't be just about listening to the next talking head. It will be about having your voice heard."

Colette looked over her shoulder at me.

"You wonder where she came up with the idea?"

"Believe me, I'm chastened. I had begun to wonder if there was *any* brain activity going on in there. Then she comes up with that. Amazing."

"I get this sense that she's just so traumatized from losing her son, she's learned to use silence as a protective mechanism."

"Sad," I said.

"Yes, very sad."

"So what do you think of David and Anne?"

"I like them."

"She really glows, doesn't she?"

"Yes, she seems very enlightened for a young woman. I was just out having a wild time at that age."

"Yes. Well here's to having a wild time at that age."

Colette kissed me and rolled over.

"I think I'll go home now. Hugo's probably ready for a pit stop anyway."

"Are you okay?"

"Hmm hmm."

I kissed her.

"Thank you," I said.

I could not think of any better words.

"Please, let's not fuck this up."

"All right. Did you want me to walk you home?"

"No, I'm fine." She kissed my ears and chest. "Stay and dream."

I lay there and watched her dress. When she was done, she leaned down to kiss me. I was about to speak but she put a finger to my lips.

"Ssshhh. Please wait. Wait until you're really sure. I'd rather say it was a good fuck and leave it at that, okay?"

"Okay." We kissed. "I'll try not to screw things up."

She started to leave.

"Oh, the play. Did you get the tickets?"

"Yes, I'd forgotten. It's a week from Saturday."

"Just the two of us?"

"I have one for Kyler too. I guess I can check and see who else is interested."

"Okay. And my car? I'm feeling completely stranded."

"I'll call. It should be done tomorrow. Please feel free to stop by for breakfast in the morning."

"I may have to. I'm running out of food."

"Okay. We'll try and get you going tomorrow."

Colette kissed me again and left. I lay there in the darkness, listening to her shoes descend the hardwood stairs, then cross the hardwood floors and go out the door. There were more footsteps as she descended the stairs outside. Then all was quiet except for the moaning of the wind in the pines. Remembering Colette's hips grinding at my loins, I moaned too. Then I remembered the old flame.

In an effort to escape her, I focused on the website. My mind flitted back and forth between work and old memories like a broken down ballerina.

Eventually I went down, poured myself a snifter of sherry and returned to read a bit of Henry the Sixth. The second part. It had always been my favorite. The same saucy characters and language you found in Henry the Fourth, Part One, but with what I thought was a broader sweep of history. A couple of pages of that and I was fast asleep.

In the morning, the same memories and dreams and regrets were there to haunt me. I jumped out of bed in an effort to escape them.

Fifteen minutes later, I was up checking on Kevin and his progress. He and his men were busy painting and installing the 2X12 ribbon. Camellia and Kyler had yet to make an appearance. I was thinking to stop by and see Colette on my way down the hill but checked in on Dale instead.

"Thought maybe you had forgotten about us," he said as I walked in.

I smiled.

"Almost did. Things have been busy."

I said hello to Jason and took a tour of the cottage. Dale had gotten his insulation inspection and was busy paneling the interior walls. The air was ripe with the scent of sweet pine.

"Looks good," I said, coming out from the back rooms. "Anything you need?"

Dale shook his head without looking up from the built-in area he was trimming.

"All right. I'll get out of your hair."

Dale looked once and went back to what he was doing. I went outside, feeling as if he had read my mind. Probably. He had probably heard about that Coastal Commission business. I almost went back in to discuss things with him but decided, screw it. I'll do everything in my powers to keep Dale busy until I have that prick Chaplin on his knees. Maybe build a barn or something on one of the new properties.

I was on the way over to Colette's cottage when an email came in. It was a young doctor, responding to my ad. He and his wife had just moved into the area. He had plans to start his own practice but my offer intrigued them. Could we meet? He had left his phone number so I called right away. A pleasant, Midwest sounding voice answered the phone.

"Is this Dr. McDonald?"

"It is."

There was the hint of a chuckle with his answer, as if he had found the very fact of his existence amusing. I liked him right away.

"This is Steven Fitzgerald. About the ad?"

"Oh, yes, yes. A cottage for a house call."

"Something like that."

"My wife Kristy and I are thoroughly intrigued. Would it be possible for us to come by and have a look today?"

"How about right now?"

"Just one second."

I heard muffled voices. Then Dr. McDonald was back.

"Sorry. Had to check with the boss, but sure, we can drive out right away. So where are we headed?"

I explained.

"When you come to the large meadow, call me back and I'll guide you in the rest of the way."

"Great. So we should be there in roughly twenty minutes."

"I'll be waiting."

Given the change of plans, I headed back to my place and called Colette on the way.

"How are you?" I asked when she answered.

"Oh, my mind's here and there, if you know what I mean."

"I do. What were your plans for the day?"

"I was thinking to go in and see how Connor's progressing with the arts center design, but of course I can't because I'm stranded."

I felt a prick of jealously. Connor was a good looking man.

God, Colette was right. The possessiveness had already begun.

"Are you there?" Colette said.

"Yeah, yeah. Just a million things on my mind."

"I know. So back to my car, I guess if that's not happening today, I'll head up and work in the garden."

"I'll check on your car as soon as we get off but this doctor and his wife called about my ad and they're stopping by here shortly. I think they may be onboard."

"So his first impression of me will be pushing a wheelbarrow."

"I had no idea it mattered."

"Oh yes. The Julliard trained bracero."

I chuckled.

"I'll explain that it's part of our cultural reorientation program."

Colette wasn't amused.

"Look, dear. Why don't you come by in half an hour and join our discussion."

"Thank you."

"Okay. I'll see you then."

I got off, a bit put off by Colette's snootiness. Maybe some cultural reorientation was in order.

Back at my place, I put in a call to Louie, the mechanic. Colette's car was finally ready. He had been thinking to call me in a few minutes.

"Perfect. We'll see you later on today."

I hung up and called Toni.

"I don't have an answer for you yet, if that's what you're wondering."

"I was but I have another question for you."

"Which is?"

"How easy would it be at this point to run a simple storage shed past the Coastal Commission?"

"Simple, as in?"

I explained about housing the golf carts.

"So no habitable space."

"None at all. You can even sell them on the green angle if you want. We're helping to save the environment."

Toni scoffed.

"I'll give my friends a call. No guarantees but we can probably sneak it through. It's residual to earlier development. You have golf carts. You need to house them safely. Some electrical. Maybe a bathroom. That's it."

"That's it."

"I'll see what I can do and get back to you."

"Thanks, Toni. I have something very special planned for you down in Cabo."

"Next week, if we could. This cold, damp weather is driving me up a wall."

"You got it."

I hung up and immediately called Connor.

"What's up mate?" he said at hearing my voice.

I explained about the storage shed.

"I want something spacious enough to work as a general workshop, repair station and storage area. Call it four bay doors with an office and bathroom to one side. Otherwise, the usual. Make it the same architectural theme."

"No problem, mate. When did you need it?"

"Yesterday." I explained about wanting to keep Dale busy. "So the sooner I can run this through the building department, the better."

"I'll tell you what, sir. You set me up for a night on the town with Colette and I'll have this done for you in two days."

I was silent.

"Oh bloody hell. I've stuck my foot in it, haven't I?"

"Maybe."

"Bloody hell, mate. My apologies, big time. I had a sense the two of you were just friends, ya know?"

"That was true a few days ago. Then things took a sudden turn."

"Promise ya won't say anything, mate. I'd hate for the poor bird to feel all clammy each time she sees me."

"I won't mention it."

"Christ, I feel bloody down in it now."

"Don't. Just get these plans done and I'll have a major perk for you. If it wasn't for trying to keep Dale busy I wouldn't even bother."

"It's no bother at all, mate. You've been as good a client as I could possibly imagine. I just feel like hell, now. Trying to pinch your bride and all."

"Connor, don't. It's totally understandable and no hard feelings. I probably would have done the same thing in your shoes."

"Thanks for that, mate. I appreciate the understanding but I still feel like I swallowed the canary."

"Connor, it's a thing between two gentlemen. It's done. Stop worrying. I think no less of you for trying."

"All right, then. I'll pick myself up and get right on this."

"Thanks, and call as soon as you have something. We'll go out for a drink, just the two of us."

"Sounds smashing, mate. I'm sharpening my pencils up right now."

I got off, feeling like hell about the whole thing too. What if the two of them were soulmates? Who was I to get in the way? I didn't feel that way about Colette. I was simply comforted by a woman's intelligent companionship and growing possessive over her coconuts for having tasted them.

I was staring out at the forest with these thoughts when the phone rang. It was Dr. McDonald.

"We're here," he said. "I can see some of the cottages." His pleasant, dry laughter came through the phone. "It looks like something out of an old catalogue."

I heard his wife's voice in the background.

"I think she's already picking one out."

"Good. Listen, take the path on your right at the top of the meadow."

"Not this first one?"

"No, the one at the very top, and then when it Y's, stay to your left and stop in front of the treehouse."

Dr. McDonald laughed and told his wife about the treehouse.

"Should we just stay on the phone then?" he said.

"No, no. You'll see it. If you get lost, call me back."

I got off and went out to wait for them on the balcony. A few moments later, their Subaru Outback appeared through the trees. I waved and watched as they parked.

"Wow, this is quite fairy tale like," Dr. McDonald said, getting out.

Surprisingly, I had guessed his appearance reasonably well. He was a bit under medium height, solidly built but not muscular, with sandy colored hair and the appearance of freckles on his face, though he didn't have them. There was just a general sunny air of cornfields about him.

"Hey, I want a treehouse," his wife said, getting out on the other side with a big smile.

She was short and compact, with short blonde hair. The build said cross trainer. The personality was type A, all the way.

"Come on up," I said and went around to meet them at the door.

"Hi, John," Dr. McDonald said, shaking my hand. "And this is my wife, Kristy."

"Steven. Please come inside."

"God, I want a treehouse," Kristy said again, looking at her husband.

I offered a smile and asked if either of them would like something to drink.

"I could use another cup of coffee," Kristy said.

I was thinking she didn't need it but led her out to the kitchen.

"You, too, Dr. McDonald?"

"Please, John will do and I'll just have a glass of water if you have it."

"Apple juice?"

"Oh sure. That's fine."

I helped Kristy with doctoring up her coffee and took them for a tour of the treehouse.

"God, I love this place," she said as we settled into our seats in the living room. "Look at the view."

"Nice prints," Dr. McDonald said of my Japanese art.

"They are, aren't they?" Kristy said.

In keeping with Zen, I thanked them without mentioning that they were actually originals.

"So, about the lodgings," Dr. McDonald said. "I'm trying to understand where this is headed."

"The truth is, I don't know."

They both laughed.

I shared my thoughts about the tribe.

"Is that what you're calling it?" Kristy said.

"Yes. It seems to me the oldest and most integral unit of our species. Families and individuals may come and go but the tribe remains. Anyway, the basic idea is to create a sense of community, whatever you wish to call it."

"And to be self-sustaining? Did I understand that correctly from your ad?"

"Yes."

"And is it?"

"Not yet."

They both laughed again.

"No, I'm footing the bill for most everything at this point. We haven't even developed a protocol for having a meeting yet."

"I can get this place organized," Kristy said. "I helped run the state offices in North Carolina while John was doing his internship. Worked directly for the governor. I was also responsible for putting together their tech department."

"Great. So you could help with our website."

"You bet. I also teach yoga and aerobics and cross training and kayaking."

Kristy did a crosswise pump of her fists. I almost laughed. She was so type A.

Before we could get on to discussing the website, I heard footsteps coming up the stairs.

"Ah, this must be Colette."

I got up and went to the door.

"Hi, come in. This is Colette, our arts director. Dr. McDonald and his wife Kristy."

"John is fine," Dr. McDonald said, shaking her hand.

"And who's this?" Kristy said while greeting Colette.

"Shorty," I said. "AKA, Hugo."

"He's going to get a complex," Colette said sarcastically.

"He already has one...Please, sit down everybody."

Hugo took a spot at Kristy's feet and looked up at her.

"Something to drink, Colette?"

"A cup of coffee?"

"Sure, the usual?"

She nodded. While I went out to the kitchen, the three of them raced off in conversation.

"We were just brainstorming on how to run the place," Kristy said when I returned.

"Good. As I said, I'm mostly winging it here. My idea has always been to get some people on board and then start fleshing things out. I didn't want folks to show up to a bunch of preset rules."

I explained about the website.

"Hopefully that will help take us in a sustainable direction. The community garden will help too."

"Oh cool. I love gardening," Kristy said. "Where is it?"

"Up the hill there about half a mile."

"Half a mile?! How big is this place?"

"1200 acres."

"Wow!"

She tilted her head with a big smile at Dr. McDonald.

"So, look. My basic thought is, everyone's time is of equal value out here, doctor, cook and Indian chief, and everybody would chip in an equal amount to help the tribe, whatever they can do to help."

"So, theoretically speaking," Dr. McDonald said. "We'd put up a timesheet and everyone would contribute so much of their energy each week."

"That's the basic idea."

"And what about the cottages?"

"At this point, everyone who's willing to jump onboard gets a cottage, rent free, and we'll continue trying to figure things out from there."

He smiled at Kristy and looked back at me.

"I guess we're game. I intend to go ahead and start my practice, but in the meantime I can see to everyone's health out here as part of our arrangements. Would that be in keeping with your basic idea?"

"Yes. It's not communism, where we have to divide up everything equally. We just give an equal amount of our time, in whatever way we can to help the tribe stay healthy, happy and thriving."

"Yeah!" Kristy said with a pump of her fist. "I'm ready to roll up my sleeves and get this thing going!"

I smiled, hearing bugles at dawn.

The Tribe

15

While we chatted, a car pulled to a stop out in front of the treehouse. I raised my eyebrows.

"I take it you weren't expecting more company," Dr. McDonald said with his affable chuckle.

"No," I said and went to look out the open Dutch door. Donny, David and Anne were just then climbing out of Donny's car. Seeing me, they all called out and waved.

"Who's that?" Kristy said.

"Three other new members of the tribe," I said quietly over my shoulder.

Anne was the first one up the stairs and greeted me.

"Wow. Very magical," she said, taking in the view.

David and Donny piled up onto the landing beside her.

"Hope you don't mind us showing up unannounced like this," Donny said with a sheepish look.

"You can blame it on us," Anne said with a smile. "We heard Donny was coming out to take possession of his cottage and arranged to get off work so we could see things too."

I smiled back as best I could under the circumstances and invited them in.

"David, Donny and Anne. Dr. McDonald and his wife Kristy."

There were handshakes and greetings.

"Donny is our eco-engineer, Anne our community organizer and David our head of tech."

"Hey, I thought I was head of tech and our community organizer," Kristy said with a pump of her fists.

"So we can organize together," Anne said.

"All right! Let's start organizing!" Kristy said.

Colette secretly rolled her eyes at me.

"Please, have a seat everyone. Drinks? I have iced teas, sodas, water? It's a bit early for a beer but if anyone wants one."

Dr. McDonald chuckled. I quickly had orders for two iced teas and a water. I retrieved them and returned to find everyone gathered around my Japanese art.

"They're originals!" Kristy said.

"She always smells money," Dr. McDonald said.

Kristy kicked his foot to much laughter.

"I love them," Anne said.

"Thank you. So, come. Let's sit."

We took our seats back in the living room.

"You know, it's just occurred to me that we'll need to build another dedicated structure, just for the tribal council to meet."

I quickly explained about my struggles with Chaplin.

"I guess we can even use one of the empty cottages for the time being but soon enough it's going to be too small."

"How about a yurt," Colette said.

"Wow, that's a fantastic idea," Anne said.

"What's a yurt?" Kristy said.

While Anne and Colette explained, David pulled up a website for yurts on his smart phone.

"Here. Check this out."

He expanded the screen and passed the phone around.

"They're very yurty," Dr. McDonald said to more laughter.

"Wow, do they come with all those rugs and accessories and stuff?" Kristy said.

"Not standard," Anne said. "But I'm sure you can buy all of it through the same company."

"Without the rugs and stuff, it definitely wouldn't be very yurty," Kristy said.

"They always look more authentic with a yak parked out front," Colette said.

"Funny," I said. "So let's see what the extra features are?"

David pulled up the accessory page. They had stoves and rugs and windows and skylights and quite a bit more.

"It's getting to be like a stationary motorhome," Dr. McDonald said to yet more laughter.

"So how much does the basic unit cost?" I asked David

"It depends on the size. They range from 14' diameter all the way up to 30'."

"Let's check out the 30' model." David quickly pulled up the details. "So maybe fifteen grand with all the bells and whistles."

"More or less," David said.

"Okay, let's buy one with everything we need."

"Right now?"

"Sure, why not. Where is this company, by the way?"

"Vermont."

"Let's see if we can find one a bit closer. There must be one of these tree hugger outfits up in the Pacific Northwest."

David went back to his Google search page and quickly had one pulled up.

"Washington state. They claim to be the original."

"Cool. As long as they can get it here yesterday."

I stood up and addressed Kristy and Anne.

"All right, ladies. You wanted to be the camp organizers. Go ahead and run with this. Order the 30' model and add in all the features you like."

"Yeah!" Kristy said, rubbing her palms together.

I went to retrieve my laptop from the kitchen and set it on the coffee table, then handed Colette a credit card.

"Colette here is my right hand gal so coordinate everything through her. Let's get this company on the phone and figure out how to have this yurt shipped down here immediately.

185

Tell them we'll hire our own truck if necessary. Whatever it takes to get it here promptly."

"Wow. Is he always like this?" Kristy said to Colette.

"Wait until he gets impatient," she said.

I stared while they had a good laugh.

"Uh oh," Kristy said. "Looks like we've angered the gods."

"That's right."

She bit her nails.

"Funny. Just get this thing rolling. If there's any hang up with the accessories, separate them from the main order so we can get that yurt down here promptly. I'm going to go talk with my builder and landscaper right now. See about having a nice clearing made and a pad built."

"Hey, what about my car?" Colette said as I headed out the door.

"Oh yeah. It's ready. We'll head into town as soon as we're done with this yurt business."

I started out the door and stopped again with another thought.

"One other rule we have at this point. Once you belong to the tribe, only the whole tribe can kick you off. So welcome. Colette, maybe you can take everyone for a tour of the cottages. The keys are in the credenza there. They're all numbered. Feel free to pick out whichever one you want."

I started to leave and stopped yet again.

"As soon as we have the yurt in place, we'll hold a tribal council."

I started out and found Kyler coming up the stairs.

"Hey, Kyler. How's it going?"

He had been working up in the garden and smelled of manure.

"Shakin' the bush, boss man. What's going on with you?"

He poked his head in the door.

"Wow. You guys are having a tea party and I'm up there sweating in the sun? Isn't somebody supposed to get kicked off the island for this?"

186

There were chuckles inside.

"Sorry, Kyler." I patted him on the back, which produced a cloud of dust and another round of chuckles. "This is Dr. McDonald and his wife Kristy. They've just joined the tribe."

They both said "hi" and waved at Kyler.

"You know everyone else."

"Okay, boss man. Guess I'll get back to shakin' the bush."

I shrugged to everyone inside and followed Kyler downstairs.

"Look, Kyler. I'm sorry. I didn't mean to leave you out. Dr. McDonald had called from my ad and Donny and David and Anne just happened to show up at the same time."

"Wow. Like I didn't say anything about Donny, and about Anne and David the other night, but I thought we were going to have a tribal council before inviting any new members."

"You're right, Kyler, but we didn't have a council meeting before inviting you in, either, or Colette or Camellia."

"But that was before we had agreed to the rules."

Kyler stared. It was the first time I had seen him be anything but his ebullient self.

"What do you want me to say, brother? Fuck. I'm blowing it here, but we needed the tech people and this doctor called from my ad, wanting to join. How the fuck am I going to say no to a doctor?"

Kyler kicked at the ground.

"Look, we just ordered a yurt to have our pow wows in and as soon as it arrives, we'll sit down together and talk about the direction of the tribe. You're absolutely right to be bummed. We all need to abide by the same rules. Christ, we need to have a pow wow about when to have a pow wow."

"I think the first order of business should be, how come I'm shakin' the bush and nobody else is?"

"Come on, Kyler. We're just shaking a different bush right now."

"Yeah. No wonder people on Survivor start fighting and shit."

I smirked.

"Come on. You're fucking tribal member number uno as far as I'm concerned. I need you."

"Yeah?"

"Of course." I waved up at the treehouse. "This was just completely spontaneous. It had been my plan to be up there helping you today. How's it going, by the way?"

"Slow. We could use a freakin' mulching machine."

"You know how that would go over."

"Yeah. I'd like to strangle her right now."

I laughed.

"And how's it going with Kevin?"

"He said he'd be done by the end of the day."

While we were talking, David, Donny and Dr. McDonald started down the stairs.

"We thought we'd leave the ladies to their business and see if we could help you," Dr. McDonald said.

"Sure."

I introduced him to Kyler again.

"Go ahead and jump in the truck everyone." I went over and opened the two passenger side doors. "Dr. McDonald, you can ride up front with me."

We were soon off towards the meadow. I explained to Dr. McDonald about the garden.

"Hey, I'd love to chip in but I'm not really dressed for the occasion."

"I have some clothes you can borrow," Kyler said.

Dr. McDonald chuckled.

"Look, I've got a better idea. Why don't you take a quick shower, Kyler? I want to concentrate the rest of the day on preparing this yurt site."

I drove around and braked to a stop at the back of Kyler's cottage.

"Make it fast. I'm heading up to talk with Dale about the foundation pad. Then we'll go track down Kevin and see what we can do about making a nice clearing."

"All right, boss man."

He jumped out.

"Hurry up. We'll be right back."

I drove up the lane of cottages, pointing out which ones were occupied and which ones were still available.

"I'd be happy with any one of them," Dr. McDonald said, "but I'm sure my wife will have her own ideas."

I smiled over at him.

"Marriage is the art of compromise. Isn't that what they say?"

"Sometimes it's the art of total surrender."

I laughed. With a look, I saw there were smiles in back.

At the cottage in construction, I braked to a stop and everyone jumped out. Dale looked up once as we walked in. I introduced David, Donny and Dr. McDonald. Dale nodded once and continued his work.

"Where's Jason?"

"I sent him into town for some supplies."

"Cool. Well, look. I have a situation here."

I explained about the yurt.

"So, as I understand it, we can pour a concrete pad without a permit. Right?"

Dale nodded.

"And the yurt?"

Dale finally stopped.

"Call it a tent, I guess. I can't see where they'd fuck with you."

"So, can I prevail on you to break off here and pour the pad for me?"

"You know where you want it?"

"That's our next mission. I'm sure we can settle on something in the next fifteen minutes or so."

"Whatever. It's your money."

"Okay. Maybe call Jason and have him bring back whatever supplies you need?"

"You want me start on it right now?"

"Maybe after lunch? I won't know until we pick a spot and I talk to my landscaper about clearing a path. Tomorrow morning at the latest?"

"All right. I'll call Jason and let him know to bring back some stakes and rebar and bender board."

"Great. Thanks. We're on our way to find a spot."

Jumping back into the truck, I noticed Dr. McDonald smiling to himself.

"You're getting a kick out of Dale, I'm guessing?"

"Yeah. He's everyone's vision of a construction worker."

"He actually grunts in two syllables at times." Dr. McDonald chuckled. "But he's very good at what he does so he's bought the right to be gruff."

"No, he's perfect. I wouldn't want it any other way."

I stopped back behind Kyler's place and honked the horn. He came out a moment later.

"Yeah!" he said, getting in. "Now I don't smell like the ass end of a bull!"

"But you still look like one."

I pulled away with everyone laughing, including Kyler.

Not wanting the yurt to be too far away from the cottages, I drove back to the meadow and around to a small knoll directly behind them.

"Let's go check out this little hill," I said, braking to a stop.

Everyone jumped out and joined me on a hike up to the top.

"Wow," Kyler said. "Ocean view and you can even see the fern grotto over there. This is perfect, boss man."

"Nice view of the cottages, too," David said.

"Yeah. Sort of looks like the Shire spreading out down below us," Donny said.

I wandered around the knoll, kicking at dirt.

"So, we're in agreement, gentlemen?"

"Unless you think we should consult the women," Dr. McDonald said.

"I'm going to take a big chance here and say fuck it." Everyone laughed. "So let's go find Kevin and drag him up here."

We jumped back into the truck and headed up towards the garden. Five minutes later, we were headed back down with Kevin following us in his truck. On our hike back up to the knoll, I pointed out where I wanted a new path.

"And place the steps over to the right here, facing the ocean."

"So, I'm guessing you want this right now," Kevin said with a chuckle.

"Right now."

Kevin patted me on the shoulder.

"This guy doesn't believe in messing around."

"Yeah, well, the United Nations is meeting here in a few days, so there's no time to dawdle."

"You're joking, right?"

"Yeah. It's actually for our tribal council. They're almost the same thing."

While the others talked and took in the view, Kevin and I took another stroll around the top of knoll.

"Go ahead and level off a sizable spot. Then I'll have Dale come up and lay out the foundation. Center things as best we can. You can dig a circle with your backhoe, right?"

"I can get it close. I'll have some guys with shovels up here cleaning out the trench behind me anyway."

"Cool. So can you drag your equipment up here right now?"

"Sure."

"All right. I'm off to get Dale. I'm hoping we can pour tomorrow."

"I'll do what I can."

"Good. So, ready guys?" I said to the others.

"I was thinking we might want to check back in on the ladies," Dr. McDonald said.

"Sure. Let's get Dale out here for a look and then we'll head back over."

Fifteen minutes later, with Dale and Kevin coordinated, we headed back towards the treehouse. Dr. McDonald's phone rang along the way.

"Speaking of the devil," he said and answered it.

While he listened, we stole glances.

"So what did you surrender?" I said when Dr. McDonald got off.

There were laughs all around.

"The word is, the women are headed down to look at the cottages."

"Got it. We'll intercept them."

Turning up the back road, I spotted them walking along the path out front and parked. Kristy pretended to pounce on one of the cottages as we walked up.

"We're fighting over who gets which one," she said with a big smile.

"Well, to be fair," I said. "Anne and David did come aboard first, so they should probably get first choice."

"Oh darn."

"It's okay," Anne said. "Go ahead. Take whichever one you want. They're all so charming."

"No, it's okay. You go ahead first."

"No, you go ahead."

"No you."

"No you."

The two women laughed.

"Okay, we'll fight about who's going to be nicest," Kristy said.

"There goes the tribe," Kyler said.

"What's happening with the yurt?" I said.

"The whole kit and caboodle is on the way," Anne said. "With everything you spent, they were willing to expedite the shipping. They said it might not be here tomorrow but definitely the next day."

"Oh, your card," Colette said. "Did you want to know how much?"

"No."

There was laughter.

"Well, no question, you're very yurty now," Anne said.

"*We're* very yurty," I said. "Let's not forget. This is all about *we.*"

We continued down the path, window shopping cottages. Half an hour later, everyone had settled on a place and we were gathered in the kitchen of the cottage Kristy and Dr. McDonald had chosen.

Kristy was going through the kitchen cupboards and drawers.

"I can't believe it. There's everything. Look at these linens. God, honey, we could have sold everything in North Carolina."

"This is amazing," Dr. McDonald said. "Did you pick out all this stuff out yourself or did Colette help you?"

"No, Colette wasn't around then. I just sidled up to first lady who smiled at me in Williams-Sonoma."

"Wow, Williams-Sonoma," Anne said. "Pricey."

"I know," Kristy said. "Is there no end to your money?"

Dr. McDonald cleared his throat.

"Let's just say the cookware didn't break me."

"Okay, foot in mouth," Kristy said with a laugh.

"It's okay. The point is, look at us. Whatever you want to call it, it's the start of something, isn't it?"

"Yeah," David said. "It'll be fun to get that website off the ground and see what happens."

"I want to help with the website," Kristy said.

"Absolutely," David said.

"Well, we should probably be heading back to town," Dr. McDonald said. "I have some calls to make and banking to do."

"I'll tell you what, everyone. Let me spring for dinner in town tonight. We need to have another meeting, just to discuss where we are and where to go from here."

"Sure, I guess we can make it," Anne said, looking at David.

"Sure. We've already chucked our work day into the trash."

"And you two?" I said with a look at Kristy and Dr. McDonald.

"Sure, I think we can make it," he said.

"And you, Donny and Kyler?"

Donny nodded

"Yeah!" Kyler said. "Another lobster dinner on Steven!"

"So, six o'clock?" I said and everyone nodded.

"Somebody should go up and let Camellia know," Colette said.

"That's Kyler's job."

"All right. I'll go see what she's doing."

Kyler shook hands with everyone and headed up the path towards his cottage.

"All right, everyone," I said. "Whoever needs a ride back to my place, let's go. And see you in half an hour, Colette. We'll go grab your car."

"Make it forty-five. I'm still a woman."

Dr. McDonald winked at me and everyone headed out the front door.

Back at my place, there were more jovial goodbyes before all the cars were headed off. I went upstairs to shower.

On the way into town with Colette, the gray clouds lifted off the horizon just far enough to reveal the red glow of sunset out over the sea.

"What's with the big smile?" she said, seeing my pleasant mood.

"Oh nothing. Just glad you're here with me."

I reached out for her hand and gave her a kiss. Having called ahead with instructions for Louie, he knew to pretend he couldn't find Colette's Celica upon our arrival and his

194

helpers played the ruse to the hilt. With increasing urgency, they searched all about the sea of cars on his lot for the Celica without finding. Finally, after a long minute, a young man pulled it around from the back of the building and Colette gasped, then threw herself at my chest.

"Oh, you," she said in tears.

"Like new," I said.

"Oh Steven. How will I ever repay you?"

"Don't worry about it. It's all taken care of."

Colette hugged me again, got in, looked at the detailed interior with the new top, then climbed back out and went around thanking everyone. Having expressed her appreciation several times, she gave me a kiss and headed off with a final wave to the crew. Louie gave me a wink and a thumbs up as I pulled off the lot.

We were the first ones at the restaurant so I asked the hostess to seat us at a booth in back. Colette did not mention the car as people arrived and otherwise sat there holding my hand under the table in silence. It was as if she had had a spiritual experience.

As soon as the drinks arrived, I clinked my glass with a knife. The chatter slowly subsided. I smiled and waited until it had ceased entirely.

"I just wanted to say for starters how truly thrilled I am about our growing tribe."

There were cheers and glasses held up as a toast.

"Motley crew that we are."

That elicited jeers and howls of protest. I held up my hands.

"So, now that I have your full attention, I need to address something that's come up, which is adopting an official method for adding or removing people from the tribe. When there was just Tyler and Colette and Camellia and me, we had agreed to have a vote but you can see what's happened. Which is my bad. I unilaterally welcomed Donny and Kristy and Dr. McDonald onboard and shouldn't have done that."

"Oh man, does that mean we're out?" Kristy said.

"Me too?" Donny said.

"Yeah! You're all off the island!" Kyler said.

Kristy shoved him.

"There will forever be an asterisk by our names," Dr. McDonald said with a chuckle.

"So how would you vote?" Anne said. "By a simple or super majority?"

"A good question and one that we should take up at for our first tribal council. The point being, we need to make some rules and stick to them. Kyler reminded me of this earlier in the day."

"Oh, thanks a lot, Kyler."

I waited patiently until this next round of razzing had died down.

"Look, violating rule number one *was* a breach of protocol on my part, but you are now fortuitously saved by rule number two."

"What's rule number two?" Kristy said.

"Once you're in the tribe, it takes a vote to kick you out."

"Yeah, we're in," Kristy said with a pump of her fist.

"Yes, you're in…So, back to business. Once we get our yurt up…"

"Yeah! I'm all about getting my yurt up," Kyler said.

Everyone at the table started riffing on that theme.

"Okay, okay. So we should have our yurts up here in a few days and we'll have a meeting, wherein we will discuss all of our issues, including when to have a meeting."

"Every time somebody pisses us off," Kyler said.

"Which will be abundantly if you keep interrupting me."

"Too bad because you need a majority to kick me off."

"All right, who'll take ten grand to vote Kyler off the island?"

Everyone raised a hand.

"Oh man."

I smiled at Kyler.

"So, we'll have a meeting, in which we'll start to sort out everyone's vision of the tribe. As noted, my basic idea was for everyone to chip in his or her fair share. Dr. McDonald had mentioned having a weekly time sheet, where everybody keeps track of his or her hours but I don't know if I want to see us getting that formal. Whatever. I guess my vision was, we'll figure all this out as we go along."

"Well, if I may play the devil's advocate for a moment," Dr. McDonald said. "Let's say I want to spend a nice, quiet Sunday afternoon at home and one of my neighbors decides to play Boston at 150 decibels. What do we do then?"

"Go next door with a shotgun," Kyler said. "Yeah!"

"Look, no doubt a thousand little things will come up but that will be the purpose of our meetings, right? To sort out our differences?"

"So, will we have to have cops?" Kristy said.

"God no. Well, I hope not. Do we want to go there?"

There were shrugs and a general shaking of heads.

"So, I say, rather than making rules for every damned thing, why don't we simply agree to the spirit of mutual respect and cooperation? Then if two people can't resolve their differences, we take it before the council. Okay?"

Again, there were shrugs and a general shaking of heads.

"Now, finally...."

Cheers broke out.

"Ha, ha. So finally, let me just reiterate where we stand. We're building a website around Camellia's national roll call idea. Hopefully that will bring in revenue and she and Kyler have brought us well along the way towards a functioning community garden and there we are."

"Here we are," Anne said.

"Here we are, embarking on an unknown journey."

"Cool," Kristy said and held up her glass. "I just want to say that John and I had a long talk about things on our way home today and we're really excited about being involved. We never imagined anything quite like this but we've been

197

talking about a more meaningful way to live ever since we met in college and just think this is so cool. So, thank you, Steven. It's really generous of you to get this whole thing started."

There were cheers for me and I held up my glass in acknowledgment.

The Tribe

16

Colette followed me home in her newly painted and upholstered car that evening and loved me like a woman does when she really loves a man. When she and Hugo left around midnight, I lay there feeling physically content but with the same dark cloud hanging over my thoughts. I had once loved a woman, heart and soul, but did not love that way now. Not knowing what else to do, I tried to cram all that down into a dark corner of my mind somewhere and forget as best I could.

Greeted by these same thoughts in the morning, I quickly jumped into some work clothes and drove up to the yurt project. Dale was already there laying out the foundation with stakes and string lines. I stood to one side and observed his methods. Dale had chosen a spot more or less centered on the knoll, had driven a stake at that position and was using a long board as a compass, ensuring that the bender board created the proper arc of a circle.

So simple and practical. I would have been consulting Archimedes.

The plastic and sand base quickly went in and Dale set about adding his rebar. I walked over closer at that point. He glanced up at me.

"I'll set up the pour so it slopes slightly from center. Water runoff. And there'll be a depressed six inch ribbon all the way around the yurt so you can do a nice tile trim."

"Sounds good. You did arrange for quick setting concrete, right?"

"I did."

"Good. And as soon as all this is done and the yurt is up, you can go back to what you were doing."

"No concrete paths or platforms or anything up here?"

"No. I'm going to have Kevin do some stone work and stuff. I want it to have a real Zenny feeling."

"You got it."

Having inspected Dale's work, I went down to talk with Kevin. He and his crew were sand setting the steps with broken pieces of sandstone.

"Looks great."

"Yeah. I anchored everything down below with a concrete pad so it won't go anywhere. Plus I'm interlocking the steps as we go."

"Yeah. It looks beautiful, Kevin."

"Thanks," he said with the usual chuckle.

"One thing. Why don't you install some kind of border along each side so the mud doesn't wash in with every rain?"

"Maybe some big slabs of this same sandstone?"

"Sounds perfect."

I slapped him on the shoulder and headed off to check on the garden. My phone rang along the way. It was Connor.

"What's the good news, sir?"

"Got those drawings done for you, mate. What would you like me to do with them?"

"You want the short answer?"

"Bloody bastard. I still feel like hell about sticking my foot in it, ya know."

"Good."

"Bastard."

"Look, don't beat yourself up."

"It comes naturally to me, mate."

"Well don't. So about the plans, I'd like you to forward three copies over to Toni and three to Frank Wheeler at the building department. I'll call Frank to let him know they're coming."

"Mate, you want me to run this project through plan check for you?"

"Do you mind?"

"It's the least I could do."

"You're a scholar and a gentleman."

"And a bloody bastard to boot."

"And the arts center project?"

"I've been dreading the encounter but we're ready to have a final design review before I run off the blueprints."

"All right. I'll talk with Colette and arrange a meeting with the three of us as soon as possible. In the meantime, stop worrying. I haven't said a word to her. And never will."

"Thanks, mate. I'll run the shed blueprints over to the city this afternoon. And wait to hear from you on the other."

"Don't forget about Toni. I need her help ramming this shed through the Coastal Commission."

"Consider it done, sir."

"Thanks, Connor and keep me posted on the city."

Out at the garden, I found Camellia mulching away all alone. Somehow, with Kyler's earlier help, she had three-quarters of the work done.

My phone rang as I was stepping out of the truck. It was Colette.

"Hello, darling," she said.

"Hi, sweetheart. How are you?"

"I just looked out and saw my car and got all teary eyed again."

"Aw."

"You are a dear, sweet man."

"Thank you. It made my heart swell to see you so happy."

"Oh, it's more than happiness. You remind me that there are really good souls left in this world and reason for hope."

"Well, *you* are one of the good souls and you were really sweet to me last night."

"Did you feel it?"

"Oh, sure. I felt it real good."

"Good. I wanted it to feel real good."

"It did. So what are your plans for today?"

"I don't know. I was thinking to call Connor and check on the status of things but I called him yesterday and he never called me back."

I explained that I had just spoken with him and related what we had discussed, the personal stuff left out.

"He asked me to apologize to you. I guess he's been swamped."

"So, are we headed in there today?"

"Yeah. Let's see how things play out but maybe this afternoon?"

"Sure. Let me know."

"I will."

"So, is there anything I can do to help in the meantime?"

"Coordinate with David and Kristy on the website?"

"I don't know what I'd be doing."

"Talk with them about the design. And if they ask any questions, you tell them I wanted your artistic eye on the final product."

"Okay. I'm kind of feeling adrift without the arts center."

"Want to come up and shovel manure with me?"

"I'm suddenly feeling focused again."

I laughed.

"I know. Call Kristy and work with her on setting up one of the cottages as a temporary tech center. Get a list of whatever they think we need. Work stations, chairs and computers. Whatever and call when you need a credit card."

"Okay. I'll call her."

"Would you like to come over for dinner tonight?"

"Would you like me to come over for dinner tonight?"

"Sure…Or were we supposed to be having dinner with everyone in town tonight?"

"That was last night."

"Yeah. Okay. Jesus, I'm losing it here."

She laughed.

"Yeah. I'm definitely losing it. Okay. Let's just talk later."

"I'll wait for your call."

"Yeah, I'll be up here in the garden mulching away with Camellia for a few hours."

I hung up and headed over to the garden. Camellia looked up briefly as I approached but continued working without saying a word. I grabbed a shovel and jumped in. When sweat got into my eyes, I stopped to wipe them with a sleeve. Camellia wiped a hand across her forehead. It was my thought to say "nice day" but it wasn't. The sky was gray and dreary again.

I went back to work.

"Are you happy here?" I said, trying to make conversation.

Camellia kept shoveling so I kept shoveling.

"My son died from an overdose," she said some moments later.

I glanced over from my work.

"I know. I heard. I'm really sorry."

She did not look up. More time passed.

"I was an addict all his life. It's the only way he ever saw me."

I nodded, not knowing what to say. Another minute passed.

"I'll never forgive myself for not getting sober sooner."

I slammed my boot down onto the shovel and dug a bit deeper. I stayed there for two hours with nothing but her words going around in my head.

Towards noon, I dug my shovel into the dirt a final time.

"I need some lunch. Are you hungry too?"

She shook her head.

"Do you need anything? Anything at all out here?"

She shook her head. I gently rubbed her back.

"All right. I'm glad you're here, Camellia. I'm really really glad you're here with us."

She nodded and kept working. I lingered a moment before walking away.

Back at the house, I took a shower with Camellia's words still rolling around in my head. Nothing could wash them away. The things we did for which we could not forgive ourselves. But there had to be a way. There had to be a way to forgive and let go or we'd all go mad.

Out in the kitchen, I was overcome with nostalgia and whipped up a peanut butter and jelly sandwich. The bread was coarse whole grain, the peanut butter crunchy, the jelly boysenberry preserves. I ate, wavering between my dearest childhood memories and Camellia's grief.

When I was done, I called Toni. She quickly answered.

"Did you receive the blueprints?"

"I did."

"So where do we stand?"

"I think I can make this work."

"And how many trips to Cabo is this going to cost me? That's my new standard of currency, by the way."

"Charming, but I don't think it will cost you nearly that much. Let's make sure things go smoothly. If it does, a few hundred dollars."

"It's worth a Cabo trip to me."

"Don't worry. I'm saving up for the big one."

We laughed.

"Hell, if it wasn't for his lordship next door, I'd be having a grand opening to our arts center in a few months. I could have feted you in style."

"So how is everything going out there?"

"It's going."

I explained about the growing tribe and the yurt.

"Yurts are very in."

"So I've learned. Necessity being the mother of invention, I've grown rather fond of the idea. It should add a ritualistic atmosphere to our meetings."

"So give me a few more days Steven and I should have things worked out for you."

"Thanks. I will await your call."

As soon as we hung up, I called Jolie. She answered after many rings.

"Where do we stand?"

"You need to run in and sign the papers at the escrow office."

"Right now?"

"You're the one in a great rush."

"Tell them I'm on my way. Should be about half an hour."

I called Connor but he did not answer. I called Colette to let her know why I was running into town and that I had been unable to reach Connor.

"Well, call me if that changes?" she said.

"Sure, or we'll do it another day."

She was antsy, as I was, but there wasn't a goddamned thing we could do, short of skinning Chaplin alive.

On my way down to the highway, I called Kevin.

"What's up?" he said.

"I had to run into town but I can hook up with you when I get back and cut you a check on the garden."

"That would be nice."

"No problem. I should be back in about two hours."

In succession, I called Dr. McDonald, who quickly put Kristy on the line, and then David, to make sure he was in communication with everyone else.

While I was still at the escrow office, Connor called.

"Where are you, lad?"

"Sitting in the building department right now, sir, waiting my turn. A lot like grammar school detention, as I remember it. Caught me looking up Sally Gilmore's britches or some such heinous act."

"And what have you learned over the intervening years?"

"Not much."

"So, what else is on your mind, sir?"

205

"Oh, calling to see about that dreaded meeting with you and Colette."

I checked my phone for the time and explained about being in town to sign some papers.

"The plan had been for us to come in together and review the plans today but it's probably getting to be a bit late for that."

"Putting it off is just fine by me, mate."

"Yeah, I know. Care to grab a drink with me anyway? I can cut you a check."

"Does the pope wear a pointed hat?"

"Say, McCormick's, on the waterfront."

"Sounds dreamy to me. Oh, here. They're getting ready to stamp the prints right now."

"Good. Call it fifteen minutes?"

"I'll be there."

I was already sloshing some Scotch around in my glass when Connor walked in.

"What have ya there?"

"A bit o' Balblair. Fancy some?"

"I would, yeah."

I waved to the bartender and pulled out my checkbook.

"What'll make you happy today, sir?"

The bartender came and poured another glass of Scotch. Connor handed me a slip of paper.

"Can make you out a proper invoice but wasn't sure if we were done."

"We'll never be done."

"Just fine by me, of course."

I wrote out the check. Connor had invoiced me for a little under forty grand. I made the check out for forty-five.

"You're too generous, sir."

"It's a pleasure doing business with you."

"Likewise, sir."

We drank.

"Never been to Cabo," Connor said. "Been thinking I should try it."

"The old Cabo is best, in my book. If you're serious about going, I'll set you up in one of the private residences at the Hotel Cabo San Lucas for a few weeks. That and some fishing and you'll be right for a year."

"I'll take two birds in the bush over a fish in my hands."

"Haven't learned a damned thing, have you?"

"Not a damned thing, except that I haven't learned a damned thing."

"I'll drink to that."

We did.

"But seriously, the view there at the hotel is exquisite, the atmosphere unhurried, the charm old world. It was the first big hotel built down there. Back in the sixties. Have lunch out on the point and go fishing with the cook in the morning. Then go into town to chase the birds at night."

"College girls on spring break, I'm guessing."

"For the most part."

"Can you talk to them in that state?"

"Probably not, but do you care?"

"Probably not."

We toasted and drank again.

"What's it like?" Connor said after a long moment.

"What do you mean?"

"The money."

I looked out at the coast in thought.

"You'd be an idiot to think it changes everything. You can buy your way out of a lot of feelings, but sooner or later, something will come along that money can't fix, and then you'll know despair all right. I was in that place not long ago, where my money was useless against the anguish I felt."

I sipped at my glass of Scotch.

"That's when this tribal vision came to me. Like how can I be one of these selfish pricks? Take the money and wall myself up behind my multi-million dollar estate? I'm not religious

207

but that line from the Bible always got to me when I was a kid. You are your brother's keeper. How can I have all these riches and not have some connection with all the poor son of a bitches suffering out there, you know? What am I going to do, buy a two hundred foot yacht?"

"Christ, mate. I'm just trying to survive from one moment to the next, if you know what I mean. I've no time to be worrying about such things."

"And believe me, Connor. There have been times when I thought, what the hell have I done to myself? I've wanted to take dynamite to the whole thing. Then a moment comes along like yesterday, where the whole tribe is gathered out at the property, making some decisions together and you're suddenly struck by the goodness of it. People working as one. It's what I've always wanted. A part of me would just as soon be alone, but I know that kind of life ultimately has no meaning or purpose."

"No knock on you, mate, but it still seems to me a function of the wealth. Money gives you freedom that other people don't have."

"Sure, but even with the old man there over the years as my fallback position, I never thought in those terms. Like money would fix me?"

I sipped from the Scotch.

"No. If anything, a woman's embrace has been my downfall. What profit it a man to gain sweet kisses and lose his soul?"

"And there the two of us are joined at the hip, sir."

"On the sweet road to perdition."

"Aye, but what a sweet road it is."

"And to hell and back it has taken us."

The bartender came and I had him splash a bit more Scotch in our glasses.

"Here's to hell and back, sir."

We toasted.

"So, to your original question, I suppose anyone would like to have my problems, but I think only a fool would see it as a lasting solution. It doesn't hurt, but it doesn't solve everything. I have more options, but that means nothing if you're not grounded. Why don't you come out and join us, by the way."

"I admire you, sir, but I'm not there. You're more likely to find me shacking up at the Playboy Mansion."

"So, Sodom and Gomorrah it is."

"It was the goat business. Gave it all a bad name."

I laughed, polished off my Scotch and threw some bills on the countertop.

"It's been a pleasure, sir, but I must get back to the tribe."

"I can see where that would be comforting, mate."

"You're never alone."

We both made frightful eyes and stood up. Outside, in the fleeting hours of a late afternoon, I patted Connor on the back.

"Did you say you had a set of plans for me?"

"I did, sir, along with an inspection card."

He pulled them out of his car.

"Splendid. Now all I need is the Coastal Commission to bend over."

"Good luck with that."

"Thanks. Let me know when you're ready for that Cabo trip. I know the owner personally. I was practically a permanent resident there at one time."

"Might take you up on that. Soon as we're done with the Met."

"Talk soon, in either case, and keep this little meeting a secret. I expect Colette will feel wounded to hear she had been left out."

On the way out of town, I saw a roadside florist and stopped to buy a dozen roses. The road to perdition, it was nothing if not colored in red.

Back at my place, I realized I had not exercised in several days and jumped into my jogging togs. I was on my way up the trail towards the garden when Kyler and Donny came up behind me in a maintenance golf cart. Kyler was wearing a big straw hat.

"Need a ride, boss man?"

"No, just follow along and we'll talk while I'm running."

We discussed the garden and the yurt foundation and the situation at the cottages.

"Kristy's moving some stuff in and I guess David and Anne are planning to do the same after work today."

"Good. And you're all settled, Donny?"

"Pretty much. Just looking after the eco equipment, as you had asked, and lending Kyler a hand wherever I can."

"Feel free to pitch in at the tech center whenever you want, too."

We moved along side by side through the quiet of the forest for a spell.

"So, what about the pour?"

"Dale said the trucks will be here in half an hour. That was about fifteen minutes ago."

"Okay. Let's go check it out."

We arrived to the site and saw the trucks weren't there so I decided to keep going.

"Why don't you guys just hang loose here and see if you can lend a hand."

"You got it, boss man."

"I'll be back in ten minutes or so."

Not wanting to miss the action, I did a quick hill climb up through the forest. The pump was there by the time I returned and the trucks were pulling up. All of us helped with dragging the hoses around as Dale and his crew worked the pour. Within half an hour, the concrete was in and the pump guy was cleaning out his equipment. Dale and his crew were busy finishing the concrete.

"Good job," I told Dale. "Give these guys a bonus and put it on my tab."

"You got it."

"So you'll be good with installing the yurt the day after tomorrow?"

"You have it here already?"

"As far as I know, it'll be here tomorrow."

"Sure. With this hardener, she'll be dry enough by then."

"Good. We're all eager to have our first pow wow."

"Smoke a little peace pipe, eh?"

"Something like that. By the way, I have city approval for that work shed so if Toni can ram it through the commission somehow, you can start on that right away. Otherwise, just keep going on the cottage."

"You got it."

I pulled Donny and Kyler aside.

"How are you two doing on funds?"

"I'm fine," Kyler said.

"I've got about a week and then I'm broke," Donny said.

"Okay. One of the things we'll do at our first tribal council is set up a fund so nobody goes hungry. You know, whatever other essentials come up, we'll make sure everyone's safe and secure, okay?"

"Sure, boss man."

Donny nodded.

"We'll build on that as far as salaries and stuff goes but for now I just want to get this website up and running and see where it leads us."

Both of them nodded.

"We'll be all right. The two main things are, plant the garden and set up the tech facilities so whatever you two can do to chip in, just do it."

I shook their hands and headed down the open slope in a run. My head had been a tangled ball of string before I left. I returned flush with endorphins and a reasonable degree of serenity.

By the time Colette showed up at six, I already had some swordfish steaks thawed out and was preparing a stuffing.

"What's all this?" she said, inspecting my work. "I smell saffron."

"That and garlic and chopped dried cherries and pine nuts among other things."

"Sounds delicious."

"Yes, and like all good recipes, you're into it two hours before you look up at the clock."

I noticed Colette wearing the shoes I loved and dropped what I was doing. We kissed bone to bone for a spell.

"Dinner first?" she said, pulling away.

"Tough call. You're awfully hard to resist."

She slapped at me.

"What beautiful roses," she said and went to smell them.

"They have your name on them."

"Aw. Did you really?"

"I did."

She came back over.

"It's such a slippery slope, Steven."

"What the hell. Once on the road to perdition, you may as well go down in style."

"So, dinner first?" she said again.

I laughed.

"You rascal. No. I just want to fuck you really good and sweetly right now."

With a deft move, I lifted Colette up onto the heavy, oak dining table and got my muzzle into her panties.

The Tribe

17

First thing the next morning, I brewed a cup of coffee and drove up to see the pour. Dale and Jason had already stripped off most of the forms. Instead of the concrete being green and steaming in the morning cold, it was gray and dry from the quick setting agent.

"It's already cracking," Dale said matter-of-factly.

"I don't care. Do I?"

"I guess not too much with a yurt. I'll have Jason come up and caulk all the cracks before we leave this afternoon."

"Thanks."

He knew what he was doing. I didn't.

Having a thought, I went down and grabbed Kevin from his work on the steps.

"Ah," he said, seeing the depressed, six inch ribbon Dale had created around the perimeter of the pour. "So you want me to install the same stonework around here."

"No. I'm picturing something more colorful. Maybe a mosaic of tiles?"

Kevin chuckled and stared, clearly wanting some direction.

"I'll tell you what. Let's have Colette and the gals coordinate with you on the design. The yurt is going up tomorrow so it'll have to wait until the day after that at least."

We agreed to have a pow wow about the design before we did anything more and went our separate ways. I returned to the house and started making phone calls. With this Coastal

Commission business, it felt like my life was frozen in place. I leaned back in my chair, daydreaming of Colette's sex.

Knowing Donny and Kyler were up top, helping Camellia hoe the garden rows, I considered joining them but was not in the mood. I made breakfast instead and was eating when David and Anne showed up with a list of all the hardware they needed for the tech center.

"I'd recommend Dell," David said. "They've got full product and software support."

"I know. I use them. Did you want to help me do this right now?"

David looked at Anne.

"We have a car load of stuff we need to unload."

"Go ahead you two," Anne said. "I can do the unpacking myself."

"Look, I've got a better idea."

I explained about the mosaic ribbon around the yurt.

"Let's grab Colette so you two can coordinate on the design. Are you good with that?"

"Absolutely. That'll be fun."

"Okay, so go take care of unpacking and I'll see you over at your place in a bit."

I gobbled down the rest of my meal, took a quick shower and went to grab Colette. Not wanting to barge in unannounced, I called her on my way. She was putting away dishes in the kitchen when I walked in. She looked over her shoulder with a smile. I put my arms around her from behind. When she turned to kiss me, I pinned her hard against the countertop.

"I'm going mad," I said. "The more we fuck, the more I want it. There's no satisfying me now."

She searched my eyes.

"Did you mean right now?"

"Yes but there's something else that needs your attention. Goddamn it."

She laughed. I explained about the design work.

"Okay?"

She nodded. I kissed her hard.

"Come see me tonight, all right?" She nodded. "Good. That knowledge will provide me with some measure of sanity for the rest of the day."

I kissed her again.

"Come. Let's go talk to Anne."

Five minutes later, I had deposited her with Anne and was driving back up to my place with David.

"What about the office furniture?" I asked him.

"Kristy's taking care of that."

"Let's call and confirm."

David was doing that as we pulled to a stop out in front of my place. I heard him talking to her on our way up the stairs. He cupped the phone once we were inside.

"She says everything's ready. She just needs your credit card."

"Ha! Get the number for the place and I'll call them when we're done."

"Coffee?" I said as David got off.

"Sure, and Kristy said 'darn' about the credit card."

"I'll bet."

A minute later, David had a Dell sales rep on the line and handed me the phone.

"It's the small business end," he whispered. "The personal computer support is all overseas now."

I got on the line with a guy in Texas and quickly spent about thirty grand. That included an install team. The warranty and tech support was good for four years. I expedited delivery. Installation was scheduled for Friday.

"Anything else in the immediate?" I asked David over our coffee.

"No. I'm already engineering the site. By the time we get the computers up and running on Friday, I should have something preliminary for you to look at."

"Good. Where is Kristy, by the way?"

"She said she was on her way out here with a load of stuff."

"Okay. Let's go find her. I want to start lining up our contributors and advertisers."

"Yeah, that's more her gig. Anne's too."

"That's fine. Let's go find them."

We ran across Kyler and Donny in the maintenance golf cart on our way.

"What's up?" I said, stopping next to them.

"Donny and I have decided to have a peasant revolt. We want better pay and work conditions. It's that or pitchforks."

"Funny thing. David and I were just looking for rebellious peasants we could burn at the stake."

"Shakin' the bush, boss man, shakin' the bush."

"Yeah. I thought that might quell the rebellion. So what about the garden?"

"The rows are almost all done. All we need now are some seeds." Kyler reached into his pocket. "Camellia gave me this list to give you."

"What am I going to do with it?" I pulled out my money clip and handed him a hundred dollars, along with the list. "Go into town and buy them."

"So what else is going on, boss man?"

My phone rang just then so I held up my hand. It was the yurt delivery guy, saying he was down on the highway somewhere. I told him I'd send someone down right away to guide him in.

"The yurt guy's here," I said, hanging up.

"All right!" Kyler said.

"Yeah. Go find him and guide him in. I'll be back to join you in a minute."

Kyler and Donny headed off towards the coast. I headed up behind the cottages with David. We found Kristy back there unloading her car.

"Hey!" she said with a big smile and an armful of boxes.

David and I jumped out to give her a hand.

"All right. Nothing like a little help around here."

Kristy dropped her first load and started right back out for another one.

"Hang on, Kristy," I said. "I need to talk to you about something."

She kept going. I followed and had to grab her by the arm after she dropped the next load of boxes.

"Stop!"

She ran her palms straight forward from beside her head, as if creating parallel lines.

"I'm focused."

"Yeah, I can see that but I was wondering if we could get some of that focus on the website marketing."

"Sure. As soon as I'm done unloading the car."

Seeing she was not to be deterred, David and I continued lending her a hand. Two minutes later, we had everything stacked inside.

"Okay, can you stop now?"

She ran her two palms forward with a laugh at herself

"Okay Ms. Focus. Come join us down at David and Anne's place for a minute."

"Let me use the restroom and I'll be right there."

Five minutes later, we were in David and Anne's kitchen, having a pow wow about the marketing end of things.

"Bottom line, I don't know a thing this crap," I admitted.

"This *crap*," Kristy said to David and Anne with a big smile.

"Well, I don't. I just know David was right. We need our name splashed all over the news and internet all at once. Full page ads. On the morning shows. Boom. *THE* name for this concept before anyone else can catch up. We dink around at the start and somebody'll clean our clocks. So, can you handle this, ladies?"

"Sure," Anne said in the slow sensuous way she always said that word, like she was a southern belle agreeing to another mint julep. Meanwhile, Kristy had done her hand focus thing, indicating a readiness to go.

217

"Okay. So let's start with some big time names. NY Times and Washington Post columnists. Faces from your major online political sites. Left and right. You find out what they want to write a guest post and I'll give it to them. Just don't let on to anyone what we're doing yet."

"That's fine but I think there are other issues we need address first," Anne said.

"Like what?"

"Like having some serious money in the bank. As in, a Dunn & Bradstreet type reference. You know? We need substance behind us so when people look, they'll know to take us seriously."

"So, how much are we talking?"

Anne looked at Kristy and back at me.

"I don't know. Millions. It depends on how big of an image you want to project. I'll do some research this afternoon and give you an answer."

"You do that but I don't care what it is. Consider it done."

"Yeah?"

"Absolutely. I'm not Bill Gates but I've got a junior membership in his club."

"Wow, this is such a trip," Kristy said with a laugh. "I love spending his money."

"All right. Enough clowning around. We ordered the computers. They're scheduled to be installed on Friday. Let's try to get those work stations in here tomorrow if we can. With any luck, we'll have a preliminary website up and be ready to fine tune things next week. Sound good?"

Kristy did her hand focus schtick. Anne smiled and nodded. David was taking it all in with a serious look.

"Okay. I've got to run. The yurt's here."

"The yurt!" Kristy said. "I want to see it!"

"Hell, I don't know if there's anything to see. It's probably all packaged up. Let's just plan on reviewing things tomorrow while Dale's installing it."

There were groans. I did Kristy's 'focused' hand gesture.

"Let's just get this office going!"

"Okay, boss man," Kristy said.

"Ha." I started out the door and stopped. "By the way, first official yurt council is scheduled for Friday evening. Make sure we have everything we need."

"Money," Anne said.

"Yeah, give us some of that good old fashioned green stuff," Kristy said.

"All right. Do we have a cookie jar?"

"I do," Anne said.

She produced one from the cupboard and I stuffed five, one hundred dollar bills into it.

"General fund. You take money out, you replace it with a receipt."

Kristy saluted.

"All right. I'm off to find our yurt. If it's worth seeing, I'll let you know. Otherwise, you'll find Dale installing it first thing in the morning."

When I caught up with Kyler and Donny, they were guiding the truck driver out to the site. I followed them and parked at the bottom of the knoll, alongside the truck. Everyone climbed out. I went over to inspect the load. The driver was uncovering it from beneath a blue plastic tarp.

"The canvas is the single heaviest part," he said.

That was in a giant bundle with a big box for the stove. The skylight and door came separately, as did the rugs. The rest was bundled together as rafters and wall parts.

"Where's it going?"

"Up there."

The driver looked up.

"This is as far as I take it."

"That's fine but can I buy the tarp off you. Looks like rain tonight."

The driver hesitated.

"Whatever it costs. Two hundred bucks?"

"Yeah, that should cover it."

"Fine. Let's get everything unloaded, guys."

Kevin came around from the other side of the knoll to check things out.

"Hey, do we have any scrap wood left over from the fence?

"Yeah. There's some still stacked up out there at the garden."

"Good. I want to use it for dunnage. Go ahead and get things unloaded, you guys. I'll be back in a minute."

I grabbed Kyler's maintenance cart and ran up to the garden. Camellia glanced up from her hoeing and smiled, as much as she ever smiled. I waved and tossed a bunch of loose lumber onto the cart.

Back at the yurt site, we got everything up off the ground and covered it with the tarp.

"You heading into town for those seeds?" I asked Kyler.

"Yeah, boss man."

"All right. In the morning, why don't you guys head over here and see what you can do to help Dale. Then get back to whatever else you were doing."

I jumped in my truck.

"First yurt council is scheduled for Friday evening."

"Cool, boss man."

"Yeah, it should be fun. I'll see you guys in the morning."

I stopped by to let Dale know the yurt had arrived and headed back home. It was lunch time. I whipped up a chicken sandwich, with cheese, tomatoes and red onions.

When I was done, I went online to check for messages. Nothing from Toni or anyone. My impulse was to make calls. I was juggling a dozen balls and none of it was moving fast enough for me. I tried not to dwell on Colette but did. Lust had taken hold of me. Several times, I almost drove over to her place.

Finally, it was twilight and she was knocking at my door. Hugo came in first with his big rabbit ears. I petted him and got hold of Colette.

"Did you bring a bone for him?"

"You're wasting no time this evening."

"No. It was hard enough, waiting all day."

We got Hugo situated with his bone and headed upstairs. Any more fervently and I would have ripped Colette's clothes off of her. I got my mouth onto her cunt first thing, then savaged her all over the bed. There was no peace until I was done. Then there was calm, as if after a tornado.

Later, we made a pasta dish with sundried tomatoes, Kalamata olives and gourmet sausage. Some hard crust bread and a salad it was a fine meal.

Later we returned to our passions and Colette slipped home after midnight.

In the morning, the entire tribe had found its way up to the yurt site, save for Dr. McDonald and Camellia. Where possible, we helped with bucking things up the hill. Mostly, we stood out of the way and watched the installation.

Colette and Anne went into town for some tile samples at one point and came back to experiment with designs for the border. Kevin was nearly done with the steps and came up to discuss the landscaping around the yurt with us. One and all chipped in with their ideas.

While we worked and joked around, my phone rang. It was Toni.

"You got the okay," she said.

"All right!" I cupped the phone. "Hey, Dale! We got approval for that shed! You can start work on it anytime!"

He gave me a thumbs up. I got back to Toni. When I got off, there was a round of high fives.

"All right, ladies and gentlemen," I said. "What's next on our agenda?"

"The office furniture is arriving this afternoon," Kristy said.

"And the computers tomorrow. I love it! Action! We're really moving forward now, folks!"

I threw my arms out and head back and hollered to the sky. There were feigned attempts to restrain me and laughter.

All the energy quickly shifted to the temporary tech center.

221

"Shouldn't you be up there planting seeds?" I told Kyler.

"Oh, man. I hate being like the serf guy."

"Come on. I'll give you a hand. We're not doing anything here."

"I can join you," Donny said.

"Me too," Anne said.

"All right, I surrender," Colette said.

All of us jumped into the maintenance cart and headed up the hill, pretending to sing peasant songs about stomping grapes and harvesting crops.

At the garden, we found the seed packets spread out everywhere.

"Wow, look," Anne said. "Broccoli...peas...spinach and cauliflower...cabbage...carrots...lettuce."

"Will all these crops actually grow in the winter?" I said.

Camellia nodded while working.

"As long as it doesn't freeze."

"Cool."

We went around, examining how things had been laid out. With the garden not being level, the rows went up and down and all around.

"We really need some way to label the things," Anne said.

"I know, Kyler," I said. "Drive back down and grab some of those stakes from the stripped out concrete pour."

"You got it, boss man."

"And a stapler from the office."

Once he had returned, the two of us went along, driving stakes and stapling the seed packages to them.

Colette came by again that night to an orgy of food and sex, broken up briefly by some Glenn Miller and a lesson in swing dancing.

The next day was another flurry of activity. While David and Kristy oversaw the computer installation, the rest of us decorated the yurt's interior. By noon, we had a list of things to add, made a run into town and returned with a truckload of large, Oriental themed pillows, two battery operated lanterns and a tea set to go with the stove.

Once everything was in place, we stood back to admire our handiwork.

"All right," I said. "What do you say we grab a bite to eat and meet back here at six for our first council?"

"All hail the mighty council," Kyler said.

"Yes. Weighty decisions will soon be rendered on an intergalactic level. Be sure to bring your ideas."

All of us went off laughing and chattering and filled with anticipation.

A few hours later, with twilight settling among the trees, we trickled back through the woods. The atmosphere was that of monks ascending to the temple. I gathered Colette along the way. We came across Anne and David near their cottage. David had brought along his laptop. I saw Dr. McDonald and Kristy mounting the stone steps ahead of us. Dr. McDonald had something wrapped under his arm. The two of them stopped at the top and waited for us to arrive. I looked back and saw Donny, Kyler and Camellia coming through the trees.

"What's in the package?" I asked Dr. McDonald.

"It's a surprise," he said with a smile.

"He won't even tell me," Kristy said.

While we talked, the other three arrived.

"All right, the tribe!" Kyler said.

"It seems like we ought to have a ritual just for going inside," Anne said at the door.

"How's this," Dr. McDonald said and unwrapped his package.

It was a gong. He struck it and the deep, melodic tone echoed off through the forest.

"Perfect!" Anne said. "Our first tribal session is now in order!"

One by one we filed inside. Someone turned on a lantern to yikes and groans.

"That's definitely not very Zenny," Donny said.

"Yes, first order of business will be to find more suitable lighting," I said.

"Shall we make tea?" Anne said.

"We'll have to have a council vote to decide," Kristy said to laughter.

"I say go with the tea," I said.

"The boss man speaketh," Kyler said.

"Oh Christ. Let's just get the stove going. The tea will follow."

Donny took the lantern and set it off on the far side of the yurt.

"It's too big…big…big," Kristy said, pretending to make her voice echo.

Earlier in the day we had scattered the pillows around the perimeter of the yurt but it was clear now that this was too large a circle so several of us spontaneously rearranged things into a smaller circle towards the center.

There was random chatter and laughter while Anne and Colette finished making the tea. Then we were all sitting down in our ceremonial positions.

"Perhaps we should strike the gong again," Anne said.

Dr. McDonald did and we exchanged looks as the melodic tone slowly subsided.

"The first tribal council is now called to order," Anne said.

18

There were puzzled looks and smiles around the circle. Now that we were all gathered together, no one knew quite what to do next.

"I know," Kristy said. "Let's choose someone to chair the meeting."

She beamed, as if expecting to be coronated.

"I nominate Anne," I said. "She's the mellowest person among us."

Kristy gave her husband a playful elbow.

"I guess I'd better nominate my wife," Dr. McDonald said.

"Oh great," Kristy said with a smile that was struggling to stay in place. "What a stirring endorsement."

Dr. McDonald looked down, smiling.

"So, are there any other nominations?" Anne said.

"I nominate Hugo," Kyler said. "Yeah!"

Hugo sat there sphinx like, ears up, perplexed by the whole proceeding.

"Okay, if there are no more nominations, all in favor of Anne say aye."

It was unanimous, save for Dr. McDonald.

"You're it, Anne," I said.

"Okay. Where should we start?"

"You're the chairperson," Kristy said.

I raised my hand.

"One thing I should probably mention. I had to organize this place as a foundation in order to get it approved by the county board so we'll need to deal with that issue at some point soon."

"Wow," Kristy said. "That *is* a big deal. I remember studying them in college and it's like a corporation, only on steroids."

"That's what my attorney said."

"Well, *I* know how to deal with them," she said.

"So you can chair the foundation meetings."

"Is this going to be a foundation meeting too?" Anne said.

"Good question. I just thought I'd better throw that out there before we get too far."

"And you didn't tell us this because…?" Kristy said.

"I forgot." Kristy laughed. "Pesky little details."

"Ooookaaaay. Well we'll definitely need to have a pow wow about *that* one sometime soon."

"Maybe we should discuss what constitutes a tribal meeting and when to call one," Dr. McDonald said."

"How about having one every Friday," Donny said.

"That sounds cool to me," Anne said. "But what if there's an emergency?"

"I would agree with Donny's basic idea," I said. "Whether on Friday or whatever day of the week, we should hold a regular meeting. Then we can call for emergency sessions whenever it seems necessary."

"So how do we decide what constitutes an emergency?" David said.

"Yeah!" Kyler said. "We're going to have to have a meeting in order to discuss whether or not to have a meeting so we can decide if we need to have a meeting."

There were chuckles and a lot of spontaneous chatter about how to decide the issue.

"People, people!" I said. "Let's be practical. We'll know if there's something really, really urgent. Maybe we can have a quick head count around the village and hold an emergency meeting if there's a simple majority. All other issues can wait until the next regularly scheduled gathering."

"How about a yes/no push button in every cottage?" Kyler said.

"I'll give you a button," I said.

"Yeah!"

"Let's get serious, guys," Kristy said.

Her comment was met with mock faces of fear and the biting of nails.

"I think emergency meetings should require a super majority," Anne said. "Otherwise we'll have nothing but meetings."

"And you see why empires crumble," Dr. McDonald said with a chuckle.

"Yeah and we can thank you for starting this," Kyler said.

"I was just posing a reasonable and necessary question."

I sighed as more cacophony erupted.

"People, people," I interjected again. "I have to go with Anne on this one."

"Going with Anne on what?" David said.

"On requiring a super majority to hold a special meeting. If we already have a regularly meeting scheduled each week, it should be something really pressing for us to schedule another one. Come on. We'll know when something comes up that just can't wait. Right?"

There was a general consensus of ayes and grunts.

"Are you taking all this down?" I asked David.

"A condensed version, yeah. By the way, did we decide what constitutes having an official foundation meeting?"

"You have to hold one once a year," Kristy said. "Just like shareholder meetings for corporations and I think we should deal with that later."

"Okay," Anne said. "Let's vote on whether or not to keep the foundation meetings formally separated from our tribal meetings."

There were groans.

"Wow, far out," Kyler said. "We're never going to have a meeting because we can't stop discussing what it means to have a meeting."

"Discussing what it means to have a meeting is part of the meeting," Anne said.

"Then I vote to order pizza."

"And I vote for Kyler to be tied and gagged," I said.

"Yeah!"

Colette laughed.

"I'm serious," Anne said with a determined smile. "We should formally decide each issue that comes up. Otherwise we'll have to come back and deal with the same issues over and over again."

"All right," I said. "I vote that we keep this foundation business separate from our tribal meetings."

"Hey, what are we calling these meetings, anyway?" Kyler said.

"The High Council of the Grand Poohbahs of the Intergalactic Tribal Federation," I said.

"Yeah! I love it!"

"But it's a point well taken. I think, to avoid any further confusion, we should call this a tribal council. Then we'll know the difference right away between a *meeting* and what we're doing right now."

"I think that's a good idea," Anne said. "All those in favor of calling this a tribal council?"

Everyone raised a hand.

"All right, we finally decided something," Kyler said.

Everyone laughed.

"All right, how about this, Anne? Kristy and I will discuss the foundation this week and report back to the tribe at next week's meeting."

"That sounds good."

"Okay, so can we move forward now?"

"Sure. So, what's next on our agenda?" Anne said.

"Well, I have a couple more items," I said.

228

"He's hogging the whole council meeting," Kristy said.

I pretended to strangle her.

"So, first thing. I'm asking everyone here in the tribe to convert their car so it runs on methane."

"Wow, that's a big expense," Kristy said. "Who's going to pay for that?"

"The methane conversion is a few bucks, yeah, but then your fuel is free."

"From where?"

"From the do do factory down there."

"Oh."

"Well, that sounds really green and cool," Anne said. "But like Kristy said, it's sort of a big expense, isn't it?"

"*And* a major intrusion into our freedoms," Kristy added.

I pretended to strangle her again.

"Look, every major car today comes off the assembly line as a flex vehicle. They just install some software so it won't work as one."

"You're kidding me," David said with a laugh.

"No, and there's a guy in town who can tweak the software so the car will run on any kind of fuel."

"Cool."

"Well, I just don't like being told what to do," Kristy said.

"Kristy, please. Don't be a stubborn jackass."

She kicked me.

"Well, seriously folks. I don't want to be telling anybody what to do but living a sustainable lifestyle is at the core of everything we're trying to do out here."

I looked around the circle.

"We have to walk the walk."

"Yeah, sure," David said. "I can see your point."

"So, all agreed?"

I looked around the circle and everyone nodded, Kristy reluctantly.

"So what else did you want to say while you're hogging the whole meeting?" she said.

"How about calling a vote to have you shot?"

Kristy kicked me again to more laughter.

"Okay, look. I think we should formalize our two existing tenets. No one new can be admitted to the tribe and no one can be kicked off without a super majority vote by the entire tribe. And I think any of the really important stuff should require a super majority. It would be like changing the constitution or impeaching someone. But everyday stuff, we just agree by simple majority. Otherwise we'll never get anywhere."

"What would constitute *really important stuff*," Dr. McDonald said.

"You would have to ask me that."

"I'm only trying to anticipate possible problems."

"Duly noted. So how about this? We'll agree to make a list of things that require a super majority vote, and agree that the list can be amended as necessary."

"Would that be by a super majority vote too?" Dr. McDonald said.

I hung my head.

"Yeah!" Kyler said with a laugh.

"Okay, let's vote on that," Anne said. "All in favor of making a list of things that require a super majority vote that can only be amended by a super majority vote say aye."

Without further ado, everyone raised their hand.

"Good," Anne said. "So let's get back to admitting new members. There should be some sort of vetting process in place, right?"

"Yeah! Tax records. Rap sheet. Character references."

"I'm being serious," Anne said. "I mean, how would we know what we're voting on if we don't get to meet this person first?"

"So, what are you thinking? That each potential member should have to attend a council meeting first?" I said.

"Yeah," she said. "Don't you guys think so?"

"Sounds like that could be rather awkward," Dr. McDonald said. "For them and for us."

"Yeah," Kristy said. "Maybe the member sponsoring this person should just submit their name and some background information to the council first. Then if we feel like proceeding to the next level, we arrange to meet that person somewhere in town, like over dinner. Then we discuss it and let it sit for a week and vote up or down at the next council meeting."

"That sounds fair to me," I said.

"Yes! Another notch for me," Kristy said with a pump of her fist.

"So what are we deciding?" Dr. McDonald said.

Kristy elbowed him again.

"We're back to deciding if we should have a meeting to discuss whether or not we should have a meeting," Kyler said.

"Okay, I'm going to try and simplify this," Anne said. "I think we should just keep it informal for now. If anyone wants to recommend a new member, bring it up at a regular council meeting, then do as Kristy suggested. Meet this person, like over dinner, and see how it goes from there. And then we'll discuss things again at the next council meeting."

"We might want to create a special board to vet people and report back to the council with what they've learned," Dr. McDonald said. "The same sort of thing you would do if you were considering a new tenant."

Anne looked around the circle.

"I'm good with that too. Does anyone else have any input?"

"Just one thing," I said. "I hope we're not turning this thing into some kind of exclusive country club. A few tough breaks in life shouldn't be a disqualifier."

"So, what are you saying?" Dr. McDonald said.

"I guess that there ought to be some sort of appeal process."

"But if we're voting by super majority, that should be good enough," Kristy said.

"And what if it's someone in your family? Or someone you really love? Wouldn't you be bummed if they got turned down?"

"Not if that person was a known criminal."

Kristy smiled.

"That's a straw man," I said.

"What's a straw man?" Kyler said.

"You," I told him.

"Wow. I don't think boss man likes me anymore."

"I'm serious, Kristy. And all of you. This is what Madison meant when he spoke of the tyranny of the majority. In fact, I think this should apply both ways, with either being admitted to the tribe or being kicked off. There should be some kind of appeal process. Our bylaws shouldn't be anything less than what our constitution affords a person."

"I agree," Dr. McDonald said.

"Me too," David said. "With something this serious, I think we should have a week or two cooling off period so everyone has a chance to reconsider things and there's an opportunity to submit new evidence."

"Something that speaks of compassion," I said. "That's all I'm saying."

"Okay, are we all good with that?" Anne said.

Everyone nodded.

"So all in favor."

With hands and voices, everyone agreed.

"Yeah! We can finally move on," Kyler said.

"I think we forgot one thing," I said.

"Oh man."

"Well, no one asked if there were nominations for new members."

Eyes searched in the shadows. Finally, Donny raised his hand.

"I guess I do. My girlfriend, Yvonne."

"Okay," Kristy said. "Isn't this where we're supposed to submit something to the council in writing about this person?"

"I thought we agreed to keep things informal for now," I said.

"No, we agreed to submit something in writing first and then arrange a dinner or something."

"Oh boy. Here we go."

"Jesus, Kristy. Let's just hear what Donny has to tell us about his girlfriend."

"I'll second that motion," Dr. McDonald said.

Kristy gave him another playful elbow.

"I agree," Anne said. "I think we risk overcomplicating things. Why don't we just allow members to nominate someone and if we feel the need, we can request more information in writing? All in favor?"

Everyone agreed and looked at Donny.

"So, what can you tell us about her," Anne said.

"She's my girlfriend. She's smart. Actually, she's a real high end nurse over at the hospital. Emergency room. ICU. That sort of thing."

"How long have you known her?"

"A couple of years."

"Any prison record?" Kyler said.

"I don't know. I never asked."

"Aren't we being sort of ridiculous here?" David said.

"We all know Kyler's just joking," Anne said, "but it is a legitimate question."

"Look, if she's a nurse, she can't have much of a record," Dr. McDonald said. "Maybe something minor, but even that's doubtful. The guidelines for being licensed are pretty stringent."

"I can ask her," Donny said, "but I don't think so. She's pretty much by the book. I don't think she'd drive over the speed limit."

"Wow," Kristy said. "That is by the book."

"So I make a motion that we invite her out to dinner next week," I said. "She sounds like someone who would fit in."

"Who's paying for the dinner?" Kristy said.

"Yeah. Guess."

"Okay, I'm always up for a free dinner."

"So, can we move on again?" Kyler said.

"Sure," Anne said.

"Yes!" Kyler said.

"So here's my question," Anne said. "I guess it's actually two. How do we establish what is a fair amount of work for each person to do around here and how do we make sure that everyone is doing their fair share? Steven?"

"My basic concept was, everyone chips in equally and everyone's time is valued the same. Doctor, lawyer, Indian chief."

"And serfs," Kyler said.

"And serfs. It doesn't matter who you are or what your skill is. Then it's just a matter of keeping track of the hours."

"That sounds very fair on the surface of it," Anne said, "but I can see the potential for a lot of problems."

"Me too," Kyler said. "Like how is a guy ever going to get rich around here?"

"I'm serious," Anne said. "David and I can conceive of a situation where we quit our jobs and are working here full time on the website, and maybe on some other things. We'd *love* to do that but we can't survive without income of some kind. So any ideas about how and when we would start paying people for their time?"

"I suggest we defer that question for the time being. I've guaranteed everyone a roof over their heads, food on the table, clothes on their back. You've got free basic medical care here with Dr. McDonald. If any other problems come up, we can discuss them. In the meantime, I say we get this website up and running and try to generate some income. Then we can discuss how to distribute the funds fairly."

"So we are allowing that there would be incomes," Anne said.

"I've always assumed as much," I said.

Colette looked down and petted Hugo.

"So, I'm still a bit confused," Anne said. "There are…"

"No, I get it," I said, interrupting her. "Some people will have jobs outside the tribe. Some people will work solely for the tribe. The ones who work solely for the tribe will definitely get a salary but everyone still has to contribute some of their free time to maintaining things around here, whether it's in the garden or maintenance or health care services or whatever."

I looked around the circle.

"Does that sound reasonable to everyone?"

"I can see that a lot of work still needs to be done on this subject," Anne said. "But I'm okay with the general idea for now."

Everyone else seemed to agree.

"So, what else is there to discuss?" Anne said.

"I think we should vote on not having any more meetings," Kyler said.

"You idiot," I said and leaned back to stare at the ceiling.

"It does seem like this should be more fun," Kristy said.

"I'm telling you, pizza," Kyler said.

"You're making me hungry," Kristy said.

"I think we should discuss the website," David said.

"Good idea," I said. "So where do we start?"

"Well, we looked into the question of establishing our credentials," Anne said, "and we're guessing you'd need to deposit something in the order of ten million in the bank to be taken seriously. Then we'd need print and TV advertising, buys on all the major internet sites, book radio and TV talk shows, whatever it takes so that there's a major, major buzz on day one of our launch."

"And we have to pick the first issue to vote on," I said.

"And pick two major figures to write their opinion pieces," David said.

Anne kept staring at me.

"What?" I said.

"Well, we went right by the question of money."

"I'll do the ten mil," Kyler said.

"I'm serious," Anne said.

"Don't worry, Anne. I'll take care of the dough."

"Okay. I think Kristy and I can do all the footwork in terms of advertising and marketing."

"Well, not without some serious support," Kristy said. "We'll need people running errands and making phone calls and doing whoever. So who's in?"

Everyone stared.

"Oh great."

There was laughter and everyone agreed to jump onboard.

"Except for me," Kyler said. "I'm with the grounds crew."

"And what about you, Camellia?" Anne said. "Are you planning just to stay working in the garden?"

She nodded.

"I'll have to beg out too," Dr. McDonald said. "I'll be available for sick call but otherwise I need to focus on opening my new practice."

"Okay," Anne said. "Why don't the rest of us meet in the office on Monday morning and get to work. Whatever time you have, come lend a hand. Kristy and I will be working up a checklist of things to do in the meantime."

"By the way, what's my official title going to be?" Kristy said.

"How about the CEO of micromanaging," Dr. McDonald said with a smile.

"I know who's not getting any tonight," Kyler said.

"That's right. He's sleeping in the car."

"It's probably a valid point, though," Anne said. "We may want to consider having titles and specific duties."

"Sure, in the future," I said, "but can we just wing it for now? Get this website off the ground and see where we stand once the dust settles?"

Everyone agreed.

"Oh shit," I said.

"What?" Anne said.

"It's just occurred to me that I need to run a DBA in the local paper before I can open a bank account."

"Maybe the paper's open tomorrow?"

"Yeah. I'll check in the morning."

"You know," Anne said. "It's occurred to me that maybe this isn't the appropriate forum for our business meetings either."

"Yeah. I think you have a point. If we make this a meeting for everything that goes on with the tribe, we'll be here 24/7."

"Yeah, let's just keep minutes of any other meetings we have and offer up a written summary at each council meeting," David said.

"That means committees," Kristy said.

"Yeah, and I can see who's loving that idea."

"That's right."

"Okay," Anne said. "So we'll create committees whenever various issues come up and have those committees offer up a summary for consideration by the whole tribe whenever the council meets, agreed?"

Everyone did.

"So, is there anything else for now?" Anne said.

"Pizza," Kyler said.

"It's actually starting to sound pretty good," I said.

"Do they actually deliver out here?" Dr. McDonald said.

"I'm sure they will, for enough money."

"So, are we being serious here?" Kristy said.

"I'm serious," I said. "Shall we call this a wrap and have them deliver it to my place?"

"Okay. Things have degenerated into a pizza party," Anne said.

"Don't call me a degenerate for loving pizza," Kyler said.

"Well, anything else before we close?" Anne said. "You, Colette? You've hardly spoken a word."

"I'm the arts director. You can ask me about that."

"Oh, is there an arts center?"

I explained.

"The minute I close on the other properties, we're going to have a pot and pan banging party alongside Fatty Arbuckle's fence."

"Is he really named Fatty?" Kristy said.

"No, his name is Chaplin but he looks more like Arbuckle. Picture one of those Babbitt type goofs from a '30s movie, wearing jungle fatigues and a pith helmet."

"How funny."

"Yeah, I wish it was."

"So, are we done for the night then?" Anne said. "All in favor say aye."

It was unanimous.

"Okay, somebody order the pizza," Kyler said.

"Wait," I said. "Why don't you invite your gal Yvonne over to the pizza party, Donny?"

"Sure, if everyone's cool with that."

I made eyes at Kristy.

"Hey, I'm not the cop around here."

"Oh. Okay. Wow. I was confused."

She elbowed me and we laughed. People started to get up but Anne held out a hand.

"Dr. McDonald? The gong?"

He struck it and everyone sat in silence as the harmonic vibrations slowly receded into the quiet of the forest.

"The meeting is now officially closed," Anne said.

With that an animated discussion broke out over what kind of pizzas to order. I punched the list into my phone; one large combo, a chicken with basil and feta cheese, a sausage with mushrooms and black olives and a vegetarian number for Camellia.

David and Anne had busied themselves with turning off the stove and lights and soon everyone was outside as they buttoned up the yurt.

"Let's meet at my place in half an hour," I said.

We started down the path toward the cottages and went our separate ways with voices echoing off through the woods.

The Tribe

19

The last ones down the steps from the yurt, Colette and I came to the road behind the cottages with everyone else having already disappeared off into the woods. We paused with a cold, damp wind stirring high up in the trees. The forest smelled strongly of evergreen.

"It's going to rain again," I said.

"Not exactly pizza weather," Colette said.

"Really. I didn't know there was such a thing."

"Sure. Hot summer nights. Days at the shore."

"I suppose. So, did you need to stop by your place first?"

"No. I'm fine."

We turned left and walked along with the trees stirring against the stars. Hugo had gone out ahead of us on his leash.

"You *were* particularly quiet tonight," I said.

"I don't have much to add when it comes to tech stuff. Or politics."

"You see? That's one more benefit of a tribe. Someone else is always there to fill in these other roles."

"To which I say, thank god."

I laughed and pulled Colette closer.

We came to the meadow and the saw storm clouds barging in from the coast. The night had turned raw. The trees were suddenly swaying and howling raucously above us.

A few minutes later, we arrived to my treehouse. Upstairs in the kitchen, I busied myself with placing several extra bottles of beer in the freezer. Colette got the leaves out of a closet and we added them to table. We had barely set out the plates and silverware when we heard the sound of voices out front. It was Anne and David coming up the stairs. I went to greet them.

"I'll never get over how enchanting this is," Anne said on the landing.

"Come in, come in."

"And why can't be build one of our own?"

"A beer?" I said, closing the door.

"Yeah. See how you are?"

"I'll have a beer," David said.

"I'll have red wine, if there's some," Anne said.

"Of course. Colette, do you mind helping Anne?"

I grabbed two beers and handed one to David.

"To the peace and health of our tribe," I said.

Our bottles clinked and we drank.

"What did you think of the meeting?" David asked with a smile.

"It was not at all how I had imagined it."

"I know," Anne said from across the room. "I was thinking of Buddhist monks or the plains Indians having pow wows in their tepees, not a corporate board meeting."

I heard the sounds of more voices and footsteps outside, followed by a knock at the door. I opened it and found everyone but Donny gathered out on the landing. Kristy was bundled up in a parka with rosy cheeks.

"We're having a sudden arctic blast," she said with a big smile.

"Come in, come in," I said. "Where's Donny and his gal?"

"He drove down to meet her at the highway so she wouldn't get lost."

"Hey Kyler, Camellia. Come in," I said and closed the door.

A great commotion ensued as refreshments were handed out.

"I bought some Perrier for you, Kyler. And Camellia. Is that okay?"

"Oh yeah, great," Kyler said with mock wretchedness.

"I can add a splash of cranberry and a twist of lemon," I said.

"Yeah. That's even better. That's the way I used to drink my vodka."

I threw my hands up and Kyler laughed.

"It's okay, dude. I figured out. I guess I can do everything in life but drink."

I patted him on the shoulder and made his drink, and one for Camellia.

"So I guess everyone agrees that the meeting sucked," Kristy said from across the kitchen.

"Let's just say it wasn't what I had expected. Come. Let's go sit in the living room and discuss things."

I helped corral everyone in that direction.

"Delegating everything minor to subcommittees will definitely help," Anne said as she sat down.

"Perhaps we should set an agenda with the issues we plan to discuss," Dr. McDonald said.

"I feel another council meeting breaking out," Kyler said.

"Hell, it was only the first time," I said. "Perhaps we're overreacting."

"I still think it sucked," Kyler said.

"It totally sucked," David said. "Like Anne said, I was expecting monks chanting or something. Instead we sounded like hedge fund managers."

"I didn't," Colette said.

"You didn't say anything," Kristy said.

"And you see why."

"Okay," I said. "So let me pose a question. Of all the things we had discussed, which of them would you eliminate?"

"Everything," Kyler said.

"I'd really love to know what you think Colette," Anne said. "You *have* been so quiet throughout all of this."

"I just recently escaped a job in the corporate world. You do not want to know how fucked up I thought that meeting was."

Anne looked at me with a bemused smile.

"No, I never really expected her to say 'fuck' either but she claims it's one of her favorite words."

"Sometimes *the* favorite word," Colette said.

"Maybe we should run it like an AA meeting," Kyler said. "We have no organization at all. Everybody just takes their turn sharing and at the end we say the Lord's Prayer."

"You must have business meetings of some sort from time to time," Dr. McDonald said.

"Yeah, I guess so."

"So how do they go?"

"Totally fucked up."

Everyone laughed.

"I still think it's not so much what we discussed but how we went about it," Anne said.

"I think what we've already proposed will solve things," Dr. McDonald said. "Limit the agenda and have subcommittees."

"This is definitely starting to sound like another meeting," Kristy said.

"Yeah, probably it's best if we drop it for now," Anne said.

"Maybe if we smoked a joint first," I said.

"Yeah!" Kyler said.

"I thought recovering alcoholics couldn't smoke weed either," Dr. McDonald said.

"We can't, but I still think it's a great idea. Let's just smoke a big doobie and talk about dreams and shit."

"That does bring an idea to mind," I said. "We could play meditative music and burn incense and such."

"Strike the gong every time things start to drift off center," David said.

"Yeah, I love that sound," Kyler said.

Hearing more footsteps on the stairs outside, I went to open the door. It was Donny with his girlfriend Yvonne. The pizza man was getting out of his car down below. It had started to rain.

"I saw him going by out on the highway and flagged him down," Donny said.

"Good job." I held out my hand to the kittenish Yvonne. "Welcome. I'm Steven."

"Yvonne."

"I know. Please come in, both of you."

They did. Yvonne was lean as a gazelle and tall in high heels. She had a ready smile, an intelligent forehead and beautiful hazel eyes.

"I suppose you've already been told countless times how magical this place is?" she said.

"Many times, yes."

"Well, it definitely is," she said. "I'm envious."

"Please don't be. And Donny, introduce Yvonne to everyone else. I'll take care of the pizza guy."

He was just then coming up the stairs. I had him place everything on the credenza inside the door and took the bill. The total with antipasto was a bit under $200. I handed him three, one hundred dollar bills.

"Are we good?"

"Oh yeah, totally."

"Cool. Thanks again for coming out."

He started down the stairs.

"Really cool place, by the way," he said with a look back. "Wish I lived here."

"What's your name?"

"Brent."

"So, what do you do besides deliver pizzas?"

"I'm taking some classes on how to repair computers and stuff. I love fixing things."

"We might need you."

"Out here?"

"Yeah. Give me your number."

I quickly put it into my phone.

"I'll call you. And thanks again for coming out. Drive safely."

I sniffed the damp wind before closing the door.

Inside, Kyler and Dr. McDonald had already ferried the pizza boxes and antipasto out to the kitchen. I joined them. The ladies were buzzing back and forth, spreading things on the dining table.

"It's started to rain," I said and jumped in with the preparations.

"What a perfect night for pizza," Kristy said.

I looked at Colette with a smile.

"Wow. Antipasto," Anne said, opening the container. "Great idea."

"Man cannot live on pizza alone."

"I can," Kyler said.

"And you see the results."

"Yeah!"

"Listen kids," I said. "What do you say we set some pizza out and leave the rest to warm in the oven?"

"Good idea," Anne said.

I dug out some large serving dishes for her.

"I know you," Yvonne said suddenly to Dr. McDonald with a big smile. She chuckled and touched Kristy on the arm. "I mean I knew I had seen your husband somewhere before and just remembered. It was at the hospital the other day. Right?"

"Well, I was there for an orientation, yes."

"See, I knew I had seen that face somewhere."

Off they went on a professional discussion as we worked.

"She fits right in, doesn't she?" Anne whispered going by me.

I nodded. She did, without even trying. It was clear from her actions and smile that she had already developed a pleasant rapport with both Anne and Kristy.

"Okay, everything's ready!" Kristy announced from the table.

Final drinks were dispersed and the conversation drifted towards the dining room.

"Wow, what a wonderful mix of people you have out here," Yvonne said to everyone in general as we sat down.

"Here, here," Dr. McDonald said and held up his beer bottle. "I would like to toast to the wonderful challenge before us."

"There's a challenge?" Kyler said.

I bopped him.

"And to our success," Dr. McDonald added amidst the laughter.

"Here, here."

We toasted and started passing around the pizza platters.

"Hmm, pineapple and anchovies," I said.

"What?" Kristy said with a desperate look at all the platters. "I hate pineapple and anchovies."

"Oh, I thought you said you loved them so I had it added to everything."

"You didn't," she said with more nervous looks at the serving plates.

Kyler took a big bite out of a combo slice.

"Finally! Pizza!"

"Here everyone, try the antipasto," Anne said. "It's really good."

Yvonne passed me the plate.

"You kids be sure to eat your greens," Kristy said like someone's mother.

While dishing out some antipasto, I caught the threads of a discussion about presidential politics and drilling for oil in the Arctic across the table.

"I'll bet the farm he approves it," Dr. McDonald said to David.

"But who else are you going to vote for?" David said. "A Republican?"

246

"I'm just saying, it doesn't seem to matter the party, they always end up in bed with big oil and big business.

"So you think they're all sold out."

"I'm just saying, however well-intentioned, the fat cats always end up calling the shots."

"I don't know," Anne said. "I can think of a number of politicians who aren't sold out."

"Until they run for president."

"Never discuss religion or politics over dinner," Kristy said with a triumphant bite into her pizza.

Anne had continued staring at Dr. McDonald.

"But that's like saying your vote doesn't matter. I mean, we have to have hope."

"You must be kidding," Yvonne said with an ironic chuckle.

"No, I'm not," Anne said. "And why would you say that?"

"Because I think having hope is delusional at this point. We need to change everything and it's like the battle is already lost."

Yvonne smiled at everyone around the table.

"No?

"You can't think like that," Anne said. "Bit by bit, we can make this a better world."

"It's not that I disagree with your sentiment, and if we were having this discussion forty years ago, I would say, yes, absolutely. We're going to change the world for the better. But look what's happened since then."

"I know, sure. Everyone can see what's happened," Anne said. "But do you really think it doesn't matter who we elect? That there's no chance of making this a better world?"

"Look, don't get me wrong. I do my part. I donate to the Sierra Club and the World Wildlife Fund and half a dozen other organizations but I don't see where it's doing much good. The world just keeps going down the wrong path."

Yvonne looked around the table and chuckled self-consciously.

"God, I can't believe you think like that," Anne said.

"But it doesn't matter how I think, Anne. There were two paths we could have gone down forty years ago and unfortunately we've been dragged down the one where big oil and big business won out. Remember the EV1 electric car that GM made?"

"Yeah. They were really cool."

"Yeah, but the minute the government let them off the hook, GM scrapped the program. I know. I had one and fought them all the way when they came to recall it. Even tried to hide it in my sister's garage but they finally came with a court order."

Yvonne laughed her skeptical laugh.

"I was actually going to *jail* if I didn't relent!"

"So?" Anne said. "Things have changed. Now we have all kinds of electric cars and hybrids. You can even get fuel cell vehicles now."

"I know. But even if every American bought an electric vehicle right now, it's still such a small percentage of the total world market. Meanwhile, we've rocketed past 400 ppm carbon dioxide in the atmosphere, our oceans are turning acidic, we're choking in plastics and the Greenland and Antarctic ice sheets are melting away so you can figure that every coastal city will be underwater in twenty years. I know that people deep down in their hearts want to change things but they keep electing representatives who are beholden to the special interests, like Dr. McDonald said. I've tried to have hope, Anne. I really have but I can't see a scenario where we're not heading over the cliff."

"God. I can't believe how pessimistic you are."

"But I don't see it as being pessimistic," Yvonne pleaded sincerely. "I see it as being realistic. I mean, isn't it true that a few people have all the money now and that the government is all about doing whatever those people want them to do?"

Yvonne looked around the table. Colette spoke up.

248

"I didn't want to be the one to say it out loud, but I'd have to agree with Yvonne. If things keep going the way they are right now, we're fucked."

"I don't see where it does any good to think that way," David said.

"But how else can you think?" Yvonne said. "Do we just stick our heads in the sand and pretend we don't see what's happening?"

"No, but you still have to try and make things better," Anne said.

"Believe me, Anne, I'm trying but it just seems like the die has been cast. Mordor won the war." She chuckled. "You can do little things around the edges but you're just rearranging the deck chairs on the Titanic at this point. I just can't see where this is going to have a happy ending."

"God, how depressing. If I really thought that way, I'd just shoot myself."

"It's not what we think," Yvonne pleaded again to Anne. "It's what's already happening. We have to open our eyes and face things as they are."

Yvonne smiled at everyone around the table. There was silence in return.

"Never discuss politics and religion over dinner," Kristy said again with another bite of her pizza.

"Yeah, I'm like totally depressed now," Kyler said. "Let's talk about something else."

"What else is there to discuss if the world's coming to an end," Anne said.

"There's a Shakespeare play running in town," I said. "Colette and I already have tickets. Would anyone else like to come along?"

"Which play is it?" Dr. McDonald said.

"Henry the Fourth, Part One."

"Is that good?" Kristy said.

"It's a fun play," Colette said. "Ribald."

"Saucy," I added.

"Hey I'd like that," Kristy said. "I've never seen a Shakespeare play."

"Anyone else?" I said. "Dr. McDonald, I presume."

"Sure. Consider me in."

"David? Anne?"

"Sure," David said.

I looked at Anne, who was still brooding over her discussion with Yvonne.

"Think I'll try a slice of that chicken and feta cheese number," I said.

Kristy handed me the plate and I grabbed a slice.

"Some more antipasto too?" she said.

"Sure. Gotta eat your greens."

I smiled at Yvonne and bit in.

"Hmm. Great sauce."

"Yeah, great pizza," Donny said.

"Delicious. I heard this place was good but had never tried them before."

"So I was thinking," Donny said. "You told me were interested in doing whatever we can to increase our green energy and I stumbled across this site the other day. A mom and pop operation that invented a solar road."

"Get out of here."

"No, I'm serious. They're still testing it out but it sounds like we could totally use it for our pathways and stuff. Wouldn't that be cool?"

"Yeah. Are they looking for investors?"

"I'm sure they are."

"Yeah. Let's look into it. Do some installations out here and see how it works."

"I think we should follow through with Anne's idea," David said.

"What's that?"

"Doing a kind of Poor Richard's Almanac website and blog about our tribe and how we're trying to live in a sustainable way."

250

"That sounds great, Anne."

"Yeah, well, with the end of the world at hand and all..."

Yvonne set her piece of pizza down suddenly and stood up.

"I'm really sorry. I should probably be going."

"No, no, Yvonne, there's no need for that," I said.

"No, it's really for the best. I can see I've ruined everyone's evening."

She went and grabbed her purse. Donny went after her.

"Great pizza," Yvonne said at the door. "It was nice meeting all of you."

I got up but she was already out the door. Donny shrugged back at everyone and followed her down the stairs. I returned to silent stares at the table.

"Well, that was fun," Kristy said with a sarcastic smile.

"I never thought I would say this about a person, but I'm so glad she left." Anne looked from face to face. "Well, wasn't she just totally negative?"

"I couldn't really *disagree* with her take on things," I said.

"So? We all know how bad things are in this world. What good does it do to simply give up?"

"Yeah. I understand your take too."

"I'm sorry," Anne said. "I just found myself feeling utterly depressed, like Kyler said."

"Yeah! Our first chance to boot someone off the island!"

"What? Simply for speaking her mind?" I said.

"Well, a person has to fit in, don't they?" Anne said. "God, I just can't picture listening to that negativity all day long."

"What do you think, Kristy?"

"About whether or not she gets to stay?"

"Yeah."

"I don't really care what she thinks, as long as she contributes around here."

"And you, Dr. McDonald?"

"We could use a good nurse," he said.

"And you, Kyler?"

"To the sharks. Yeah!"

"Seriously, you dumb shit."

"Hey, I don't care. I guess I wouldn't want to be the one to reject her."

"And you, Colette?"

"If you knew my thoughts, you'd probably reject me too. The only difference between Yvonne and me is, I know enough to keep my mouth shut."

"And what about you, Camellia?"

"Poor Donny," she said.

She dabbed her delicate little mouth and looked from face to face. The rest of us exchanged looks all around.

"Yeah, poor Donny," I said and bit into the crusty remains of my last slice.

"So, I guess that's it," Anne said. "I'm the only one who votes no."

"Looks like it."

"Wow. I don't even know what to say. I feel totally disconnected from everyone now."

"Don't, Anne. If we're going to give up every time we don't get our own way out here, we are doomed"

"I'm sorry but I do. This place was all about making it a better world and how can we make it a better world if we think like that?"

"Maybe that's part of the challenge. To change the way people like Yvonne think. Otherwise we're just preaching to the choir."

Anne dropped her last piece of pizza and sighed.

"Anne," I said. "And all of you. If any of you thought this was going to be easy, you're kidding yourselves. The world got the way it is because peace is hard. War is easy. A bit of friction and the next thing you know, people are at each other's throats. Just like this."

"So, what do you suggest?" Anne said.

"Accept dissent and forge ahead with what we're doing. Hell, she was civilized. Expressing your opinion shouldn't be grounds for banishment."

252

"But to listen to that negativity every day?"

"Let's just do good things, like we've been talking about. She'll be won over."

"I don't know."

"None of us do. How was that sausage and mushroom and black olive number," I said, reaching for another slice.

The Tribe

20

With all the goodbyes having been said and everyone out the door, Colette and I drifted back out to the kitchen. Seeing the pizza boxes open, I was unable to resist another bite of the chicken and feta. Hugo watched me with ears perked up. I gave him a morsel and took another bite.

"Hmm, so good but I must stop. Please get this stuff out of my sight."

Colette finished pouring herself a half glass of wine and obliged me by consolidating all the leftover pizza into one box and shoving it into the frig.

She came over, pressed her body against mine and looked up.

"I found myself very much admiring you this evening."

"What? It's taken you this long?"

"I thought very highly of you from the start but this was different."

"How so?"

"Well, it would have been all too easy to agree with Anne. She's such a sweet soul and probably right at the heart of it. I'm a giddy '60s idealist compared to Yvonne. You wonder what made her so cynical."

"The EV1, apparently."

"That would do it, I suppose."

"So, your point?"

"Oh, it wasn't until you said something that I realized we were suppressing dissent."

"It's easy to jump on that bandwagon."

"Almost everyone did, except you."

"Don't get me wrong. I was as inclined as the next person to grab Yvonne by the throat."

"Do you think she'll even want to join us?"

"I don't know. Maybe she'll save Anne the trouble."

"She might."

I kissed Colette.

"Let's get back to you admiring me."

Colette laughed and pushed away.

"It's fading fast."

She drank from her wine and finished placing some glasses and utensils into the dishwasher. She drank again and returned to press her body against mine.

"Let's fuck," she said.

"What a wonderful word."

"That describes a wonderful thing we do."

"Yes."

She stared up.

"So?"

"Yes, let's go fuck."

We left Hugo with his obligatory bone and went off to play with our own bones and flesh. While we did, it began to rain in earnest outside.

In the morning, I awakened to blue skies. I thought of Colette and wanted to do it again. Over the first cup of coffee, I called her.

"Are you still vibrating?" I asked.

"I am."

"I would love to know how that feels."

"Imagine ejaculating from the fifth chakra."

"Okay. Wow. I'll never be able to think of the chakras in the same way again."

"Did you have plans for today?"

"I hadn't until just a moment ago. What do you say we go up and play in the garden?"

"I think that's a splendid idea. It had crossed my mind too. A very organic way to heal all the energy."

"Perhaps you can pass the word."

"I will. I think maybe David and Anne are already up there. I saw them headed that way and they seemed to be dressed for the occasion."

"Did you want to drive up with me?"

"Sure."

"Okay. I'll jump into some work jeans and head over in a few minutes."

I took the golf cart and headed that way. Whizzing across the meadow, I spotted Kyler in his golf cart and honked. He saw me and turned back from the direction of the garden.

"Hey boss man."

"How are you doing?"

"Good. What's going on?"

"I'm on my way over to grab Colette. We're heading up to work in the garden. I was thinking to grab everyone else."

"You're too late, boss man. Everyone's up there already."

"Dr. McDonald? And Kristy?"

"Yep."

"And Donny?"

"I haven't seen Donny today."

"I suppose he went back into town with Yvonne last night."

"Yeah, his car's not here."

"Do you happen to have his number?"

"Yeah. You want to call him?"

"Yeah. Dial the number for me."

A moment later he was handing me the phone.

"It's ringing."

"Hey, Donny," I said when he answered.

"Hey, Steven."

I explained about the vote, without telling him who voted which way.

"Wow. I never would have expected that."

"She's a nice lady. I don't know that any of us really agree with her point of view but dissent is not a crime. I guess it really comes down to whether or not she wants to live out here. We hope so, and you too."

"Wow, thanks Steven. I've been feeling like an outcast ever since we left last night."

"Hey, my apologies. I should have called you right away. I wasn't thinking."

"It's cool. So I'll talk to her and see what she says."

"Good. For the record, everyone is headed out to work in the garden today. Why don't you come out and join us?"

"Sure. It's a lovely day. I'll drive out as soon as I can."

"Bring Yvonne."

"I'll see but it might be a bit too soon."

"No problem. We'll hope to see you in a bit."

I handed Kyler back his phone.

"Hey, is there anything to drink out there?"

"I don't think so, boss man."

"All right, listen. There's a cooler in the storage area out in back of my place. Why don't you head over there and grab everything we need. You'll find a couple of bags of ice in the freezer and lots of sodas and bottled water in the frig."

"All right, boss man. I'll see if there's any money or shit lying around I can steal."

"You're off the island, sucker."

"Yeah!"

Kyler laughed and gave me a high five.

"I'll see you up at the garden in a few."

I found Colette wearing jeans, boots and looking quite fetching in a straw hat. My heart flinched a bit at the sight of her. Her love was a gift. Why couldn't I let go to it? Instead I remained crucified on the cross of my screwed up emotions.

"Good morning, beautiful," I said and kissed her tenderly.

"Good morning to you."

"So, are we ready to go?"

"Sure. I was just wondering. Should we take along some refreshments?"

"I already sent Kyler off on the detail."

"Then we're off."

Coming out of the woods, we saw all the bodies from a distance, some standing, some bent over, all of them busy. The garden had a whimsical feel, the way the rows wound up and down over the contours of the land.

Everyone looked up at the sound of our golf cart crunching in the gravel.

"Hey! It's about time you guys showed up!" Kristy said.

"We're with corporate. We just came by to check on your progress."

That was greeted with boos and jeers.

"Did you happen to think of refreshments?" David said.

"I sent Kyler on a beer run."

There was laughter.

"No, seriously. He's coming up with some refreshments."

"Yay!" Kristy said.

I said hello to Dr. McDonald, shook David's hand and gave Anne a hug.

"How are you?"

"I'm good. This is really therapeutic."

"Isn't it? It's amazing that we all got up with the same idea."

"It's very bonding," she said.

"Okay, enough with the bonding," Kristy said. "Let's get to work!"

I laughed at her.

"So, what are we doing?"

"Plantin' crops," she said with a crossways pump of her fists.

"Okay, you tell us where to start plantin'."

Kristy walked along, showing us where all the latest seed packets had been placed.

"Okay, I guess I'll jump right in here with the broccoli."

258

"And I'll take the spinach," Colette said.

"I fights to the finish 'cuz I eats my spinach…"

Kristy laughed and went back to what she was doing. As I bent down to start planting, the sun went behind the clouds. A moment later, the sun was back out brightly, making my shadow in the dirt.

I looked over and met Dr. McDonald's smile.

"Ancient stuff, isn't it?" I said.

He chuckled.

"Mesopotamia."

"Are you kidding. Those were the days. Nebuchadnezzar. Harems and hanging gardens."

"Conquering kingdoms, destroying temples and dragging home slaves."

"And I've heard that Nebuchadnezzar played a hell of a shortstop."

"You guys are nuts," Colette said.

"What we need are some crop planting songs?" Kristy said.

I did my best impression of Paul Robeson.

"Winter time, and the living is breezy."

"Wow, you missed your calling," Colette said.

"Ah, and there you have uttered the bitterest words of all."

"Do you know what yours is?" Dr. McDonald asked me.

"Not sure. Planting broccoli, I guess."

We laughed.

Overcome with emotion, I stood up to face everyone.

"You know what? I love all of you."

"Awwwww," Kristy said.

"Yeah, how sweet," Anne said.

She came over and gave me a hug.

"No, seriously. I suddenly felt this great goodness in what we're doing. Like, wow, working together here is part of some great destiny. You know?"

"Yeah, our tribe," Anne said. "In the bigger tribe of the world."

"Yeah."

259

I heard the crunch of tires on gravel and looked up to see Kyler pulling to a stop.

"Yay, refreshments," Kristy said. "Let's toast to our new beginning."

Kyler came over with the ice chest.

"What's everyone standing around for? Come on, start shakin' the bush!"

"We're having a moment," Anne said.

"You mean, like tripping."

"Kind of."

"Yeah! That's the kind of tribal shit I want to see."

I gave Kyler a hug.

"I love you, you crazy son of a bitch."

"I love you, too, man."

Kyler dug out some drinks and started passing them around.

"Here's to the real frickin' billionaire hero. He could have disappeared into the Caribbean somewhere but instead he's screwing around here with us."

I reluctantly clinked bottles with everyone and drank.

Kristy was staring at me with a big smile.

"Are you really a billionaire?" she said.

I hung my head.

"Okay, wow. I guess you are."

"Kristy, please. I'm a member of this tribe. That's all I am right now and none of the other crap really matters."

"Well not that it changes anything about the tribe but having a billion dollars would sure matter to me! You could have started a rocket company or something like that."

"Yeah, and instead I set up this stupid little outfit."

"That's not what I meant."

"Yeah, sure."

She made a face.

"No, I dig what you're saying and it's all crossed my mind too. I could have gone to Mars and done all this flashy stuff with my money. Instead, I've planted my little lily of the valley."

Dr. McDonald slapped me on the shoulder and offered his sunny smile.

"I get it," he said. "You went for substance over excitement and I think you've done the right thing. The world will remember what we've done here, long after the next rocket launch is forgotten."

I looked over at him.

"I hope so. I really do hope so."

We had been working in silence for a spell when another car approached. It was Donny and Yvonne. She had come. I stole glances that way while continuing to work. She came cautiously but confidently and graciously went around saying hello to everyone. Anne was last and the two women hugged.

"I feel like I should apologize," Yvonne said, "but I honestly don't know what to apologize for."

"It's all right," Anne said.

"No, I want all of you to understand that I've had a heavy heart lately and I can see where my perception of life has been filtered through that prism. You have every right to think I'm just this totally negative person..."

"Yvonne," I said, interrupting her. "Let's just say it made for an interesting conversation. No one is obligated to think in a particular way around here."

"No, but I want everyone to know. I get why you would feel totally frustrated with me and I do appreciate your positive approach to life. I really do. I just can't ignore what's being done to the planet anymore. And to *us*. I just feel like in a hundred years, civilization will be back in the dark ages."

"Did you want to plant seeds with us?" Anne said.

Yvonne chuckled in her warm but ironic way.

"Sure."

"And from a little seed, something bigger can grow."

"You're right. It can."

"That's all I was trying to say. Let's plant a seed and watch it grow."

"Okay. Let's plant a seed."

A spontaneous cheer broke out and everyone came around to hug the now self-conscious Yvonne.

I went back to work, watching every little hole my fingers made in the earth and the little seeds going in and the loose earth covering them over and was aware of the simple holiness of this act, the Isness of it, the supplication, this act of faith between man and God and Nature, that there in its sacred tomb, the seed would unfold and life would begin anew. I heard the conversations going on around me, Dr. McDonald talking with Yvonne about their profession, David talking to Kristy about the website and Kyler talking with Donny about stupid men's stuff. I heard the chatter of human beings, the miracle of communication and how it somehow wedded eternity to humanity's fleeting hopes and dreams.

Like Camellia, and me, Colette had been mostly quiet all morning but came over to me as noon approached.

"I'm famished," she said.

"Yeah, pizza!" Kyler said, having heard her comment.

"There's still some in the frig," I said. "Probably enough for a slice or two apiece."

"Yeah!"

I looked around and the general consensus was, sure, let's have a bite to eat, so Kyler zipped off in his golf cart. When he returned, each of us took a slice of the leftover pizza and stood there eating with earth on our hands. When we broke off an hour later, nearly half the garden had been planted.

"Want to drop by and see a preliminary mockup of the website?" David asked me as we were gathering in our cars and golf carts.

"Sure."

"Hey, I want to see it too," Kristy said.

"Sure," I said. "If anyone else wants to have a look, feel free to join us."

"I'll join you," Anne said.

"Me and Camellia are going into town to stock up on supplies," Kyler said.

"I have some business in town too," Dr. McDonald said.

"What about you and Yvonne, Donny?"

"I think she'd like a tour of the place first, but yeah, we can meet you over there in a bit."

"Okay, well let's everybody take showers and meet up in the war room," Kristy said.

"What? You don't like the way I smell?" I said.

Kristy made a panicked face.

"Great out here. Not so great in a closed room."

I was already climbing into the golf cart with Colette.

"All right, then. We'll see the rest of you there."

When we came to the road that ran behind the cottages, I paused. The sun was high overhead. The world was bright and clear.

"Maybe we should shower together," I said with a big smile. "Save on water."

Colette chuckled.

"You're devious."

"All right. We'll save it for later."

I drove around back, dropped her off with a kiss and headed back to my place. Half an hour later, I was walking in through the open door of the tech center. Kristy was already there with Anne and David. Everyone had wet hair.

"Here, have a look," David said and pulled up the home page.

"Oh, I like the two characters."

They were Colonial Era looking men, with buckled shoes and rolled up scrolls in their hands, ready for fisticuffs. David took me on a quick tour of the site.

"There'll be a dated log of old articles but the main thing will be the vote tab here on the front page. I was thinking to keep a running tally of the vote but then thought maybe that's not the best idea. Keep it a mystery? What do you think?"

"Yeah. I've kind of settled on keeping it a mystery too."

Colette walked in just then and we asked her.

"Yeah, I say keep it a mystery."

"Is there some way to certify the vote?" I said. "We'd lose all credibility if people thought it was rigged."

"I've set it up with Google analytics. You can't get any more reliable than that."

"And what about that issue of people voting multiple times?"

"Kind of the same thing. I've set it up so you have to give your email address and a phone number and then we run everything through Google analytics. We can't stop fraud 100% but I have this disclaimer here when they sign up. See? If anyone is found to be voting more than once on the same issue, they will be disqualified from further participation."

"Yeah, it's still cause for worry though."

David laughed.

"I've sort of come around to your way of thinking. Like it's not meant to be exact, right? It's just a barometer of how the country is feeling. So if the vote is really close, people can argue, but when the trend is clearly running one way or the other, and if this thing really does take off? Politicians will have to listen. It'll be like the Daily Show or something."

"That would be far out, wouldn't it?"

"Yeah. I'm hoping it'll take off that way."

"We'll be famous," Kristy said.

"That's not the point," I said with a face at Kristy.

"Could happen though," Anne said.

"Yeah, I suppose it could."

"So, what do you think of the overall design?" David asked Colette.

"Do you mind?" she said.

"That's why I asked."

"And this is where I get out of the way."

"Did you file that DBA?" Anne asked me.

"Oh shit, no. I forgot. I'll do that right now."

I heard Colette saying that she thought the front page looked a bit cluttered as I was heading out the door. I did a Google search for the local paper out on the front porch. As I was listening to the phone ring, Donny and Yvonne appeared through the woods. Yvonne smiled warmly. I cupped the phone.

"Go on in. The politburo is in session."

A few minutes later, I returned to the war room.

"Success?" Anne said.

"Well, there's good news and bad news. The bad news is, you have to run the ad once a week, for four weeks in a row. The good news is, you have thirty days from the moment you open your doors to get it done, so…"

"…so you can start a bank account."

"I can. I'll go in Monday to take care of business. We'll be hefty looking, I can guarantee you that. So how's the site going?"

"Oh, cool," David said. "I moved some of the stuff I had at the top of the page down here and created this logo thingy in between the two guys."

"That's cool looking."

It was a scrolled image, all red on one side, all blue on the other with the arms of the scroll interlocking in the middle.

Colette looked at me.

"I thought there should be something that said red/blue but I didn't want it to be just this 'us against them' mentality. I think this suggests a meeting of the minds in the middle."

"Which of course never happens anymore," Yvonne said.

Everyone looked at her.

"But we're hopeful," I said with a smile.

"I know. You're all so hopeful," she said. "I do admire that about you."

"So, where do we stand on everything else?" I said.

"Anne and I have looked into a bunch of ad buys but we need to know what day before we pull the trigger," Kristy said.

"And the guest bloggers?"

"I thought you were going to take care of that?" Anne said.

"Oh boy. If you want something done around here, you have to do it yourself."

I was pummeled with wadded up pieces of paper and pencils.

"Okay, I have an idea. Let's see if we can get those two guys who do that opinion segment on the News Hour each Friday. Can you dig up their contact information, David?"

He quickly had both their email addresses up on the screen.

"Cool. Text that to me and I'll send them both a note this evening."

There were looks all around.

"So?" I said. "Dare we try to shoot for some time this coming week?"

Everyone looked at David.

"Check on your ad buys and see what those two columnists say, but if you're asking me? I could have everything ready to launch next week."

"How about Friday?" I said.

"Sure," Anne said. "I think that would be great. Give people all weekend to vote and maybe cut things off on Monday at midnight. Then announce the results on Tuesday and put up the new issue on Wednesday."

I stood there with pursed lips.

"What?" she said.

"Well, it occurs to me that that would be great going forward but on this initial vote, maybe we need a bit more time. We don't know how quickly people will catch on."

"You're right, yeah. Maybe give everyone an extra week the first time?"

"I think that sounds better."

Everyone nodded.

"Okay, we have a target date. I'll email those two gents and throw some money at them. You line up those ad buys and I'll deal with the financing."

"I know. I'll work up a prospectus of our business plan for anyone who wants to see it," Kristy said.

"Okay, we're on a roll," I said.

"So, what's the issue you're going to debate?"

There were looks around the room.

"Details, details," I said.

Everyone laughed.

"I know," Colette said. "How about whether or not we should get rid of the electoral college?"

"Perfect," I said.

"Yeah," Anne said. "That is perfect. That's something that will definitely bring out the passions in everyone."

"That or the pitchforks."

21

I spent Saturday evening and Sunday dealing with business as necessary and otherwise lounging around my place with Colette, indulging in good food and wine, the discussion of life and great sex. There were dust worn books, music and movies, a passing shower and the wonderful scent of things being cooked in the kitchen, all the while being aroused by the sight of Colette's naked legs and painted toe nails protruding from beneath her nightgown.

Behind it all, my spirit was like a thoroughbred at the starting gate, nostrils flared, tail twitching, ready to bolt forward at the sound of the bell. I had sent off invitations to those two guest columnists but had yet to hear anything back. All that remained was waiting with anticipation for things to unfold over the upcoming week.

First thing Monday morning, I dashed off to find Dale in my truck and had him join me in a search for a suitable storage shed location. Having settled on two options, I dropped him back at the cottage. The final decision would be up to the tribal council to make.

Back at my place, I scrambled up some eggs, took a shower, downed one more cup of coffee and headed for the bank. Agnes, the investment manager, a tall, upright woman in her sixties with the name from a bygone era, took me back into her office and set about dealing with the money transfer. Back and forth she went with the paperwork. It took most of an hour to get everything straightened out.

I watched Agnes with fascination — the white blouse, the black pumps, the red lipstick — her every movement pregnant with all that was feminine, despite the fact that she was not particularly attractive. Some women just had an animal magnetism and left you staring.

Back at the property, I stopped by the tech house and found Kristy working with Colette.

"Get that ten mil transferred all right?" Kristy said with a big smile.

I nodded.

"Darn. I wish John and I had ten mil to transfer around."

"Where are Donny and Kyler?"

"Up plantin'," Kristy said with her comical, crosswise fist pump.

"So how are we looking?"

"Getting there. For the print ads, I used a service. It costs a bit more but with one click of a button, they take care of all the major newspapers."

"What do we mean by major?"

"I did a Google search and basically drew a line at the thirty biggest American cities. Less than that and we were cutting off things like Boston and San Francisco and Oklahoma City."

"Wouldn't want to leave out Oklahoma City."

"There's not much else in Oklahoma."

"Fair enough. So…"

"So, past the thirty biggest cities, you quickly got into places like Omaha and Fresno. But there were a few others down the list that I cherry picked, like Atlanta, Miami and Honolulu. Would have thought them in the top thirty, wouldn't you?"

"I stand here astonished."

Kristy laughed.

"Anyway, I think the final count was thirty-seven."

"So, what are we talking about, money wise."

Kristy smiled.

"Oh, just a little over a mil. Or as you would say, pocket change."

I suddenly felt an itch on the side of my nose.

"Too much?" Kristy said.

"No. What about the internet buys and TV?"

"We were just working on that. Did you want to do the same? All the big names?"

I nodded.

"The TV part is probably going to cost you a few mil alone."

I nodded.

"Should I feel guilty about spending all your money?"

"No. There's no half-assing it now, Kristy. I'm more worried that we might have left something out."

"That 65' yacht I've always wanted."

"I'll keep it in mind. Meanwhile, let's get the copy ready for the ads."

She did her crosswise fist pump and we sat down to brainstorm. Half an hour later and we had things roughed out for print and the internet.

"Here, I'll make the buys. You two start thinking about a concept for the TV stuff."

Fifteen minutes later, I leaned back in my chair and closed my eyes.

"Weary?" Colette said.

"No. Just clearing the brain cache."

"Hungry?"

"Yeah."

"Pizza again?"

"God no."

"Okay. Want to see what we've got for the TV ad."

"Sure. Hit me."

"So, we were thinking archive images of the Florida recount and clips of all these new voter suppression laws.

With a somber narrator in the background. 'While American politicians are busy trying to take away your vote.' Then we flash to an image of our logo and the narrator saying, 'National Roll Call is making sure that every vote counts'. What do you think?"

"Love it. Missed your calling. Think we can get it down to fifteen seconds?"

"That's what we're shooting for," Kristy said.

"Good. Let's get these folks on the phone and start talking demographics and ad slots. I'd like to do a cross section but really go after the younger crowd. The Daily Show. Saturday Night Live. That sort of thing."

An hour later, we had an ad agency mocking up the ad for us and the ball rolling with all the major networks. The slots were secured. I had made a deposit. All that remained was final approval on the ad itself.

"I'm starving," Kristy said.

"We need to get a café opened out here."

"Hey! Now there's a great idea!"

"Help you pay for that '65 yacht."

"I'm all over it."

"In the meantime, I could do with a turkey sandwich."

"Who has turkey?"

"I do."

"Yum. I guess we're all headed over Steven's house in the clouds."

We jumped in the golf cart and started off through the woods. Back at my place, I let the women whip up the sandwiches. I grabbed my laptop and checked my emails.

"Hey!" I said, carrying the laptop out to island in the kitchen. "I have messages from both of those columnists."

"What? Their people want to talk to our people?" Colette said.

I chuckled.

"Yeah."

"Cool," Kristy said.

271

I grabbed my phone and dialed the number of the right wing guy. A woman answered who sounded as if she worked in human resources at a major corporation. I explained who I was. She wanted to know if I was serious about the money. I cupped the phone and whispered.

"She wants to know if I'm serious about the money."

I un-cupped the phone.

"Absolutely. The deadline is the only string attached."

She wanted to know more about who I was and our operation.

"Do you accept payments through PayPal?"

She did.

I explained about our launch strategy and that I could not reveal anything more without a signed NDA. I had offered fifty grand each for these opinion pieces.

"Get me an NDA and I'll transfer half the funds up front."

We went through the 'this is somewhat unconventional' conversation but I ultimately prevailed.

"Just to be clear, this opinion piece is to be delivered no later than Thursday, midnight, Eastern Standard Time."

If the money was there, they would deliver.

"I'll transfer the funds the minute I receive your NDA. The balance will be transferred for a piece delivered on time. No other strings attached. I know the man's work. We won't engage in any second guessing."

While waiting for the NDA, I called the second number. In contrast to the first woman, the second woman sounded like somebody's mother had answered the phone. When I explained who I was, she readily admitted that, for that kind of money, her husband was ready to do just about anything, as long as it was legal. We both laughed and I explained again about our launch and the need for confidentiality. She had no problem whatsoever with that. The NDA was on the way. I stood ready to transfer the deposit immediately upon its receipt.

I got off the phone to a turkey sandwich and a pickle on my plate. Kristy passed around some kettle cooked potato chips.

"We're having flavored seltzer," she said. "Did you want some?"

"No. I should be going for a jog but it's too late for that now. May as well have a beer."

I went to grab one.

"I'm glad you brought that up," Kristy said with a shake of her finger. "Because I'm thinking to start an aerobics class out her. She punched the air a bit and went back to her sandwich. "Too bad we don't have a big activity center."

"Blame Chaplin and the Coastal Commission."

"What a jerk. I'd like to kick that guy in the shins."

"I'll pay you."

Kristy laughed.

"Look, you two can't say a word about this, but as soon as escrow closes on the land parcels around his place, I'm going to file for a 200 home subdivision."

"Oh no!" Colette said.

"It's only a bluff. To bring him to the bargaining table."

"You're mad," Kristy said. "You bought 1500 acres just to bluff the guy?"

I nodded and bit into my sandwich.

"God, I want that kind of money. So I can mess with every jerk who's ever tried to screw me around."

"Yeah, well, don't be fooled. It has yet to bring me peace of mind."

I heard the 'ding' of incoming mail and checked my in box. It was the NDA from the left wing guy. Figured. The other NDA was probably working its way through legal.

I attached my signature and sent the NDA back, followed by the payment.

"Do we have a prefab spiel on what we're doing here?" I asked.

"Good idea," Kristy said with her crosswise fist pump. "Let's work something up right now."

273

Five minutes later, we had an overview of our website worked up and I sent it off to the left wing guy's people.

"You know," Kristy said. "You really need to get your books going on all of this. The website, the foundation. The longer you wait, the more of a nightmare it's going to be."

"I thought you were going to take care of it."

"Not without some money..."

I laughed and looked to the heavens.

"All right. How much is this going to cost me?"

She pretended to be doing a web search.

"Let's see, 65', deluxe cabin, hmm hmm hmm hmm hmm."

I stared at her.

"Go ahead, put a number on it."

"Well, it's probably going to take me all week and I think with my business degree that I deserve to make five hundred dollars a day, so three or four grand?"

"That's fine."

"Darn, I knew I should have asked for more."

"Yep."

"Okay, let's renegotiate."

"Too late. And don't go telling anybody about it either."

"Okay," she whispered.

"Now, if you'll excuse me, I'm going to finish up my turkey sandwich."

I had been sitting there for several minutes, eating in peace and listening to Kristy and Colette chat when my email inbox 'dinged' again.

"It's the right wing guy's people," I said, checking my messages.

I quickly signed their NDA and sent a payment, along with our company spiel.

"Hmm. Darn good sandwich," I said, taking the last bite.

"I know," Kristy said. "It's the cheese."

"It's the cheese, Gromit."

Kristy smiled blinkingly at me.

"Who's Gromit?"

I explained.

"And that's one of his favorite lines. 'It's the cheese, Gromit. The cheese'."

"How funny."

"So," I said, standing up. "Is there anything else on our agenda today?"

"I need a workout," Kristy said.

As I was setting my dish in the sink, I heard Kyler call out from down below.

"Hey, boss man!"

I went out onto the landing.

"What's up, my friend? Are we all done with the planting?"

"Pretty much. I left Camellia doing the last row."

Seeing he looked depressed, I went down to talk with him.

"What's going on, man?"

"Oh, I'm just fucked up in the head today."

"About what?"

"About everything. That legal bullshit. Dealing with Camellia. Just being a fucking alcoholic and never being able to drink again. I've been feeling like I just want the whole fucking struggle to be over with."

"Hey, man. Don't even talk like that."

I gave him a hug.

"This is exactly why we have a tribe, man. So our lives aren't empty and meaningless and all alone. We have people who love us and an important role to play, you know? Don't you realize how bummed we'd all be if you were gone?"

"You really think so?"

"Fuck, I know it."

He seemed unconvinced so I encouraged him to sit with me in the golf cart.

"Look, Kyler. I have those feelings too."

I explained about my old relationship.

"You know, you go around pretending like everything's fine on the surface but you're dying inside. Don't you people say 'one day at a time'?"

"Fuck, it's one minute at a time right now."

"I know. Sometimes it's like that and all you can do is put one foot in front of the other."

"Or fucking hide in bed."

"Yeah, that's okay too but don't do something that's permanent when the feelings are fleeting. I wake up feeling terrified half the time but by lunch I've forgotten all about it. It would be pretty stupid to off myself over that."

"You really feel that way?"

"Sure."

We stared at each other.

"So was there something specific about this legal business?"

"No, just worrying about shit."

"Okay, well. If it ever comes to that, I'll get you the best fucking attorney that money can buy. Worst case scenario, we'll get you off with a wrist slap."

"Are you serious, boss man?"

"Absolutely. I'll get you F. Lee Bailey or some shit."

"Wow, thanks."

I threw an arm around his shoulder and touched my head to his.

"So let's make a pact right here and now that we'll talk about this shit rather than holding it inside of ourselves. Agreed?"

"Okay, boss man."

"And we won't do anything stupid."

"Okay, boss man."

"All right. So what else is going on?"

"Camellia says we need a scarecrow."

"Yeah? That'd be cool. How about an animated one?"

"That would be way cool."

Kristy and Colette had come out onto the landing, looking for us so I called up to them.

"Camellia says we need a scarecrow. Why don't you look into that, Kristy? Animated would be really cool. They must have them for sale somewhere."

She quickly did a search on her smartphone.

"Got it on Amazon," she said. "$95 bucks, batteries not included."

"What? Some plastic shit?"

Colette leaned in to have a look and laughed.

"No, it's a perfectly old-fashioned looking scarecrow."

"Cool. That's a buy," I said.

"All I need is a credit card," Kristy said.

"You give them a roof over their heads and food on the table and this is the thanks you get."

"Yeah, yeah."

"You ready?"

Kristy nodded and I called out the number to her, then the expiration date and security code.

"Wow, it worked," Kristy said a moment later. "Let me jot that down."

"Funny."

They went back in the house. I looked back at Kyler.

"So what else is on your mind? I can see you're still thinking."

"Oh, I just want to help people in recovery, you know, and I was thinking about this guy I met at an AA meeting last night. A homeless vet."

"How the hell does that happen?" I said.

"I know. Bummer, isn't it? So the poor fucker's living on the streets and I was thinking, wow, wouldn't it be cool if we could get this guy out here."

"Sure, but you know the rules. Put something in writing and we'll throw it out there on Friday."

"Yeah. Meanwhile, this guy's living on the streets."

"Well, you can talk to everybody and see if it's possible to arrange a council meeting sooner."

"Yeah, we have to have a meeting in order to see if we can have a meeting."

"All right, Kyler, I'll tell you what. I need the tribe to approve a location for that work shed so let's both work on trying to arrange something for tonight."

"All right, boss man. Thanks."

I gripped Kyler by the shoulder.

"Hey, I love you, brother."

"I love you too, man."

"All right. Tell everyone you see about the meeting and I'll check in with you later on."

We hugged again and Kyler whipped his golf cart around with a final wave goodbye. I watched until he had disappeared down the path into the woods.

Upstairs, I told Kristy and Colette about our conversation.

"Wow, scary stuff," Kristy said.

"Yeah, we need to keep an eye on him."

"Lots of hugs," Colette said.

"Yeah. I'm wondering if he has clinical depression or something that needs special attention."

"Kyler?" Lori said. "I don't see depression. Maybe bipolar. I don't know."

"Yeah, Christ. Well there's another item on the tribal checklist. A shrink."

"I'll try and get him to talk to me alone," Colette said.

"Yeah. Anything but holding it in."

I yawned.

"God, I'm depressed all of a sudden."

I went over and flopped out on the couch.

"Don't hold it inside," Lori said.

"Oh shut up," I said.

After a quiet moment with my eyes closed, I explained about the tribal council we were trying to arrange.

"So, suppose can you get in touch with your husband today?" I asked Kristy.

"He usually takes my calls."

I smiled at her.

"I just hope like hell this meeting turns out differently than the last one."

"I'm sure it will," Colette said.

"Well, guess I'll go work on my accounting," Kristy said and started for the door. "How and when do I get paid, by the way?"

"We work on 2/10/90," I said.

"Bummer. Guess I'll just have to rig the books."

"You do that."

Kristy said goodbye and headed down the stairs.

"Call me about the meeting!"

"I will!" she called back.

Colette curled up next to me.

"That is scary stuff. About Kyler."

"I know. I feel like the tribe is failing somehow if you can end up feeling so completely alone out here."

"He'll be okay. I'll talk to him."

"Yeah. It's definitely nothing to take lightly."

"I know," she said.

I looked down. Colette still had her open toed slides on and they were hanging seductively off her feet. Knowing what aroused me, she was always wearing them now.

"Can we shut out the world for a while?" I said.

She took hold of me through my pants.

"Is this your answer to everything?"

"Well, when all else fails."

She smiled, stood up, closed and locked the Dutch door, pulled me up by the hand and left Hugo with a bone on our way up to my bedroom.

Later, we lay sprawled under the sheets, our hands still slowly exploring.

"Thank you," I said.

Colette reached over to kiss me and stood up to dress.

"You're welcome. I'd better go walk Hugo and see if I can help down at the tech center. I'm beginning to feel adrift without the arts center."

"Let's go talk with Connor tomorrow and give a final okay on the design."

"Okay."

Now dressed, she leaned over to kiss me. "Shall we plan on something for dinner?"

"Sure. Sushi?"

"That sounds good."

"Okay. Give me a call if you have any word about the council meeting tonight."

"I will."

I watched Colette leave, wanting her again.

Within the hour, I received word back from Colette. Everyone had been contacted and the council meeting was on for six o'clock.

A few minutes before the hour, I was ascending the steps to the yurt with Colette and Kristy.

"Oh, wow, look at the tile mosaic," I said. "It's beautiful. I had no idea Kevin had been up here working."

"There's a lot you don't know about," Kristy said.

I made eyes at her.

"You'd better not be rigging those books." She smiled. "And you'd better have forgotten that credit card number."

She smiled again as we slipped inside the yurt. Everyone was already there, including Dr. McDonald. There was a fire in the stove and the battery operated lamps had been replaced by ones with oil.

"Much better," I said to Anne.

"Yeah," she said.

How she could make one word sound so sexy was beyond me to explain, but she did.

A moment later, Dr. McDonald hit the gong and Anne pronounced the meeting in session. I raised my hand.

"Yes, Steven."

"First thing, I wanted to welcome you to the tribe, Yvonne."
She smiled.

"Does this make it official?"

I looked around the room and everyone nodded.

"Secondly, I make a motion that we quit being so goddamned formal about this business." That was met with universal agreement. "Let's just throw things open to discussion and if it seems like things are getting out of hand, Anne can step in as a referee. Agreed?"

"Here, here."

"I second that motion."

"I third it."

"I fourth it."

"We fifth and sixth it."

"All right. Agreed. Thirdly, I want to reiterate what was suggested last Friday. Let's not get bogged down into the mud of actual business matters. Let's stick to the overview and agree to set up subcommittees whenever it's clear that a matter is too complicated to be resolved here conveniently. This is the grand council. We don't want to be dealing with minutia."

"Here, here," Kyler said.

"But how will we know when we're dealing with minutia?" Yvonne said.

"I think you just crossed the line right there," Dr. McDonald said.

There was laughter.

"All right. So simplify, delegate, and stick to the elevated."

"Fair enough," Anne said. "So why are we here?"

"First thing, I have approval for the work shed so we need to decide on a location. I've chosen a few preliminary places for the tribe to consider."

"Isn't this where we'd choose a subcommittee to decide things?" Kristy said.

"No. This is where we decide things quickly and create a subcommittee if we can't."

"Ooookaaaay," she said.

"I'm not kidding, Ms. Subcommittee. If it's a big deal, delegate. Otherwise, let's get things done."

"So, what are the choices?" Anne said.

I explained.

"See, my original idea was to keep everything organized around the main meadow. You know, keep the clutter down? But..."

"I don't want your maintenance yard anywhere near my arts center," Colette interjected.

"Well I don't want your arts center anywhere near my maintenance yard."

Everyone laughed.

"But Collete's right. It's become more and more apparent to me as things progress around here that we need to designate separate areas for development. Commercial, industrial, whatever."

"I definitely want to see a grander vision for the meadow," Anne said. "Where the town center is also our spiritual and cultural center."

"I agree," Dr. McDonald said.

"I'm onboard with that," Kristy said.

"And everyone else?" I said.

From the nodding of heads, it was unanimous.

"Okay, then we'll plan to build it up by the garden. And, for the record, can we agree in principle that that area will be our so called industrial sector?"

That suggestion met with blank stares and the shaking of heads.

"I wouldn't consent to anything but the maintenance shed being built up there right now," Anne said. "I don't know if *garden* and *industrial* really go together in my head."

There was quickly a consensus on that point too.

"Wow, shot down twice in a row, boss man," Kyler said.

"I'm having a Kristy moment."

She kicked at me.

"So, on to my second point of business. Kyler here has someone he wants to nominate for consideration by the tribe."

Kyler explained about the vet. Yvonne spoke up.

"I can see on the surface where that would seem like a very noble thing to do, but you can't ignore the potential danger involved."

"How do you mean?" Anne said.

"I mean a lot of these guys...no...probably most of them come back from war with symptoms like PTSD and depression and for the most part it goes untreated. I'm sure Dr. McDonald has seen this in his work too. It's a ticking time bomb. You don't always know what's going to happen with them."

"So you're saying we should just treat them like lepers?" Anne said.

"Nooooo...I'm only suggesting that we should be careful. This could explode in ways that none of us can foresee."

"Is that your perception too, Dr. McDonald?" Anne said.

"Obviously I have no opinion on this acquaintance of Kyler's but in general I would have to concur with Yvonne. My heart goes out to this gentleman and I think we should give him fair consideration, but if he's basically living on the street and not actively seeking support for his problems through the VA and such, I think that's cause for some real concern."

"Maybe we could just meet him over dinner?" I said. "It would give us a chance to assess his temperament firsthand."

"Sure, why not?" Anne said.

Save for Yvonne, everyone else quickly concurred.

"By the way, did you suggest the idea of joining the tribe to this guy?" I asked Kyler.

"No, boss man. I guess I understood that would be a no no."

"Which brings to mind another thought," I said.

283

"Absolutely," Anne said. "I think I know where you're going with this one. We should never invite someone out here until the tribe has met that person on neutral ground, yeah?"

"It's only common sense. Never mind how awkward it could become, having to say no. We have to consider the potential for danger."

With looks all around, everyone concurred.

"Okay," I said. "That's all the business I have. Anyone else?"

I looked around at a circle of heads shaking.

"Maybe we should smoke a peace pipe now," Donny said.

"Depends on what's in the peace pipe," I said. "We have to remember that there are sober members among us."

"How about if we just go around the room and share a bit about our day and shit," Kyler said. "That's what we do in an AA meeting. I think it would be kind of cool for the tribe. So we can get to know each other better."

"Sounds good to me, but before we get on to that, dinner anyone?"

"I'm hungry," Kristy said.

"Pizza," Kyler said.

"Colette and I already went through that today, and our answer was sushi."

"Ooooh, that sounds good," Yvonne said.

We quickly learned that Kristy, Kyler and Dr. McDonald had never tried sushi.

"There's always a first," Anne said.

"I vote we table that decision until after the meeting," I said.

All agreed.

"Okay," Anne said. "So who's going to share about their day first?"

"Oh, I will," Yvonne said. "I had a doctor on our staff driving me absolutely crazy today. I swear he was going to kill one of our patients. Sorry, Dr. McDonald."

"It's quite all right. I often feel the same way."

Yvonne laughed and started in on her tale of how this doctor had screwed up a patient's meds.

22

The sky was gray and overcast the next morning. A mist drifted in among the treetops. God was brooding along the northern coast.

I gulped down an extra cup of coffee and went off in search of Dale, wanting to show him where the tribe had agreed to build the maintenance shed. The two of us kicked around the site a bit with our boots.

"So I take it you want me to drop everything and jump on this."

"If you don't mind, please."

Dale's mouth pursed up.

"Sorry, my friend. I know how you feel about finishing what you've started but that cottage will be there as soon as you're done here."

I dropped a less than happy Dale back at his work and drove around to Colette's place. She was still in her robe, sipping coffee. I searched beneath the robe while we kissed. Her flesh was as soft as rose petals and as warm as fresh baked muffins.

"So easy to get started," I said and growled in her ears.

"You are relentless."

"A man's hunger is relentless." I pulled back to look at her. "Are we still going in to see Connor today?"

"I was planning on it."

I kissed her again.

"I have several other things on my to do list. Shall we go in together?"

"Sure. You can drop me downtown if it comes to that."

"All right. Half an hour then?'

"Make it forty-five."

I kissed her passionately again.

"How about an hour, beautiful?"

"Steven."

"Ah. I feel a sudden fall from grace."

With her eyes fixed on me intently, Colette set her coffee cup down and said "Come."

Moments later, I had Colette bent over her bed, the robe pulled up over her back, that pale erotic hourglass in my hands and her ears blushing pink in the way only a woman's ears will blush during sex, and they were still blushing that way when we walked into Connor's office at a little past ten. He seemed to notice while welcoming us in and offered me a furtive smile.

"Come have a look," he said and led us back to his drafting table.

Connor kept the drawings in an old oak cabinet with a dozen shallow drawers and brass corners, like the specimen drawers of a 19th century botanist. One could picture the dusty rooms and glass cases filled with pinned butterflies.

"How goes the adventure out there?"

I told Connor about the website launch on Friday.

"Sounds terrific. So even a bloke like me could cast a vote."

"You could."

"I'll be sure to do that, then. Give the Tories a regular pranging."

I laughed.

"Now there's a word that needs no explanation."

Connor laid the plans out and flipped through them, explaining the final design changes. Colette and I watched from either side.

"So, your thoughts?" he said with the last page.

"Looks great to me," I said.

Colette nodded.

"Smashing. I'll go ahead and run off some prints then. Any word from the Coastal Commission?"

"No. We're years away from that if you're waiting."

"Bloody hell," Connor said.

"Don't you worry. I've got something else in the works."

"Thinking of the rack, are you?"

"More along the lines of mental torture."

"Best kind."

"I'm hoping. The science center's next," I said.

"Great stuff."

"Once this launch is off the ground, we'll arrange a meeting with my tech team."

"Any time, mate."

We shook hands.

"So, we're good for now?" I said.

"We're good."

Colette and I started out of the office.

"Keep me posted on that rack business," Connor said from the door.

"You'll be the first to know."

Downstairs, Colette and I climbed into my truck and looked at each other.

"Great stuff," I said with Connor's Scottish accent.

She smiled.

"So what now?"

I placed both hands on the steering wheel and shook it.

"I just want things to move forward."

"An early lunch while you're waiting? I'm living on coffee and a muffin."

"Sure. How about back to the scene of the crime?"

"Where would that be?" she said.

I started the truck with a look over at her.

"Stella's Café? Where else?"

"Oh. That seems like years ago now."

288

"Doesn't it, though."

Five minutes later, we were getting settled at the same table. Hugo seemed to know the place and took his spot on the floor. The sky outside was still dark and brooding. The waitress came to take our orders.

"Soup and sandwich?" I said to Colette.

"Perfect."

They had tomato bisque or clam chowder. We both ordered the bisque and club sandwiches. My phone rang while we waited. It was Anne. An old friend had just pulled into town and Anne wanted us to meet her. I invited them to join us for lunch.

"Was that Anne?" Colette said when I hung up.

"Yeah." I explained about the friend. "I've got a feeling she's going to pitch this chick for the tribe."

"This chick…"

I shrugged.

"And the rules?"

"Yes. The fucking rules."

"You're definitely in a state."

"I am…Anyway, we're just having lunch."

"With Anne and this *chick*."

I shrugged again.

Anne and the woman came in a few minutes later.

"Hi, you two," Anne said. "This is my friend, Elicia. Steven and Colette."

We scooted over to make room for them. Anne sat next to me, Elicia across the table. Elicia could have been Anne's beautiful sister. Dark, wavy hair, intense dark eyes and white sparkling teeth full of mirth. Her whole persona seemed to be bubbling over with gaiety.

"So," she said with a smile at Anne. "I know this could get Anne in trouble but I kept asking her where she was living until the truth finally came out."

"Well, we did agree to a process."

"I know," Anne said. "I'm sorry."

"Oh well, we're here now. So, tell me, Elicia. What's your story?"

She explained about having run an organic farm on leased land up in Oregon for the past five years. Then the owner decided to sell the property to an investor.

"Everyone was really bummed of course but that's the way of the world, isn't? Plow up the earth, build more houses and sell them to a family with five kids and a dog."

"The poor dog," I said. Elicia laughed. "So what are you going to do now?"

Elicia looked at Anne with a big smile.

"Well, obviously I'm here to pitch you, hoping you'll pitch me to everyone else."

"Pitch what?"

"That I'm an old fashioned farm girl who knows how run a garden. Among my many other talents."

Her smile was cheerier than white clouds after a good rain. I looked at Anne.

"I'm sorry," she said. "I just heard you were in town and thought it would be a chance for you to meet Elicia personally."

"No, this was my idea, not hers," Elicia said, interjecting.

"Look, no apologies needed. Either one of you. And I'm happy to put in the good word for you, Elicia, but ultimately I'm just one voice. All this stuff has to be run through the council."

Elicia kept staring at me with her big glowing smile.

"Okay, okay. I'm sold," I said. "You're just the kind of person we need to help us with the garden.."

"I can do lots of other stuff, too, like jarring for the winter and raising animals. We had chickens and cows and pigs on our farm. They're really helpful. Pigs eat all your garbage, cows give you milk and cheese, chickens give you eggs, and of course you can eat them."

I made a face and Elicia laughed again.

"I had you pegged for a vegan."

290

"Hardly. I'm just against these giant livestock factories where they use soy and corn feed and there's no environmentally safe way of dealing with the waste. It's like ten times worse for the environment than all the motor vehicles on the planet put together."

"So I've heard."

"Yeah, but with a bit of pasture, the animals can feed themselves and their waste turns into fertilizer and it's not any stress on the planet. It's not like I'm going to gorge on animal flesh all the time but I'm also not going to have a tofu turkey for Thanksgiving."

I chuckled.

"Hey. We did it all on our farm. I can even help you build up a blog and website."

"Look, I already told you. I'm sold."

I turned to Anne.

"You want to set up an audition on Friday?"

"Yeah, thanks, Steven" Anne said again with a touch of my hand.

"Yeah, thanks from me too," Elicia said. "I'm dying to come out and see the place."

I looked at Anne and she looked at Elicia.

"Steven's reminding me that we agreed to have these first meetings on neutral ground, like at a restaurant."

"Sure," Elicia said, her beaming smile unfazed.

The waitress arrived with our soup and sandwiches.

"Order something?" I said.

Elicia ordered the bisque, Anne the clam chowder, both with no sandwiches.

Amidst the ensuing chatter, my phone rang. It was Jolie.

"Excuse me," I said and headed out the door.

"What's the news?"

"Your escrow is done."

"Fantastic. So the properties are mine."

"Well, they have to be recorded first, but yes."

"Will that be done today?"

"I can assure you that the papers will be delivered to the courthouse today. Whether or not they record them today, I can't say. Tomorrow at the latest."

"Okay. Then call me as soon as you have news."

I got off and headed back inside.

"This looks like good news," Anne said as I sat down.

"The escrow closed on those two properties. All I have to do is wait for the county to record them now."

I bit into the rest of my sandwich.

"More land?" Elicia said with a look around at everyone.

"Sorry," I said. "Can't discuss it right now. As soon as the deeds are recorded, I'll explain."

I excused myself and called Richard.

"The escrow closed," I told him when he came on the line. "How's it going on your end?"

"Come on over and I'll show you."

"I'll be there in fifteen minutes."

I took two more quick bites and slurped down the rest of my soup.

"Looks like we're off," Colette said.

"You don't have to come if you don't want."

"Sure, hang with us," Anne said.

"No, I think I'll follow along with Mr. Excitement here."

I was already up and out of my seat. I checked the bill and threw some money on the table.

"It was nice meeting you, Elicia."

"It was great meeting you."

"And we'll see you back at the ranch later on, Anne."

Colette and I were out the door and on our way across town. Ten minutes later we were dashing into Richard's office. He was on the phone when his secretary ushered us into the office. Richard pointed at the chairs. Colette received an especially warm smile.

The two of us sat there listening to Richard discuss the law. His pink Irish face was particularly ruddy that day. I presumed he had been out playing golf with the likes of Chaplin.

When the conversation dragged on, Richard fished around on a side desk and unearthed the subdivision papers. Before turning them around to face me, he thumbed through to a page with the tract drawings and pointed. I nodded and took them. The development was laid out with roads and markets and green space.

"This ought to get Chaplin apoplectic," I whispered.

"It's scary looking," Colette whispered back. "I hope to god you never go through with it."

"Hmm. You know, there is the potential for some serious money here."

She hit me with an elbow. A moment later, Richard was finally off the phone.

"Hi," he said with a big smile and outreached paw for Colette. "Richard."

"Colette."

"And where has Steven been hiding you?"

"Off in the woods somewhere."

"Well, I'm certainly glad he dragged you out. What do you think?" he said to me."

"What do I know? It looks fine to me. Will it pass muster?"

"I did as you asked, sir. All the I's are dotted and T's crossed. I imagine the Coastal Commission will have a field day with you, if you ever get that far, but no one could take this filing to be a joke."

"Good. So what now?"

"As soon as the deeds are recorded, we can file an application with the Bureau of Real Estate. They'll want some money to start. They'll especially want proof that you have the wherewithal to go with this madness. It can drag on for months and years from there. Which I assume is just what you want."

"More or less, yes."

"So, if this is all you need for now, give me some money and I'll take it from there."

"How much?"

"I'll have to ask my secretary."

Richard called through to her and she presently brought in some papers. I walked out of the office a short time later with several copies of the filing and roughly fifty grand lighter in the pocket.

On the way back to the ranch, my mind was swirling. I hardly saw the wet, gray coastline. Much had moved forward in the past few hours but I wanted more.

"Ready for dinner?" I said as we pulled off the highway.

"Actually, a moment to myself is what I'm thinking right now. Do you mind?"

"Not much." We smiled at each other. "I'll drop you off on my way to the tech department."

Kristy was there alone, working on the accounting. I gave her Richard's number.

"Call him if you need anything or have any questions."

Kyler and Donny zipped by in the golf cart right then. I rushed out to flag them down.

"Is Dale up top yet?"

"Yeah. I saw him up there laying out the foundation. I guess he's got someone coming in tomorrow to trench things."

"Good. Let's drive up there to have a chat."

I jumped into the golf cart and we rode along with the quietude of the forest somewhat stilling my busy mind.

"So how is our recycling plant going, Donny?"

"Great. It loves shit and making methane."

"I don't know why but that fact just gives me a thrill."

Kyler laughed. I smiled at him."

"So otherwise, you guys have plenty to keep you busy?"

"Not really, boss man. We're kind of just driving around today. Anything you need?"

"Not right this second. Why don't you two start making a list of things we might need around here. Stuff for the garden.

Trash cans? Whatever comes to mind. Just jot down your ideas and I'll arrange for the funding."

"Gotta go through the tribal council, boss man.

"I'll give you a tribal council."

"Yeah! Putting the boss man in his place!"

We found Dale and Jason sitting down for lunch.

"Gentlemen," I said, walking up.

Dale bit into his sandwich and took the subdivision filing from my hand all in one motion.

"Where's this?"

"On the other side of Chaplin."

"You own it?"

"The deed is being filed at the courthouse as we speak."

"And you're serious?"

I looked around from face to face.

"No, but I want Chaplin to think I am."

Dale slowly shook his head.

"And you want from me?"

"Get some survey people out there. Make some commotion along that property line. Anything to ensure that we've gotten Chaplin's attention."

"Should I be worried about legalities here?"

"Not a bit." I tapped my finger on the subdivision map. "As far as anyone is concerned, that fucker's going in. Whatever you need monetarily to get the ball rolling, you got it. I'll take care of Chaplin, as soon as he blows his top."

"You fuckers are crazy," Dale said and handed the filing back to me.

"No, that's yours. Keep it. Just get some people out there. No jackhammers but make sure that son of a bitch knows we're here."

I left Dale eating his sandwich and headed back to my place. A pit stop later, I was seated at my desk, twiddling my thumbs. For all I had accomplished that day, I still felt like the world was locked in amber.

Around ten the next morning, I got word that the deed had been recorded. I let Dale know and dragged Donny and Kyler over with me to inspect the new property. We skirted the property fence in my truck for a mile but I never saw Chaplin and assumed that he had not seen us.

It started to rain in the afternoon. I invited Colette up to my place and the two of us spent the rest of the day and evening being hedonists. We ate and drank and whiled away a rainy evening entwined in our pleasures.

The next day broke with towering white clouds, like saints riding in high in a brilliant blue sky. I drove over to the new property first thing and found Dale's surveying crew out there pinning the roads. Back and forth I went along the property line, parking here and there, doing everything I could to make myself visible and had been there an hour or so before I finally saw Chaplin driving out through his woods in a brand new Avalanche. When he noticed me, I waved. Chaplin stopped and sat there with his motor idling. The surveyor's truck was parked up over my shoulder, company logo and all. Chaplin remained there staring at things for another long minute before he turned around and slowly headed back towards his mansion.

I smiled to myself. The hook had been set. It wouldn't take long now, twenty-four hours at most and that chubby fop would be railing at the world, or at least at various California institutions within it.

I called Toni on my way back to the ranch.

"Chaplin knows."

"You'd better hope this doesn't backfire."

"You just keep your eyes peeled and let me know the minute you hear his footsteps. I want to know everything he's doing. Meanwhile, picture me savoring the moment."

"You're a sick man."

"I am, but there will come a time for me to hold out the olive branch, and I will. Do you think that stuffy old gas bag would ever hold out the olive branch to me?"

"I'll keep you posted," she said with a laugh and hung up

I headed over to the tech center. Only David and Kristy were in the war room when I arrived.

"D-Day's tomorrow," I said, walking in. "Why is this place so quiet?"

"Anne's at work," David said. "I don't know about anyone else. I'm just testing the website again before I launch. I found a little glitch in the code for Macs but I think it's good now."

He brought the site back up on his test server and we watched as he navigated through the pages.

"Looks good, huh?"

"Yeah."

"So I think we're ready to roll."

"What about the two opinion pieces?"

"Oh yeah," Kristy said. "They came in this morning. You need to forward the remaining funds."

"Greedy bastards."

She laughed.

"I'll do it from home in a minute. In the meantime, how about the ads? Everything done? We're all signed off?"

"Good to go."

"Far out. I'm...starting...to get...excited."

Kristy did her comical fist pump, several times.

"Yeah," David said. "I guess with the east coast papers, we'll need to be manning the fort here in the middle of the night."

He glanced at his watch.

"I'm going home to catch some shut eye. I'll be back around two."

"I'll be here too."

"Me too," Kristy said.

"It'll be like watching elections results."

"Yeah," she said. "I hope everyone else is planning to show up. We'll need help with the phones."

"I was told they will," David said.

297

"Well, guess I'll head home and take care of those invoices."

I offered Kristy and David high fives.

"See you in the wee hours of the morning."

"I've got my fingers crossed," Kristy said.

"So do I."

I headed off through the woods in my truck, wondering if this fool had spent his money at all wisely.

23

Later that afternoon, I reached for the phone, thinking to invite Colette over for dinner but stopped. Something wasn't right. I could feel it in my bones. When Colette called shortly before six, I cited the impending all-nighter and told her I needed to get some sleep.

That evening, while listening to Pandora, Frank Sinatra came on, singing *I've Got You Under My Skin* and suddenly there was no denying the truth of it. Whatever those crazy, dangerous feelings were that we felt when we fell head over heels in love, I did not feel them for Colette. I cared about her deeply and loved her in my own way, but the love songs were still all about somebody else.

I went to sleep unsettled by that knowledge and awakened at a little past two, tangled up in troubled dreams. Eager to escape them, and myself, I quickly dressed and started off through the woods on foot. It was a pitch black, moonless night and I could hardly see ten feet in front of my face. The rustling I heard off in the brush might well have been a bear. I was greatly relieved when the lights of the cottages came into view off through the woods.

Nearing Colette's place, I saw that her lights were on but hurried past and on to the tech center. David and Anne were at the computers when I walked in.

"Any votes yet?" I said on my way back to make coffee.

"Not so far," David said.

"Any traffic?"

"A trickle."

I found coffee already made and poured myself a cup.

"Probably early risers on the east coast," I said, sitting down next to David.

"Could be," he said. "Could be the Twitter blasts or the internet ads."

"But nobody's biting."

"Not yet," Anne said.

David had a real time traffic gauge set up with what looked like an earthquake monitor oscillating alongside of it. We were waiting for the big one to hit but the oscillations were yet minor. I pulled my jacket more tightly around me and settled in to watch. The bank of phones was sitting there with red lights on, silently waiting.

"I don't know what terrifies me more. This thing taking off or becoming a complete flop."

I looked at David.

"What the hell do we do if it does take off?"

"Hire some people fast. That or seriously grow the tribe."

"Yeah."

"There's Elicia," Anne said.

"Yeah, there's an army."

She smiled.

"We'll need twenty more like her."

A few minutes later, Kristy came in.

"Are we knocking 'em dead yet?" she said.

"Not yet," I said.

"Coffee anyone?" she said on her way into the kitchen.

"It's already made," I said.

I got up and joined her. She poured the last cup.

"Better make some more."

I leaned back against the counter while Kristy ground up some fresh French roast beans. Once the coffee was brewing, she leaned back with her cup and a smile.

"I'm going to be big time bummed if this thing flops. I'm counting on that 65 foot yacht."

"You're nothing, if not focused."

"That's right."

She did her little number, but with only one upright palm going forward.

A minute later, the water stopped gurgling and we poured two fresh cups.

"Anyone out there?"

"Sure, I'll have another one," Anne said.

"Me too."

"Sugar? Cream?

Anne came out.

"I know how he likes it."

I went back with my cup.

"Why don't we log some votes?" I said. "Prime the pump."

"That's a good idea."

In less than a minute, all four of us had voted. When Kristy voted to keep the electoral college, we threw pencils at her.

"Hey, somebody had to vote on that side. I would look rigged, otherwise."

"Sure," I said. "I knew you were a right wing hack all along."

"Hey, I'm conservative about some stuff, yeah."

"I say we vote her out of the tribe."

"Oh boy. You're the one who said we don't all have to agree."

"Yeah. I take it back."

"Too late."

"Oh hey, look," David said.

Quickly, a few dozen more votes had been posted on both sides of the issue. You could see the traffic monitor spiking in unison.

"The votes are running almost even so far," Kristy said.

"Yeah, right wing pricks are more likely to get up early in the morning."

"I'm sure," she said.

"It's true. I read an article about it."

"Ooookaaaay."

"No, it's true. The ruling class has to get up early to check on their stock portfolios. The peasants are still in bed, sleeping off their bacchanalian adventures."

"I believe it," Anne said.

"I'm sure."

All of us looked back at the computer screens. The traffic wasn't huge, but steadily growing, along with the vote tally.

"It's still mostly even," Kristy said.

"It's early," I said. "You wait until the bacchanalian vote comes in."

"I'm sure."

"Okay, valley girl."

We sat sipping coffee and watching the screens. The vote tally had eclipsed one thousand by the time Colette came in.

"How's it going?"

We filled her in.

"There's coffee in the kitchen."

I felt obliged to join her out there but didn't.

"Oh look, comments on Twitter!" Kristy said.

Colette hurried out to join us. I touched hands with her but skipped the kiss.

Meanwhile, Kristy was scrolling down through the thread on Twitter. Some people were voicing their opinions. Some were saying what a great idea the website was. The votes kept piling up. Not an avalanche yet, but they were piling up.

At a little past four in the morning, I went to take a leak and was still in midstream when a great cheer broke out in the living room. I hurried back.

"Look at that!" Kristy said. "It's an avalanche!"

The totals were spiking. David dug deeper into the stats.

"Wow. In a matter of a few minutes, the traffic jumped to over a million visitors."

There were high fives and more cheers.

"Look," Anne said. "It's *trending* on Twitter."

"Hey, we're cool!" Kristy said.

As we watched, the vote tally steadily surged and swung to almost 70% against keeping the electoral college.

"See?" I said. "The bacchanalian crowd is finally getting out of bed."

"Hey, the electoral college has worked just fine for over two hundred years. We can't just go changing things on a whim all the time. Where would we stop?"

"You're right. Let's go back to the good old times, when women couldn't vote."

"Shut up."

I razzed Kristy a bit more and focused back on the screens. The traffic kept exploding, as did the vote count. We spent the next several minutes, wandering around the office, in a bit of a shock over our seeming success.

"Hey, let's pull up the morning shows," I said. "They're already airing on the east coast, right?"

"Yeah," Anne said and pulled up one of them on her computer.

Their social media expert was just going over what was trending that morning and it was *us*. We let out with another cheer.

"Come on, come on, let's hear what she's saying," I said.

Anne turned up the sound. The woman had our site pulled up on her laptop and was relating the traffic stats. One of her male counterparts had unfolded the NY Times and was holding up our full page ad.

"T r e n d i n g," Kristy said.

The voting had exploded into the millions. We were high fiving each other again when the phone rang.

Kristy screamed.

"Look, it's them! They're calling us!"

"Well, answer it, stupid," I said.

"Me?"

"Well, somebody better."

"I'll do it," Anne said and reached for the phone. "National Roll Call."

We huddled around Anne, both listening to her and watching the screen. From the show itself, we could hear the questions that went with Anne's answers. What is National Roll Call? Whose idea was it? How did it get started? Anne did a deft job of explaining how one of our team had come up with the idea in a meeting. But who was our team? It's kind of a tribe of people up here in Northern California. A tribe of people? The questions kept coming and Anne kept answering then, while maintaining a veil of intrigue.

The door opened behind us and Donny came in with Yvonne. Yvonne was wearing her nursing uniform. I held a finger up to my mouth and led them over to the screen. Their jaws dropped when they grasped what was going on. I gave them a thumbs up and focused in again on Anne's conversation. The hosts wanted someone from our company to be on the show the next morning. Anne told them, sure and the hosts passed the call to one of their offstage underlings. The show moved on to the next item. A few minutes later, Anne finally hung up.

"So, what?" Kristy said.

"They offered first class plane fare back to New York, five star lodgings and five grand."

We were engaged in a round of high fives when the phone rang again.

"Shit," I said. "It's probably another show wanting us on."

"I'll get this one," Kristy said.

"No, no. Let it go to the answering service," I said.

"Why?"

"Because we can't be on every show."

"Then why do we have these phones?"

"I think he's right," Anne said. "We need to discuss a game plan before we start committing to every offer."

"Ooookaaaay," Kristy said.

"Seriously," Anne said. "Let's check our phone messages throughout the day and answer them in an orderly fashion. In the meantime, we need to decide who's going back there to be on the show."

"I'll go," Kristy said.

"I think David should go," I said. "Or maybe Dr. McDonald."

Anne shook her head.

"What?"

"Come on, Steven. You know there's only one person who can do this."

"I don't want to."

"Yeah, but who else can really speak for us? We're a tribe, but you're still the one who started it. This was your vision. You need to go and explain it to the American people."

"I hate New York."

"You'll be going in style."

"I'll go with you," Colette said.

"There you go," Anne said. "Colette used to live there. She knows the ropes."

I looked around from face to face. The phones were ringing away and Kristy was blowing a rod, wanting to answer them.

"All right, goddamn it."

I got up, pacing.

"Jesus. With all the transfers, we'll need to get on a plane here by midmorning."

"I think it should be exciting," Anne said.

"Real exciting. You don't know who you're talking to here."

"So? Shall I call them back?"

"Yeah, yeah. Call them but tell them it has to be two plane tickets."

"What should I tell them is your title?"

"I don't know. The grand poohbah of the intergalactic tribe."

Anne smiled.

"I'll just tell them you're the founder and main investor."

"Fair enough." I looked at Colette. "I need to get some sleep before we go."

The very thought of it made me yawn.

"Will somebody answer the phones?!" Kristy said.

"Just call the answering service and sort through them as they come in," I said. "Selling ad space on our website should be foremost. You'll need to put together some kind of pricing structure, David. You know the drill. Based on the level of our traffic. Work with him, Kristy."

"Oh, like we don't know what to do."

I pretended to strangle her again.

"Go," Anne said. "We can handle this."

"All right. Will you take care of the flight arrangements?"

"I will. Go. Get some sleep."

"Okay. But don't make it any earlier than ten from the local airport. And can someone give me a lift home? I walked over."

"I'll give you a ride," Yvonne said. "I'm headed off to work anyway."

"Great. I'll see you in a few hours," I told Colette and gave her a hug.

The gang started singing *New York, New York* as I walked out.

"And no more shows for now," I called back to them.

"Wow, you're really taking off," Yvonne said as we drove away.

"We're taking off, Yvonne. Remember. It's a tribe."

"But I don't feel as if I've done anything to help so far."

"You helped with the garden."

She scoffed with a smile my way.

"That's like saying I pulled some weeds."

"Yvonne. I don't get you."

"What do you mean?" she said, still smiling.

"You're important. You can do great things if you want. I don't get why you diminish yourself so much."

She chuckled.

"Well, I just think that's easy for someone like you to say, you know."

"Look, my idea was, everything we do out here is equally important. It all has to be done. Why should one person be held in higher esteem than another? Let's say down the road that you help people with their health issues. That's a special contribution. Everybody is going to bring something unique to the table. So in the meantime we each pull some weeds or whatever it is that needs to be done. Are we happy? Are we content? Isn't that the real question?"

"Is it?"

"It is to me."

We rode along with our own thoughts until Yvonne was pulling to a stop in front of my house.

"Thanks."

"You're welcome."

"You know, I just want to see you in the spirit of things. We're happy to have you. I want think you're happy to be here."

"I am," she said with a big smile.

"So why doesn't it feel that way?"

"I don't know. I guess I'm accustomed to being very skeptical of the world."

"Is that because you're a nurse? I mean, like a cop, you're dealing with depressing crap all day long, until you can't see anything positive."

"Maybe."

She chuckled.

"Well, this is a really big day for the tribe, so let's see some of that old time positive spirit, okay?"

She chuckled again.

"What?"

"Well, see, I think you should be really excited about going on this trip and you're not. So we're not all that different."

"Okay. You win. We're both depressed."

"That's not what I meant."

I leaned over and kissed her on the forehead.

"Peace, sister. I'll see you back here in a couple of days."

She stared with a dumbstruck smile, as if my kiss had thoroughly surprised her. I left her that way and headed upstairs.

It was a few minutes past five in the morning. I had at best three hours to get some sleep. The effort went as expected. Tossing and turning with ever greater anxiety as the hour drew near. I was just getting into some serious Z's when the alarm went off. I wandered into the kitchen, brewed some coffee and called Anne.

"Is everything arranged?"

"Yes. Aren't you going to ask how things are going?"

"I'm too groggy."

"Steven. It's an absolute phenomenon. We've clipped past three million visitors and half of them have voted. And it's only the first day. The morning of the first day."

"I'm absolutely thrilled. I just wish I didn't have to go to New York."

"Speaking of which, we had a quick discussion and thought it was only fair to put off meeting with any new potential members until you get back."

"No, no. Go ahead. We obviously need to get Elicia onboard. She's got my vote. Don't know what to say about that vet. I'll leave that in your hands."

"Don't worry about it. We'll take care of it."

"So, about the flight?"

"You're outbound from Eureka at 10:15. Your connecting flight in San Francisco goes out at 12:00 noon. That puts you into JFK a little before 9:00 tonight. The network will have a limo waiting for you and you're staying in a five star hotel. Sounds like fun."

"Yeah. New York, New York. Does Colette know?"

"Yeah. She called here a few minutes ago."

"Okay. I'm brewing up some coffee and jumping into the shower right now."

"Did you want a ride?"

"No. I'll take my truck. Best not to pull anyone away from their duties."

"All right, sir. Everything you need will be waiting for you at the airport. Have a fun trip. We'll be looking for you on TV tomorrow morning."

"Yeah. Hope I look good in pancake makeup."

"I'm sure you will."

I got off and called Colette.

"Are you ready?"

"Not yet."

"Okay. I'll see you at nine."

"I'll be ready by then."

"Good."

I got off, gulped more coffee, showered and dressed, all the while wishing I could go back to bed.

The terminal in Eureka was essentially the great room in somebody's contemporary mansion. Cedar planks with arched glue lam beams on the ceiling, chrome and black Naugahyde seating below. Efficient and Scandinavian looking.

Our plane was a Horizon prop jet, seating about forty and capable of 300 knots. We touched down in San Francisco at a little before 11:30 AM, giving us just enough time to dash across the terminal and catch our nonstop flight to JFK.

Before long, we were rocketing down the runway. As soon as the first class stewardess came around with a bottle of champagne, I held up my hand. She filled one of those plastic goblets. I took it and offered some to Colette.

"Just a sip, thanks."

She took one and coughed. I tossed back the rest and looked down at the Sierra Madre Mountains gliding by. I looked down at Colette's feet. She was wearing the shoes. I considered whether or not we could pull it off in the bathroom.

"Are you nervous?" she said.

"I don't think nervous is the right word. More concerned. Like, am I going to be able to articulate what we're doing back there?"

"I assume they'll be eager to hear about the website more than anything."

"Which all gets back to the tribe, as far as I'm concerned."

"It should be fun, trying to explain it."

"Yes, like Newhart's shtick on explaining baseball to someone who's never seen it."

"Never heard that one."

"It's a laugh. 'So you have two white lines. And you hit the ball and run'."

The stewardess came back by with the champagne bottle and I had her top me off. Colette watched.

"Don't even say it." I looked at my watch. "It's almost four o'clock in New York."

She smiled.

"I've always hated the time change going this way. It's so much easier gaining three hours than losing them."

"Maybe we can order something from room service once we're settled and watch a movie, then get to sleep early."

"Sounds perfect. I brought a sleeping pill."

"Only one?"

"I might have two."

Somewhere over Kansas, they served us a lunch of beef medallions and fresh steamed vegetables. I had two glasses of sauvignon and slept through most of the ensuing movie.

All was a tapestry of lights on black velvet as we came in for a landing at JFK. A chauffer with a sign was waiting for us as we disembarked. He took us to the Omni Berkshire Place, a short walk from the studio. We were treated like royalty and were soon unwinding in our suite.

"Nice view," I said, taking in the skyline from the 15th floor.

"Are we still going for room service?"

"Sure."

I found the menu and had a quick look.

"Well, it's five-star all right. How about some sushi and beer?"

"Sounds good."

We both picked out some rolls and four imported beers. I added two slices of a lemon/coconut cake.

"Should go with sushi," I said.

"I'm sure it will."

We took a quick shower while waiting, put on the sumptuous robes the hotel had provided us and were soon having a minor orgy with the rolls.

"Oh, damn the wasabi," I said at one point and rushed to blow my nose in the bathroom. "I love that stuff," I said, coming back.

A short time later, we were curled up in bed with our second beers and a movie.

"I feel like I've been dragged across the Seven Seas."

"Think you can sleep?" she said.

"Yeah. The question is, will they be able to wake us up in the morning? These sleeping pills are pretty powerful."

"Maybe we should tell the desk to break down the door if we don't answer."

"Good idea. Give them a call."

24

The call from the desk rang through at a quarter to five. I reached for the phone, thanked the desk clerk, fell back on my pillow and threw in a few swear words for good measure. Colette chuckled. I looked over my shoulder at the windows. A crack in the opaque curtains revealed it was still dark outside.

"You have to be out of your mind to get up at this hour."

"The early bird gets the worm," Colette said through her pillow.

"Yeah, funny. I hated hearing that crap when I was a kid. Like there was only one worm, and he was only available at five in the morning…Besides, who the hell wants a worm?"

Colette chuckled again. I slapped her on the ass and got up.

"Easy for you to laugh. You get to sleep in."

"No, I want to go too," she said from under her pillow.

"Yeah, we'll see about that."

Fifteen minutes later, I was coming out of the bathroom, wearing the monogrammed bathrobe and drying my hair with a towel.

"Your turn, soldier."

When Colette failed to respond, I went over and ripped back the covers. She quickly jumped out of bed and disappeared into the bathroom.

There was a thought to go in and nail her against the sink. That was followed by a stab of conscience. The memory of

Catherine would not go away. It had become like a corpse, looking up at me from the bottom of a lake.

I called down to room service and ordered breakfast and was all dressed in pleated cords, Clarks boots and a plaid sports shirt by the time Colette reappeared from the bathroom. She quickly retreated when room service knocked and promptly reappeared when the young man was gone. She nibbled at the scrambled eggs and sausage while dressing.

"No tie?" she said.

"No tie."

I pointed to my suede sports coat hanging from the back of a chair.

"It's my brawny guy look. All I need is a mustache."

"You'd look good in a mustache."

"They tickle."

She laughed and continued dressing between bites of the breakfast. Finally, I stood up and pulled her to me.

"I miss fucking."

She searched my eyes.

"I thought you had lost interest."

I kissed her mouth tasting of toast.

"Just a bit distracted the past few days."

"Hmm," she said and pulled away to resume dressing.

Women. They didn't miss a goddamned thing.

At six o'clock, a limo picked us up out front. Insane. All that trouble to take us two blocks.

Following a warm welcome at the door, a gaggle of female aides swept me off down a long hallway. Wardrobe first, then hair and makeup. I cast a longing look back at Colette for help.

"She's with me," I said as they hurried me off.

"Don't worry. We'll take good care of her," one of them said.

True to her word, an aide accompanied Colette as I was dragged into wardrobe A middle aged woman with too much lipstick and a cigarette voice was waiting for me.

"Going to have to get rid of this plaid shirt, hon. It'll strobe on TV."

I came back out wearing a blue dress shirt. They had tried to sell me on a tie but I refused.

Colette smiled as I was swept from there into hair and makeup and finally into a waiting room. A woman who did a splashy afternoon cook show was already seated there, gabbing away with a guy who had jumped into an icy river to save a young boy and his dog. He was the hero of the day. They hardly noticed us.

Shortly before show time, Megan Starr, the female host quickly made the rounds, introducing herself.

"I'd swear I've seen you somewhere before," I said when she got to us.

She smiled her glorious white smile, set against a mulatto face.

"Well, quite something, your website. Were you ready for all this hubbub when you launched yesterday?"

"No."

"Have you been on TV before?"

"No."

"Well, don't get stressed out."

"I won't. Not much. I'd just rather be back in my treehouse."

"Does he really have a treehouse?" she said to Colette with big eyes.

Colette nodded back.

"So you're a bit of a wood elf."

"I couldn't have said it better myself."

She smiled. Just then, an aide poked her head in the door and Megan excused herself. It was time for the big show.

Another aide came in and led me to the side of the stage. A moment later, the stage manager gave a signal and the show went live. It was strange watching things ramp up without the music and flashy graphics.

After the obligatory morning banter about traffic and weather and whatever trouble was going on in the world that day, Megan introduced me.

"Our first guest is the scion and sole heir of Robert Fitzgerald, renowned Silicon Valley entrepreneur, and a successful entrepreneur in his own right, whose simple idea has just exploded onto the internet. So, please, let's give a big welcome to Steven Fitzgerald."

I walked out into the bank of blinding lights. I had been told to wave but made do with a respectful nod of my head in the direction of the audience. After shaking hands with the other two hosts, I sat down and waited for the applause to abate.

"So, my god, where to begin," Megan said.

She held up several papers, each of them with a front page article about our company in their media section. George, the male cohost turned his laptop to face the cameras.

"The lead story on Huffington Post. And dozens of other sites. You're literally everywhere. How does that make you feel?"

"Uncomfortable," I said.

The audience laughed.

"But why?" Erin, the other female cohost said bouncily. "You're young. You're rich. You're famous."

She made eyes at the audience.

"Even good looking. What's not to like?"

I looked at George.

"I was born rich by accident, I'm human by necessity."

Clearly intrigued by my play on Montesquieu, George leaned forward in his chair with a wry grin animating his craggy face, his eyes squinting as though peering through heavy fog.

"Did I miss something?" Erin said with a pleading look at the audience.

George answered for her.

"I believe he's saying that in the world filled with so much suffering and inequality, it's unseemly for a man to parade about his riches. Is that correct, sir?"

"Something like that."

"I'll tell you what I'm dying to know," Megan said, jumping into the conversation. "A representative from your company said something about a *tribe* when I spoke with her yesterday."

Megan pretended to be perplexed for the audience.

"So, what is this *tribe* and would it have anything to do with how National Roll Call got started?"

"It would, yes."

"Okay, so do tell."

"About the tribe?"

"Sure. About both."

"Well, about the tribe, I happened to be watching this PBS special about indigenous tribes in the Amazon one day and thought, now there's a gig."

With the audience in an uproar, George leaned farther forward in his chair, his smile even wider.

"But it was a revelation for me. You know, this idea of working together collectively. You make the spear tips, I'll skin the hides. Anyway, it was in that spirit that I laid the foundation for what we're doing back in California."

"So, are you suggesting that we abandon the comforts of modern civilization and return to our pastoral roots?" George said.

"Sure, why not? I believe my mates are out in the parking lot with their spears and fur loin clothes right now."

The audience broke out in laughter again. George remained staring at me with his craggy smile.

"Look, I'm not suggesting that *anyone* do *anything*. I'm just saying that, for me, it was a revelation. Like, wow, that's us ten thousand years ago, a tribal tradition that must reach back hundreds of thousands of years and probably even millions in our DNA. So civilization comes along and plucks us out of that tribal framework and then what? Is it possible that every social experiment from that moment forward has been our attempt to regain a lost sense of belonging?"

"Fascinating. So, you're clearly not an admirer of the rugged individualist."

I scoffed.

"One of the great fictions of all time, in my humble opinion."

"For all your money, you're sounding like a communist," Erin said.

"Funny. I'm feeling like one too."

Erin stared aghast as the audience laughed.

"Look, all I'm saying is, every fortune is built on the backs of the common man and woman. Without the salt of the earth, the whole thing collapses. Einstein had alluded to this. His sense of guilt over being glorified, when his whole life was propped up by the work of countless others. Anyway, I'd prefer to think of myself as a tribalist. It's not the same as communism but I suppose they're close."

"But don't you think that families already serve the role you're ascribing to your tribe," Megan said.

"Sometimes, sure, but you can hate your parents and still find someone within the tribe to admire as a role model. Again, you watch how these indigenous tribes function and the tribe is the core social unit, not the family. You grow up learning from everyone. The wisdom is communal."

"Something like the role small towns once played in America," George said.

"Exactly. Like Rockwell's painting of a town hall meeting. A man gets up to speak his peace and everybody listens respectfully. You're getting close there. It's the equivalent of sitting around a fire and retelling the myths."

"That painting was one of my favorite images growing up as a girl," Megan said.

"Yeah, it's the image of togetherness. Of a *tribe*. Now look at us today. We have our families, hopefully, and friends, but

317

too often we live out our lives as isolated social units, in our separate little cubicles, in jobs that demean us. I think a lot of people are dying to get out of that trap."

"What you're attempting to do sounds very idealistic," George said. "But is it practical?"

"Probably not." I looked at the audience and waited for their renewed laughter to subside. "But that's what our tribe is trying to figure out. Can a group of people, founded on such principles, long survive?"

A warm glow washed over George's smile with my allusion to Lincoln.

"Okay, so you have a tribe," Megan said. "Please tell us how National Roll Call evolved out of that."

"We needed some dough."

There was more laughter.

"So, your tribe is not above capitalism," George said.

"Not above free enterprise."

"And you're saying there's a difference."

"I think so. Commerce is natural to human beings. Silk and spices from the east. Tobacco and sugar from the New World. Trade. Innovation. Entrepreneurship. You can never suppress the human spirit but these increasingly large oligarchies today? Or this madness on Wall Street? Flipping burgers has become a derogatory term, but guys and gals like that serve a real purpose in life. What godly good use are credit default swaps? It's not even capitalism anymore in its original sense. It's like some Monopoly game these people have dreamed up to make a quick buck and justify their ever increasing existence. So, no we're not capitalists, but we're not communists, either. The abiding principle is, everyone's work is of equal importance and everything is done for the good of humanity and this earth as a whole. The environment, the community and the value of human lives come before profit. Money is a means, not an end."

George stared at me, smiling. The entire studio had grown silent.

"I can go on if you'd like," I said.

"No, no. I understand, sir. You're trying to live holistically, but we're still back to needing some dough."

I shrugged.

"Sure. We needed some dough. I've been bankrolling the entire operation up to this point and ultimately that's artificial. You want to be able to say, this thing can stand on its own merits."

"Well, exactly," Erin said. "It's like anyone with a billions of dollars could start their own tribe."

"To which I would say, why not? Would it have been better for me to buy an island and hide inside my fifty thousand square foot mansion?"

Megan pointed at herself and nodded at the audience with a comical face.

I stared until she looked at me. The Namaste sign followed, in response to my obvious disgust. Meanwhile, Erin was gesturing plaintively at the audience.

"I know we're going to get to the bottom of this website idea, sooner or later."

"Okay, look. It was this simple. We had the start of a tribe, I think nine of us at that point, and we were sitting around a restaurant one night, trying to come up with a way to generate income. Now, two or three of us could be said to be truly techy..."

"Would that include you?" Megan said.

"No. I know enough to be dangerous."

"I know someone's father who would be greatly disappointed," Erin said.

I looked at the audience.

"I know we're going to get to the bottom of this website idea, sooner or later."

"Touché," Megan said. "So go on."

"So, out of the blue, this lady Camellia throws out this national roll call idea."

"And is she one of your techy ones?" Erin said.

"No, not at all. She was...how can I put this delicately? Camellia had recently suffered a great personal tragedy and was like this wounded bird we had taken in."

The audience gushed with empathy.

"Yeah. Truly heartbreaking stuff. She was just completely locked up in her shell, hardly speaking, and then...poof...out comes this idea."

"So you stole the idea from her then," Erin said.

I laughed and shook my head at the audience.

"I can see you're really not getting the idea of this tribal business."

Erin made eyes at me and I made them back.

"Look, using our resources for the mutual benefit of every one is the essence of the tribal idea. What? You think she should have patented the idea first and licensed it to the rest of us?"

"Well, I guess I would have."

While the audience laughed, George spoke up.

"So you're saying that the tribe engages in free enterprise, yet shares everything in common?"

"Yes and no. It's not that simple."

Megan smiled at the audience.

"I know we're going to get to the bottom of this tribal business, sooner or later..."

"Okay," she said over the laughter. "We'll be right back with Steven Fitzgerald and talk more with him about National Roll Call and *the tribe!*"

As soon as we were off camera, a master of ceremonies came forward to entertain the audience. A flurry of aides appeared onstage to check our makeup and offer refreshments.

"You're doing great," Megan said with a pat on my arm. "You've got the audience eating out of the palm of your hand."

I nodded as she was being whisked away by some of the production crew. George and Erin were otherwise engaged, leaving me alone. I looked side stage for Colette but she was obviously still stuck in the green room.

A few moments later, Megan rushed back onstage, the production manager started counting with his index finger, three, two, one and you're on.

"Welcome back everyone and we're still with Steven Fitzgerald, scion of the Fitzgerald fortune and self-described founder of a new age tribe."

I felt a sudden itch behind my ear.

"So, Steven, before getting back to our discussion of National Roll Call and *the tribe*, please tell us a bit about your relationship with your father. It appears that you were never the least bit involved in his empire."

"No. I was never inclined towards his line of work. And the two of us were never all that close."

"A difficult childhood?"

"Not a particularly warm and fuzzy one, no. My parents had a fairly loveless marriage and my father was always consumed with his work. I hardly saw him as a boy and my mother had her own demons."

"So, you were neglected."

"Oh, I wouldn't say that. I had everything I could possibly want. How can you complain? But I was raised mostly by nannies and butlers. It was hardly the stuff of Ozzie & Harriet."

"So then you lived the life of a playboy for a number of years," George said with his smile. "Drifting around the Mediterranean…"

"…waiting for the old man to croak."

The audience gasped. George's sagacious smile never wavered.

"Look, my mother is gone and my father had a brother and two nephews, all three of whom are thoroughly entrenched in his software business, so quite honestly, I had pictured them inheriting the fortune."

"So it was a complete surprise to you," George said.

"Not entirely, but I certainly never expected to inherit the whole thing."

"And what was your first thought upon learning that you had?"

"What would your thoughts be to awaken and learn that you're a billionaire?"

"I suppose to think, and now I can do everything I have ever wanted."

"Exactly. And so the question becomes, what is it that you have always wanted to do? There are people starving in India and all that."

"And so you had a Siddhartha moment and thought, I'll go find a way to use this money for the betterment of mankind."

"Yes, but that did not come immediately."

"Ah, so you did think of a new Ferrari and the villa in Cannes."

I squirmed a bit in my chair, cleared my throat and darted another glance out at the audience. Everyone was waiting.

"Look, the truth is, I had met a lady and, foolish as it seems now, I went about trying to fashion a little paradise for the two us."

Every woman in the studio gushed, Erin and Megan included.

"And then she was gone. I was sitting around with my wounds, that PBS program came on and I had a revelation."

"About a tribe," George said.

"About a tribe."

"So tell us a bit about how your tribe is structured?"

"It's not very much, really."

George smiled and waited for the laughter to subside.

"So, it's not a commune?"

"Oh god no. In fact, my concept of it was precisely the opposite. Let's not lay down a bunch of rules beforehand. Let's just gather a group of people together and see where things grow organically from there."

"So you literally started with no rules," George said with fascination.

"No rules. We have a few of them now. The two basic ones are, you can't be admitted to the tribe or kicked out without a super majority vote."

"And that's it?" Erin said.

"We have a few more. About how to run our council meeting, for instance, but for the present, no. I'm sure we'll dream up more as things go along."

"But this sounds like it would lead to total chaos," George said.

"It has."

Megan looked at the audience with an ironic smile and waited for their laughter to subside.

"But seriously," she said, looking back at me. "It's just whatever goes? In whatever direction?"

"The ultimate form of moral relativism?" George said, his brow wrinkled up and squinting through even heavier fog now.

"Call it moral relativism if you like, but I think it's more contextual."

"Contextual. Please explain."

"Well, I go back to those indigenous tribes. If a child breaks the tribe's mores, the punishment is ostracism. That's it. If you wish to do these things, fine, there's the jungle. Have at it. So the child wanders alone for a day and decides, okay, you've got me. I'll play along, since I'm nothing if I'm not part of the tribe. When your survival and the survival of the tribe are synonymous, you instinctively choose what preserves both, because belonging to something is in your best interest. I can't see where it's any different from what our founding fathers had called the common good. Or your small town. People are healthier when they feel part of community. It's in our DNA."

"It just sounds so unwieldy and chaotic somehow," Megan said.

"Have you read the news lately?"

323

"You've got me there. It certainly is a fascinating idea."

George was leaning forward in his chair and staring at me with his smile.

"I can see the attraction on an organic level but it does seem to me that you'd soon run into trouble. Even if it's just one warring tribe against another. Won't conflicts inevitably arise? Isn't that ultimately why mankind found sanctuary in the laws and mores of civilization? To avoid the warring tribes?"

"It's a valid point, to which I would say, we're still evolving as a species, right? Take the peace movement of the sixties. That could not have happened without an explosion in technology and communications. The war was ten thousand miles away but we were all witnessing it from our living rooms. And that fact is even more true today. We watch it from our phones. You can no longer commit some horror without the whole world seeing it and I believe an aversion to this kind of brutality is now being passed down from generation to generation. However haltingly, the urge for peace has entered our gene pool."

"But still there is war," George said.

"Sure. Some people don't get it yet. In fact, for some, war is still a very profitable enterprise, but that does not negate that fact that we're on an evolutionary path."

"So you would agree with the Seville Statement," George said with a sage smile.

"Not entirely. Probably the last tenet more than the others. I suspect the environment did program us towards violence to a large degree, but we're also capable of being programmed towards peace, as I think you're now seeing."

"What's the Seville Statement?" Erin said.

I looked at George and shrugged.

"A refutation of the Standard Social Science Model, I guess you would say."

"And what's the Standard Social Science Model?"

I looked at George again

"Behaviorism writ large? We're a blank slate, which culture has largely influenced?"

"You can read the likes of Cosmides and Tooby," George said.

"Or Pinker and Dawkins and really get your head screwed up."

"Well, we're really digressing down into the weeds here," Megan said.

"Exactly," I said. "And I'd rather keep things on a practical level. Let's say you're commuting back and forth to work two hours every day. And you're in a job you really don't like. So you lie there at night, tossing and turning and wondering, how in hell do I get out of this rut? Now juxtapose that with our tribe. Instead of spending ten hours every week on the freeway, you spend ten hours working in the community garden. If you're a doctor, you look after the health of the members. If you need a doctor and you're a carpenter, or an accountant, you do some work on his house or on his books in exchange. In the meantime, you're surrounded by nature, you're living a sustainable lifestyle and have a sense of wellness because you're connected to something. I'm not saying this is a solution for everyone and every problem facing humanity, but it's *one* viable alternative. Everyone knows we can't keep on going the way we are."

"And what way is that?" Megan said.

"A Ponzi scheme in which we explode the population, ravage our natural resources and pollute the world until it's uninhabitable."

"Wow," Erin said. "Aren't we talking about young people falling in love and having dreams and starting a family and stuff like that?"

"Sure. But the way I see it, you can no longer have four or five kids and not realize that you're contributing to the death spiral of our species."

"God, this is sounding so grim."

"Well, can you imagine 15, 20, 30 billion people on the face of this earth?"

Erin shrugged.

"But that's where capitalism's headed. The only way to keep it afloat is more mouths and more consumers. What do politicians tell us whenever we're having hard times? 'We need to get people consuming again."

"Well, I'm thoroughly depressed now," Erin said with a forlorn look at the audience.

"So, come join our tribe. We're actually doing something to turn this thing around. Clearly our leaders are helpless to stop things."

"Anyone else for joining a tribe?" Megan said with a hand raised to the audience.

The response was a huge cheer and hands raised throughout.

"So, what are your plans going forward for National Roll Call, Steven?"

"Our only plan is to stay relevant and I think the only way to do that is to stay focused on the truly important issues of our time. Economic fairness. Going green. Population control. Protecting the environment. I'd like to see humor be a part of the equation, but more than anything I want this to be a go to place where people feel their voice can be heard on the most important matters in this world."

"So no Kardashian updates?" George said.

"God no. Nothing even remotely like that."

"And you will come back to share with us how the tribe is doing," he said.

"I would love to. In fact, I'd love to have all three of you out there on location someday. As things mature, of course. We just had our first official tribal council the other day, in a yurt."

"In a yurt," Megan said.

"Yeah. Long story. We're dealing with some local zoning issues. Anyway, we spent most of the meeting deciding how to have a meeting. You wanted to get drunk afterwards."

The audience laughed.

"Actually I think we did, but we have big plans. A cultural arts center. A tech and science center. There's a foundation at the core of it so we'll be doing things to help disadvantaged people of all ages."

"Thank you so much for coming on," George said in his silky, academe style.

"Steven Fitzgerald!" Megan said with one hand pointed at me and one hand urging the crowd on.

"We'll be back with more," George said before the network went to commercial break.

Seeing the hosts stand up, I did too. Megan and Erin came over to thank me. When it was his turn, George shook my hand and leaned in close to my ear.

"Perhaps you'd like to come on to my evening show at some point. I'd love to discuss what you're attempting to do out there at greater length."

"Sure. I'd love that."

"Good, and I wish you the best of luck, sir. I've always admired the compassionate risk takers of this world."

The master of ceremonies had come out to entertain the audience again. The stage was flooded with aides. One of them guided me back towards the dressing room. Colette came out and greeted me with a big hug and a smile.

"You did great," she whispered.

"Thanks. I think it went all right."

"No, it was great."

"Thanks. So, come on. I guess they want their shirt back."

The aide smiled and led me first to wardrobe, where I retrieved my plaid shirt, and then to a bathroom, so I could remove my makeup.

"Are we done then?" I said to her.

"Yes. Your check will be mailed to you."

I thanked her and started out the door with Colette.

"Oh, didn't you want a ride back to your hotel?"

"No, thanks. We'd rather walk."

Colette and I hurried down the sidewalk on a frigid winter morning.

25

In passing another side street, Colette and I were hit with a blast of cold arctic air and laughed. The wind coming up from the harbor had cut right through our clothing.

"Jesus, it's cold."

"Welcome to New York," she said.

"Yeah, thanks and goodbye."

We huddled closer together and hurried on among the morning pedestrians, all of them bundled up like Eskimos.

We passed the sign for a show and Collette squeezed my arm.

"Should we stay over? Seems like we ought to see a show or something."

I groaned.

"No?"

"No, I just want to go home. Are you okay with that?"

"Sure. I lived here for years. I've seen it all."

"Good. We can be home in a few hours and snuggling up in bed."

We came to the next side street and hurried across, laughing again.

"I'll bet you the gang is dying to hear the news," Colette said. "Want to call them?"

"You do it." I handed her my phone. "Anne's number is in there in my recent cache."

A few moments later, I was listening to Colette's end of the conversation. She cupped the phone.

"They thought you did great too." Colette started to un-cup the phone and covered it again. "And Kristy's bummed because you didn't mention her by name."

"Tell her I was too *focused*."

"Steven said to tell Kristy he was too focused."

A moment later, I heard laughter through the phone.

"She's laughing."

"So I heard."

Colette went on talking.

"I'd better get off," she said. "We're almost to the hotel and it's absolutely freezing out here. It's in the teens but feels like twenty below."

Colette exchanged a few more words with Anne and hung up. I took the phone.

"God, it is cold," she said with a shiver.

We came to the hotel and rushed in past the doorman. It was like stepping into the tropics. Upstairs, we quickly gathered our things, left a tip on the bed and rushed back downstairs.

Within the hour, we were on our way home and sipping champagne. I could see my treehouse up ahead and felt greatly relieved to have the episode behind me.

It was going on late afternoon when we finally pulled off the highway and onto our road. All I wanted was to hide out for a couple of days but Colette needed to pick up Hugo at the tech center, which meant there was no escaping the gang and relating at least some of our story.

We were met with cheers at the door. Everyone was there save for Yvonne and Dr. McDonald. We hugged all around. Hugo barked away at seeing Colette. I gave Camellia an especially long hug.

"You see what you've started?" I said, standing back.

She stared with her faraway look.

"We can all thank you. And welcome to you," I said to Elicia. "I see you made the cut."

"Yeah," she said and threw her hands out playfully.

"And the vet?" I said.

There were looks all around.

"We'll have to discuss that later," Anne said.

"Dude, some weird shit went down," Kyler said.

"We all agreed to hold a council meeting and discuss it then," Anne said.

Kyler made eyes at me.

"You did great, by the way," David said.

"Yeah, it's so cool that they let you go on about the tribe," Anne said.

"Yeah. I guess we can thank George for that. He seemed to be sincerely interested. Even asked me to come on his evening show."

"Wow, cool," Anne said.

"And no mention of me," Kristy said with a crosswise pump of the fists.

"I did but they edited it out."

"Oh, sure."

"So, how's it going here?"

"Can you say, overwhelmed?" David said.

"Yeah. Mainly with the phones," Anne said.

"The website is pretty much taking care of itself," David added. "Had one glitch but I quickly fixed it, and we had to increase the size of our server. Otherwise, everything's cool."

"So the votes are still rolling in."

"Oh yeah, over twenty million total so far," David said. "And it's a wipe out. Almost five to one for ditching the electoral college. Dig this. There's talk on Capitol Hill about appointing a committee to consider the matter."

"Yeah, far out. We saw that on our phones while we changing planes in San Francisco. Have you taken ad buys?"

"That's one of the things we need to discuss," Anne said.

"What's to discuss?" Kristy said. "I say take that money."

331

"Surprise, surprise."

"Yeah, I think we should be careful with who we accept as advertisers," Anne said. "It goes to our brand. I mean, do we really want Shell Oil on our site?"

"Maybe we could have left and right advertising," I said.

"Hey, that's an idea," Kristy said.

"She's all about money," Donny said.

"You bet I am. So are you two going to roll up your sleeves and chip in or what?"

I groaned.

"Okay. Out of the tribe," Kyler said.

"Look, I'll jump in here tomorrow, for sure, but right now, I'm exhausted. I just want to grab something to eat and crawl into bed." I yawned involuntarily and so did Colette. "We've hardly slept the past two days."

"Well neither have we," Kristy said.

"All right, kick me out of the tribe but I'm going to bed."

"Go ahead you two," Anne said. "There's a ton to discuss but it can wait until tomorrow."

"Thanks."

I yawned again.

"As soon as we're back on planet earth, I'll come down and chip in."

Outside, I asked Colette if she still wanted to come over.

"Do you want me to?"

"Sure," I said.

We stopped at her place to grab a change of clothes, drove over to mine and were soon putzing about in our robes as evening settled over the forest. I put a frozen gourmet lasagna dish into the microwave and the scent of red sauce filled the house. We made a salad, poured some red wine, sliced some bread and were soon indulging ourselves at the table.

"Hmm, good," I said.

"For frozen, it's pretty savory."

"I wonder what they meant about the vet?"

"He must not have fit in."

"Yeah, but they could have just said that. Something weird must have gone down."

"Remember Yvonne's warning."

"Yeah, sad. You have to feel for those guys."

After the meal, we made love, then let Hugo join us in bed for a movie. I kept yawning and eventually fell asleep with the movie still on. When I awakened, Colette was asleep and the TV was off. I slipped off to the bathroom. Colette stirred when I came back.

"I'm hungry again," I said.

"Which hungry?"

I pulled the covers down and kissed her neck and back.

She moaned and reached out a hand.

"Hugo's bones are in my purse downstairs."

At hearing the word, his ears had pricked up.

"You want one?" I said.

In response, he immediately jumped off the bed. With bone in maw, he was content and I slipped back upstairs.

Colette moaned again when I resumed kissing her back. I continued down until I was at her soft buttocks, then deftly flipped her over and got my lips into her womb. It was a sweet, salty pungent scent that I loved to savor.

Once she had orgasmed, I crawled up and gently swam in a sea of ecstasy.

Later we had ice cream and watched the movie again and fell asleep before midnight with Hugo lying at our feet.

I awakened early the next morning with Colette curled up on the other side of the bed. It was raining and I still did not want to face the world. I closed my eyes again but found my mind racing with a thousand things.

I started out of bed, hoping not to disturb Colette but she noticed the movement and reached out a hand. I kissed it.

"The world is calling."

She touched my face tenderly and dropped her hand. I went down to make coffee and took Hugo out while it was brewing. Back upstairs, I sliced some hard crust bread and stuck it in the toaster. The first cup of coffee went down like a bum guzzling wine. When the toast came up, I slathered it with butter and strawberries preserves. Hugo got the remnants of my slice.

Colette was sleeping again when I went up to shower. I tiptoed through getting dressed and was weighing whether or not to kiss her before running off when she spoke.

"Is there coffee?"

"Yes. Would you like me to bring you a cup?"

"No, I'll go down and get it."

I went to kiss her now.

"Thanks for letting me sleep."

"You're welcome."

"Should I come help?"

"All hands on deck."

"Okay. I'll be over in a bit."

I kissed her again.

"Hugo's already been out."

"Thanks."

"Just take one of the golf carts home."

"Thanks."

I threw on my bomber jacket and suede fedora and hurried down to my truck. Kristy and David were at the helm when I walked in. I said good morning on my way in for another cup of coffee.

"So, where do we stand?" I said, coming back out and taking a seat.

"The phones are the biggest problem," David said. "Or at least the most immediate one."

"So we made an executive decision this morning and hired a professional answering service," Kristy said. "Anne and I wrote up a short script."

"So we're good for now."

"For now," David said. "We weren't sure if we were supposed to run this through the council."

"We'll we operating a twenty-four hour council if we have to run every little idea through it."

"Yeah."

"So what else? What's going on with the ads?"

"The requests keep coming in."

"It's endless," Kristy said.

"I wouldn't be surprised to look out the windows and see them parked in front."

"Why can't we just take their cash?" Kristy said.

"I think that is one thing we *should* run by the council."

"I'm freaking out," she said.

"Yeah. I can tell. So, is everyone coming in?" I asked David.

"I haven't talked to everyone yet this morning but yeah, I think so."

"So what else needs to be decided right now?"

The door opened and Elicia and Anne came in. Elicia was glowing. Her very white teeth were rarely hidden.

"Did you sleep well?" Anne said.

"Enough. I'm back from the dead. So what's the deal with the vet?"

"All of us agreed not to discuss it until the next council meeting."

"Oh fuck that. Come on. I wasn't here. What the hell happened? Elicia?"

Her smile acquired a tinge of concern.

"I guess *loose cannon* comes to mind? *Unhinged*?"

"Is that what you think, Anne?"

"Maybe not as much as everyone else but I can see why they'd feel that way."

"So, what the hell did he do?"

"It was like he was on meth or something," Anne said.

"I thought he was supposed to be sober?"

"That's what Kyler thought too," she said.

"You know what we gleaned," David said. "That he did most of his time in the war zone as a private contractor."

"Oh, so he's a mercenary."

"Yeah, I guess."

"No, he is, David. That's what they are. Don't even get me started on that one. Instead of paying our soldiers decent money, we're giving it to those fuckers. Fucking Cheney and Halliburton. It drives me insane just thinking about it."

Everyone reflexively backed off a few paces. I smirked in response.

"So, is this kind of how things went the other night?"

They all nodded.

"Yeah, sorry but privatizing war just pisses me off. So, if this guy's a bummer, forget it. We don't need that kind of energy around here."

"I think it's the way he left the restaurant that has everyone freaked out," David said. "We didn't lay down a verdict on him or anything but I think he knew he wasn't welcome."

"So?"

"So, it was like you could feel he was planning something."

"Okay. So we might need a restraining order?"

"Maybe our own special forces unit," David said jokingly.

"Oh brother. So I imagine Kyler really has his tail between his legs."

"You know Kyler. He pretty much takes everything in stride but you could tell he didn't want to run into this guy at a meeting ever again."

"All right. Well, that's one more thing for the council to decide. What's next?"

"I think we should call all these potential advertisers," Kristy said.

"Old money bags here."

"That's right."

"All right. How about this? Let's write up a spiel to tell them. 'We were caught a bit flat footed by the volume of traffic and requests for ad space so we're working up a pricing schedule. We'll be making calls and taking orders tomorrow morning. All calls will be returned in the order they were received.' Does that sound fair? I mean, that's our basic message but everybody's free to wing it from there."

"Sounds good to me," Anne said.

"I'm typing it up right now," David said.

"More coffee," I said and headed for the kitchen.

"So tell us about New York," Anne called after me.

I returned with my coffee and recounted our journey.

"George Cross is a trip." I pretended to be him. " 'And what exactly do you mean by *the tribe*?' He's like a hookah smoking caterpillar and Cheshire cat thrown together. Nice guy though. I could tell he was sincerely interested."

"What's it like being in a big studio?" Kristy said.

"Come on. You've seen these shows. I don't know where they get these people but I'm sure they're all high on caffeine and Tupperware."

They laughed.

"So what about Dale? And the garden? And anything else that's been going on around here?"

"You were only gone thirty-six hours," Kristy said. "Relax."

"Yeah. I'm focused."

She laughed.

"So?"

"So, Dale started the work shed foundation yesterday and I don't know about the rest. It's raining. I need more coffee."

"All right, Christ. So what about this pricing schedule, David."

"Here. I printed these up for you to look at. This is what sites with similar stats are charging for space."

I flipped through the sheets.

"Okay. So we put something together that mirrors these rates and run it by the council this evening?"

Everyone agreed.

"Great. What else?"

"Nothing except for deciding who gets to advertise on our site," Anne said.

"Do we have a list?"

"There were hundreds of calls. We haven't had time to work through all of them yet."

"Why not?"

"Because we don't have enough bodies!" Kristy said coming back with her coffee.

"Well, get them."

"God. I thought this was a tribe. Who appointed you the boss?"

"Me!"

I made eyes at her and she made them back.

"I'll start calling right now," Elicia said.

"You know what? You're perfect for it, Elicia. Let's make a list of all the messages in the order they were received and start calling."

"There are hundreds of calls," David said.

"So, who types the fastest here?"

"That would be me," Kristy said.

"Okay, pull up a document and get ready. Anne do you know the number?"

"For?"

"The answering service message line."

"Right here."

"Okay, you ready, Kristy?"

"For what?"

"I'm going to put the messages on speaker phone, you start typing and I'll pause the messages each time you fall behind."

"Wait a minute," David said. "What are the rest of us going to do? We won't be able to think if you do it like that. Why don't you just have Kristy put on these headphones."

"Because I didn't know we had headphones."

David handed them to Kristy.

"So, are you all right? You still need me to pause the messages for you?"

"No, I'm fine."

She went to work.

"So, what else?" I said.

"More bodies," David said.

"You've said that. Any ideas?"

"I have a friend," Elicia said. "She's a graphic artist and would love to join us."

"Okay. I guess we need one of those, don't we?"

"We do," David said.

"All right, what else do we need in terms of staff?"

"Mostly techy people," Anne said. "Artsy, techy people. Between me and Elicia and Kristy, we can run the office."

"What about Donny? Where the hell is he?"

"He worked really late last night," David said. "He'll probably be in here soon."

"But he's techy, right?"

"More artsy techy, but yeah."

"So how many more do we need?"

"I think at least four besides me. We can't really count on Donny since he's your eco management guy. We can use him to fill in a bit but…"

"All right. Everyone make a list of people you know. And try to strike a balance. You know, male and female?"

"We already have some people in mind," Anne said.

"Okay. I can see where this is headed. It's going to start looking like a college dorm around here. So what else?"

"We have over a week yet but we need to start working on our next issue and our guest columnists."

"I have an idea," Elicia said.

"We're all ears."

"Why don't we set up a place on the site where people can vote on which issue to vote on?"

"That's a great idea," Anne said.

"Yeah," I said. "But we should give people a list to choose from, right David?"

"Yes, please. We let them make their own suggestions and I'll need a Google like algorithm. I don't even want to think about it."

"That's cool," Elicia said. "I just think it will get people more engaged."

"More *i n v e s t e d*," I said.

"Whatever," she said.

I pretended to strangle her too.

"All right. Let's look at the headlines and cull some options."

"There are some obvious ones," Anne said. "Abortion. Funding the Ukraine war. Supreme Court reform."

"Yep. Definitely those. Let's see what else is in the news."

All of us stood over David's shoulder and watched as he surfed from site to site. Donny came in as we stood there.

"What's going on?" he said.

"Just moving the ball forward," I said.

He joined us and the conversation continued about which issues to choose. Kristy hit the pause button, took off her headphones and headed for the kitchen.

"God, I see everybody's having fun but me."

"I can spell you," Anne said. "You're right. No one should have to do it all."

"Thank you," Kristy said, coming back with her fresh cup of coffee.

"How far did you get?" I said.

"Fifty calls…Out of over five hundred!"

"And that's it?" I laughed at the sour look on her face. "All right, we'll all spell you. At least anyone who can type."

"More bodies," she said.

"Council meeting," I said.

"The sooner the better," she said.

"Fine. I'll call Colette and get her down here. What about Kyler? Dr. McDonald? Yvonne?"

"Yvonne's working."

"So's my husband."

"I think Kyler's in bed," Donny said.

"So somebody go wake him up."

"Says Henry the Fifth."

I pretended to strangle Kristy now.

Donny shrugged and went back out into the rain. I looked back at the others.

"It's time to start talking money. How much to pay everyone and what to do with what's left over."

"Isn't that council business?" Anne said.

"Sure, but I think it's best if we come up with some recommendations. Otherwise we'll be there for hours just listening to everyone's BS."

"Wow," Kristy said.

"Okay, ideas! Is that better? So let's roll up our sleeves and get to work."

"Ya vol, mon commandant," Kristy said and gulped her coffee.

26

The storm broke just before dusk. Gray clouds clung to the highest tree tops as darkness settled over the wet forest. I opened my windows to the cool air and heard that woodcock calling off in the distance.

After a moment's reverie there on the shore of evening, I looked back at the list of prospective advertisers in front of me. Five of us had taken roughly one hundred names a piece and I had called most of mine. A day of that and you wanted a drink. I poured a snifter half full of brandy, drank and looked again at the list.

Enough for now, I decided, polished off the brandy and headed down to the forest floor. The damp evening was pregnant with the scent of wet bark and pine needles.

Near the back of the cottages, I ran into Dr. McDonald and Kristy. Dr. McDonald smiled, patted me on the back and spoke with his chuckling, cheery Midwestern voice.

"A bit more than you had bargained for?"

"In my wildest dreams, maybe. At least now, everything is possible."

"When I saw my wife perusing '65 foot yachts, I knew things were going well."

Kristy kicked his foot.

"Actually, I've decided that we should donate everything to a foundation serving needy kids."

"Forget it," Kristy said.

Dr. McDonald and I chuckled.

"Hey, I earned that yacht," she said.

"Yeah. But why don't we focus on the welfare of the tribe first, huh? The idea is to create a life worth living out here. Not to get rich."

"Easy for you to say."

"Yes, and there are some things that only the rich will ever understand."

I laughed at the look on her face.

Hearing more voices, I turned and found Donny, Yvonne, Kyler, Camellia and Colette coming up the path behind us. I went back and joined them with my arm around Colette.

"Wow, I love the forest right now," Kyler said. "It's like something out of a magical fairy tale."

"It is a magical fairy tale," I said.

"Yeah! I love that!"

We had come to the steps and started up the knoll towards the yurt in pairs. At the top, we all paused in a moment of reverence. The sky was burnished red with the last light of day. Lingering storm clouds hugged close to the darkening sea. Then, with the fire having faded from the sky, we turned and went inside. Anne and Elicia already had the stove and tea going. David was lighting up a second oil lamp. I sat down and made myself comfortable among the pillows.

"So," I said. "Other than for the, uh, vet episode, was the last meeting generally better than the first one?"

"A little," David said.

"It was a lot better," Anne said.

"It's still really easy to get lost in all the minutia."

"It will be interesting to see how all this newfound wealth affects things?" Yvonne said.

"There's a positive thought," Anne said.

"I'm a realist," Yvonne said.

"I'm an impressionist," I said.

That brought laughter.

"I'm an abstractionist," Dr. McDonald said.

"I'm a cubist," Colette said.

"What am I?" Kyler said.

"Pop art," I said.

"Yeah!"

"So what am I?" Kristy said.

"A determinist," I said.

"Real funny," Kristy said to everyone's laughter.

As Anne and Elicia were passing out the tea, Dr. McDonald hit the gong.

"Welcome all grand poohbahs," I said. "The high order of the intergalactic council is now in session."

"So what's first?" Anne said.

"I'm curious about this list of potential new tribal members," I said.

David pulled out a piece of paper and unfolded it.

"Only one copy? What, are you paying for the paper?"

He pretended to shrug sheepishly and read off the names with their qualifications. There was Ashley, web design, mobile application developer, Hans, software engineer, cloud architect, Kato, IT consultant, data modeler and Tara, a graphic artist who could do web design and mobile application development. They were variously, from 22 to 27 years old.

"By the way, we consolidated these from a list made by me, Anne and Elicia."

"Sounds like they're all worthy of consideration to me," I said.

"The king has spoken," Kristy said.

"Grand poohbah of all grand poohbahs will do, and all I said was, they *sound* like they're worthy of consideration."

"So we should discuss them," Kristy said.

"So discuss away."

I looked around the circle. No one spoke.

"What?"

"I guess we're all just a bit skittish from last Friday," Yvonne said.

"Yeah, I meant to thank you, Kyler, by the way."

"Hey, boss man. I just thought, wow, this is the perfect guy for us to help. How was I supposed to know he was a nutcase?"

"Wow," Kristy said. "I don't know what you guys think but the men who go to war are the real heroes and patriots of this country to me."

"Look, Kristy. I already told you. This guy was a hired gun, a mercenary. He went over there to get rich, not to serve his country so don't get me started."

"Wow," Kristy said.

"Yeah. I'm not even sure I'm onboard with all this bleeding heart BS in the first place. 'War will exist until that distant day when the conscientious objector enjoys the same reputation and prestige that the warrior does today'."

"I'm sure. I suppose that's a famous quote from someone," Kristy said.

"President Kennedy," Dr. McDonald said.

"Oh."

I nodded at Kristy.

"So, please, let's forget about this guy and move on. I assume these four new individuals don't have a rap sheet."

"Not that I'm aware of," David said.

"Maybe we should at least run a background check on them," Kristy said.

"Like we did on you."

"I'm an all American girl."

"Indeed. So…getting back to reality."

Kristy pretended to kick me with everyone laughing.

"Okay, I make a motion that we have dinner with these four individuals tomorrow night and if we all get along with them, it's thumbs up on the spot."

"Without a formal council vote?" Kristy said.

I went for her throat and she fought with my hands.

"The whole tribe will be present. How's that not a council vote? What do you folks say in AA, Kyler? Keep it simple, stupid?"

"Yeah! I'll second that motion."

"Look, Kristy. We need to grow the tribe with qualified people, and fast, so?"

I looked from face to face. There were looks all around and a raise of everyone's hand.

"So, what's next, Anne?"

"I think we need to discuss salaries."

"Well, it seems to me that we need an income stream first so why don't we discuss this advertising business?"

"What's to discuss?" Kyler said. "Just give me some of that big time money."

"I'm with Kyler," Kristy said.

"Gosh, I never would have imagined."

She went to kick me again.

"Okay, Anne, you were the one who brought it up. Are we going to let Scumbag Oil advertise on our site or not?"

"I liked your idea of having right wing and left wing advertisers," David said.

"Who decides which is which?" Yvonne said.

"Not them," I said. "That's the whole point. If we let the advertisers decide, they'll just put themselves in whatever column makes them look good."

"Like the oil companies running one of those 'we're all about the environment' ads," Donny said.

"Exactly. It's a tough one. You don't want to discriminate. It wouldn't be in keeping with the spirit of our website. You know, a fair and honest forum for the American people to voice their opinion. But I'd still like to see these fat cats being called out for what they are."

"As expressed by another fat cat," Kristy said.

"There goes your 65' yacht."

"Hey."

"I wonder if we're getting into first or fourteenth amendment issues here," Dr. McDonald said.

"You mean, if we pigeonhole them as right wing pricks?"

"Yeah."

"Probably. I guess I can run it by my attorney,."

"But we are calling them right wing pricks."

"Funny," Elicia said. "But no one ever gets called a left wing prick."

"And I suppose we all know why."

"Oh boy," Kristy said.

"So, are we ready to vote?" Anne said.

There was a general agreement.

"Wait a minute," I said. "What are we voting on? There are two issues here. One, do we pick and choose our advertisers and, two, do we have left and right accreditation?"

"I think they're the same thing," Anne said.

"Here we go," Kyler said.

I flopped backwards on the pillows.

"Look. Here's my position. I don't want Shell Oil on our website *unless* we can call them out for what they are. Like Donny said. I don't want one of these, 'we're all about the environment' ads on our site when they have a record of being environmental pigs."

"I think that approach is entirely wrong," Yvonne said.

"How so?" I said.

"It's like the scarlet letter. You're just trying to shame someone in public."

"And your solution?"

"Either allow them to advertise or don't take their money at all."

"She has a point," Anne said.

"Okay. I'm taking my football and going home."

"See?" Kristy said. "If the grand poohbah can't have his way, he blows up the ship."

"You'll be lucky to get yourself a dingy and a pair of oars at this rate."

"Ha. That's up to the council to decide."

"Now kids," Kyler said.

I threw up my hands.

"Okay, you know what? Yvonne's right. This really comes down to, do we want to take Scumbag Oil's money or not. You know my feelings, but I *am* only one vote."

"Thank god."

"Yeah, yeah."

"Okay, why don't we just have a couple of quick nonbinding votes," Anne said. "To see where everyone stands."

"Sounds fair to me," I said.

Again, all were in agreement.

"Okay, so who's in favor of allowing *all* advertisers?"

Kristy, Dr. McDonald and Yvonne were in favor. Everyone else was opposed.

"At least we now know who the right wingers are," I said.

"Not necessarily," Dr. McDonald said with a chuckle. "I just think in the spirit of impartiality, we should let everyone in."

"Sure."

"So," Anne said. "Shall I assume that the rest of you are in favor of picking and choosing our advertisers?"

There were nods among us. Kristy stared.

"Look, folks," I said. "Here's what I propose. Let's hold off on any final vote until I can run the legal issues by my attorney. In the meantime, can we agree to avoid the most controversial elements in terms of advertising?"

"Who gets to decide that?" Yvonne said.

"All right. How about this? Let's form a committee comprised of three individuals and they'll decide who's in and who's out."

"So, who's going to be on the committee?" Kristy said. "You?"

"No. But you can be."

"Yeah!" she said.

"All right, all in favor of having a committee to decide on our advertisers?" Anne said.

It was unanimous.

"So," Anne said. "Nominations."

I raised my hand.

"I vote for Kristy, David and Anne."

"That sounds like a fair mix to me," Yvonne said.

"Anyone opposed?" Anne said, looking around the circle. "No? Okay, all in favor."

Everyone raised a hand, save for Kristy. She stared at me with a dumb look on her face, like she had been had.

"Great. You stacked the committee."

"It's a trick I learned from John Marshall."

"Who's John Marshall?"

I explained.

"See? You let the other person win the battle while you win the war."

"Great, you rat."

I laughed.

"So, any other business?" I said.

"Salaries," Anne said. "David and I both took a week off work but we'll have to quit our jobs if things keep on the way they are. It's got to be one way or the other."

"Okay," I said. "But if we're going to pay one person, we have to pay everyone, right?"

"Not me," Yvonne said.

"Or me," Dr. McDonald said.

"Well, I was going to make that point. Pay everyone whose fundamental job is working around here to maintain things."

"Like me," Kyler said.

"Exactly, and Donny."

"So what about Colette and you," Anne said.

"Don't worry about that. That's a matter between the two of us. When we build the arts center and she takes over as director, we'll need to discuss the tribe compensating her at that point but not now."

"Isn't it fun to be the topic of discussion?" she said.

"Sorry, dear."

"May I speak for myself?"

"Of course."

"Thanks. I just wanted to say. I don't need to be paid but I'll gladly help out in any way that I can."

"Great, Colette," Anne said. "So, we have David, Kristy, Donny, Camellia, Kyler, Elicia and me. And possibly four new members of the tribe as of tomorrow. So, are we all going to be paid the same salary and how much will that be?"

I raised my hand.

"Yes," Anne said.

"I think we've already discussed this. Equal contribution, equal pay."

"Does everybody agree with the idea?"

Kristy pretended to grouse and I laughed at her.

Eventually everyone raised a hand.

"Okay, then how much should the salaries be?" Anne said.

"I suggest we start at twenty grand," I said.

"It figures old money bags would say that."

"I think you're down to one of those two dollar Styrofoam boogie boards from 7/11."

"Shut up. The whole council is supposed to decide."

"How about a life vest and some swim fins?"

"Shut up."

"It is a fair question," David said. "Who can survive on twenty grand a year?"

"We can always increase them," I said. "Besides, the deal comes with a free roof over your head."

"Maybe I'm not the right one to speak up on this issue," Dr. McDonald said, "but I tend to concur with Steven. It doesn't seem prudent to overburden the website's cash flow at the start."

"You're right," Kristy said. "You're the wrong person to be speaking up."

"Maybe just a life vest," Dr. McDonald said.

Kristy kicked him.

"All right," Anne said. "I would have to agree too. David and I can do just fine for now with forty thousand a year."

"Sure, because there's the two of you?"

"Kristy, please. You have your husband's income too, and all of us, I'm sure we can survive in the short term. I feel that twenty thousand is adequate for right now and we can agree to readdress the issue whenever it seems warranted. Does anyone want to second the motion?"

"I will," I said.

"Okay, everyone in agreement?"

Again, Kristy pretended to pout before raising her hand with everyone else.

"So, can we order pizza now?" Kyler said.

"First we need to decide on how and when the salaries are to be distributed."

Anne looked around the circle.

"I suggest that we assign your new committee to decide that question too."

"Oh good," Kristy said, rubbing her hands together.

"I second the motion," David said.

"All in favor?" Anne said.

It was unanimous.

"Okay, pizza!"

"Just hang on, pepperoni brain. We need to open up the meeting and air out any other thoughts and concerns."

I looked around the circle.

"I wonder about privacy and security," Dr. McDonald said. "It seems to me that with your appearance on national TV, we've opened ourselves up to hordes of gate crashers."

"I've thought about that too and have reluctantly concluded that I'd better install a gate down at the highway."

"So we're going to be a gated community," Elicia said with a forlorn smile.

"Personally, I'm glad," Dr. McDonald said. "I'd hate to think of that vet guy barreling up here in a personnel carrier."

"Like he'd have one," Kristy said.

"I'd be wary of him too," Yvonne said. "That guy is a classic time bomb."

"Maybe we're getting a little carried away with this?" Elicia said.

There were looks around the circle.

"No, I'm serious," Yvonne said. "He should be getting help. Look. You have to take psyche classes to get a nursing degree and that guy is right out of a text book."

"We all know he's disturbed," Elicia said, "but I prefer to think positive. I don't see him as a guy who would come back here to hurt us."

"I think that's being naïve," Yvonne said.

"Well maybe it is but that's how I prefer to see the world."

"Okay," Anne said. "Shall we leave that as unfinished business for now?"

"No," I said. "Sorry but this is one time where I have to make an executive decision. I do consider this a serious safety issue and I'm not content with leaving that road open to the world."

Everyone looked at me and around the room. I shrugged.

"I'd have to agree," Dr. McDonald said.

"Me too," Yvonne said.

"Okay," Anne said as if speaking for the whole tribe. "Agreed. So let's go around the circle and share something personal."

"You go first," I said.

"Yeah, so I was going to announce this earlier but we've been so caught up in all this other stuff. So, yeah, I'm pregnant."

There was a chorus of oohs and aahs and congratulations.

"Wow," Kristy said. "We've been trying too but I guess you beat us too it."

"And all the more reason to be wary," Yvonne said.

"So, you just found out?" I said.

"Yeah, yesterday. I missed a period and went to see the doctor."

"So what, about six weeks?" Dr. McDonald said.

"Yeah. In fact it's just occurred to me. We were already seeing this one doctor but maybe we should use you now?"

"I'd be happy to keep an eye on things between checkups but I'm an orthopedic specialist. I wouldn't pretend to be an obstetrician."

"Okay. I just thought it would be more in keeping with our tribe and everything."

"No, you're better off with an expert, but day to day, if you need anything, you just let me know. I'm here."

"Yeah, thanks."

David was next and told us about his growing photography website. Camellia thanked everyone for the love and support and said she was just really happy working in the garden. We went around the room, one by one and Elicia was last.

"So, I've had this idea stuck in my craw for a really long time and would love it if the tribe and foundation would look into it with me."

"So, tell us," I said.

"It's about cooperatives. About combining sustainability with bringing back good manufacturing jobs to America. You know, like instead of having the usual top heavy management structure, we'd invest in companies where the employees own everything and call it Co-Opportunity."

"I love the name," I said.

"Yeah, cool, isn't?" Elicia said with a big smile. "I already pitched the idea on the Clinton Foundation website but it didn't get much interest. But maybe now?" she said with another big smile for everyone.

"So, where would you start?" I said.

"Okay, dig this. So now that hemp is legal to grow again..."

"...that evil weed."

"I know, huh? So now that the government has stopped freaking out about it so much, I think hemp clothing is going to be really big and it's totally sustainable and I saw that there's this perfect old abandoned factory in town that we could probably get for nothing."

"I like it," I said and looked around the room. "Anyone else have thoughts?"

"So, what? Would this be part of the tribe?" Kristy said.

"I'd like to see that. This is totally what I think the foundation should be doing. We could help train high school kids at risk. Single moms. *Real vets*? We could do a lot of good on a lot of different levels."

There were nods all around.

"Even you're for it, Yvonne?" I said.

"I'm not against everything," she said with a laugh.

"Okay. So shall we set up a committee to explore this?" I said.

The vote was unanimous. Elicia and Kristy and Donny were chosen for the committee.

"Co-Opportunity," I said. "I love that name."

"Cool, huh?" Elicia.

"Yeah."

There were looks all around.

"Oh, one other thing," Elicia said. "I know this might kind of freak some of you out but I'd really love it if we could trip together."

"Forget it," Kristy said.

"I would have to be with Kristy on this one," Yvonne said.

"But what about the rest of you?"

"Trip on what?" I said.

"Oh, I have some friends who pick magic mushrooms."

"I'm sure. We'll probably all die," Kristy said.

Elicia smiled at her.

"Have you ever taken a trip before?"

"No, and I don't intend to start now."

"What kind of magic mushrooms?" Dr. McDonald said.

"Just forget it, John," Kristy said.

"I'm only asking. What kind of mushrooms are we talking about? There are quite a few psychedelic species."

"Just psilocybin."

"Just psilocybin," Kristy said.

"Well, there is a big difference between those and say, amanita muscaria."

"Of course."

"And why do you think we should do that?" I said.

"I just think we'd end up bonding together better as a tribe. It's like we would see our true selves and have a better understanding of how we fit together. A totally ritualized experience, of course."

"Of course," Kristy said.

I shrugged.

"Is anyone else interested?"

"Wow, I think that would be like totally breaking my sobriety," Kyler said.

"I'm game," Donny said.

Yvonne looked at him and chuckled.

"I'm game too," Anne said.

"I can't believe any of you are actually considering this," Kristy said.

"I'll do it," Camellia said.

"Oh my god," Kristy said.

"Yeah, I don't know," Yvonne said.

"Are you sure?" I said to Camellia.

She nodded.

"I need to pass through to the other side. I need to see where my son has gone."

"This is so weird," Kristy said.

"Why don't we have a show of hands," Anne said. "Who's willing just to consider it?"

Everyone raised a hand except Kristy and Yvonne.

"Are you nuts?" Kristy said to her husband.

He chuckled.

355

"She just asked if we were willing to consider it."

"I'm sure. It'll probably ruin your career. And all our chances of having children."

"That's nonsense," Dr. McDonald said with another chuckle. "And from a clinical standpoint, I must admit to being curious. Are you sure of the quality, Elicia?"

"Oh, absolutely. These people go out picking every year and no one has ever gotten sick. They know what they're doing."

"I can't believe we're even discussing this."

"Well, it seems to me almost settled. Everyone's in but you and Yvonne."

"Well, I'm not going to be the last holdout," Yvonne said.

"Oh great."

"So, you can be the chaperone," I said to Kristy.

"You'll probably all end up in the nuthouse."

"So, you'll own the website and can buy yourself that yacht."

"You bet I will."

"So, dinner tomorrow night with the new potential members of the clan?" I said.

"I'll text them in a minute," David said.

"Anne?"

"Yeah. If that's everything, we'll conclude the meeting."

"Hey, wait a minute," Kyler said. "When are we tripping?"

There were looks all around.

"How about Friday," Dr. McDonald said.

Everyone agreed.

"I want a divorce," Kristy said.

"And on that note, I say we conclude the meeting."

Dr. McDonald struck the gong and after a long moment of silence, everyone stood up.

"Pizza!" Kyler said.

"Is everyone game?" I said.

"Yeah."

"Yeah."

"Sure," Kristy said. "It'll probably be our last supper."

"So, what kind does everyone want?" Kyler said.

There was a general discussion and several pizzas ordered.

"And what about you, boss man?"

"Think I'll have the mushroom special."

There was a moment's pause before everyone broke out in laugher.

27

I awakened the next morning from more unsettling dreams, dreams of a world closing in on me, dreams of things that could never be reached. I rolled over and looked out the windows. A memory came of when I had been wildly, madly in love and I wanted to feel that way again, even though being wildly, madly in love had never worked out all that well for me in the past.

Without answers, I climbed out of bed. It was a beautiful, clear day. The coffee was soon going. My mind was all over the place.

Unable to find peace, I did a splash bath and drove up to find Dale. He was working on the new foundation forms.

"Saw you were on TV," he said with barely a glance up from his work.

"Yeah. Famous now. So how goes it up here?"

"Good. If the weather holds, we should be able to pour tomorrow. What's up?"

"I want to install a gate down at the highway. Would it be too much trouble to distract you again?"

"No. You just need a bit of concrete poured and electrical. Otherwise I'll turn you onto Dennis, my wrought iron guy."

"Fair enough. You good with everything else?"

"Like to get some funds."

"Just drop off an invoice with Tillie and I'll make sure she takes care of you."

"Much obliged."

"No problem."

I left with the name and number of a wrought iron operation.

Back at my place, I called and Dennis promptly answered. He was out on an installation but could stop by that afternoon. I poured another cup of coffee, had some cereal and jumped in the shower.

Toni was next on my list.

"I was just going to call you," she said. "Chaplin has been poking around the city and Coastal Commission, trying to figure out what you're doing."

"So?"

"So, from unnamed sources, I know that when he heard about your subdivision filing, he stormed off."

"Good. Let him stew for a few days and I'll ask him out to lunch."

"I'd make sure he wasn't wired."

"Consider me duly warned. Perhaps I'll have him meet me at my attorney's office."

"Sounds like the prudent course of action to me."

"So? Shall we let this play out a bit longer before we discuss your bill?"

"That's fine."

I hung up and headed over to the tech department in my golf cart. The tech team had decorated the front of the cottage with Christmas lights and a holiday wreath. It was a fine wintry day in the woods.

"Ho ho ho," I said, walking in.

The office was buzzing with activity.

"Cool, isn't it?" Anne said.

"Yes. Thanks. You've reminded me to get out my Christmas stuff."

I rolled up my sleeves and went to work. Those of us who had no other skills answered the phones and made calls and ordered lunch.

At four that afternoon, I dashed down to meet Dennis at the highway. He was a taciturn fellow, but cheerful, with a barrel chest, yellow hair and a tinge of iron dust around his face and ears. He smiled with a tinge of soot on his teeth.

We discussed the gate and he gave me a price on the spot.

"That doesn't include concrete or running the electrical."

"Dale said he'd take care of that. And if I wanted it done yesterday?"

Dennis smiled his sooty smile.

"I usually don't jump clients."

"We had a threat out here. I consider it a serious security matter."

"All right, but if I'm going to bump you, now's the time to do it. I won't have another window for at least a month."

"I'll add 20% for your troubles."

"That's all right."

"No, I insist."

"Let's just get it done. I require a 50% deposit."

I walked back to my truck and wrote out a check.

"Have Dale touch base with me about the concrete and electrical as soon as you can. If it's all a go, I can have the gate out here day after tomorrow."

"I'll take care of it."

We shook hands and went our separate ways.

At seven that evening, Colette and I were walking into the darkened atmosphere of our usual restaurant. As with the entire town, the place was done up with Christmas lights and Christmas cheer. The usual laughter and tinkling of glasses went on in the background

The rest of the tribe was already there. Anne and David introduced us to the potential new members. All of them had fine faces. All of them smiled and said hello as we sat down, save for Hans. He was the software engineer and cloud architect, sported a goatee, was already shaving his head at 27 and had all the expression of a Botox treatment gone wrong. His maroon shirt and black pants fit the image.

360

Kato, the IT consultant and data modeler was a patrician looking Japanese fellow, tall, pale, with black hair and eyes and a face that possessed a measure of warmth, even though it was as expressionless as Hans' was.

Ashley, the graphic artist and web designer, who also doubled in mobile application development, had exquisite porcelain skin, gay, upturned, Oriental looking green eyes and red lips.

When I got to Tara, the web designer and mobile application developer, my heart skipped a beat. Her mane of long auburn hair and pale skin instantly swept me away. She had a fine face, but not too pretty. Just lovely enough that you could look at it for a long, long time. She even made her baseball cap look fetching.

Aware again of Colette's presence next to me, I waved and called for more drinks. With that done, everyone drifted back into conversation. In our thirties, Colette and I looked like the chaperones.

"I feel like someone's parents," she whispered.

"Maybe generations have succumbed to Moore's Law. You're out of date every eighteen months now."

"Daunting thought."

I noticed Tara stealing another look my way and smiled. She smiled back.

"Someone's intrigued," Colette said to me.

"Oh, we were all young and curious once," I said.

"You're not really all that old, Steven."

"According to my theory of generations, I'm Tara's great, great, great, great, great, great, grandfather." I thought about it for a moment. "There might even be another 'great' in there somewhere."

"You know, you can be charmingly full of shit at times."

"Thank you."

I dared not speak my true thoughts. That Tara's beauty had swept me away and caused me to dream, in a way that Colette never had, and probably never would.

I noticed Hans stealing glances at Colette.

"Who's intrigued now?"

"You must be kidding," Colette whispered back. "I'm seeing dungeons."

"I suspect he's very clinical about it."

Kato too snuck a look at Colette.

"Ah, more intrigue."

Amidst the hubbub, folks kept sneaking looks this way and that. I did my best to mind my own business.

The waitress arrived to take our orders. Then the conversation resumed. When the drinks came, everyone paused again for a toast.

"Speech, speech," Kyler said to me.

"I'll save my remarks for the tiramisu. Suffice it to say, I'm delighted to see you kids here. Now make sure you're all home by ten."

"Ha ha," Kristy said. "We don't feel part of this generation either."

"You and the doc are more young *generationny* then me."

Dr. McDonald smiled his sunny smile

"I think as a function of being in college all these years, I still feel connected to the younger crowd. You can't help but be aware of the next and the next and the next permutation as new students come in."

"Yes, you're definitely more permutationny than me."

"So, we're all dying to know," Tara said. "Are we in or out?"

I looked at Colette and shrugged.

"I guess if it was up to us alone, you're very much *in*."

Tara and Ashley high fived each other. I pointed at Kristy.

"We're easy. Here's where you're going to run into trouble."

"I'm sure. I'm the happiest go luckiest person in the whole world."

"Yes, and meanwhile, back on planet earth."

Kristy shoved me.

A short time later, our meals began to arrive. I grabbed the wine list and ordered several bottles of pinot noir—Lynmar Quail Hill Vineyard, Calera Jensen, Mt. Harlan, Etude Heirloom, J. Rochioli West Block and Williams Selyem Westside Road Neighbors—along with several Chardonnays from Mount Eden Estate, all of them vintage 2001-2003.

When I handed the waitress the wine list and looked back at the gathering, Tara was stealing glances at me again. I smiled and put my arm around Colette.

During the meal, I grew lost in a meditation on the growing tribe around me, enjoying the mix of new personalities but also aware of the increased potential for fissures. We were not one amorphous thing anymore, if we ever had been, but an ever more complicated body of moving parts that was morphing into something new as I sat there. Realizing the whole thing was completely out of my control, and that I either accepted that or went mad, I kicked back and tried to enjoy the wine, meal and camaraderie. All the while, the darting exchange of glances with Tara continued.

Finally the waitress and bus boys were gathering up the plates and handing out dessert menus.

"So what, do we all have to have tiramisu?" Kristy said.

"Yes, it's mandated by the communist party," I said.

She made a face.

"So, is it a commune?" Ashley said.

"God no."

"Then what is it?"

"Order your desserts and I'll tell you."

"The grand poohbah is about to speak."

I smiled and ordered the tiramisu. There were more orders for that and the chocolate cake and a few for the orange/coconut hummingbird cake, some a la mode.

Once everything had been delivered, I tinged my glass with a fork and the buzz of conversation paused.

"Hail to the grand poohbah," Kyler said.

"Yes, well, let me start by saying to our four guests. Or new members of the tribe? You don't look like people who would willingly sell yourselves into bondage."

"Yeah!" Kyler said. "Welcome to our dungeon!"

"Don't let Igor here scare you off. He's mostly harmless."

I waited for the laughter to subside.

"But seriously. I wanted to offer my welcome. You seem like a fine lot, and personally, I'd be delighted to have you onboard."

"Here, here," David said and held up his glass.

We all toasted and drank.

"Hurry up. My tiramisu is getting warm," Kyler said.

"We'll have police soon for this sort of thing."

There were feigned looks of fright and more laughter.

"But seriously. I've been struck this evening by how completely beyond my control things have become."

"Hey, I know that feeling," Kristy said.

"Yeah. For instance, I had an impulse to buy a half dozen more golf carts for the tribe the other day..."

"Yeah! Free golf carts!" Kristy said.

"She's nothing, if not insatiable."

"My tiramisu is getting warm," Kyler said.

"So eat the damned thing."

"Yeah!"

He dug in."

"Please," I said with a wave of my hand. "No need to forestall your epicurean delights on my account. I'm almost done anyway."

There was a facetious round of applause.

"God, I know the madness of kings right now."

Colette gave me a comforting pat on the shoulder.

"So, I was saying. What the hell was I saying? Oh, about cutting down our fossil fuel footprint and making unilateral decisions but who really gives a shit at this point?"

There was applause and more laughter.

364

"I'm suddenly having second thoughts about my previous invitation."

There were sad faces and offers of submission.

"Okay. Forgiven. So it seems to me that we get along just fine, and if you're sincerely interested in joining us, I see no reason why we shouldn't have a vote right here and now."

"A bit of my chocolate cake for a yes vote," Ashley said.

"Actually, Anne is our informal council leader, so I should probably turn things over to her at this point."

"Okay. So, I feel the same way about you guys. Of course David and I already know you, but this just feels so good to me, the energy and everything. So what do the rest of you think? Are we all in favor of them joining?"

There was a unanimous raising of hands, followed by congratulations and cheers.

I raised my glass as the hubbub died down.

"Welcome, and your indoctrination begins tomorrow at seven."

"Oh," I said, tinging my glass another time and leaning forward with a whisper. "There is one more order of business I should mention. The trip. I'm not sure if you all were informed about this impending initiation rite."

"Ha," Kristy said. "This is a free country and a free tribe, so don't expect me to join in."

"That's quite true," I said. "But just so you know. The majority of the tribe has agreed to go forward."

"Look," Elicia said over the buzz of voices. "I'll just make sure there's enough for everybody. That way you can participate if you want, or you can just sit around and chaperone the rest of us."

Our four new members shrugged as if they weren't overly concerned about the decision, one way or the other.

"Oh, also, just so you know," Anne said. "We've chosen this Friday for the trip. That way those of us with day jobs will have ample time to mellow out."

With no further formality, everyone dug into the desserts. I went on stealing glances at Tara and took her home in my heart.

The following morning, I met Kristy in town and introduced her to Tillie.

"Tillie here does my books. Kristy is serving that role for the tribe, Tillie. I just need you to interface with her in whatever way my finances and the finances of the foundation may get intertwined."

"Sure, sure," Tillie said with her awkward laugh.

"That's it. You two are now officially connected. You know I'm an idiot about this stuff, Tillie, so please, both of you, make sure things don't run off the rails."

I left them talking and went in search of Toni. She was in her office, pouring over some plans and papers on her desk, as usual. The horn rimmed glasses went up on her head upon my entrance.

"Haven't really heard a word," she said. "If that's what you were wondering."

"I was."

She shrugged. I sat down.

"Should I be getting nervous here?"

"I don't know. Should you?"

I shrugged.

"Any skeletons in your closet?"

"Maybe."

"Hmm. Do tell."

"I'd rather not. The question is, how do I approach this fop without appearing to blackmail him?"

"I'll pretend I didn't hear that."

"Hmm. Just thinking out loud. And off the record."

"Well, on the record, you could hire me to act as a liaison for your subdivision. Interfacing with the neighbors. Addressing any local concerns. That sort of thing."

"You're hired."

"A check, please."

I pulled out the check book.

"You don't mess around."

"It will appear that I'm messing around unless you have paid me."

"How much?"

"How much interfacing do you want me to do?"

"Why don't we start with two grand worth and go from there."

"I can make a few phone calls for that much."

"I'll bet." I signed the check and slid it her way. "So, what to tell him?"

"Just like I said. I'm contacting all the adjoining property owners on behalf of Steven Fitzgerald, to see what we can do to make this development go forward as painlessly as possible."

"He'll love that."

"My question to you is, what do you want him to do?"

"Meet me in a quiet bar somewhere, for starters, so we can talk without witnesses."

"There's no reason he couldn't wear a wire in a quiet bar."

"Don't worry. I'm sufficiently wary of the bastard."

"You should be. You're walking a very fine line here."

"All right. See what you can do. I'm going to go talk with someone who doesn't make me nervous."

"Who would that be?"

"A bartender, probably."

She smiled. The glasses came down and she resumed her work.

"Did you know you're very beautiful without your glasses on, Ms. Peabody?"

"Get out of here."

When I looked back, she gave me a smile. I closed the door and hustled downstairs to the street.

Low on supplies, I stopped at the market and headed back to the property. My phone rang along the way. It was Anne.

"Where are you?"

"Heading home right now. Why?"

"I need to talk with you about all these requests we're getting for interviews."

"Send a surrogate."

"Sorry. They're only interested in talking to Mr. Billionaire."

"Christ. All right. I'll be by as soon as I drop off some supplies at home."

At home, I changed into my jogging togs and ran over to the tech center. The place was buzzing when I walked in. Heads turned. The able bodies present were Kristy, Ashley, Kato, Hans, Anne, David, Donny, Colette and Tara. Like north and south poles, my eyes locked with Tara's immediately. I squeezed Colette's shoulders going by and waved to everyone else.

"Ladies and gentlemen, here's the master key." I handed it to Anne. "Feel free to fight over which cottage you want and settle in anytime. Once you decide, I'll make sure you each receive a proper set of keys."

All four of them waved and went back to their work.

"Got you licking stamps," I whispered in Colette's ear.

"Yeah, working for Mastuh again. What are you doing?"

"I'm going for a jog and then up to work in the garden."

"May I join you?"

"It all pays the same."

She leaned in closer and whispered.

"Anything would be preferable to me. I think they thrive on adrenalin and Red Bull. Lots of Red Bull."

"Don't worry. The next generation will come along in eighteen months."

She made a face.

"So, are you ready to go over these requests?" Anne said.

"No, but let's see what you have."

Anne took me into a back bedroom, which served as her office and quickly ran through them. And I quickly dismissed the great majority.

"Let's just go with the local paper and the Rolling Stone. Did George Cross' people happen to call?"

"No."

I looked at the list of cable and broadcast programs again.

"As far as I'm concerned, this just amounts to over exposure and hawking ourselves. Maybe the News Hour, but beyond that, I'd prefer to maintain a bit of mystique."

Anne shrugged noncommittally.

"Okay." I went to the door. "Kristy and David, could you two join us please?"

"Is this an official meeting of the grand poohbahs?" Kristy said, coming in.

"Yes."

I explained my reasons for not wanting to overexpose ourselves and showed them the interviews I was willing to do.

"It appears that Anne has some reluctance about my take so time to put it to a vote."

"I say go for the money," Kristy said with bug eyes.

"Surprise, surprise."

"Well?"

"Well, let's say overexposure ultimately hurts our brand, and that leads to diminished interest and income. Then we've sacrificed long term success for short term gain. It's like the latest celebrity fad. One month and you're a nobody again. I think one of our greatest strengths is dignity. You know, being aloof from the marketplace. So you know how I feel. Go ahead and vote."

"You know, the more I think about it, Steven's right," Anne said. "We need to have a long term strategy of trust. If we grab for every dollar, we've lost that."

"David?" I said.

"I totally agree. I don't want to look cheap."

"I knew this committee was stacked," Kristy said.

"Oh shut up. We're looking out for your best interests too."

"Okay," she said with her crosswise fist pump. "I'm going back to work."

"Hey, wait a minute," I said.

She came back.

"I know we need to run this by the whole council, but one thing we didn't discuss was when and how do we divert funds from National Roll Call into a tribal account and how much?"

"For what purpose?" Anne said.

"Like for buying those extra golf carts."

"Already got you covered," Kristy said.

"How so?"

"I'm working with Tillie to set up the website as a working arm of the foundation. That way, whenever the tribe needs something, the money is there. You just have to get approval."

"From who?"

"We'll need to set up another committee."

"I can see where this is going."

She smiled.

"I need to get back to work. I'm focused."

"I want those golf carts!"

Kristy threw up a hand and kept walking.

"Okay, you two. Do I need to know anything else before I go?"

"Where are you going?"

"For a jog and then up to work in the garden. I need something to center my mind."

Anne and David looked at each other and shrugged.

"We're fine," he said. "Did you run that question by your attorney?"

"Oh, damn. I forgot. I'll call him this afternoon before his office closes."

"It's fine. We have time. We already sold out all our ad space for next month without needing Scumbag Oil."

"Okay. I'll call Richard and see what he says. And that's it? Things are humming along like a well-oiled machine?"

"It's a constant challenge," David said. "I already have Hans and Kato working on version 2.0, and Tara and Ashley are constantly revamping and improving the design and graphics. Keeping things fresh. And I'm handling any glitches that come up. Plus I've set up a rotating graveyard schedule. Glitches know no time or boundaries."

"But you've got it all handled and enough manpower?"

"So far, so good."

"Okay, then let's set up an interview out here with the Rolling Stone and the local rag. And with the News Hour and we'll go from there."

On the way out, I whispered in Colette's ear.

"Dinner?"

She looked up and nodded.

"If you can escape somehow, you'll know where to find me."

I waved another time to the crew and headed out the door. The vision of Tara's strange beauty followed me off through the forest.

28

I took a trail up through the fern grotto, past where Donny's friend had tried to turn my property into a sativa plantation and ran along Chaplin's property fence for half a mile, looking for any sign of the prick but saw none. I finally gave up and headed over to the garden. Kyler was out there wearing a straw hat and setting up a trellis for string beans. Camellia was weeding and pruning nearby.

"Hey boss man!" Kyler called out. "Coming out to work with us peons?"

"The salt of the earth, baby. That office work is enough to drive a man mad."

"Yeah!"

I gave him a hand holding up stakes while he pounded them into the soil. The day was sunny and cool with a gentle wind blowing in from the sea. We talked while working away.

Eventually I helped Camellia with pulling weeds. The soil was rich and black from all the mulch and the sun was warm on my back.

After an hour or so, I ran over to check on Dale. He had poured that day and was already gone. Several large stacks of lumber and beams had been dropped off close by. I ran back home, feeling refreshed and centered from the exercise and having worked in the garden. I went in to shower with black soil under my fingernails.

Cleaned and wearing washed cotton clothing, I pulled some salmon out of the frig and called Richard while starting dinner. He listened to me explain the advertising issue and reminded me that he wasn't a constitutional law expert.

"I'll look into it," he promised and hung up.

Colette called a few minutes later and walked over around dusk. I kissed her with another woman's beauty in my heart.

"How goes it down there?" I asked.

"I'm praying for your victory over Chaplin."

"Not cut out for office work, are we?"

"Steven, I have to tell you, those folks are just amazing. It's as if they've been working together their entire lives. It's humbling to watch."

She came and pressed her body against mine.

"And you know how infinitely grateful I am for everything you've done for me, but god how I long to be at my passion."

"Come," I said while searching for my I-pod.

A moment later, I had some Tito Puente blaring and swung Colette out into the living room for a bit of mambo.

We danced.

"You're good," she said when the song came to an end.

"You're better," I said.

Back in the kitchen, I explained my meeting with Toni to her.

"I'm not so sure the bastard will meet with me again. Not after the way I harangued him the last time."

"I would be very wary of the man. Pretend he's wearing a wire."

"Everyone keeps saying that."

I rinsed and dried the salmon with paper towels."

"How shall we prepare it?" Colette said.

"Just lemon and freshly ground pepper. Here, help me julienne some veggies and I'll do up a honey and garlic reduction sauce. A salad too?"

"Oh, how about something a bit sweet. Do you have mint?"

"I do."

"Go ahead. Do your sauce and I'll make the greens."

We were soon indulging ourselves in good food and wine. Hugo lay on the floor with paws up, contented from a dinner garnished with salmon.

Once we had cleaned up the kitchen a bit, Colette left him the usual bone and we disappeared upstairs. The woman aroused me on a physical level to no end but my heart was everywhere but in that room now.

I shuddered to think of how my father had stuck out forty years in a cheerless marriage. A life built upon guilt and a sense of duty. Can't let the kids and the little missus down. I recoiled from that fate as though from fire, and yet there I was, at war with my own happiness and passions.

Colette fell asleep with me around ten. At a little past midnight, she was kissing me goodbye. Fully awake again, I emptied my bladder and went out to sit the back balcony. The night air was cold and damp. High clouds were streaming in from the coast. Rain was in the forecast again.

I awakened in the morning with the forest drenched in rain and the same troubled heart.

My phone rang around the third cup of coffee. It was Toni.

"Chaplin's willing to meet you but he wants to do it up at his place."

"Forget it. You tell him we meet on neutral ground. The country club will do again."

"I'll call and see what he says. Do you care when?"

"Preferably today or tomorrow afternoon. I can't do it Friday or over the weekend."

"I'll see what I can arrange and get back to you."

"I'll be sitting by the phone."

I got off, leaned back in my chair and considered all the balls I was juggling. There were maybe a half dozen of them up in the air though it seemed like hundreds. There was Dale, but with the rain, I knew he wouldn't be working. I had the interviews to consider. There was Toni and Chaplin and this crap with the Coastal Commission. There was the subdivision filing. I had a thought to call Connor and get him started on the tech and science center building but decided to wait. Best to let some of these other balls come back down to earth first.

I was about to call Anne and see about those interview requests when the phone rang. It was Toni again.

"Let me guess. He caved."

"He did. Can you make lunch today?"

"Sure. At the Baywood again?"

"Yes. At noon, he said."

"Tell him I'll be there."

I got off and immediately called Anne.

"Any news on those interviews?"

"The local paper said they would have a reporter get in touch with you. No further word from the News Hour but Rolling Stone called. They were wondering if you could do the interview tomorrow."

"Sure. Tell them to make it in the afternoon. Say three o'clock? I'd like to take them for a tour and then we'll sit down at my place for the interview."

"Yeah, I'll give them a call and confirm with you."

"So how's everything down there?"

"Fine. We posted those ten categories for next week's issue and the response has been off the charts. People really like the idea that they can have a say in things."

"Yeah. We kind of figured as much. So everything's good otherwise?"

"Yeah, we're good."

"Okay, because I have a lunch date with Little Lord Fauntleroy from next door and I'll be heading into town."

"Oh, is this good news?"

"I don't know yet. We'll have to see. Just figure I'll be out of commission from roughly eleven to two."

"Okay. Good luck...Oh, can you stop by with the keys to the cottages on your way into town? I guess everybody's decided on their place and wanted to start moving in."

"Sure. What numbers?"

She rattled them off and I pulled the keys.

"I'll see you around eleven."

I got off. The rain was pouring down. I felt like a caged tiger.

I headed over to the tech center with my mind fixated on Tara. I wanted her madly, but in a spiritual way, from the fifth chakra up. Colette was splendid companionship and intellectual camaraderie. Tara was inspiration. The mere thought of Tara and Catherine was finally forgotten. Finally forgotten.

Inside the cottage, I waved to everyone and pretended to ignore Tara. Stiff upper lip and all that. Duty first.

"Lunch with Chaplin," I whispered in Colette's ear. Her eyes lit up. "Don't get your hopes up too high. He hasn't agreed to anything yet but at least he's come to the table."

"I'll keep my fingers crossed."

"You do that." I kissed her on the forehead. "I'll call you as soon as I have news."

The rain had begun to let up as I pulled into the country club parking lot. It was still coming down but no longer in buckets. The golf course was a lake from the rain. Ducks had the front nine to themselves.

I gave the hostess my name and she promptly led me to Chaplin's table. He stood up to shake my hand.

Chaplin ordered Scotch with a look my way. I nodded and the hostess ran off.

I stared at Chaplin, imagining his thoughts. *It's a hundred grand to get in on the ground level here these days and I've earned every penny of it.*

"It's hell on your golf game," he said, looking out at the rain.

"What's your handicap?"

"Eight," he said.

Liar. I knew it was more like eighteen. Maybe.

The Scotch came and the waitress asked us if we were having lunch.

376

I looked at Chaplin with a smile.

"We're not sure yet," he said. "Please check back with us in a few minutes."

She left. I saluted Chaplin with my glass and drank.

"So, why are we here again?" I said.

"Oh, well, surely we're not going to play games today."

I set my Scotch down and leaned forward.

"What do you mean, play games? You filed a complaint with the Coastal Commission and I'm assuming you've had a change of heart."

"Come, Steven. Surely you know I didn't arrange this meeting over your…whatever it is you're doing over there."

"No? Then please explain."

"Why, I'm talking about this proposed subdivision of yours, of course."

"Oooooooooohhhhhh. So you want to talk about my subdivision. Well, why didn't you say so? I don't read minds, you know."

Chaplin sat there fidgeting with his glass. His face looked like a tea kettle ready to blow again.

"And?" I said.

"Well, good god, man. You can't be serious. A subdivision? Up here? Along this pristine coastline?"

"Why not?"

"Better if I asked you. Why in god's name would you want to despoil this beautiful countryside?"

"I suppose my energy's just looking for someplace to go. Seeing as I'm all bottled up in every other direction."

"Are you proposing that if I relent on the one matter, you'll relent on the other?"

"I said nothing of the sort. Good god, man. That could be construed as blackmail."

"Well then, what are you proposing?"

I reached for my Scotch and smiled acerbically.

"You proposed this meeting. I came to hear you out. I don't know where you got this notion that *I* had something to propose."

"Oh, this is ridiculous."

"I suppose it is."

"Well, if you refuse to lay your cards on the table, we'll never get anywhere."

I leaned forward again.

"May I suggest that *you* lay your cards on the table? You apparently have something in your craw."

"Well, obviously I want to put an end to this subdivision business of yours."

"So, file another complaint with the Coastal Commission. It's a free country."

"And you can be assured I will."

"Good."

The waitress reappeared.

"So, have you gentlemen decided on lunch yet?"

"The prospects aren't looking good," I said.

The waitress blushed and left. I smiled back at Chaplin.

"You were saying."

"I was saying, fine. I will file another complaint. And I'll keep filing them until I put an end to this nonsense of yours. All of it."

"So, we're back to who can outspend whom, which is a war I'm thoroughly prepared to wage."

He was really boiling over now. I smiled at his apoplectic state and tossed back the rest of my Scotch.

"So, now we both know where we stand. Shall we call it an afternoon?"

He stared without answer.

"By the way, Chaplin, there's one thing I've been wanting to tell you. About that incident over in the Mediterranean?"

He stared.

"Let me tell you exactly what happened. We had both been drinking and I passed out on the deck of my boat. When I awakened, she was missing. They found what was left from the sharks two days later. You don't think that broke my heart? I loved that woman. So, the sins of youth? Perhaps, but nothing compared to the greed and hubris you displayed down there in Sonoma. So you got that one judgement buried and walked away looking squeaky clean. Or relatively so. I won't bring it up, since I believe people have a right to redemption. So now that all our skeletons are out of the closet, you tell me how you think we can settle our differences."

For all his boisterous rotundity, Chaplin seemed to have shrunk, as if someone had let the air out of a balloon. He ordered another drink and belted down a good slug of it before he could go on.

"All right. If you'll agree to cancel that subdivision, I'll pull my complaint from the Coastal Commission."

I nodded slowly and studied him.

"I'll tell you what I'm willing to do. I'm willing to shake hands with you for now. A gentlemen's agreement. You pull your complaint and I'll shelve the subdivision. Then in a year or so, if we've built up a sufficient degree of trust, I'll place the whole goddamned parcel in conservancy. To remain undeveloped into perpetuity. I can use it for recreational purposes with some limited development, like a lodge or the likes, but no residential, no commercial and no industry. It this starting to make sense to you?"

He stared for a long moment before nodding.

"Are we speaking of both parcels?"

"Both parcels. But you leave me and the tribe the hell alone. No more interference. Not one more goddamned complaint. Fair enough?"

Again, he took a long moment before nodding.

"Come on, Chaplin. Have we disturbed you one single time in all the time I've been here?"

He seemed to want to weigh the question but ultimately shook his head.

I held out my hand.

"Shake?"

Again, with the same reluctance, he did so.

"All right. You pull your complaint and notify Toni the minute you have. As soon as I get word from her, I'll pull the plug on the subdivision and we'll see if we can get along for a year."

The waitress approached our table as if there was a bomb beneath it.

"So, did we decide on lunch, gentlemen?"

"No, we've decided that we each have urgent business to attend to."

We stood up together.

"How much do I owe you?" I said.

"Just go ahead and put it on my tab," Chaplin told the waitress.

She left. I threw a fifty dollar bill on the table for a tip.

"As soon as I get word, I'll have my attorney pull the filing."

Out in the parking lot, I almost did a jig. The Red Sea had parted. Pharaoh had let me go. I immediately called Colette.

"Get ready to see your dreams come true."

"No."

"Yes. He completely caved."

"On everything?"

"Well, on the Coastal Commission BS. I'm waiting to hear from Toni, but assuming Chaplin is a man of his word, he agreed to pull his complaint if I shelve my phony subdivision."

I heard the phone cupped and hubbub in the background.

"What's up?" I said.

I heard Colette come back.

"Oh, I just got a bit teary eyed there and everyone wanted to know what was happening. I'm not sure they quite understand the import but..."

"...they will, so get your ballet shoes out. If all goes as planned, we can break ground within the week."

"Oh Steven. I'm so excited."

"Good. Hey, I've got a few more calls to make but let's do this. Invite everyone over to my place for dinner tonight. I'll have it catered. Who knows how long we'll be able to fit everyone at the same table. Anyway, I'd like the new folks to see my place and what better time to celebrate."

"Should I ask them now?"

"Yeah."

"Okay, just a second."

I heard the phone cupped again and she was back.

"Yeah, everybody's in."

"Okay, call it six o'clock."

"I'll see you then. Oh, Steven. This is such wonderful news."

I got off and immediately called Toni. Chaplin had already called her. We shared a restrained celebration and I called Richard, then Connor when I was done with Richard.

"The bastard caved."

"You mean Chaplin?"

"One and the same."

"Bloody beautiful, mate. Did you catch him with his pants down in a house of ill repute?"

"No. Meet me for a drink and I'll explain."

"Fifteen minutes and I'm there. The usual place?"

"I'll be waiting for you."

Connor walked in, gave me a firm handshake and ordered a Scotch. I gave him the condensed version of what had gone down.

"The bastard was trying like hell to get me to say it for him. I'm telling you, I would have sworn he was wearing a wire."

"Bloody brilliant. So now what?"

"We get the arts center going. In the meantime, I want to start designs on a science and tech center."

"Brilliant. Any ideas?"

"No. I'm clueless but we brought on four new nerds so I'll set up a meeting between you and the bunch of them and you can start throwing ideas around."

"I've a career just building up your utopia, mate."

"So why don't you join us?"

"The minute the hot tubs go in, I'll have a tour."

I laughed, then looked off and shook my head.

"What, mate?"

"Oh, you should have seen the man cave. Once he realized he had no more cards to play, the air completely went out of him."

"What cards did he have?"

I tossed back my Scotch and looked down at my hands.

"None, really. The only one he had, he had already spent."

I looked back at Connor.

"It was about a boating accident over in the Mediterranean. Years ago now. Chaplin must have hired someone to dig into my past. A young Irish lass named Laura I had met in Barcelona."

I saw her face and felt a knife in my heart.

"We had set sail for the Balearics one night on my boat and the rest is bloody hell history, as you would say."

I ordered another Scotch and finished telling him the story.

The Tribe

29

Tara and Ashley were the last of the tribe to arrive for dinner. I heard their knock and found them standing under the porch roof outside, shaking the rain from their clothing. The weather had turned raw. A steady mist was drifting down through the trees

"Welcome! Welcome! Come in!"

"This…place…is…such…a…trip," Ashley said, wiping her feet and stepping over the threshold.

"That was the idea. Here, let me take your coats and scarves."

I took them and closed the door.

"You know everyone, of course."

"Never seen them before," Tara said. "Oh wow, Ashley. Look at these Japanese prints."

She and Ashley went over to have a closer look.

"Originals?" Tara said.

I shrugged noncommittally.

"Wow. They must have cost you a fortune."

"We don't talk about that."

"I'll bet. They just transport you."

"That was the idea."

Tara laughed.

"Well it definitely works."

"Help yourselves to the bar," I said and headed for the coat closet. "Cold beers and wine down below. Hard stuff up above. And everyone, please, start taking your seats! Dinner will be served momentarily!"

There were several offers to help in the kitchen but I waved them off. Kristy followed me anyway.

"Hey, I want to help," she said with her crosswise fist pump.

"Very well. All these cold platters need to go out to the table."

Kristy grabbed one with shredded cabbage and cilantro, and one with tomato and avocadoes. I followed her with the salsas, lime wedges and serrano peppers. Other people followed me back out to the kitchen but I shooed them off.

"Please, take your seats. The hot platters will be out in a minute."

In a final last flurry of activity, Colette and I delivered the carnitas, rice and beans.

"We'll be keeping the windows open tonight," Dr. McDonald said with a chuckle.

"Funny," Kristy said. "Maybe I'll have *you* sleep on the couch."

"Maybe I will."

"Sounds like a lot of hot air to me," Donny said to much laughter.

"And on a lighter subject," Anne said to even more laughter.

"Yes, cheers everyone," I said. "Please enjoy. Speech to follow."

There were groans and a scramble for the food.

"How about some mariachi music, boss man?"

"That's a good idea," I said and got up.

"Spare us, please," Ashley said.

"Yes, mariachi music verboten," Tara said.

"Somebody shoot the band," Hans said.

I put on a Poncho Sanchez CD and returned.

"That doesn't sound like mariachi music to me," Kato said in a comical voice.

"It's Cuban mariachi," I said. "You just add a little more hot sauce."

"And hot air," Kristy said.

The lively banter went on throughout the meal and soon everyone was kicking back with full stomachs. I looked around the table.

"I sense a speech coming on," Tara said.

"Yes. And in keeping with the Latin theme, it will be a Castro style, two hour harangue."

"A walk anyone?" David said.

"Bolt the door, Kyler."

"Yeah!"

I stood up.

"But seriously, we slew a dragon today and now I need to clear the air about a few other things moving forward."

"Uh oh. Here come the beans," Kristy said.

I waited for the laughter to subside.

"Okay, okay. I'm determined to get this out."

"Stampede!" Ashley said.

I threw up my hands.

"Okay, everyone, let's let Steven say his peace," Anne said.

"Thank you. So, I've been attempting to say, I set some things in motion before most of you arrived. And certainly before our current largesse. Things that I had intended to bequeath to the tribe, which I realize now places me in the position of acting unilaterally and without tribal consent one more time. So, as noble as my intentions might be, I'm here to beg both your forgiveness and indulgence."

"He speaketh much and sayeth little," Tara said.

"Kyler, go make sure that door is good and bolted."

"Yeah!"

"So, yes, to make a long story short."

"And if you have to say that, it's already too long," Hans said.

I acknowledged their razzing with upraised wine glass.

"I remember a time when kids respected their elders."

"Out with it, out with it."

"All right, so I had already arranged to build an arts center out here, using my own money, and I intend to go through it. The tribal council be damned."

"Three cheers for the Fitzgerald Center for the Arts," Dr. McDonald said.

"Yes. Thank you. We all want to leave something of ourselves behind to the world so I'll be expecting a monument out in front."

"Hey, if you're giving away free gifts," Kristy said. "Why don't you just give us those yachts?"

"Speaking of hot air…"

"Darn. I want that yacht."

"Yes…So, it was always my plan to also build a science and tech center to go along with the arts center and I would love to bequeath that building to the tribe, as well, with your permission."

"Yachts! Yachts!" Kyler said, which soon became a chant.

"I'll not dignify this nonsense any further."

"Boo!'

"Thank you. And as a final note, I'd like to arrange a meeting between my architect Connor and the entire tech team so you can offer up all your ideas on the design of the building and any of its practical needs."

Everyone stared, waiting.

"Yes, that's it."

I sat down to more applause

"Thank you, thank you. I know it wasn't quite Castro-like but…"

"So, dessert and coffee anyone?" Colette said, getting up. I started to get up with her but she placed a hand on my shoulder. "I'll take care of it. Enjoy your company."

Kristy went to join her in the kitchen and the rest of the tribe resumed their conversations.

"Oh, with all the hubbub," Anne said from across the table. "I forgot to tell you that I confirmed the interview with Rolling Stone for tomorrow."

"Gonna get my picture on the cover," Ashley sang with Tara.

Several others around the table quickly joined in.

"So, what time is it?" I asked over the chorus.

"Three o'clock, as you had requested."

"Good. Let's hope the weather clears. And I'll expect the rest of you to be on your best behavior."

"So, no joints or beers after three?" Ashley said.

"No, and none before."

There were quickly sounds of rebellion.

Just then, Colette and Anne and Kristy came in bearing cake plates and coffee mugs. The sugar and cream went around the table and everyone dug in.

"Hmm, great cake," Tara said.

"Doesn't seem to be in the Latin theme," Dr. McDonald said.

"That's because Mexicans can't bake a cake, any more than they can bake a good loaf of bread."

"There goes the Latino vote."

"Hey, come to think of it," Ashley said. "We do kind of look like the Republican Party around here."

"I'm Japanese," Kato said.

"Yeah, well, if you hadn't noticed it, you're also white."

"Okay, that will be our next mission, tribal members. Diversify our demographics. Bonus points for anyone who can bring in a minority."

I fended off a barrage of wadded up napkins and dug back into my cake.

Around ten the next morning, I drove up to give Dale the news. He and Jason were busy erecting an exterior wall for the maintenance shed so I jumped in.

"What's up," Dale said once he had the braces in place.

"I got the road cleared on building the arts center."

"Yeah? What happened?"

"I made that fucker next door an offer he couldn't refuse."

Dale smiled one of his rare smiles.

"So, I suppose you want me to drop everything and start over there."

"No, get this done, but anything you can do to move both projects along simultaneously. I would love to have that arts center done in the spring."

"Once I'm weathered in up here and the mechanical's going in, I can jump down on that foundation."

"Be much obliged. Did Tillie take care of you?"

"She did."

"Good. Oh, Rolling Stone is coming out to do a piece on the place this afternoon so if you see me wandering around in a golf cart with some folks, you'll know who it is."

"Wow, the Rolling Stone! Cool!" Jason said.

"Yeah. Gonna be on the cover."

We laughed.

"I'll see you guys later."

I stopped by the garden but only Camellia was out there working. She smiled when I waved from my golf cart.

From there I headed down to the tech center. Several faces turned my way as I walked in. The place was a hubbub. They were at home in their element. I was out of mine.

I noticed Colette missing and nodded at Tara. She smiled and went back to work.

"Where's Colette?" I asked Anne.

"I guess in town with the architect. I know he had called."

"Oh. So how is everything going here?"

"Good. Are you getting excited?"

"About the interview?"

"Yeah."

"What's to get excited about? I'm only concerned about them portraying us in a positive light."

"I'm sure they will."

"Yeah, we hope. I can see the 'Jonestown style cult takes root along the Northern California coast' headline."

"Noooooo. Yeah, I'm sure it'll be fine."

"Okay, if you say so. I'll be home practicing my speech."

She gave me a hug.

"You'll be fine."

"Thanks. And, hey, the rest of you, remember, no hooters until the Rolling Stone people leave."

"Come on, it's the Rolling Stone," Ashley said.

"As in, let's go get stoned," Tara said.

"I'll be sure to remind them."

I waved a final time and whizzed home silently through the forest in my golf cart.

At a quarter to three, my phone rang. It was Jenner Doyle, down at the highway with his photographer and wanting to be sure of the directions.

"Yeah, just drive straight up until you see a large meadow and gravel parking area. I'll be waiting for you there."

A few minutes later, the car appeared out of the forest. I climbed out of the golf cart to greet them.

"Jenner Doyle," he said with a shake of my hand. "This is Sara Willoughby."

I shook her hand too. She was a young slender blonde with gray eyes and no makeup. Jenner was a craggy veteran of the forty year culture war.

"Quite a spread you have here," he said. "Is this as far as it goes or is there more?"

"It goes another mile in every direction. Come on, jump in and I'll show you around."

I took them first to see the cottages.

"Oh wow, we'll have to get some shots of this," Jenner said. "You don't mind do you?"

"Just don't give out my address."

He laughed. The two of them went about framing up various photos.

"Can we see inside?"

"Of course."

I opened up one of the unoccupied cottages.

"Wow," Jenner said. "This is truly classic craftsmanship."

"Look at this," Sara said from the kitchen.

Jenner went out and marveled with her over the beveled glass doors and old-fashioned dishes.

"This is quite something," Jenner said. "And every cottage is like this."

I nodded.

"Wow. You've really done something here. And this was all done with your own money?"

I nodded.

When they were done inside we jumped back into the golf cart and wound along cottage row again. Jenner asked me to stop several more times so Sara could photograph the cottage exteriors.

From there, I took them on a quick tour of the waste recycling plant and the power grid. Finally we arrived at the tech center.

"Come on in. This is the temporary home of National Roll Call."

"Temporary?" Jenner said.

"Yeah, long story. Come have a look and I'll explain everything when we sit down for the interview. Hey, everybody!" I said, going inside. "It's the folks from Rolling Stone. Put out the joints."

"Hey, we want to be on the cover," Ashley said.

"Yeah," Tara said and made a pose with Ashley.

Jenner nodded at Sara, who went to work taking shots of them.

"You just might make it," Jenner said and continued around introducing himself. As he did, asking questions, Sara followed behind, clicking off photos.

"Okay, so how about a group shot?" Jenner said.

I stood back while Jenner and Sara arranged everyone.

"Let's get you in here, Steven," Jenner said. "Sitting down in front somewhere."

"No, no. This is about them."

"No, I insist," he said.

"Yeah, come on and get in here," Tara said.

Reluctantly, I did.

While Sara was photographing, Tara posed her baseball cap on my head in various stupid poses.

"Are we good?" Jenner said to Sara after a few minutes.

She nodded. I stood up.

"Okay, we're off to new adventures," I said.

Jenner went around shaking hands with everyone and expressing thanks as we headed out the door. I took them up to the yurt next.

"Wow, what a trip," Jenner said on our way up the steps. "So this is your ceremonial lodge."

"Basically. It's where the council meets anyway. It wasn't my original intention but necessity being the mother of invention and all."

Jenner stared at me with a curious smile.

"Like I said, I'll explain everything once we sit down for the interview."

After several photographs of the yurt, I took them up through the fern grotto and along Chaplin's fence. Sara had me stop for more photos along the way.

We came to the maintenance shed next and the garden. Dale was working away with Jason on the exterior walls. Camellia and Kyler were working away in the garden.

"He doesn't talk much," I whispered about Dale.

Jenner nodded and had Sara take a few photos of him working with Jason. Then he had Kyler and Camellia pose together in the garden.

"All right! Cover of the Rolling Stone!" Kyler said when they were done.

"Page 41," I said. "Maybe."

"Yeah!"

Kyler introduced himself before we drove away. Back at the meadow, I stopped and explained about the plans for the arts and tech centers.

"That's what I was going to tell you. Everything was put on hold because the prick next door filed a complaint with the Coastal Commission. I was stuck in the mud until yesterday. I made him an offer he couldn't refuse."

"Oh, I'd love to hear that story."

"You will but let's head over to my place and we'll knock things around over some refreshments."

"Oh wow!" Jenner said, seeing my treehouse come into view. "Is this your place?"

I nodded and pulled to a stop.

"Yeah. We definitely need to get several shots of it from the outside here."

"Here, let me pull the golf cart back out of the way."

"No, no. Pull it up closer. Let's get it in the shot. It plays nicely into the green angle."

Once they were done photographing from the forest floor, I led them upstairs. Sara was clicking off photos the entire way.

"Wow," Jenner said. "It just makes you want to move in."

I opened the door and waved them through ahead of me.

"Enchanting," Sara said. "May I?"

"Go right ahead. Photograph whatever you want. My bedroom and office are upstairs. I even made the bed."

She smiled.

"Drinks you two?"

"Uh, juice will do," Jenner said.

He looked to Sara and she nodded her head.

"You'll forgive me if I have a Scotch."

While I made the drinks, I heard the doors to my upstairs balcony open and close. A minute later, the two of them came back downstairs.

"Please, have a seat. Your juices are there."

The three of us got comfortable. Jenner turned on his tape recorder.

"So, you were saying about this neighbor."

"Okay, turn that thing off for a minute."

He did. I explained about Chaplin.

"So, never mind his parading around the old Hollywood name, like anyone gives a shit at this point, or his great white hunter BS, he had dug up this dirt and figured it would set me back on my heels."

"And what was the dirt?"

"I'm guessing you already know that."

"Are you referring to that boating incident over in the Balearics?"

I nodded.

"And you said?"

"Knock yourself out. I don't give a damn what you do. I had assured him at the start that I could outspend him a hundred to one, and that I was fully prepared to do so, if that's what it took to put an end to his bullshit but that didn't seem to faze him. He went right ahead with his complaint, so I went ahead with my development plans and suddenly he got real cooperative."

"How much of this can I print?"

"That he filed a complaint against me with the Coastal Commission and that the two of us were ultimately able to work things out."

"It makes for a far better story the other way."

"Sure it does, but if I rub dirt in his face, I risk him reneging on our deal."

"Understood."

"So, what else did you want to know?"

Jenner pointed at the tape recorder, I nodded and he turned it back on.

"So," he said with a wry smile. "What the hell got into you?"

I smiled.

"I know, huh."

We laughed.

"Look, I had these ideas, where it was just easier to do something than trying to explain them."

"So, explain. What does this place represent to you?"

"You name what's wrong with this world and this is my alternative to it. Greed? Corruption? War? Overpopulation? Addiction to oil. GMOs. Destruction of the environment? More greed? Egotism? Many of these problems are as old as the sun. Some aren't. Either way, I can't see us surviving much longer on the path we're headed down."

"And that path is...?"

"The one with runaway population? The one where we're getting the entire third world addicted to our own insane addiction to fossil fuels?"

"Interesting. I wonder if you've seen the recent reports on livestock production. Like from the UN and the National Academy of Sciences?"

"Yeah, yeah. To be honest with you, I was a bit behind the curve on that issue until recently, but yeah, I know. It's huge."

"Yeah, the methane production from raising cattle alone just dwarfs that of CO2."

"So I've been reading. Yeah, it's sobering. The thing is, I can't see where you're going to get people to stop eating animal flesh...but maybe we can all cut down to once or twice a week? And look for more sustainable ways of raising livestock? So, yeah, we're all about doing our part on that front too."

"Yeah. So, sorry to distract you. You were saying about population growth and weening ourselves from fossil fuels?"

"Well, Brazil has proven that you can get off the juice, and as to overpopulation, I think that goes to the heart of everything. And that goes to the question of capitalism itself."

"How do you mean?"

"Well, this ought to fire up some right wingers but I see capitalism as the ultimate Ponzi scheme. You have to keep producing crap or the whole thing collapses. Which means you're dependent on an ever increasing population, and any fool can see where that's headed. Forget what you're seeing now in terms of climate change and the collapse of ecosystems. What happens once we double or triple the population? Billions of people will have to suffer and die apparently before the light finally goes on. It'll be like this migration out of the Middle East and Africa right now, only on a colossal scale."

"And this is your answer to all those problems?"

"Well, a stab at it, anyway. A sustainable lifestyle, where the focus is on quality of life, not on consumption. Something more akin to the medieval pace of life, where you can take a week to make a chair, but with the best of modern technology still at your fingertips."

"There are some pretty big organizations out there, already doing some pretty important things to help change the current trajectory of the developed world. Why not just throw your lot in with them?"

"Because I don't see them getting at the basic problem."

"Which is?"

"I've already stated it. We can't just keep rearranging chairs on the Titanic and expect things to change much. The question for me is, how do we maintain freedom, innovation and free enterprise without destroying the planet? Because capitalism as it's currently defined is incapable of confronting the problem. It's only goal is to produce more and make profit. We're at each other's throats as we career off a cliff. There's no thought for where this ride is taking us. The same with our leaders. So, the point of all this? To create an alternative model. A tribe of people who remain individuals, with their own separate goals, but work around a common goal of living in a sustainable manner. I just figured, if we do this ourselves, you have something concrete that might catch on."

"Well, setting aside the specifics of how it's run and what it means for the moment, we've got 'billionaire starts alternative community.' How is the everyday guy or gal going to emulate what you've done here?"

"Look, you can take a hundred people anywhere and if they throw in their lot together, they can get something like this off the ground. Ten grand a piece and you've got a million dollars. A hundred grand a piece and you have ten million. You can buy some land and get something similar going."

"Is a hundred people the number you're working with?"

"I am but it doesn't have to be that. Just something that will give you a good cross section of skills…My point is, it doesn't take a billionaire. I just happen to be one and had the money to make this happen. So, did I wait around five, ten years for the thing to mature? I'm too damned impatient. Anyway, the real question was, could I find a group of people willing to take part and work together in this way and from that standpoint it's been a resounding success. You saw those folks down in the tech center. They gladly took a cottage and twenty grand a year to be a part of this, when they could be out there making three, four, five times as much in the corporate world."

"But to be part of what? I still don't get it. So you have a green platform and you're working together as a community…"

"…a tribe."

"Okay, a tribe, but with your National Roll Call, you're still basically operating in the capitalist system…"

"Look, let's stop right there. I got into this same discussion with George Cross the other day and you know damned well it's a straw man. Either capitalism or communism? BS. There's a world of difference between commerce of old and the function corporations serve today. Not to mention this wild west BS on Wall Street. What we have today are the greediest, most avaricious and unenlightened human beings holding the levers of power and that's what they'd like you to think. It's one or the other. Bullshit. No, we're not above making a buck, but when our commercial interests are so at odds with the basic needs of humanity, something's terribly wrong. It's the spirit of it, you know? The enlightened spirit. Thrive, sure, but as part of a whole. We belong to a tribe and our tribe is part of the greater global tribe."

"It's beginning to sound like Rousseauian idealism."

"There's that word again."

Jenner smiled.

"Look, Rousseau's noble savage was just a rehash of what Plato had said, and Confucius before him, up and down the line. This belief that there is some essential goodness in mankind and that it only needs to be nurtured."

"And you're saying you disagree?"

"No, I'm only saying that they've taken it out of context. You take an individual and place that person within the safety and security of a group and those instincts will flourish. Take them out of the group and those instincts wither. Or, worse, go very, very awry. Think of all these horrible mass killings. They start digging around into the killer's past and it always leads back to same thing. A loner who has grown completely severed from his community."

"And that's it? Simply provide a sense of community?"

I smirked.

"I'm sorry but that's a lot. I think Joseph Campbell was getting at this when he suggested the Earth rise shots from the Apollo missions could be a new mythic symbolism. It was like an evolutionary moment. Like, wow, we *are* all just one tribe here on our little blue planet. And you'd think our direction over the past fifty years would reflect that realization, but no. Things are more fucked up than ever."

"And why do you think that is?"

"I don't know. Blame the Chinese and Soviets. They gave working collectively a bad name."

Jenner smiled.

"Look, I'm just following the archeological evidence. We're going back to Lucy here. Millions of years in this tribal framework and suddenly, in relative terms, civilization yanks us out of that structure. It's like asking wolves to eat salad. They're not designed to digest it and we as a species are not meant to be loners...For the most part. Obviously some individuals thrive better in solitude, but the vast majority of people are happiest when functioning within the fabric of a group. And we're all connected anyway, no matter how goddamned independent we'd like to think we are."

"So, any wars break out around here so far?"

I smiled.

"Differences, yeah. Like whether to order sushi or pizza."

Jenner laughed.

"Seriously, though. There's been some fractious energy, like on the night of our first tribal council but I got up the next morning thinking, I'm going up to work in the garden. I need to get centered and guess what? Everybody was already up there when I arrived. Nothing had been said among us. It was just a communal sense welling up within everyone independently. Hey, this garden is core to our physical and spiritual well-being and there we were. By the way, there's some real solid hippie energy here among our members so who knows where that will lead us. We'll probably have a pottery shop at some point and things of that sort. Classes in organic gardening. The website has helped move us towards financial sustainability, but this isn't about money. We'll be working with the local community on an organic level. You know, try to produce everything we need and barter for the rest. Whatever it is, it has not been necessary for me to explain what I mean by a tribe. Everybody around here just got that instinctively."

"And what about rules?"

"I think we're up to three of them at present."

Jenner laughed again.

"Yeah. A super majority of the tribe is required to vote someone in. The same to vote you out and everyone's time is of equal value."

"Well, it sounds like it's a hell of an experiment. Any regrets so far?"

I smiled acerbically.

"And my options were? Build a couple of castles? Jet set to Monaco? Whatever the hell billionaires do with their money these days."

"I suppose you still can."

"Sure, I can do whatever the hell I want but I really do believe that our species is headed into the abyss. Meanwhile, 99% of the people on this planet get up every day, face with a life and death struggle. I feel it's my duty to get up and face that struggle with them. To do whatever I can to help turn this thing around. I am my brother's keeper, when all is said and done."

"That's a hell of a burden to place on yourself."

"Well, it's a burden I accept."

"Yeah?"

"Yeah. It's life. I mean, I have my Zen moments. Like it's all in a dream, right? But the cat still climbs a tree and we still have to deal with our problems."

"So, you said you'd like to see more of these tribal units spring up."

"Sure. I can hope it catches on. Again, it's not a belief system. It's just people working together in a sustainable way. To anyone listening out there, I would say, hey, it's fun. It really is. We have a dynamic, malleable core that can go wherever we want it to go. I'll be the first to admit that we're winging it, which has led to some awkward moments, where this or that person's ego gets in the way, mine included, but the spirit of cooperation quickly brings you back in line and we have a good laugh. Basically it's humble yourself and go with what's best for the tribe, because the sense of harmony and brotherhood is ultimately more rewarding than having your own way."

"Well, look, before we get any deeper into that discussion, I'd like to ask you a few questions about your personal history. Your family, your relationship with your father and how you got from there to here. I trust you don't mind."

"No, I was expecting it."

"By the way, how *does* it feel to wake up and realize you're a billionaire?"

"I suppose that depends a lot on your state of enlightenment."

30

I stood on the balcony, watching the Rolling Stone people disappear off into the forest. Once they were gone, I went back inside and called Colette. Her phone rang four times and went to voice mail. Remembering that she had gone into town to meet with Connor, my ears burned. So, the two of them were getting chummy. I shook my head. You're dreaming about Tara and thinking revenge? Lord, how fucked up can one man be…

Out of courtesy, I called Anne and filled her in about the interview. Yes, everything seemed to have gone well and, no, I did not have time to stop by and relate all the juicy details. I had a lot on my plate that afternoon.

Twilight had settled over the forest by the time Colette finally called. Did I want to get together for dinner? She was dying to know how the interview went. I begged off, citing exhaustion, and sat there stewing as darkness set in. There was a thought to charter a private jet and drag Tara off to St. Moritz. Screw Colette, and everyone else.

In the end, I shelved my worst impulses for one day and tried to get some sleep.

At a little past eleven that night, my phone rang. I looked at the caller ID. It was Kyler. Why in hell would he be calling me at this hour?

"What's up?" I said in answering.

"Boss man, I ran into that vet guy tonight at a meeting."

"So?"

"So, that fucker's crazy. He totally went off when he shared. Fuck this, fuck that. I sacrificed all this shit for my country and all they do is treat me like shit when I come home. The next thing I know, he's crying, then he's going off again."

"So?"

"So when he got to this part about how people keep rejecting him and how there's always a price to pay for your actions, I just knew he was talking about us."

"Did he say anything specific?"

"No, but he kept looking at me."

"Yeah…What's his name again?"

"I don't know his real name. He calls himself Sage."

"Well, I don't know what we can do about it without an explicit threat. The new security gate is going in tomorrow morning sometime and I guess we'll have to leave it at that. At least he won't be able to drive in here with his car."

"This guy is totally special forces, boss man. I don't think he's going to give a shit about a gate. He'll probably show up in a tank or something."

"I think you're going a bit overboard, Kyler. Anyway, unless he says something specific, the cops aren't going to get involved. You can't get a restraining order on somebody for just shooting off their mouth."

"Okay, you're the boss. I just thought I'd better tell you."

"Yeah. I appreciate it. Let's just pray for the best and see what tomorrow brings."

Around nine the next morning, I received a call from Dennis, saying he would be out there in half an hour to install the new security gate. I phoned Dale to let him know, gobbled down some breakfast, made a few other calls and drove down to the highway. Dale had poured the concrete the previous day and his electrician was already down there dealing with the power.

Once Dennis showed up and it became clear that my presence wasn't required, I wrote Dennis a check and drove up to the tech center. My arrival there was met with a barrage of questions about the interview. Still feeling petulant over this Colette and Connor business, I walked past her with a quick smile and sat down to field questions from the others. About the article itself, I had to plead ignorance. Jenner had promised to forward me a copy before it went to press, but as of that moment, I honestly had no idea what tone he would take.

Having answered everyone's questions, I went around the office with David, getting briefed on the status of the website.

"Here's what's winning hands down for next week's vote," he told me. "Should we have a national election law?"

"Makes sense. Everything comes back to that one thig. Imagine having to stand in line for eight hours to vote."

"Yeah, well, whatever it is, the issue really has people going. Doesn't seem to matter which side you're on."

I had stolen a quick glance at Tara while he was talking. Just the sight of her swept my heart away. David was smiling when I looked back.

"Oh, sorry…So, is it decided?"

"Pretty much but the nominations are open for another day."

"Okay…So, is that it for now?"

"Pretty much."

"Okay, so here's the new gate code. Make sure everyone has it. I'm headed back home. There's some stuff on my desk I need to attend to."

I started to leave.

"Oh, are we still on for the council meeting tonight?"

"As far as I know, yeah," Anne said.

"And?" I said to Elicia.

"Yeah, we're all ready for takeoff," she said with a big smile.

"You guys are nuts," Kristy said. "I can just see Camellia. She'll probably end up in a straightjacket."

Tara and Ashley bit their nails then raised their hands, signaling their intentions. Hans, Kato and Donny acknowledged me with three salutes. I looked at Colette. She nodded and went back to what she was doing.

"And you?" I said to Kristy.

"You can count me out of this *trip* you're planning to take."

"And Dr. McDonald?"

"I'll disown him if does."

"I guess that's between the two of you. Wouldn't hurt to have a couple of chaperones. So, see you all at 6:00 then."

I gave Colette a passing squeeze of the shoulders and headed back to my place.

As the hour to trip drew nigh, I grew increasingly tremulous. I had passed through the looking glass before and knew what to expect — my heart ripped open and the truth revealed. There would be no more escaping my feelings for Tara.

I grabbed some veggies and chicken out of the refrigerator and made up a giant stir fry. I also knew everyone would be hungry at some point later on and lack the wherewithal to boil an egg.

At the appointed hour, I started off through the forest on foot in the dusky light. Nearing the cottages, I ran into Tara and Ashley.

"To the sacrifice," Ashley said when they were beside me.

"The steps definitely have an Aztecy feel to them," Tara said.

"And the Aztec altar ran red with blood," Ashley said.

I glanced over at her.

"Hard to imagine," I said.

"You mean having your heart cut out?" Ashley said.

"I wasn't going to say it out loud."

"I said it for you."

"You did."

We walked along in silence.

"So, are you really just one of us peasants?" Tara said.

"I'd like to think so."

Tara smiled in response. Hearing voices, I looked to find Colette with Kyler and Camellia behind us and excused myself.

"Hi," I said, meeting up with them.

"It seems like there should be banners and trumpets and shit like that," Kyler said.

"With emphasis on the 'shit like that'," Colette said.

I nodded and fell into place beside Colette.

Hearing more voices, I looked back to find Dr. McDonald and Kristy coming up behind us. Hans and Kato and Donny and Yvonne were behind them another fifty yards.

"It's starting to feel like a sacrifice," Kyler said.

"Ashley was saying the same thing."

"I'm thinking more along the lines of the Dionysian Mysteries," Colette said. "Thank you very much."

"Yeah. So how are you?" I asked Camellia. "Are you okay with this trip?"

She stared at me with her searching eyes. That was her answer.

At the steps, Tara and Ashley were waiting for us.

"Watch out for bouncing heads," Ashley said.

"Please. I don't even want to think about it," Colette said.

"You had to be on drugs," Ashley said.

"I believe they were," Tara said.

"And so will we pretty soon!" Kyler said.

"What are you guys talking about?" Kristy said, coming up the steps behind us.

"Aztec sacrifices," Ashley said.

"The still beating heart," Tara said.

"You guys are giving me the creeps."

"Are you still chaperoning?" I said.

"Yes."

"And you, Dr. McDonald?"

"You know, ever since reading about Huxley and Albert and Leary and their early experiments at Cambridge, I have wondered."

"If you do, I'll kill you," Kristy said.

"Being familiar with anatomy, Dr. McDonald should be very helpful with the sacrifice," Ashley said.

"Will you guys stop it!" Kristy said.

"Hey look," Tara said. "We have ghosts in the yurt."

"It's Anne and David," I said. "They always come early to set things up."

"There's a third ghost too."

"It must be Elicia."

More jokes were made about sacrifices on our way up the steps but most of the silliness had dissipated by the time we took our seats in the yurt. David had arranged candles on a low table in the center of our circle. Anne came around with the tea. Elicia passed out the mushrooms in little ceremonial bowls.

"I had started to put them in plastic bags but that just seemed totally not green and tribally, right?" she said.

"Are we supposed to take them now?" Ashley said.

"Nooooo!" Elicia said and laughed. "No, we should all get comfortable and have a little ceremonial introduction before embarking."

"You can keep ours," Kristy told Elicia.

"I haven't said no yet," Dr. McDonald said with a smile.

"That's it. I want a divorce."

"I recommend waiting until *after* the trip before making any major life decisions," Elicia said with a smile.

Finally everyone had their tea and mushrooms and we sat staring at each other in the flickering candlelight.

"So," Elicia said. "Does anyone have any doubts or concerns?"

"Yeah, me," Kristy said with a look at her husband.

"I'm just curious," Dr. McDonald said with his sunny smile. "How much experience have you had with this particular mushroom, Elicia?"

"Enough."

"And would you say it's along the lines of an LSD trip or milder?"

"Oh, much milder, yeah. You will definitely have a psychedelic experience but it will seem very gentle and almost comforting."

"I'm sure," Kristy said.

"No, it's true," Anne said.

"So, no one would be inclined to jump out of a second story window," Dr. McDonald said with a chuckle.

"No. There will be a period where it seems as if you have penetrated into the mysteries of life and then it will just feel like a magic carpet ride for several hours."

"And you think I'll be able to get back to work on Monday morning?"

"No problem."

"John, please. Don't even think about doing this."

"No, I'm curious. I often thought about it in college but it just never seemed like the right timing with my studies, but now this seems entirely safe to me."

Kristy threw up her hands.

"I can't believe this. It's like we're from different planets all of a sudden."

"Why don't you just come along?" Anne said.

"No way."

"Well, all right," Elicia said. "If everyone else is onboard, we're ready to begin. So, you chew them. They'll taste just like regular mushrooms. And then it will take anywhere from half an hour to an hour to come on. At that point, we'll see everything differently, including each other. Our relationships will change, but I can assure you that we will love each other even more deeply and profoundly than before. We will really be a tribe then."

407

"Here, here," I said.

"So, ready?" Elicia said.

She began to chew her first mushroom and everyone else followed suit, save for Kristy. She sat there with a forlorn look on her face, as if we were waving goodbye to her from a departing rocket ship.

Each of us had roughly five mushrooms and it took the better part of five minutes to chew them all down. There were looks of intrigue among us and jokes about intergalactic travels.

"God, I feel completely left out now," Kristy said.

"So join us," Elicia said.

"Yeah," Anne said. "It's not at all like that bad stuff you've read about. It's just like this really mellow, joyful experience."

"I'll be here with you," Dr. McDonald said.

Reluctantly, Kristy bit the cap off one of the mushrooms and began to chew.

"Maybe I'll have just one."

There were looks around the circle.

"They're kind of tasty," she said. "Okay, two."

She smiled when everyone laughed.

There had been something on my mind all day and I decided that this was a good time to express it.

"So, listen, everyone."

"The grand poohbah speaketh," Ashley said.

"Get yer, get yer, get yer, get yer poohbahs out," she sang with Tara.

"It's a wonder anything gets done around here," Kristy said.

"It is, isn't it?" Anne said with a bemused smile.

Seeing me wait, Ashley and Tara pretended to bow.

"Thank you. So I've been thinking about our need to grow and wanted to make a motion for each of us to nominate a new member of the tribe."

"I thought we weren't going to conduct any tribal business tonight," Yvonne said.

"Yeah, what if *everybody* decided to make a motion?" Kristy said.

"Okay. I just thought while we're waiting to come on, you know."

"When *are* we going to come on?" Kyler said.

"You mean unglued?" Donny said.

"Yeah!"

"I understand Caesar at this moment."

"There there," Colette said with a pat on my arm.

"So, like Ashley had said, and Jenner with the Rolling Stone was saying too, we look a lot like the Republican Party, so how about we strive for diversity in our nominations?"

"Face black?" Kyler said.

"Bigotry," Elicia said.

"All right, I think Steven has a good point," Anne said. "We need to grow and diversify, but I also think we need to find ways to uplift people and help the less fortunate."

"I think I'm coming on," Kyler said. "No, just kidding."

"Yeah, is this really what we want to be doing right now?" Yvonne said.

"Look, it's not going to hurt anything to have a quick vote," Anne said. "So all in agreement."

There was a majority consensus.

"So any comments first?"

"Yeah, get me some bracero helpers," Kyler said.

"I'm serious," Anne said.

"Me too!" Kyler said with a laugh.

"All right. Let's just have a vote. All in favor of nominating a new member raise your hands."

Without any great enthusiasm, but without dissent, everyone did so.

"Does Irish qualify as a minority," Tara said.

"Hey, I resemble that," Donny said.

"How about Italian?" Kyler said.

"I know a single mother with a little girl who's really fantastic with crafts and environmental stuff," Elicia said. "So, are we considering kids?"

"That's a really good question," Anne said.

"Maybe we can agree to consider each nomination on its merits?" I said. "Without prior prejudice?"

"I can agree to that," Anne said.

"I'm hungry," Kristy said.

"You won't be for long," Ashley said to great laughter.

I had been sitting there for a spell, staring at the flickering candles, when all of a sudden I awakened on the other side. There was no past, and no future. There was only the mysterious now, and it felt as if I had been in that 'now' for all eternity.

Too, the faces around me were now archetypal. Elicia was the earth mother, Anne the benevolent judge, David an elf, Ashley an elfish princess, Kyler was Tom Bombadil, Colette the Queen of Spades, Dr. McDonald the corn god. When I got to Tara, I stopped. She was staring back. Our hearts were as one.

"Oh wow," Kristy said to Kyler. "I know you from another lifetime. You are my ancient brother."

"I *am* an ancient brother," he said.

"Wow, you're a samurai warrior," Yvonne said to Kato.

He had stood up and was pretending to do tai chi with a sword.

Everyone around the circle had gravitated towards someone. I looked at Colette and her beauty was flat, like the face of a card, but Tara radiated to me.

Suddenly, a strange voice was calling from outside the door and it opened. A medieval highwayman stood there. Everyone turned to look.

"Bloody hell, you all looked shanked, mates."

"Connor, the Viking warrior," I said.

"You kept telling me to come out, sir, so here I am."

Everyone stared.

"I can see I'm interrupting something, right?"

Elicia went over to him.

"We're on a journey. You have to join us or leave."

"Bloody psychedelics?"

She nodded.

"Well, if you've got some on hand, guess I'll join you. Must be some reason why the gods dragged me out here."

Elicia led him over to a bag of mushrooms by the stove. They returned and Connor took a seat on the other side of Colette. I watched him chewing on a mushroom.

"Be awhile before I catch up with you, mate."

I nodded. People talked but the words meant very little to me.

"The trees are calling," I said sometime later and stood up.

Outside, I had started off through the forest when Tara magically appeared. I stopped, stared into her eyes, touched her face. Then we kissed.

A gap in time occurred. Then we were deep in the forest together, Tara with her back against a towering pine, her dress up and one leg around me as we were joined by cock and cunt.

"I have known you forever," I said.

"Forever," she said.

"I never want us to be apart again."

"Never," she said.

Our flesh was soon satiated but our spirits remained interlocked. I spoke untold things to Tara without saying a word.

We were there a long time when the reentry began.

"Time," I said.

"It's come back."

"But a different time."

"The less of us, the greater the mystery."

We wandered off as if chasing wood sprites through the forest. Then magically we found ourselves back at the yurt.

"There he is," Kristy said as we walked in.

411

"There you are," I said.

"Yep, it's me," she said and did a funny little jig with her crosswise fist pump.

When everyone laughed, she did it again.

"I see you have found your true self," I said.

"Yep, that's me."

I looked and saw that Connor and Colette were missing; both relieved and wounded to realize this fact. Otherwise, Yvonne was off talking quietly with Kato in the shadows. Donny lay with his head in Camellia's lap. Elicia was lying next to Kyler. Hans and Ashley were lying with their bodies in opposite directions and their heads touching. Dr. McDonald lay in the center of the circle, staring up at the ceiling. Anne and David alone were still curled up together. One got the sense that they had met in this very same way.

Tara went and sat by Hans and Ashley. I went and sat by Dr. McDonald.

"How are you?" I asked.

"Who am I?" he said, turning his head to look at me with a smile. "That is the real question."

"Do you know?" I said.

"Yes, I think so. I have come to bring peace and heal the world."

"I always feel peaceful when I'm around you."

"You have done something very wonderful here. I feel…there is a sense of peace that comes with being here together. Home. I feel at home."

"We have done something wonderful here," I said.

Ashley sat up suddenly and came over to me.

"Oh, grand poohbah." She ran her fingernails through my hair. "We love you, grand poohbah. You make all things possible."

Tara joined her in running fingernails through my hair.

"We love our grand poohbah."

"I will be the grand poohbah of all grand poohbahs, if it makes you happy."

"It does. You are the grand poohbah because you don't care about being a grand poohbah."

"Yes, just being an old run of the mill poohbah is all right by me."

I sat there smiling and soaking in their affection.

"I'm hungry again," Kristy said out of the blue.

"Me too," Yvonne said.

She came over out of the shadows.

"So what should we do?" Anne said.

"I have food," I said.

"But who will cook it?"

"It's already cooked."

"Oh, grand poohbah of all the grand poohbahs," Ashley said.

"I was thinking ahead."

"When it was a world where people still thought ahead," Tara said.

"You *are* a grand poohbah," Kristy said.

I stood up.

"Shall we go find my treehouse?"

"Yes, let's go find your treehouse," Anne said.

"We're off to see the wizard, the wonderful wizard of Oz."

Everyone joined in with the song and filed out of the yurt.

"But what about Connor and Colette?" Anne said outside.

"They will find us," I said.

"There," Kristy said, pretending to pin a note on the door. "They'll know we went off to find the yellow brick road."

Tara and Ashley were already skipping down the steps, singing the song. Kyler and Elicia joined in with them. The rest of us followed along, talking and laughing.

At the bottom of the steps, Camellia came up to me, put her hands around my face and kissed me.

"Thank you," she said and stared into my eyes for a long moment before walking ahead.

413

31

On our way through the forest, Tara and I fell farther and farther behind the others. Now and then we saw faces turning back to look and slipped in among the trees with a laugh. All through what seemed like a yearlong journey, we heard the word games and nonsense of our friends echoing from up ahead.

"Man does not live by bread alone."

"But by all the stir fry that emanates from Steven's wok."

"Wok-a-doodle-do."

"Wok a mile in my moccasins."

"Wok, don't run."

"How *do* you stir up a fry, by the way?"

"Well, first you find a fry, and then you stir it up, of course."

"And then you break bread."

"Who broke the bread?"

"Did you say we're having baroque bread?"

"Yes, it's a very intricate subject."

When the ongoing laughter and jokes faded to silence, Tara grabbed my hand.

"We'd better catch up."

It did seem as if we were all alone in the darkness now and ran ahead wildly.

"There," I said, seeing the lights of my treehouse come into view.

We hurried on and found the others just then making their way in through the front door. Tara and I rushed up the stairs and into a general commotion. Anne had uncovered the lid to the wok in my kitchen but no one appeared to know what to do next.

"What *do* we do with your stir fries," Kristy asked me.

"Gas them," I said and turned on the burner.

"Oh no," David said. "He's going to burn the dear little stir fries at the stake."

"They will go willingly down our gullets," Hans said.

"A sacrifice that must be repaid with our joyfulness," Elicia said.

"And joyful we are," Ashley said.

"And if not, off with their heads," Kristy said.

"Wow, how quickly we arrived at the French Revolution," Dr. McDonald said.

"I believe Napoleon's next," Kato said.

Tara looked at me.

"Not I," I said with a hand placed inside my shirt.

"Ha, this must be your Waterloo," Hans said.

"No, this is my treehouse. Waterloo's down the road a few miles...Will somebody please break the bread?" I said above the laughter.

"Can I just slice it?" Kristy said as if overwhelmed.

"No, but you can baroque it," Ashley said.

Kristy doubled over in laughter.

"Okay, how do you baroque it?"

Ashley jumped in and the two of them started slicing. I went about uncorking bottles of wine.

"To the ancient god of wine," Ashley said as I poured her goblet full.

Glasses were held aloft and wine savored.

"I have some sparkling water for you Kyler," I said.

He came over and placed a hand on my shoulder.

"Wow, I was kind of worried about this trip and my sobriety, boss man, you know, but it's like totally made me

415

aware of how stupid drinking is for me. I'm like on this higher plane all of a sudden where drinking is just this idiotic and destructive thing."

"So you're all right?"

"Oh wow man, totally. I can see like this spiritual journey now and would never turn back. Drinking for me is like being a stupid drunken Norsemen."

I laughed.

"Hey, that's so good to hear, Kyler."

"Yeah, man. Wow. I never expected this but I'm free. I finally fucking free of all that bullshit."

"All right."

I gave him a big hug.

"Well, let's get this meal going."

"Yeah! Let's eat some stir fries!"

"Plates, everyone?" I called out.

"Did you want home plate?"

All too aware of where this was headed, I grabbed the plates myself. Kristy was still slicing bread as I passed by.

"Anyone like a slice of life?" she said with a big smile.

"It will be a miracle if anyone actually gets around to eating," Yvonne said as we took our seats.

"I'll eat some," Kyler said and took a big bite.

"Oh no! The poor little fries are going down his gullet!" Ashley said.

"Screaming and dripping down his gluttonous maw," Tara said.

"Yeah!"

"Hey, this is really good," Kristy said.

Ashley held up her glass.

"Here's to being gluttonous."

"Gluttonous maximus."

"Gluttonous minimus will do."

"Hmm, good stir fry," Tara said. "Thank you, grand poohbah of all grand poohbahs, for thinking ahead."

"Amen," Elicia said. "We would all be out hunting stir fries right now if it weren't for our grand poohbah."

Everyone touched glasses and drank to the good food and companionship. The bantering went on and on.

"I wonder what happened to Colette and Connor?" Kristy said at one point.

I looked around the table at all the faces and shrugged. I had completely forgotten about them.

"It just dawned on me," Kristy said. "How did Connor get onto the property?"

"I gave him the gate code," I said. "I knew he'd be coming out here someday soon to take a look at a building site."

"Maybe we should send out a search party to look," Elicia said.

"Why don't we just call their numbers," Anne said. "They probably don't know where we are."

I called both of them but got no answer. I shrugged and received more shrugs in return.

Over the course of the next half hour, I did grow concerned. There were bears up here in the woods and an attack was not completely out of the question.

A short while later, amidst the din of conversation, we heard footsteps coming up the stairs. The door opened and Colette came in with Connor. I stood up and went over to give Colette a hug, then Connor.

"We were worried about you."

"Yeah," Anne said. "We weren't sure if you knew where to find us."

Colette and I exchanged another look and she went over to greet everyone else.

"Sorry, mate," Connor said to me quietly.

"It's all right. The deck's been shuffled."

"You understand then."

"Yeah. It happened to me too. With Tara."

"I kind of gathered as much when you two disappeared."

"Yeah. I'm guessing everything's exactly as it should be."

"You're sure, mate?"

"Connor, I couldn't be happier."

"The same here."

"Good. So come in. There's food and drink."

"A glass of wine sounds heavenly."

I poured him a glass of pinot noir and showed him to the food. Colette remained at the table, talking with Anne and Elicia. When our eyes met, she looked away quickly so I went over to reassure her.

"It's all right, Colette," I whispered in her ear. "We're where our hearts have told us to be."

She looked at me.

"I still feel mixed up."

"No, no. Everything's fine. Come, have some wine and something to eat."

Later, with everyone coming back to earth, bodies drifted out towards the living room with an ongoing sense of awkwardness. Only David and Anne and Kristy and Dr. McDonald had survived the journey as couples. Everyone else had either switched places or had found a new partner—Tara with me, Colette with Connor, Donny with Camellia, Yvonne with Kato, Kyler with Elicia and Hans with Ashley. What of this would stick was anybody's guess, but there were looks around the room as if everyone felt unsure what to make of it.

"Is everyone okay," Elicia said.

Around the room, there were tentative nods of the head.

"Things sometimes change when you go over to the other side and come back, but we're still a tribe, right?"

"That's what's so cool," Anne said. "Different pieces can come and go and shift around, but the tribe remains."

"I just want to say I love all of you," Colette said. "Steven. You are like an ancient brother to me and I'm so glad that you came into my life."

"I love you, too, Colette. And Connor and all of you. There have been times when I've wanted to run away from what I started here, but I would not trade what we've become for anything in the world."

"Is Connor one of us now?" Kristy said with a look around the room. "Are you?"

"I thought you had to be voted onto the island," Connor said.

"That's why I'm asking," Kristy said.

"The question is, do you want to be one of us?" Anne said.

"Look, mates, I still have my vote in for hot tubs and the likes, but sure." He squeezed Colette's hand. "I'm all onboard if you'll have me."

"Shall we vote then?" Anne said.

"Wait a minute," Kyler said. "Aren't we supposed to convene all the grand poohbahs first?"

"Yeah," Ashley said. "To decide if we should convene all the grand poohbahs, so all the grand poohbahs can decide what all the grand poohbahs want to decide."

"Then I make a motion to convene all the grand poohbahs," I said.

"I second the motion," Kyler said.

"Okay, all the grand poohbahs are convened," Anne said.

"Hey, just who are all the grand poohbahs?" Yvonne said.

"If you were a grand poohbah, you'd already know," Dr. McDonald said.

"All right!" I said, channeling Ralph Kramden.

"Uh oh, the grand poohbah of all grand poohbahs is angry," Ashley said.

"Well. Can we just have a vote?"

"Okay, I agree," Anne said. "Let's just go ahead with the vote. All in favor of making Connor a member of the tribe."

There were looks all around but no one raised a hand.

"Bloody hell," Connor said. "It's worse than being booted off."

Then in unison, everyone broke out in cheers and raised a hand.

"Welcome aboard!" Kyler said.

"Jesus, brings a tear to me eyes, mates."

"Here, let's have a toast," I said and brought over the bottle of brandy with some snifters. "The couples can share one."

"I'll make us some Shirley Temples," Elicia said.

"Yeah! Screw you drunken heathens," Kyler said.

Elicia came back from the bar with two drinks and we all held our glasses high.

"So, to our latest member. Welcome aboard."

Everyone cheered and drank.

"Hey, are we still nominating new members?" Kyler said.

"Not you," Donny said.

Everyone laughed.

"Hey, I met the guy at a meeting. How was I supposed to know he was a madman?"

"Because the guy had been sober for all of three days maybe?" Ashley said.

"Yeah, we need to be careful," Anne said. "But we also need to be supportive of recovery."

"I think we need some more peasants," Kyler said. "Otherwise we'll start to look snobby."

"Personally, I enjoy my effete intellectual snob status," Hans said.

"To the garden with him for some cultural indoctrination!" Tara said.

"Yeah! That's how we'll punish people around here. Ten days of weeding in the garden!"

"You know what I think," Anne said. "We need to have a real cross section of society out here. Children and old people. So we can see the whole circle of life."

"Yeah, that's a really good idea," Yvonne said. "My mother's a widow and really struggling and I would feel so much better if she were out here with me."

"Yeah. It's not a tribe without young and old people," Anne said.

The following moment of silence was broken by someone shouting off in the woods. Then a gun went off and everyone jumped.

"What in bloody hell?" Connor said.

"Fuck. It's Sage," Kyler said. "I can totally tell by his voice."

"Great," Kristy said to Elicia. "What was that you said about seeing the best in people?"

"Let's not get started," I said.

"Who's bloody Sage?" Connor said.

While Kyler explained, I hit the lights and closed the curtains.

"Everyone keep it down," I whispered. "I think he's too far away to have seen the lights but he's definitely coming this way."

"Shouldn't we just get out of here?" David whispered back.

I looked at all the faces around the room.

"And if he sees us leaving? Then what?"

"Well, I don't know if waiting around here like sitting ducks is the brightest idea, either," Yvonne said.

"I say we call the police," Kristy said.

I darted a look her way.

"I do *not* need the police out here right now."

"Better that than being shot."

"Maybe it's best if we go down and confront him, mate," Connor said.

I looked from face to face, weighing the idea.

"All right, look. Connor and I will go down and try to disarm the son of a bitch."

"Don't," Colette said with a hand on Connor.

I looked at her hand and back.

"We'll be all right. It's two against one."

I went to the hall closet and returned with a sheepskin rifle case and two baseball bats.

"Is that really a gun?" Kristy said

I pulled a 12 gauge shotgun out of the case, snapped open the breech, placed two shells in the barrel and snapped the breech shut.

"Beautiful gun," Dr. McDonald said.

"Yeah. An Aguirre & Aranzabal. Came down from my father."

I handed him the shotgun

Forget it," Kristy said. "I don't want my husband shooting that thing."

"Fuck, I'll take it," Tyler said. "My old man used to take me hunting all the time when I was a kid."

"All right. The safety's here."

I looked from face to face again.

"We'll try to settle this peacefully but if worse comes to worse and he tries to come through that door, you drop him."

"I'll drop him. You can bet on that, boss man."

I smiled.

"The Sundance Kid here. You ready?" I said to Connor.

He took a few swings with his bat.

"The bloody Louisville Viking, ready for battle, sir. I'll clip the bastard off right at the knees."

"All right, everyone, stay away from the windows, keep quiet and if it comes to that, call the police."

Connor had started towards the front door.

"No, this way. There's a ladder down from the back balcony."

"Be careful," Tara whispered as we slipped out the back door.

Down on the forest floor, Connor and I stopped to listen. Sage was still shouting.

"I'd say he's about two hundred yards away."

Connor nodded.

"Game plan?" he said.

"I'm thinking we hide behind a big tree and club him as he's going by."

"High, low," Connor said with a swing of his bat.

422

"Let's see."

We started up the hill through the woods. When two more shots rang out, we both froze.

"Come out, come out, wherever you are!" Sage shouted. "You chicken shit motherfuckers!"

"Sounds like he's packing a bloody cannon," Connor whispered.

I nodded.

"Something big. Maybe a .45."

I motioned farther up the hill.

Once it seemed we were safely out of sound range, I pointed north in Sage's direction. Twenty yards farther ahead, I grabbed Connor's arm and pointed. Sage came into view through the trees, a hundred yards off to our north. We watched him swaying and stumbling along the path.

"He's drunk," I whispered.

"Should be an easy mark," Connor whispered back.

I pointed down the hill.

"See those two big pines?"

Connor nodded.

"You behind one of them, me behind the other? The guy farthest away calls out, the one closest clubs him going by?"

"Sounds like a plan, mate. I'll do the clubbing."

"Are you sure. I was going to offer."

"No, my pleasure. You don't have to be a yank to swing one of these shillelaghs."

"All right but be careful. I don't think he could hit the side of a barn in his condition but he's still one burly looking motherfucker and he does have a gun."

"We'll be smart, mate. Don't you worry about that."

We slipped down the hill from tree to tree in Sage's direction. By the time we had positioned ourselves behind the two big pines, he was a short ways past us on the trail. With a final nod from Connor, I called out.

"What the fuck, dude? Why are you shooting off a gun out here?"

423

In lurching around, Sage nearly fell over.

"Oh, so you fuckers finally decided to come out of hiding. Well, come on over here and we'll have ourselves a little chat."

"No, you come over here."

There was a long moment of silence.

"Fuck. You don't think I'm going to fall for that shit, do you?"

"What shit? You've got a gun and I've got my dick in my hands."

"Yeah? You're right, I do have a gun and you people are going to eat some shit for the way you treated me. Fucking bunch of hippie motherfuckers. So where are you?"

"Over here."

"Over where?"

I heard the voice coming my way.

"Where," he said again.

A moment later, I heard the sounds of a scuffle and peeked out to find Sage with his back to me and his gun pointed at Connor. Connor had his hands up. Sage motioned with the gun and Connor carefully set the baseball bat down.

"So you're the big fucker, huh?" Sage said. "Gonna help out the world but couldn't help a poor fucking vet. So where are the rest of you fuckers?"

Connor stood there silently.

"What's the matter? Cat got your tongue?"

It struck me why Connor wasn't speaking. One word of his accent and Sage would know there were two of us out here.

I took a cautious step that way but a twig snapped under my feet and Sage swung around in my direction.

"Oohhhh. So there's two of you motherfuckers. Trying to set me up, huh?"

Sage came at me now with the gun. As he did, Connor went for the bat and caught Sage a good one across the wrist before he could lurch back around. Sage dropped the gun with a yelp. For good measure, Connor whacked him again across the back of the knees and Sage went down with another yelp.

I dashed over and grabbed the gun. Connor stood over Sage with the bat.

"Bloody bastard. I've half a mind to beat your brains in."

"Yeah? Well fuck you. You'd better put a bullet in me, 'cuz if you don't I'll be back out here to waste all of you motherfuckers someday."

"Fuck, what do you do with the bloody bastard?"

"I'll tell you what we're not going to do. Call the police. Not unless it becomes absolutely necessary."

"So what then?"

"I guess take him up to my house."

"And do what, mate?"

"Try to talk some sense into him."

"Sounds like a bloody mess to me, mate. What if he goes off up there?"

"I don't know."

I handed Connor the gun and offered Sage my hand.

"Come on. Get up."

"Fuck you."

"It's come with us or you're going to jail. Or I'll personally put a bullet in you. Now what's it going to be?"

Reluctantly, Sage took hold of my hand.

"Fuck!" he said, putting weight on his wounded leg. "You're lucky I'm wounded or I'd waste both you fucking pukes right now."

"Yeah, yeah. Big tough guy. Now let's go."

Sage went hobbling along ahead of us. I took the gun back from Connor and followed. When we came to my place, Sage stopped.

"So this is where all you fuckers were hiding."

"Go on. Get upstairs," I said.

Sage did so, hopping on his one good leg.

"Hey, it's Connor and me!" I called up to forewarn everyone.

When Kristy opened the door and saw Sage, she jumped back. Then she saw that I had the gun.

"Hit the lights and have everyone back out of the way. We don't want any hostages."

We went in with the tribe members huddled together back by the kitchen. Kyler had the shotgun pointed. I motioned for him to drop it.

"Here, sit down," I said to Sage.

"Aw, fuck!" he said, taking his seat in a chair.

"I'd better have a look at him," Dr. McDonald said.

"All right. Just be careful."

I stood right behind Sage with the gun.

"Try anything and I'll drop you, pal."

When Dr. McDonald probed the bones in Sage's wrist, he yelped again.

"Right there?" Dr. McDonald said.

Sage nodded, his eyes watering.

"You may have fractured his capitate and hamate bones. Somebody bring me some ice. Let's see the leg," he said to Sage.

Again, he yelped.

"Looks like a pretty serious contusion. Probably of his lateral digital extensor tendon."

Kristy brought ice in a towel and Dr. McDonald placed it gently on the wrist.

"You shouldn't be walking on that leg."

"No shit." Sage looked around at all the faces. "You people fucked me up good."

"Well, what did you expect?" Donny said. "You were going to fuck us up pretty good if we didn't."

"Yeah? Well fuck all of you."

"Please, back off, Dr. McDonald," I said.

"Yeah, what are we going to do with him?" Kristy said.

"The least you fuckers can do is give me a drink. I'm in pain here."

Hans started for the liquor cabinet.

"No," I said. "He's had enough liquor already."

"I say we give him some mushrooms," Kyler said.

"He'd be a sight more sociable," Ashley said.

"No," Anne said. "We have no right to force that on him."

As she approached, Sage looked up in seeming awe of her regal presence.

"Remember, we had encouraged you to get help," she said. "Yeah, like a vet support group or something."

"But you said you weren't into that shit," Kyler said.

Anne held up a hand.

"And we were willing to be supportive, but we're trying to create a mellow, peaceful community out here and energy like yours has no place in it."

"Hey, I've got some really good grass," Kato said.

Anne looked around at all the faces and stopped at mine. I shrugged.

"What about that, Sage. Do you want to have a toke with us?"

He too looked around at all the faces and hung his head.

"Yeah, sure. If you're offering, I'll have a hit."

I nodded at Kato, who pulled out a pipe and a small zip lock baggie. He came over and offered Sage the first toke. Sage inhaled and held it for a moment before exhaling with a cough. I sat opposite him with the gun in my hand. The pipe went around the room with more people inhaling and coughing.

"Fuck, I'm getting a contact buzz," Kyler said and headed out to the front porch.

Camellia and Elicia joined him.

"We keep forgetting about our sober members," Anne said.

I shrugged and turned my attention back to Sage. He was looking around the room with tears in his eyes now. Anne knelt beside him.

"Hey, it's all right," she said and patted his hand.

Sage hung his head.

"It's okay. It's okay. We care. We just can't have these bad vibes around here."

"Fuck, I'm sorry. I'm really sorry, man." He looked around at all the faces. "I just feel so fucking lonesome sometimes, you know?"

He broke down, sobbing.

"It's all right," Anne said and put her arm around him.

Tara and Ashley went over to comfort him too and the gentleness of this female energy led to an even greater expression of grief.

Slowly, everyone in the room drifted closer to Sage and stared. I grabbed the shotgun and hid it with the pistol in a back room. Kyler was coming back from the front porch with Elicia and Camellia as I returned to the living room. Seeing Sage weep, Kyler came over and whispered to me.

"Fuck, boss man, he's totally losing it."

I nodded and sat down with the others. Sage looked up as though ashamed.

"Fuck, I'm sorry," he said again to everyone in general.

"It's okay," Anne said. "You see? Our tribe is all about love and forgiveness and second chances."

"So why didn't you give me a second chance? You just ran me off like I was shit."

"Maybe we shouldn't have, but your energy just didn't seem right to everyone and look what happened. You think maybe we were right?"

"Fuck, I don't know. I don't know how to deal with this world. All I know how to do is blow shit up and waste people."

"So, what do you want to do?" Anne said.

Sage looked around at all the faces again.

"I don't know. I told you. I just feel so fucking alone."

I searched the rest of the faces and nodded at the back door.

"We need to have a pow wow," I told Sage.

Out on the balcony, we went round and round about what to do before we finally came to an agreement and went back inside.

"All right," Anne said, kneeling down next to him again. "We're willing to let you participate in our tribe on a probationary basis, but only to visit for now and you have to stay sober and get help. We'll try to make you feel at home and support you as much as we can and if works out with everyone, we'll let you come live here permanently. Are you willing to try that?"

He hung his head and nodded. Everyone in the group had gathered near and offered their reassurances.

32

I awakened the next morning with Tara's auburn hair splashed across my chest, her blushing right ear exposed, her pale neck and shoulders. I wanted to kiss them all and every part of her but contented myself with watching and waiting until she finally stirred. When she did, her hand reflexively reached out and struck my face.

"Oh, sorry," she said with a sleepy smile my way.

I kissed her in place of words and those kisses quickly erupted into passions.

Afterwards, we both used the bathroom and returned to caressing in bed.

"Do you remember the words we spoke last night?"

Tara had her head on my chest and looked up at me.

"About never being apart again?"

I nodded.

"About being together forever and ever."

She nodded.

"Why? Do you think that was silly?"

"Not at all. That's how it feels in my heart. But they are only words. An attempt to capture what in the end are ephemeral feelings."

I caressed her.

"What is this lovely flesh? This journey we make among the stars?"

"You're being very metaphysical this morning, oh grand poohbah."

I smiled and pulled her closer.

"I remember this conversation between Kerouac and Ginsberg in *Dharma Bums*, where they were discussing Buddhism and Ginsberg was saying it was all a bunch of rot and he was glad that something had come out of nothing and Kerouac said, no, no, no, you've got it all wrong, that nothing had come out of something and it was all about trying to get back to that *something* and I thought, well, isn't that the great question right there? Is this *something*?"

I kissed her all over until she giggled.

"Or is it nothing? Or perhaps the two are one and the same thing and it's only us tangled up in our words that makes it seem like there's a difference?"

Tara lay there staring at me intently.

"What *are* you trying to say, oh great poohbah?"

"Hell if I know."

She laughed as if I had told a great joke and we were both quiet then.

"I suppose that human beings have been trying to understand the mysteries of this universe for what, a hundred thousand years now? Trying to find the answers for why we're here and just looking at you makes me feel like I understand it all in an instant. Like this is the whole thing right here and all I want to do is to go on feeling this sense of wonder and bliss forever and ever..."

I looked over at her.

"...and probably a bit longer than that."

She studied me for a long moment, then kissed my lips and face and nestled up more closely in my arms.

"I just pray this beautiful spell is never broken."

I had a thousand things to say in response but decided it was very wise and probably wiser than anything I had said already and left things at that.

"Will it break our spell to have breakfast?" I asked a while later

"No. Not having breakfast might."

I laughed, kissed her forehead and got to my feet.

"Shall I come help you?"

"Sure. I'll start things," I said, grabbing my robe. "You can use this bathroom."

"Thanks. I'll see you in a minute."

I relieved my bladder again downstairs and brewed some coffee. To go with the gray, wet weather outside, I made oatmeal and toast.

Tara appeared a few minutes later, blushingly wrapped in my comforter. I took hold of her, wanting to tear the comforter off and start all over again.

"You make everything look divine, dear."

We kissed standing there.

"Can I help?" she said, looking up at me.

"You're going to have a hard time with that comforter."

She smiled.

"It's all ready. Go have a seat."

She poured herself a cup of coffee and did so. I brought everything over to the table and we started doctoring things up with butter and honey.

"I'm glad I don't have to work today," she said while stirring her oatmeal.

"David gave you the day off, did he?"

"He and Anne said they would take care of things. I believe Hans and Kato are going to spell them. Ashley and I are on call in case of an emergency. Donny too."

"Let's hope there aren't any emergencies."

Tara took a spoonful of her oatmeal.

"Hmm, good. Goes with the rainy day."

"That was my thought. Strawberry preserves for your toast, dear?"

I pushed the jar her way.

"Hmm. Thank you. And what are you doing today?"

I made eyes at her. She smiled.

"I see."

"Actually I have two things on my agenda."

"Which would be?"

"Well, one, and I believe this comes under the heading of common decency. I need to go over and talk with Colette. Clear the air, you know? I trust you understand."

Tara nodded.

"And what would the second one be?"

"Well, first, let me ask you a question. How would you feel about taking a trip?"

"I just did."

"Ha ha. I mean the other kind of trip."

"I know. To go wandering. So where, and for how long? I doubt David's going to take very kindly to my absence."

"Don't worry about David. I'll buy out your contract."

"Oh, great. I'm chattel now."

"Sorry."

She quickly reached out with a hand.

"Me too. This is just a woman dealing with ancient woman stuff. You understand."

"I understand."

"So back to your plans."

"So, I'm hoping to arrange another tribal council this evening and discuss things with the whole tribe."

"And that would be?"

"Let's call it a surprise."

She wrinkled up her nose and went back to her oatmeal. I reached out and took her hand in mine.

"Are we both here, darling? Is what we've been saying really true for you too?"

She nodded.

"Okay, so I can't predict the future but I can guarantee you this much. If you come with me, you'll be comfortable. No matter what happens, you'll be comfortable. If you want, I'll

433

put money in the bank. Whatever it takes for you to relax and enjoy our journey together."

"I guess all I'd ask is that, if it ever comes to that, you'll help me to land on my feet."

"I hope it never comes to that, but I promise I will. I don't want you to ever worry again. I do love and adore you. With all my heart."

She squeezed my hand.

"I love you too, Steven. I felt like I belonged with you from the moment we first met. Money or no money."

"I know. So be patient, please. I'm going to arrange some things today, including this tribal council, and then we'll see how everyone takes to my announcement."

"Are you always this secretive?"

"No."

She stared.

"All right. Let me explain."

Tara listened as I went on for the better part of five minutes.

"So? Sound like fun?"

"Sure. Right now, a bit of Latin sun sounds delightful. Don't know how everyone else is going to take to this. Not happily, I think."

"You just come up with someone to nominate and I'll handle the rest."

"And you? Do you have someone in mind?"

"I do. But it's a secret."

"Well mine is too."

"Well, mine is more secret than yours."

I had finished the rest of my oatmeal and went to place my bowl in the sink. Tara's neck and shoulders were exposed to me on the way back so I pulled her mane of auburn hair aside and kissed her there. I heard the spoon clang in her bowl and her hand came up to touch my face.

"I want to do sweet things to you," I whispered in her ear.

When she moaned, I swept her up in my arms, comforter and all, and carried her back up to my bed.

An hour later, I tracked down Kyler and Elicia at her place.

"How was your reentry?" she asked with a big smile.

"Fine. I'm feeling a bit like a stranger in a strange land, but I'm good. And you?"

"I trip like this every few months so no big surprises here."

"That's obviously not going be the case with everyone. Can't wait to see Kristy this morning."

Elicia smiled.

"So, how are things with Tara and Colette?"

"Fine with Tara. I'm going by Colette's place right now. Are we still on for what we had discussed?"

Elicia looked at Kyler and back at me with a smile.

"We're still game."

"Yeah, boss man. I'm stoked about taking this trip."

"Good. Me too. Time for the hive to swarm."

"Good one," Elicia said.

"Okay, off on my next mission."

"Hey, wait a minute," Elicia said. "Didn't you say something about going to see a play this evening?"

"Oh god. I'd completely forgotten."

"Did you still want to go?"

"No. Screw Shakespeare this. What do you think?"

"I was looking forward to all those ribald inns and saucy wenches, boss man."

"Yeah. Another time, huh? I don't really feel like going into town tonight."

"Sure. We're happy here at home too," Elicia said.

"I'll call the box office and tell them to donate the tickets to charity."

I started out.

"Good luck," Elicia said.

"Yeah. I'm sure everything's fine. I just want to reassure her."

Hey," I said at the door. "If you see any of the gang before me, let them know about the council meeting tonight, okay?"

"You got it, boss man. I already let Donny and Camellia know."

"Donny and Camellia," I said with a shake of my head.

"Change, change changes," Elicia said.

"Yes indeed."

I found Colette alone at her place. Connor had gone off to work early that morning. We hugged and sat down together in the living room.

"Are you okay?" I asked her.

"Yeah and no."

"Yeah. It's all a bit strange, but…"

I shrugged. She sighed.

"I have to be honest, Steven. When I met with Connor the other day, I had these uncomfortable feelings. Feelings I really didn't want to acknowledge. I just know I wouldn't have done what I did last night on my own. It was only after I realized you had run off with Tara."

"It's all right. We were both just following our hearts."

"Yeah, but still. We shared a lot these past two weeks. Way more than just friendship. You can't help but feel strange, having it uprooted so suddenly."

"I know. I do love you Colette, but what's happened in my heart is so clear and inescapable to me, I…"

"It's okay. I know…So what's going to happen now?"

"Nothing. You're still here. You still have the tribe. You still have your job?"

"Do I?"

"Of course."

I reached out to touch her hand.

"Dale said he would start work on the arts center foundation this coming week and I'll make sure it gets done and that your salary continues."

"I feel a bit guilty about that one."

"Don't. Just don't tell anyone. When the tribe can afford to pay you, fine. Until then, you're on my payroll. Make this place blossom with culture, Colette. That's your job."

"I can't wait to have everything going and a dance studio again."

"You will, and it will make me very happy to know that you are happy."

"Thank you. Thank you, Steven. You are a dear sweet man."

I smiled sadly.

"So, I don't know if you've heard but I'm trying to arrange a tribal council this evening. Can you make it?"

"Sure. What's up?"

"It's a surprise."

"Of course."

"You'll find out. If I start telling people the gossip will be all over town."

She looked askance at me.

"Just don't worry, okay?"

"Okay. Thank you."

"Yeah. Everything will be just fine."

I gave her a long hug and headed off for the tech center. David and Anne were monitoring things when I walked in.

"Everything good?" I said.

"Everything's good," David said. He pushed his chair away from his bank of monitors. "Votes on the new issue have already topped five million."

"How's it trending?"

"Two to one in favor of a new voting rights act."

"As we figured."

"I'm just glad to see so many people engaged and focused on what's important," Anne said. "Look at this."

She pulled up the front page of a major online news site. Their cover story was about a former athlete who had undergone a sex change.

"He is kind of cute," I said.

437

David made a face.

"She," Anne said.

"Oh yeah, *she*. By the way, I assume you've already heard…"

"…about the council meeting tonight?"

"Yeah."

"David's going to be stuck here monitoring the site but I can make it."

"I've given her the power of attorney," David said.

"And the purpose of this meeting?" Anne said.

"It's a secret."

"That's what everyone's saying."

"Sorry. I'm not trying to be coy here but as you can see, one word and it would be all over the place."

"What would?"

"Ha. Just show up, please. It's not like I have something really heavy to say."

I passed Hans taking in the gray morning from his front porch.

"Good morning."

He signaled with one finger raised in response.

"Council meeting tonight."

"If Hans returns to planet Earth by then, I'll be sure to let him know."

Donny caught up with me as I was climbing into my golf cart.

"What's up?" I said.

"It's Camellia."

"What about her?"

"It's just all this weird energy this morning. I felt such a profound connection with her last night but now I don't know."

"You're missing Yvonne."

"Yeah, no. I guess she's where she should be. I just don't know about me and Camellia."

"Take some more mushrooms."

"Yeah, right."

"Give it time, Donny. She's damaged goods but she'll heal. I see her starting to come out of her shell a bit already."

"Yeah. I just wanted to make sure I still had my own cottage."

"Of course. Whatever people need, you know?"

"Thanks, man."

I patted him on the shoulder.

"Are you going to be at the council meeting tonight?"

"Yeah, I'll be there."

"You got somebody in mind for your nomination?"

"Yeah, I do. I know a guy who's a real Renaissance man. Metal and wood, sculpture. Whatever, he can build it and he's written a few books."

"Cool. Sounds perfect. We need practical people like that out here."

I patted him on the shoulder again.

"Buy her some flowers, Donny. She's sailing across a sea of grief but she understands kindness."

We both nodded and hugged. I climbed into the golf cart and headed off.

I had been back at my place for a few hours, making phone calls and arranging things in advance of our intended trip when I heard Kyler's voice down in front. I went out on the porch. He was in his golf cart.

"What's up, brother?"

"We're being invaded."

"What!?"

"You'd better come with me, boss man. I found these six people hiking around here, looking for the tribe. They said they heard about us on the news and it's like, you just show up and you're automatically voted onto the island."

"Fuck. All right."

I closed the door and hustled downstairs.

Kyler drove me over to the meadow and around by the cottages, looking for these folks. We finally spotted them walking along the trail out front with their backpacks. There were three young men and three young women. They stopped and turned around at our approach.

"Hello," I said, getting out. "Can I help you folks?"

"Far out. It's like the guy who was on TV."

"Yeah, that's me. So what can I do for you?"

"We just thought it was like such a far out idea and wanted to see if we could join. We were already camping in the area and exploring and stuff and thought we recognized the location from a local news story."

"Does anyone else know you're up here?"

They looked at each other.

"What? Are you going to off us or something?"

"No. I just want to know if we can expect more people showing up here uninvited."

"Wow, that's like totally not what we expected to hear," one of the women said.

"Sorry, but we can't take on the whole world. You have to know somebody in the tribe and the tribe votes together on who gets to join us."

"So it's an exclusive club," one of the other men said.

"Fuck, boss man..." Kyler started to say.

I held up my hand.

"Look. Use your intelligence. This is finite. We could have hundreds of people showing up like this. Where would we draw a line?"

"Fuck, let's just go, James," the third man said.

Just then Elicia came down the path with her big smile

"Hi. How are you folks doing?"

She introduced herself to everyone there.

"Far out. You're like what we were expecting to find out here," one of the women said. "Not like we were going to get arrested or something."

"Well, we do have to have some kind of rules, you know? So where did you guys come from?"

"We're from New England," one of the women said.

I stood there listening to them explain about their travels.

"Well, maybe we could give them a chance to rest before they go?" Elicia said to me.

"Sure. That cottage is empty over there. You folks want to rest and clean up, you're welcome."

We headed over and I unlocked the door.

"Elicia here will be your chaperone." I shook all their hands. "I really do wish you the best. But please don't tell anyone else where this place is."

Kyler and I headed back to my place.

"Fuck, you were a lot more tolerant than I would have been," he said.

"What? You think I should have run their asses back out to the highway?"

"Yeah! Bunch of hippie sons a bitches!"

"You're a sick man."

"Yeah! No, just kidding, boss man." He glanced at me. "Sort of."

"Yeah, who knows what's meant to be in this universe, Kyler, but I'm definitely a bit freaked out. That's all we need are hundreds of people showing up here unannounced."

"Electric fence, boss man."

I smiled.

"You are sick."

"Yeah!"

We had come to the front of my house and I climbed out.

"Let me know if this thing gets out of hand."

"You got it."

Elicia called me a few hours later.

"What do you think of us nominating these people?"

"Oh Christ."

She laughed.

"So who's us?"

"Me, Kyler, Donny, Camellia, David and Anne."

"I thought Kyler wanted to run them back out to the highway."

441

"He changed his mind."

"Indeed."

"So, you didn't answer my question."

"What do I think? It's your call. Everybody gets a nomination."

"They're really very cool people who can add a lot to the tribe."

"They'll definitely add a lot of facial hair."

She laughed.

"So what exactly are they going to add?"

"They all have college degrees and experience all the way from organic gardening to alternative power and techy skills."

"Sounds great on the face of it, Elicia, but I'm still concerned about setting the wrong precedent here. Show up and you get invited onto the island?"

"Think we should crucify a few of them down by the highway to send a message."

"Maybe just one."

She laughed again. I paused, reflecting.

"All right, Elicia. I'd only ask this. Arrange for them to wait at the bottom of the hill when we start the council meeting. That way we can discuss their fate in private. Right? We don't want to be doing it in front of them."

"No, you're right. That makes sense."

"Okay. Then I'll see you guys at six."

The gray, wet dreary day dragged on and faded into a gray, dreary evening. I was dreaming of Latin suns.

At the appointed hour, I headed off through the darkened forest on foot, hearing what sounded like drums and a wood flute off in the distance. The sound grew louder and louder as I drew nearer to the yurt until I could make out other instruments. Eventually, other members of the tribe appeared out of the mist and we went forward together as if drawn by a magic spell.

When we came to the bottom of the steps, we found our six wanderers seated there making music, variously playing wood flutes, a Tibetan singing bowl, gourds and a small Djembe. They acknowledged us without stopping and we in turn bowed reverentially before heading up.

Inside the yurt, I found Anne and David and Elicia setting things up, as usual.

"Cool, isn't it?" Elicia said to me.

"They're trying to make themselves indispensable."

"They're doing a pretty good job," Anne said.

"Wow, they're way more tribally than we are, boss man."

"Yeah, huh? We're like a white nerd band trying to play the blues in comparison."

There were laughs and looks all around.

I took a seat among the pillows and enjoyed the music while the rest of the tribe trickled in. Some of the awkwardness from the previous evening was still on display. Yvonne arrived alone and did not seem to know where to sit. Donny said hello to her and they were talking when Kato came in. Then Colette and Connor arrived together. Eyes were flashing this way and that, each of us still trying to assess what had happened the previous evening.

When Tara arrived, she sat down with me and whispered in my ear.

"Is it still a secret?"

"It is from my end."

"I haven't said a word."

Dr. McDonald came in with Kristy and they went around saying hello to everyone. I heard Dr. McDonald's warm, dry Midwestern chuckle and smiled to myself. Some things in life just made you feel good inside.

"That music is truly transporting," he said, sitting down next to me.

"It is. Almost makes me want to take some more mushrooms."

There were laughs and groans.

"I can see where you could kind of get hooked on that stuff," Kristy said.

"Ah, our fledgling hippie."

"That's right," she said with her little fist pump.

"Not quite what you had expected, was it?"

"No, I felt superhuman. Not so much today though. Darn."

Anne came around passing out tea as everyone got seated.

"So, what's the big mystery?" Ashley said.

"Well, first," I said and looked over at Dr. McDonald.

He obliged me by hitting the gong.

"The gathering of the intergalactic poohbahs is now in session," Anne said.

All eyes turned towards me.

"Okay, before we get into anything else, I make a motion that we vote on our visitors. Because, if we're going to invite them into the tribe, they may as well participate in our business."

"I'll second that motion," Anne said.

"I'll third it," Kyler said.

"Okay, all in favor."

"Wait, shouldn't we be discussing them first," Yvonne said. "Like the pros and cons?"

"Forgive me, but I've lost my stomach for some of our formalities over the past 24 hours."

"Yeah," Anne said. "I think we should just ask, does anyone have a reason why they *shouldn't* be admitted?"

Yvonne laughed her dry but charmingly cordial laugh.

"What?" I said.

"Well, I can't believe we're completely dispensing with our adopted rules. Come on, guys. Once they're in, there's practically no getting them back off without a constitutional amendment."

There was silence. Elicia looked at me. I shrugged in a way that said, she has a point.

"Okay," Elicia said and went into a long dissertation on who these people were and why she thought they were worthy. "Not to mention the music."

She smiled at everyone. I looked at Yvonne and shrugged again.

"So?"

"So, I certainly feel a lot better about it now."

"Fair enough. Shall we vote?"

The general consensus was, yes, we were ready to vote now.

"So, all in favor?" Anne said.

With varying degrees of enthusiasm, everyone raised a hand.

"Okay, this was your baby, Elicia," I said. "Go down and get them."

While Elicia was gone, conversation broke out among us. Then Elicia reentered with the newest members and introduced them as James, Ryan, Matthew, Katrina, Diana and Zoey.

"Congratulations and welcome," Anne said. "I guess we don't really have a formal process for welcoming new people onboard."

"Yeah, we should have that," Kyler said.

"Like kneeling down before the grand poohbah and being knighted."

"How about if I just hit the gong," Dr. McDonald said and did so.

Our newest members looked a bit lost by the patter but several of the old members welcomed them into the circle and shared some of the background.

"So, let's get on with the big mystery," Ashley said.

"I'll bet he's planning to build a twenty story resort," Kristy said.

"Or do eco tours," Hans said.

I waited as a half dozen other stupid ideas were thrown out there and the silliness finally dissipated.

"Wrong, all of you. I asked you to gather here because Elicia, Kyler, Tara and I are planning to swarm."

"Swarm?" Anne said.

"He means they're going to start a new colony," Yvonne said. "Right?"

"That's right."

There were groans and complaints.

"God, we're just getting started," Anne said. "Who's going to replace your roles in the tribe? And move forward with your Co-Opportunity idea, Elicia?"

I waved a hand at the growing tribe.

"With you and the new nominations, there'll be a total of 28 members, so I'm sure you'll have plenty of energy and resources."

"But what if we end up broke?" Yvonne said.

"You won't. You'll be just fine with the website income but if worse comes to worse, I'll take care of you. The way I see it, we're not abandoning the tribe, we're just creating a new satellite."

"So, where are you going?" Dr. McDonald said.

"We're heading down to Baja."

"That sounds cool," James said.

"Hey, you can't abandon us too," Kristy said. "You just got here."

"Yeah, it was actually Kyler's idea."

People booed him.

"Yeah!" Kyler said.

"Why Baja?" Yvonne said.

"Oh, Kyler had this idea for a recovery, retreat, rehab place and I know this old Mexican family down there that owns about fifty miles of coastline, so we're putting two and two together. We'll buy a parcel of land and start building up a new tribe, with the recovery place off to the side."

"You're just a restless soul, aren't you?" Yvonne said.

"Maybe. Probably, but I'm also thinking of the potential. If I stay here, that's one tribe. If I move on and keep creating new ones, maybe I can see hundreds of them started in a lifetime."

In the silence and shadows, I sensed the disappointment.

446

"Look, everyone. Everything will remain the same. The arts center is going up and I'll be happy to do the tech center for you, too. This place will keep growing and becoming self-sufficient, so when Rolling Stone comes back in a year or so to do a follow up piece, you'll be able to show them that the idea is really working."

"I'm going to miss you, grand poohbah," Kristy said.

"Yeah, we're going to miss all of you," Anne said.

"And we're going to miss you too but think how cool it will be to have like exchange students between the two tribes. Some of you can come visit us and some of us will visit you and we'll keep learning and growing from what the other is doing."

"Can I have your treehouse?" Kristy said.

"No."

"Darn."

"Look, in the long run this is going to be more fun, and each time we start a new tribe, that's one more chance to show the world that the idea works."

"Yeah," Anne said. "Changing the world, one tribe at a time."

"We can hope. At least we can keep changing our little corner of it."

I looked around the circle. Everyone was looking back, waiting for the next move.

"So, ten of us still get to make our nominations, right?" I said.

"Hey, if you're leaving, how come you get to make a nomination?" Kristy said.

"Oh shut up," I said and pretended to bonk her over her head.

She laughed.

"So, who are you nominating?" Anne asked Elicia.

"That friend of mine Sandra I told you about. She knows everything I know about organic farming and she worked with me on the Co-Opportunity project so she can jump right into my shoes."

"Didn't you say she had a child?" Kristy said.

"Yeah, that's something we need to consider," Yvonne said.

"Without children," I said. "We'll all grow old and die with no one to take care of us."

"It's true," Anne said. "A tribe needs children. It's part of life."

"So what about you, Tara?" Kristy said.

"I'm nominating my older brother. He's a consultant in Chicago and single and excited about getting out of the rat race."

"Cool, and what about you, Kyler?"

"I'm nominating this photographer guy I know in the program."

This was met with howls of protest.

"Does he own guns?" Dr. McDonald said with a chuckle.

"Hey, the guy's got over twenty years of sobriety and is all excited about joining us and I just thought, how cool would it be to have someone who can help chronicle the tribe as it grows?"

"That is a good idea," Anne said. "So, what about you, Yvonne?"

"Like I had mentioned, I'm nominating my mother. She has a lot of physical problems right now and needs my help but she's a tough old French gal who's wise and loves to cook and is great with kids."

"That's wonderful," Anne said. "And what about you, Steven?"

"Drum roll, please," Ashley said.

I allowed for a moment of suspense before speaking.

"The pizza delivery guy."

There was laughter.

"The pizza delivery guy!!!?"

"Oh, man, I'm going to miss pizza," Kyler said.

"Sure, now you'll probably want to stay," Kristy said.

"Maybe."

"Pizza is totally not a green food," Matthew said.

"Yeah," Zoey said. "Most of the ingredients have a super high fossil fuel footprint and when you add in the delivery, it's totally a bummer food source."

"So, we can't eat pizza anymore?" Yvonne said.

"Screw that," Kristy said. "I'm eating pizza."

As the discussion spun out of control, I laughed and winked at Elicia. We were getting out of there just in time.

"All right," Anne said finally. "This is a council meeting, and for those of you who are new, we don't usually get into such things here, let alone try to decide them. If you want to make a motion about not eating pizza, you're welcome to do so but it takes a majority of us to bring it to the table."

"Everyone in favor of pizza?" Kristy said.

All hands were raised, except for the new people.

"Motion denied," Anne said.

"Yeah!" Kyler said.

"No need for that," Anne said. "But you folks have to accept. This is how it works here. We can suggest things but no one tells anyone else what to do."

"At least we could build our own pizza oven and try to make it more of a sustainable food source," Zoey said.

There were looks all around and folks nodding their heads.

"Yeah, that would be cool," Anne said. "Shall we have a vote on building a pizza oven."

Without prompting, everyone raised a hand.

"Done," Anne said.

"We can even use it for cooking homemade bread and stuff," Zoey said.

"Yeah, that's cool."

"So why the pizza delivery guy?" David said me.

"Because he knows how to fix computers."

"Oh, cool."

"Man, am I ever going to miss pizza," Kyler said again.

"So we can build our own pizza oven down in Baja."

449

"And start a pizza parlor!"

"You'll have competition," I said.

"They have pizza in Baja?" Kristy said.

"Yeah, there's one not too far from where we're going. It's called 'I'll Be Back Pizza' and their logo is an image of Schwarzenegger as the Terminator."

Amidst the chuckles and buzz of conversation, we moved on to the remaining nominations.

Epilogue

We had traveled for five days, camping the first night in Big Sur, the second on the beach in Gaviota, the third night at a state park north of Encinitas. On the fourth day, we crossed into Mexico and indulged ourselves with showers and dinner at the Rosarito Beach Hotel.

On the fifth day, we came to a small mercado about two hundred miles south of the border. The market was little more than a crudely built palapa with a thatched roof and covered front porch. An old woman was out sweeping the porch with a homemade broom when we walked up. Clumps of bananas and papayas hung from the beams of the porch above her head, as did brightly colored mesh bags for carrying groceries.

"Ola," Elicia said.

"Ola," the old woman said with a look up from her sweeping.

"Buscamos los higos de Don Francisco."

The woman stopped and gestured with one hand. They were all around us.

"Por el mar. Los higos por el mar."

"Si, si," the woman said and rattled off several sentences that none of us entirely understood. I had caught the words El Rosario, which I knew to be the next village down the highway, but inland, not on the coast. I whispered as much into Elicia's ear.

"El Rosario, no," Elicia said. "Queremos los higos de Don Francisco por el mar."

"Si, si," the woman said and gestured in the direction of El Rosario again.

Collectively, we looked off towards a rocky point, ten miles to the south. According to our map, the coast swept back east from that cape for several miles before angling more directly south again and out to the next cape twenty miles further on. When the old woman saw the look of doubt on our faces, she repeated, "El Rosario," and went back to sweeping.

Elicia spoke up.

"I think she's saying that to find the sons of Don Francisco who live along the sea, we need to get around that point."

"I'm going to put my money on that one too," I said.

Elicia laughed and pretended to kick me in the shins.

"Ah, channeling your inner Kristy, I see."

That led to more laughter and another attempt at my shins.

We thanked the woman and started into the market. The place smelled of the bananas and papayas and freshly butchered meat. The whole chickens looked fresh so we bought two of those and an ample supply of potatoes, onions, tomatoes, peppers and fruit. We added some beer and sodas and several gallons of bottled water. We already had all sorts of dried and canned food stored inside our mini motor home, which was equipped with the usual bath, kitchen, a dining table and two beds.

"Wow. Homemade coconut ice cream," I said. "I'm getting a gallon of that."

Each of us added a particular fetish or two and left with our goodies bulging from several of those mesh bags. The old woman stopped sweeping the porch as we came out.

"El Rosario," she said and gestured again.

We thanked her, stashed our stores away and headed down the highway. The road meandered up and down along the coast for several miles. Rolling hills girded us to the left, some of them nothing more than massive white sand dunes, suggesting that they had once been part of an ancient sea. Altogether, the area could have been Southern California before the white man had despoiled it.

Ten miles to the south, the highway swung sharply left away from the coast and climbed up into the hills along repeated switchback turns. Five miles farther on, the highway descended into the outskirts of El Rosario and wound back and forth for a mile or so through a mix of sad looking block homes and businesses. The only difference between the homes and businesses was that the businesses were often painted up in gaudy colors.

Along a barren stretch of the road, we came to a gas station and stopped to top off the tank. Elicia asked the attendant where we could find a road down to the coast and he directed us back up the highway two miles, to a rutted, dirt road we had noticed along the way. It had not appeared to be going anywhere.

Returning to that spot, I pulled off the highway and sat there with the engine idling. The road before us plummeted down into a deep, dry gulch before heading off through the hills. The way was peppered with small boulders here and there.

"Wow, looks a moon mission," Tara said.

"I say we go for it!" Kyler said.

"We have AAA, right?" Elicia said.

"Oh yeah. They'll be down in fifteen minutes if we get into trouble."

With a final shrug, I eased off the brake and inched my way down into the gully, dodging boulders as I did. Driving back up and out of the gully turned out to be somewhat less perilous. The road led from there around the flank of a hill and on through rugged country for ten miles or so, with the road barely wider than our vehicle in most places.

We eventually came over a rise and were treated to a vista of the crescent coastline, sweeping out towards the next point, twenty miles farther south. The road continued dipping in

453

and out of arroyos, while angling ever closer to the shore. I had been on the receiving end of numerous calls to follow this or that arroyo down to the sea and finally took one, simply to satisfy the restless natives. Several hundred yards later, we arrived at a narrow, rocky beach with no place for a man to make a foothold.

"Satisfied?" I said, climbing back into the motorhome.

From the reactions, I gathered not.

I turned around and headed back, knowing we needed to find a place more along the lines of a river wash. Roughly five miles farther down that long stretch of crescent coastline, we came to one, the land opening up suddenly into a half mile wide plain, lush with vegetation and running up inland, as far as the eye could see.

I parked and got out. The others joined me.

"It's rich soil," I said, squatting down to grab a handful of it.

"We'll be washed away with every good rain," Tara said.

I looked up at the cloudless sky with a smile.

"Funny, but this wash tells its own story."

"They've been doing it along the Nile for five thousand years," Elicia said.

"Yes, and like I said, getting washed away with every good rain."

I looked further up the wash.

"Back there, where it narrows. We could build a dam and divert the water to channels on either side. Build an underground basin and catch a lot of it."

"Ah, but that would take equipment, oh grand poohbah, and how would you propose to get that equipment down here?"

"I don't know. Let's go have a look at the coast."

We climbed back in.

I headed down the wash, taking special care to avoid the softer sand. At the shore, everyone climbed back out. The nearest point of the crescent was several miles to the south, and the shore in that direction was roughly parallel to us now but looking north we had a long, sweeping view up the coast, with the waves breaking off for fifteen miles.

A small island straddled the coast about two miles offshore, with a collection of moai-like outcroppings dotting the sea around it.

"I like it," I said and pointed to the bluffs on the southern end of the wash. "That's a perfect place to build our little village."

"Not that I doubt you, oh grand poohbah," Tara said. "But you still haven't explained to me how you intend to get all your equipment down here. Not to mention the supplies we would need on a regular basis."

I smiled at her and looked back out at the sea.

"A big barge," I said.

"Yeah!" Kyler said.

"Oh grand poohbah, assuming you could get all this under the noses of the Mexican authorities, how would you propose to get a barge down here in the first place?"

"It's only two hundred miles up the coast to Ensenada. That's a day trip for a tugboat."

"Assuming you could get it under the noses of the Mexican authorities."

"Where there's a will, there's a way."

"We need to learn how to say that in Spanish," Elicia said with a laugh.

I looked inland again and all around the fertile, open plain.

"I like it."

"He likes it," Tara said as if my royal spokesperson.

"Let's at least set up camp and make ourselves comfortable for the night," Elicia said.

"Sure," I said. "How about up on those bluffs? That's where we'll be building our new settlement."

"Where there's a will, there's a way," Tara said.

"That's the spirit, doll."

"Yes, it will definitely give us a splendid view of our crops being washed away with every good rain."

"All in favor, say aye."

Everyone but Tara did.

"It's nearly unanimous, dear," I said.

We were about to climb back into the motorhome when we heard the drone of an engine to our north and paused, watching expectantly as it grew louder. Finally, an old battered truck appeared on the road going south and started across the wash.

We could barely make out the driver from that distance but clearly he saw us because the truck suddenly wrenched around in our direction. A few minutes later, a man in his early thirties was climbing out of the truck. He had a lean build, a good face and was wearing a soiled, white straw hat

"Ola," Elicia said. "Buscamos los higos de Don Francisco."

"Aquí está," the young man said.

"He's one of them," Elicia said.

"I'm putting my money on that one too."

Elicia eyed my shins and laughed.

"Me llamo Ricardo," the man said.

"Bueno, Bueno," Elicia said and introduced all of us.

I waved at the coastline and everything around it.

"Ask him if he owns this."

"Entiendo que, todos aqui is tu yu, verdat?" Elicia said.

"A mi familia, si. Que quieres?"

"Posible comprar la."

"Aqui?" Ricardo said.

"Si."

"No, no es bueno. Mucho juvia."

He waved at the sky. Tara smiled smugly at me.

"Tell him I want it anyway," I said with a smug smile back at her.

"Si, comprendo pero queremos," Elicia said.

Ricardo shrugged and studied us.

"Vamos a mi casa y hablamos a ya."

456

"Onde esta?"

"La punta. El otro lado."

"He's inviting us to discuss things at his house," Elicia said. "I gather it's just on the other side of that point."

"So I gathered."

Elicia eyed my shins.

A no nonsense kind of guy, Ricardo said "Vamos," and jumped back into his truck.

I pulled around and followed him up the wash and onto the road heading south, holding back as necessary to stay out of his dust. We lurched up and down through arroyos as before, until five miles farther on, we passed inside the cape and came down to a beach and a small fishing village. The coast wound in and out of a series of coves and sandy beaches from there, until it disappeared beyond the next point, another fifteen miles to our south.

Down in the camp, children ran out excitedly to greet us. Curious mothers followed them, along with three old women. Several men of various ages were down mending nets and tending to their boats in a small, sheltered cove.

We climbed out and joined Ricardo. Elicia and Tara quickly engaged with the children, who were dying to look inside the motorhome.

"You are staying tonight?" Ricardo said.

I nodded.

"Si. We stay."

Seeing a little bluff above the camp, I pointed.

"Up there?"

Ricardo waved to say, wherever you like.

"Come on, let's make camp," I told Kyler.

"Right on, boss man. This place is so cool."

By the time we had our tent up and our awning and chairs out, the sun was nearing the sea. We walked back down to the camp and found the women setting up dinner on a long picnic table. Kerosene lanterns hung from the palapa overhead. One of the old men had built a fire nearby. Everything was

457

scabbed together from loose bits of lumber and driftwood and sheet metal, yet had an enchanting beauty to it, perhaps because of the sea as a backdrop.

Elicia and Tara came bearing platters of sliced tomatoes, onion, chilies and cabbage. One of the Mexican women had set up a griddle over the fire and was heating tortillas.

"What's for dinner?" I asked Elicia.

"They're grilling up two big yellowtail on the other side of the house."

"Cool, let's go grab some cold drinks," I said to Kyler.

Soon, all was prepared and we were toasting to their food and our cold beers and sodas. In broken Spanish and English, we explained the drive down and the purpose of our journey, and that we wanted to buy that parcel of land. Ricardo shrugged. He had no particular price in mind and thought we were nuts.

Wanting to draw something, I asked Elicia to request a piece of paper and a pencil.

"That's Spanish 101," Tara said with a laugh.

"I know. I flunked out. Ask him, Elicia."

"Un lápiz y pedazo de papel, por favor?" she said.

One of the women said something to a young girl and she ran off to a tin shack. A minute later, she ran back with the paper and pencil. I drew a crude picture of a tugboat and barge and pointed at the barge.

"Tell him, like that."

"Como eso," Elicia said.

Ricardo looked up at me, raised his eyebrows and rubbed his thumb and fingers together.

I nodded. Tara rubbed her thumb and fingers together and pointed at me.

"You're giving away my secrets, dear."

"I have always found honesty to be the best course of action."

All the while, Ricardo had been studying us with a slow nod of his head.

458

Having a thought, Elicia pulled a copy of the Rolling Stone out of her big straw purse and held it up for everyone to see. Jenner had used one of the group shots from the tech center for the cover. Tara had her baseball cap on my head in a screwy fashion that seemed perfectly suited for the Mexican audience. I had never seen one Mexican male wear his cap straight forward.

"Nosotros," Elicia said, pointing. "Con el jefe."

The men nodded, mildly impressed. It was mostly the same with the older women but the young women and children were quickly fighting over the magazine. Once they realized it was us on the cover, they stared with big eyes.

"How do you say, whatever you need?" I asked Elicia.

"Todo lo que necesites? I think that's how you would say it."

She nodded at Ricardo and he nodded back.

"How do you say lumber?"

"Maderas," Elicia said.

"And a bulldozer."

Tara groaned.

"Equipo grande," Elicia said with a laugh and a dramatic wave of her hands.

"Una excavadora?" Ricardo said.

"Si, one of those. Todo lo que necesites," I said to emphasize the point.

He seemed to understand. Everyone went back to eating. The young people were still thumbing through the magazine and buzzing over us.

"Hmm, so good," Elicia said. "Muy sabroso."

The women acknowledged this comment by inviting us to have more. We did. It was an orgy.

"I wish I could call the others and tell them that the swarm has landed," I said.

Elicia pulled out her cell phone and waved it at Ricardo. He shook his head.

"Ay ya. Por la carretera."

You had to be near the highway. In my mind, I tried to picture how far it was. Twenty miles, minimum, no matter which way you went, and they would be hard miles.

"That'll be the first order of business," I said.

"What's that?" Elicia said.

"A microwave tower."

"Oy vey," Tara said. "We're already wrecking the place."

"Yeah, I want my MTV," Kyler said.

"Darling, you have to be able to communicate with the world," I said.

"Don't you wonder how they've gotten along so far without it?"

"They're not addicted yet."

"So, maybe we should get *un-addicted*."

I made bug eyes at the children and they laughed.

"Look, darling. There's good and bad technology. For instance, what if we have a medical emergency? Or one of our family members needs to get in touch with us? Yeah? No? Maybe?"

She shrugged indifferently.

"So, our first fight, dear. Here, have some more fish."

I leaned over and whispered in her ear.

"I love you."

She shrugged indifferently again but a hand came up to touch my face, as if to say it wasn't really a fight. I laughed and stole glances around the table at what was already a tribe of people, though I doubted any of them thought of their relationships in that way. They were simply acting out an ancient tradition, doing what their ancestors had done before them, since times immemorial.

I imagined our new tribe being born alongside theirs and my heart was glad. The simple spirit of it made me glad.

I looked out to sea, where the sun had just touched the horizon. A cool wind stirred up from the coast. Gulls winged by as darkness rushed over the land. The fire light flickered on our faces and the surf whispered over our meal and laughter.

How real and beautiful and ancient that moment seemed.

The George Cross Interview

George sat across the table from me, his shirt collar open, sport coat unbuttoned, hair slightly ruffled, looking stoic and urbane, his craggy face squinting into the camera as he waited for the stage manager to cue up the program. The set was darkened around us, the atmosphere that of two old friends sitting down to talk of life at a dimly lit kitchen table.

The stage manager signaled and began counting down silently with lips and fingers...three...two...one...and George's mellifluous voice broke in.

"Steven Fitzgerald. Scion of the Fitzgerald family Silicon Valley fortune, by his own account, a drifter and denizen of Mediterranean locales in years past but now the man behind National Roll Call and founder of an eclectic social experiment in Northern California he chooses to call *the tribe*. I am delighted to have him with me at the table this evening."

George turned to me.

"Welcome, sir. Good to be with you again."

"Likewise. I appreciate the invitation. Ever since you suggested it on the morning show, my mind has been spinning. So much to say."

George smiled.

"Well, before we proceed, please tell us what you've been doing with yourself lately. I understand you've started a *new* tribe down in Baja California. Why? Were you already bored with your experiment? And why there?"

"Well, to answer your first question first, I won't deny that *adventure* played a part in my decision but we thought of it simply as the first tribe swarming."

George smiled warmly.

"So a new colony. And why Baja?"

"A member of the original tribe had approached me with the idea of starting a recovery operation down there. Something that would work more or less within the same tribal framework. He already had a general location in Baja in mind and so off we went to explore. Of course, it goes without saying, he's in recovery."

"You said *we*. How many are involved?"

"For now, just this gentleman, Kyler, his girlfriend Elicia and my wife, Tara."

"Ah, so you were married recently."

"Yes. We set up near a little fishing village down there and they knew of a gringo expat who could serve as our minister of the peace. I'm not so sure any of it was legal but it worked for us."

George smiled.

"Yeah, it was cool to see everyone in this fishing village join in. The old men and women, the kids. Everyone dressed up as best they could and participated in the ceremony."

"Would you happen to have photographs of the event?"

"I do."

"With you?"

"Yes."

I pulled the photos out of my coat pocket and handed them to George. As he thumbed through them, an even warmer smiled washed over his face.

"This is your wife."

"Yes."

"Beautiful. And this is the village in the background?"

"Yes."

"Fascinating. Both primitive and enchanting."

"More or less my words upon seeing it for the first time."

"It's striking to see how truly happy these individuals appear."

"And why not? They have everything they need and you'd pay a million dollars up here to have that view."

"Do you mind?" George said, gesturing at the photographs.

"No, go right ahead."

George placed one of them on edge on the table and a camera zoomed in.

"So, this is the actual ceremony."

"Yes."

George placed a finger on the photo.

"And your wife Tara."

"Yes."

"And Kyler and Elicia, was it?"

"Yes."

"And here's another one, showing more of the village. I'm intrigued by this contrast. Here you have men mending nets alongside their wooden boats and solar panels on top of their makeshift shacks."

"I'm responsible for the solar panels."

"So you brought them down with you. When you first arrived?"

"No. Once I had a chance to assess the lay of the land, I hired a tugboat to drag a barge down there with a supply of materials and equipment."

"Why not by rail or road?"

"There is no rail system in Baja."

"I did not realize that."

"Yeah and you'd have to see the way in. The main highway going down to Cabo is perfectly navigable but this is off on twenty-five miles of very primitive dirt track. Conversely, it's roughly 200 miles by sea from Ensenada to where we are, so less than a day's journey."

George set the photographs down.

"So, your presence is transforming the landscape."

"You could say that. My wife certainly thinks so. When I mentioned a microwave tower, she groaned...*Bristled* probably better describes it."

"This collision of two worlds. Is this Africa in the nineteenth century? An opening up of commerce that brings as its price the complete devastation of the native people?"

"No. Not in the sense I think you're suggesting. To the best of my knowledge, Baja's not rich in natural resources so there's really nothing there to exploit."

"No?"

"No. Lots of sunshine and ocean views, which I'll admit does pose some potential for danger. Have you ever driven from Tijuana down the coast to Ensenada?"

"I have not."

"Nothing but clutter. The Americans invaded and dragged their cookie cutter developments along with them."

"But you don't see that happening where you are."

"Not any time soon. If for no other reason than of the roads. It certainly won't happen on our account. We went there seeking what these people have, not the other way around."

"A simpler, pastoral life."

"Yeah, that."

"It does appear from the photos that they were already self-sufficient when you arrived."

"Absolutely. It's rather humbling to see the ancient wisdom they possess about living off the land. You think, if the big one went off, we wouldn't know what to do. These people would just go on with their lives."

George smiled again.

"Yeah. They're carrying forward knowledge and traditions that go back thousands of years. And are now mostly lost and forgotten by us."

"I take it that these families have been there for a number of generations."

"Longer than anyone there can remember."

"Fascinating."

"Yeah. Consider. Three hundred miles from the border and these people have never been to America, and have no apparent desire to do so. The idea of the American dream? They have little to no idea what that would mean."

"No Mercedes in the driveway and concern for their gross median income."

"Not in the least. They live by the sun and the moon and the stars. Entertainment is sitting around the fire at night and sharing. You realize, being a part of it, how much TV has usurped that role in our lives. We gather around to watch whatever sitcom but no one's really communicating."

"But it's something of a social experiment on your part, no? You choose what to introduce into their lives and what not to?"

"Perhaps, but I'm only making the same considerations I make in my own life. Does this or that modern convenience serve me? Or is it becoming my master?"

"Your wife bristled at the idea of a microwave tower."

"Yes, she really did, but I quickly prevailed on that one."

"Communication is essential to us as a species."

"Always has been. Look at how quickly smart phones exploded into use. In our particular case, you'd have to jump in a car and drive twenty five miles to get a signal. Let's say there's a medical emergency. On a renewable energy basis alone, having the tower is far more efficient."

"You mentioned bringing a barge down. Did your wife bristle over that too."

"Yeah, big time. Especially when we started backing the heavy equipment off onto land. And the diesel run generator."

"It's not very green."

"No, but it's only there so we can build up our green energy infrastructure."

"Such as."

"The same kind of waste treatment plant we have up north. Your waste goes in. Usable energy comes out. A minor dam to help control and store water. Some solar and windmills. That together with the energy from the waste treatment plant will eventually replace the generator and the dam ensures that we don't have to drag down an endless supply of bottled water."

"So, will you be washing your clothes alongside a stream?"

"Actually, we brought down a pedal driven washing machine. Have you seen them?"

"No. Explain."

"You just climb on a stationary bike and wash your clothes while getting some exercise."

"So, an inventive new way to harness human power. And you don't see what you're doing as leading inevitably to big screen TVs and a clamoring for more modern gadgets?"

"I'm not there to control these people, but I do consider it my job to educate them. To make clear the dangers of wanting a modern convenience for every task."

"And you truly believe that reckoning is upon us."

"I do. Either we end our oil guzzling willingly or deal with the inevitable catastrophe. Only the most brazen climate deniers would assert otherwise."

"Coastal cities submerged. Drought. Heat waves. Wild fires."

"That. But with a bit of moderation and ingenuity, it's easy to imagine a sustainable and pleasant future. Or we can continue on the current trajectory and see what happens."

"Before we move on, tell us about this recovery facility."

"Oh, this is Kyler's gig, mostly. My main job is working out the logistics of getting people down there and back to the States. When I brought up the idea of an airstrip, my wife really bristled."

George smiled.

"Yeah, she won out on that one…For now."

George's smile glazed over.

467

"But about the recovery home, it's been truly illuminating for me to see how similar their framework is to our tribal concept. These folks sit around the fire every night and share their stories. The many parallels are fascinating."

"So, does recovery relate to your personal journey in any way?"

"No, but the minute I understood what Kyler was going through, I thought, far out. I really want to support his vision. I mean, you look at how drugs and alcohol have torn at the fabric of our society and you can't help but get involved."

"Understood. So, the other reason for your *swarm*?"

"Simple. A realization that creating one tribe was a very poor use of my resources."

"So, continue incubating new tribes as time goes by."

"I plan to. Not that I want to see it turned into a franchise but given my resources, I have the ability to do this many times over. If I really believe in what I'm doing, why would I be satisfied with just one?"

"You make an interesting analogy there. Franchise. It brings to mind quality control and I believe we had touched on this earlier. The laws and mores of civilization. Mankind's ongoing effort to maintain order and avoid the warring tribes. Isn't that why your experiment is bound to run into problems along the way? Chaos will overtake you?"

"That's a straw man, in my estimation."

"How so?"

"Well, let's take a law that says you can't cross the street in the middle of a block. Now, the purpose of that law is safety, obviously. But let's say it's late at night. There are no cars around and it means you have to walk an extra quarter mile to get home. What are you going to do? The practical? Or obey the law?"

"So laws become unwieldy."

"When applied on a mass scale, sometimes, yes. They can be rigid and unyielding. Whereas, when you're talking on the scale of a hundred people or so, you can play things by ear and adapt on the spot. I remember you using the phrase 'on an organic level' and that's my point. Why frustrate yourself with a bunch of rules beforehand? Why not let life evolve and see how things play out? I am also reminded of that phrase, 'what if everybody did it'. Same straw man. It's the spirit of it. If you're consciousness is sufficiently evolved, you'll play along. If not, you wouldn't want to be there in the first place."

"You mentioned Rolling Stone. I read the interview and also went back to watch the tape of your appearance on our morning program and came up with a list of references you have used. Do you mind going through them with me?"

"That's why I'm here."

"Montesquieu."

"Oh. What was the phrase I had used? 'I was born rich by accident, I'm human by necessity'?"

"Yes."

"And Montesquieu had said, 'I was born French by accident, I'm human by necessity'. I believe that was just a handy line to get out of being cornered by Erin."

George smiled.

"So, not a student of his works."

"Not really. I should probably confess here that I'm an inveterate dabbler when it comes to my reading habits. And learning in general. Always found it difficult to sit still in a classroom. Great idea man. Great starter, but when it comes to the fine details and management? I grow bored and want to move on. But back to Montesquieu, I get this sense that we would have been kindred spirits. You can't help but admire his contributions to the separation of powers and early anthropology. Definitely ahead of his time."

"Lincoln."

"Oh yeah. Whether or not a tribe, so founded, can long endure."

George nodded.

"We shall see. Dare I say, the past twenty years have given me occasion to revisit Lincoln?"

"How so?"

"Like maybe we should have let the South secede?"

"So, you would undo the idea of our nation."

"Our empire?"

"Our empire. But what would this country have become? Another Europe? A group of squabbling nations?"

"Like we aren't already?"

"But here I'm trying to imagine a world in which the United States had not served as a buttress against imperial Japan and Nazi Germany. Or to Russia and China currently."

"There's that...I suppose my point is more sociological. In Sweden, you're Swedish. In Denmark, you're Danish. In the United States, what are we? If you're from Alabama, you hardly feel any affinity with Vermonters. I struggle to find much in the way of social cohesion in this country."

"So your inclination is to tear things apart."

"Have you read *The Breakdown of Nations*?"

"Leopold Kohr."

"Yes. I think he was on to something. I can envision a more enlightened future where civilization reorganizes around, in your own words, smaller more *organic* social structures."

"Like the tribe."

"Or the city states of old. Of course, with the post World War II liberal democracies under assault, that vision does appear to be more of a pipe dream than not. For the present."

"But not your tribe."

"I'm just trying to create an alternative path within the system. Plant some dichondra and see how it grows. I guess my personal vision is a future where a significant portion of our society has returned to a more rural, agrarian way of life and the big cities are diminished but still vibrant commercial centers."

"Our society just migrated from that place in the last century and now it's time to go back."

"That migration was for economic reasons, mostly. Kicks, too, I suppose, but if you obviate most of the economic

470

reasons, wouldn't it be possible to spread out again? Clearly being able to live comfortably in the country is no longer an issue and if you want some big kicks, you can always go visit the city."

"But not for everyone?"

"God no. This is an incentive program, not a dictatorship. Some people will want to go on living in the city, which is the way it should be. I'm talking about proportions. More people in the country and less in the cities, and about a way of living. If we continue down the path we're on and foist our consumer economy off on the developing world, I think we're back to that inevitable catastrophe. The planet will be a hellhole before the end of this century."

"Playing the contrarian here, with billions of dollars at your disposal…"

"For want of which, I would not be sitting here at your table tonight."

George smiled.

"It has given you a platform. But aren't there better ways for you to utilize those resources than putting together…?"

"A tribe."

"A tribe."

"So give me an alternative."

"Working with an NGO. You could have enormous reach within one of those agencies."

"Or find myself swallowed up by another bureaucracy. Look, I admit to being a stubborn ass but I have my own vision and I'm determined to follow it through. Let's say in the next decade or so, 20 million Americans find their way off the grid and into one of these collective situations because of my efforts. That's more than I could ever hope to achieve through the next platform."

"But aren't we back to giving up our Suburbans and Sunday afternoon football?"

"The Suburbans, maybe."

"But you're still uprooting people."

"It has to be by choice, so I assume much of the initial energy will come from the disenfranchised, the young, apartment dwellers, the inner cities, perhaps the aging faced with end of life decisions. But I can also envision folks on a suburban block tearing down fences and turning their backyards into a collective garden. Pooling resources to install a neighborhood solar panel system. Pooling their skills in the same way we're doing it with the tribe. It's a way of thinking that can easily be adapted to the situation at hand. Or you can go on living out your lives as separate units in your separate cubicles. That's ultimately a very barren choice, in my estimation but it's one that people are certainly free to make."

With that, George turned to the camera.

"We'll be right back with Steven Fitzgerald."

With the cameras off, George excused himself and disappeared stage right. I was offered refreshments and pointed towards a guest bathroom, stage left. I called Tara and quickly explained how things were going.

"I wish I could watch it live."

"You should have come."

"I don't want to watch it live *that* much."

I laughed.

"We'll watch the show when you get back," she said.

"All right. I should be there in about an hour."

"We'll order room service and snuggle up in bed."

"Sounds lovely…Oops, they're waving me back. Gotta go."

"I love you."

"Love you, too."

I turned off the phone and hurried back to the table.

"Tara was wanting a blow by blow account," I said, sitting down with George.

"You should have brought her."

"We just discussed that. She said she didn't want to see the show live *that* much."

He smiled and looked at the camera. The stage manager silently counted down again and we were on.

472

"I'm back with Steven Fitzgerald."

George turned to me.

"Before we move on, anything more you'd like to say on what we've already discussed?"

"Yes, if you don't mind. For me, this is critically important. For instance, you have referenced *giving up comforts* several times, to which I would say, so you really love the rat race? You really love being stuck on the freeway for two hours a day? I have to believe that a lot of people secretly dream of an alternative. And so much the better if that alternative leads to a sustainable platform."

"So, your more agrarian society."

"You saw the results of the recent environmental forum. Victory was saying, 'Yeah, we know we're screwed if we keep doing what we're doing, but we're really not ready to stop doing it yet'."

"We're up against some very powerful economic forces."

"So we foist off our fossil burning economic model on the rest of the world and live with a disaster of Biblical proportions."

"You're king for one day. What would you change?"

"What we've already discussed, of course. But there's also the shortsightedness of our government."

"Explain."

"Well, take for instance one of our initiatives, *Co-Opportunity*. We're funding start-ups that run their business cooperatively. No top down management. No shareholders. The people who work in the company own the shares equally. It has allowed one group of people to revive a textile mill and make hemp based jeans at prices that are competitive with China. Our government could fund such initiatives. Instead, they subsidize businesses that are busy offshoring American jobs. Which is in the best interest of our country?"

"The national debt."

"Yeah, there's another one where we come up against our government's inherent shortsightedness. It's taken the Reagan

473

tax cuts and 40 years to get into this mess. So let's put together a 40 year plan to dig ourselves back out. But no. The government only works in 10 year budget cycles, so again and again, we fail to tackle our most intractable problems, and mostly because it's beyond the scope of our modeling."

"There was nearly a budget deal along those lines a few years back."

"Don't remind me. The debt was what? Roughly sixteen trillion at the time and the grand bargain proposed to slash it by twelve trillion over ten years? One can only dream now."

"When it comes to tackling the debt, there's always the elephant in the room. Defense and the welfare state."

"First of all, I hate that term, welfare state. If we accept that capitalism is a pyramid, that means the vast majority of people will always be at or near the bottom of the economic scale, so I think there will always be a need to help the less fortunate in our society. But let's say in exchange for more taxes on the wealthy now, we envision a leaner government down the road, where much of what the government provides in terms of social services is done on a more *organic* level. Small groups cannot build bridges and highways and major infrastructure projects, or provide defense, but we're certainly capable of filling in some of these social service needs. That's intrinsic to my concept of a tribe. Smaller, self-contained communities that provide these sorts of services on their own and thereby significantly reduce the demands on our government."

"I'm trying to envision the algorithms for such a program."

"Like I said, I'm an ideas guy. I wouldn't pretend to know how to put such programs together, but I have no doubt it can be done. You know, if we can send a man to the moon? We just have to start by thinking long term. Agree to a goal of no national debt and a leaner government however many years down the road and work our way steadily towards it."

"And if such a vision leads to diminished production, recession and economic hardship?"

"So Congress slaps together another budget deal that allows them to say, there, that ought to get the economy moving again. Meanwhile, we're rushing blindly towards that cliff. There's no room for standing back and saying to ourselves, hey, is there another way of going about this?"

George furrowed up his brow.

"You seem certain that catastrophe awaits us."

"Look around you, George. Do you really think it's not already happening? Even this recent environmental forum acknowledged as much in issuing their toothless climate deal."

"We're trying to turn around a battleship."

"While rearranging the deck chairs on the Titanic...Maybe our best shot *is* trying to change the trajectory in third world countries. Aggressively put renewable energy to use in Africa and India and South America while they're still mostly living a pastoral existence and hope that it boomerangs back here. I can imagine someone thinking, hey, that looks like a hell of an alternative to the rat race I'm in."

"So," George said, looking back at his list. "Einstein."

"You may as well throw in Pinker and Planck there."

"In what sense?"

"That our everyday perceptions of reality have lagged so far behind the science. Relativity. Quantum mechanics. Cognitive behavior. Together they present a picture of life that doesn't comport at all with our daily existence."

"The world works quite well in Newtonian terms so why worry ourselves over what we can't see."

"Yes, but when you apply a force-reaction mindset on a geopolitical level, you get Iraq. The Bush people invaded Iraq like it was an inanimate object. You kick it and it will move wherever you want. And then, when the thing exploded in their faces, they were astonished to see it had a life of its own."

"Your thoughts on Pinker."

"A good place to start on the subject of cognitive behavior. I have a mental note to follow up on his sources. And on his antagonists."

"The Integrated Model versus SSSM."

"Yes. As the layman, I was fascinated by Pinker's first few books. Then you come across intellects like Sampson and Richardson, who have called his theories 'rhetorical' 'untenable' a 'straw man' and you wonder. I guess what really interests me is how the effort to create artificial intelligence revolutionized our understanding of our own minds. You try to make a model of us and realize, wow, we have no idea how this thing works. So we're back to breaking down the mind, trying to figure out how the hell it *does* work. Like how do you get a 3-D perception of reality up here from a 2-D image in our retinas? Of course it's 3-D out there but the mind has to reconstitute it. How?"

"I am reminded of the arguments against intelligent design. We've very much been jury rigged together by nature."

"Yes, a vestigial nerve from an ancient fish now keeps us from inhaling food down our windpipes. Hardly intelligent design."

George smiled.

"Dawkins."

"Yeah, I don't know why I had brought him up. Not a big fan. And that's where I leave off with Pinker. You don't believe in God, that's fine. It absolutely should not be a factor in scientific inquiry. So stay out of it."

"So you believe in God."

"I don't particularly like the word *believe*. I'd rather say, certain experiences have informed me that there is one. Science does the same thing. I don't know how you can look at one of those Hubble deep space shots, or go outside and look up at the stars on a really clear night and think, yeah, this is all just an accident. It's interesting that two of our greatest minds, Einstein and Hawking, both came to accept the idea of a higher power. What that is, I have no idea but a universe without purpose makes no sense to me."

"And that purpose?"

I shrugged.

"To love? To give? To learn? I think those three things right there will put you on a solid spiritual path. Conversely, religion has become so laden with dogma over the millennium, it's now monstrous in its arrogance. When I think of God, I think of humility."

"Rousseau."

"I am reminded of Voltaire's response to him. Why, you make me want to get down and crawl around on all fours."

"The Romantic notions have not comported well with our growing knowledge over the ensuing two hundred years."

"Not much, but you know what I've said. Taken out of context, none of this makes sense. We have an innate desire to do good. But we also have an innate capacity for evil. I believe there has to be a framework that encourages us to do good instead of evil and that brings us back to the tribe."

"A place with no laws and no organized means of enforcement."

"Now you remind me of Lenny Bruce's caveman shtick."

"Refresh me."

"So the caveman explains to his mates, 'We eat here, we sleep here, we crap here. So just don't crap where I'm sleeping'. So he wakes up the next morning and discovers someone has crapped by his bed. 'Hey, you crapped where I'm sleeping. What's the matter with you?' Of course the impulse is to smack the other guy around but he quickly realizes the inherent complications and brings in a third party to enforce the laws. 'Okay, here's the deal. We eat here, we sleep here and we crap here. So if you see anyone crapping by my bed, pow! You give him a good one'. To which the guy asks, 'Well, why don't you just do it yourself?' 'No, no, I can't. You see, I have to do business with this prick."

George smiled without comment.

"Am I digressing?"

"No, I see your point. So how *do* you enforce things?"

"Mostly on the spot. And if that fails to resolve things, we have a council meeting."

"And if that fails?"

"Banishment...No, trust me. There's no cookie cutter solution and we do have friction, but we're continuously finding new ways to work things out. Because we want to."

George stared, waiting. I waved for him to go on.

"Zen."

"Oh, everything is Zen. No resistance to the state of things. No wanting, no duality. Frustration is Zen. Stubbing your toe is Zen. It's as close to religion as I'll ever get."

"So, no Hindu scripture? Buddhism? Taoism?"

"That's a mouthful."

"All right, Hindu scripture."

"I could reread the Bhagavad Gita for the rest of my life and never grow tired of it. As D. T. Suzuki said, when it comes to the metaphysical, there is no richer tradition than the Hindu mind, but for the same reasons that the Chinese monks revolted against Buddhist dogma in the sixth century AD, I wither when confronted with Hindu dogma. Or dogma of any kind."

"Zen is unique in that regard."

"It is. Here is the Buddha experience. It's inside of you and you don't need anything but yourself to have it. And if you're *not* having it, you and you alone are responsible for that failure."

"Religious fanaticism does seem to have reached a crescendo in this world."

"To which Muslims have no exclusive. You see abortion clinic doctors being gunned down here in America and ultra-orthodox Jews in a ruthless land grab on the West Bank and realize, we're but a code of laws away from our own form of ISIS."

"Even uttering such things often leads to a more incendiary environment."

"Yeah. You speak freely about the Israeli situation and you're soon on the Jewish Defense League's hit list."

"But you would make a distinction between Israeli policy and Jews in general."

"Of course. The Palestinians aren't blameless but the Israelis have an existential problem. They can't really acknowledge their own genesis. Listen to their policy makers. None of them ever refer to 1948. Their reference point is always to a time two thousand years ago, when they last owned the place, or to the present. To acknowledge how they displaced two million Palestinians in founding the Israeli state is too damning."

"And no matter what we do, the problem remains…"

"Intractable. But not unsolvable."

"So what would you do?"

"I think the Israelis will ultimately have to turn the other cheek. It doesn't seem to be in their DNA but until they reckon with the *Palestinian* diaspora and accept a two state solution, there will be no peace. They're right to fear. Some will never accept the existence of a Jewish state, but as with the wider Muslim vs West conflict, I think you can take the gasoline out of ninety nine per cent of it. Perhaps the Israelis could use their largesse to assist the Palestinians with some grand rebuilding projects. This is a generational problem. It takes time and patience, but I can envision a future where we're talking a minor skirmish here and there, not an endless and intractable state of war. The sad thing is, the Palestinians are the very sort of secular and moderate Muslims we should be embracing in the Middle East."

"Joseph Campbell."

"I was inspired by his work but also have my reservations. Nietzsche comes to mind. The power of the will. Campbell seemed convinced that this life could not be changed. The struggle goes on ad infinitum and you just accept it in some

Byronesque fashion and thereafter catapult into the black abyss of nonexistence. And maybe he's right, but then I have no explanation for my conscience or my altruistic tendencies."

"There will always be a chasm between our aspirations and the reality of the human condition."

"But we must go on trying, or we cease to be human."

"Who has most influenced your thinking?"

"It's not whom. It's what."

"What, then?"

"Pain."

George smiled.

"And I'm being serious here. I imagine that's what informed Jesus and Buddha and St. Francis de Assisi. When you can no longer ignore the suffering in this world, you feel beholden to do something about it."

"National Roll Call," George said.

"Another platform from which to do good. I spoke with Anne, one of the members up north just this morning and they're now funding a program to help disadvantaged youth. You know, if every kid had a reasonably happy, healthy start, what a difference it would make. You only have to look at how similar we all are, up to, say, five years old and then how so many lives start to run off the rails."

"Your father."

"I forgive him now."

George smiled.

"You know, I've had pause to consider my own redemption these past few years and I can only hope my father found his before he passed away."

"Perhaps in you."

"Perhaps in me."

"Next challenge."

"Oh, I've got my hands full down there for the next year or so. We'll see. I'll be keen on seeing our tribes continue to swarm. That and connecting with people who are already on the ground in developing countries. See what we can do to stop them from turning into us. To encourage a desirable alternative to consumerism before we're all doomed."

"Have you thought of working with other activists? Clooney, Damon and Bono come to mind."

"They haven't called. No. I wouldn't mind meeting those guys and seeing what we can do together. It just hasn't happened yet. Give them my address down in Baja."

George smiled.

"It's been a pleasure, sir. You will come back and see us again."

"Sure. As soon as there's more to share. In the meantime, I'd just like to say that I think you've done a great service to humanity in your own way. Your show is always about the great ideas and there's something comforting in the constancy of it. Same format, same theme song. Which I love, by the way. Please don't ever change it."

"Steven Fitzgerald," George said into the camera. "We'll be back with you tomorrow evening."

George and I parted ways after a brief conversation. I took a taxi across Manhattan on a cold, wintry night. There was snow on the ground and I was very glad in my heart to know that Tara was there awaiting my footsteps.

About The Author

The product of an Irish/Italian family, Mr. Corcoran was transplanted from the clapboard New England of his youth to the cookie cutter, stucco subdivisions that increasingly littered the old ranches and disappearing orange groves south of Los Angeles in the 1960s. Ever rebellious, and true to the folk music/coffee house idealism that helped shape my early worldview, he chose to resist the Vietnam War, was a man without a country for several years and can count incarceration in a Mexican prison as one of his many colorful experiences from that era.

Having pursued a love of reading and writing in various forms all his life, Mr. Corcoran finally took that passion seriously around the turn of the millennium and has dedicated the remainder of his days to authorship. In completing the circle of destiny, he has returned to the New England of his youth and presently resides along the Rhode Island shore.